HILDA

WILLOW'S WEDDING VOWS

Debbie Viggiano

ISBN: 9798639715822

www.debbieviggiano.com

Unicorn Publishing Limited

For Debbie Brown, a true friend.

There aren't many people willing to share a gall bladder and liver cleanse!

Chapter One

'Did you have a good weekend?' Willow asked her superior, Jean.

The two women were huddled over the staff room kettle on this bleak Monday morning in early September.

'I've had better,' Jean replied, pulling her cardigan around her ample bosom. 'Our Julie broke her wrist.'

'Oh no. How did that happen?' asked Willow, pouring boiling water over coffee granules.

'Believe it or not, she did it when trying to open a jar of jam. The lid wouldn't come off, so she gave it some welly and the wretched thing flew up sending Julie's wrist smacking into an overhead cupboard. She's now in plaster.'

'Oh dear,' said Willow, sympathising. 'Nothing worse than being in plaster.'

Except, she thought privately, getting plastered. Which was exactly what she'd done on Saturday night. But it hadn't been in a jolly let's-get-tipsy kind of way. Instead it had been in a let's-blot-out-the-misery way.

It had been her thirtieth birthday and boyfriend Charlie had taken Willow out for a slap-up meal at the local pub. She'd almost stuffed herself to a standstill on the huge plate of tender slow-cooked lamb, green beans and divine buttery mash. Throughout, Charlie had entertained her with anecdotes about work, including some rather bitchy criticisms of staff.

'It's about time everyone realised what a plank the MD is. *I* could do that job with my eyes shut.'

There'd also been a dig about the scatty new receptionist who Charlie had nick-named Ditzy Di on account of how she always cocked things up. Last week's faux pas had been booking the boardroom for twelve different clients... all at the same time.

'Gorgeous looking girl, and sweet enough, but nothing between the ears.'

Willow had privately tutted thinking that, much as she loved her clever accountant boyfriend, it wasn't a nice trait to be so quick to put people down.

Sometimes Charlie put Willow down too. Not nastily, but in such a way as to let her know that being a library assistant wasn't rocket science, and no matter how irritating or rude some members of the public could be, Willow's days were surely never as stressful as Charlie's. But she forgave him this flaw, and one or two other niggles because, after all, nobody was perfect.

Or quite so good looking, eh? the little voice in Willow's head had piped up.

Willow had quietly sighed in agreement. There was no doubt about it. Charlie was a "babe". His rugged blond looks and come-to-bed blue eyes played havoc with her heart — and that of other women too. At times he was an unashamed flirt, but Willow told herself it was excusable given the amount of female attention Charlie received. He was like a particularly glorious golden sunflower that towered over everything — and everyone, in his case.

But flirting didn't mean anything, did it? After all, Willow's good-looking postman had winked at her last week. He'd made her smile and blush, but she hadn't run after him, scattered his letters in all directions and panted, "Quick, deliver me to Heaven", had she? And as far as she was aware, Charlie had never taken his flirting any further.

Are you sure about that? the little voice had sneered.

She'd ignored it. The little voice was always taunting her, probably because she had body issues and lacked self-confidence.

Willow was a curvy girl. Friends said she looked just like Amanda Seyfried but with hips and boobs, and a bum that meant she always needed the next size up in jeans which left the waistband gaping. She hated standing next to her bestie, Emma, who had a metabolism faster than Usain Bolt, and almost disappeared whenever she stood sideways. Emma had recently come out of a disastrous long-term relationship and was living back home with her mother. There had been many tears, with Emma sobbing that she felt like a failure.

Emma had been sure her boyfriend was going to pop the question. Instead he'd asked Emma if they could take a break. An indefinite one. It had been Emma's situation that had prompted Willow to start thinking about her own long-term relationship with Charlie. Wasn't it about time the two of *them* got married?

When Willow had opened her birthday cards and found every single one of them sporting the numbers "three" and "zero", it had set something off in her brain, as if to remind her she'd reached a significant landmark in her life. The sneery little voice in her head hadn't wasted a second in pointing out that Willow's biological clock was now ticking. Whilst having a baby before marriage wasn't an issue, she was old-fashioned enough to want a wedding band and loads-of-sex honeymoon before stretchmarks and nipple shields.

Sipping her birthday champagne while Charlie chatted away, she'd quietly weighed things up. She and Charlie had lived together for almost a decade. It wasn't like they didn't know each other's little foibles. Okay, he drove her slightly mad with his habit of leaving clothes inside-out and dumped on the floor, but she irritated him by nicking his socks and borrowing his razor. Charlie's flirting had never got out of hand – other than when she'd gone on a girly night with Emma to a club where Charlie just happened to also be. He'd been snogging another girl. But Willow had mentally shaken the memory away. That was *waaaay* back, and not long after they'd met. They hadn't been living together. They hadn't even been "exclusive". And he'd never done it since, had he?

I wouldn't trust him, sniffed the little voice in her head.

Good, she silently replied, *because you're not the one who wants to marry him, so why don't you just bog off, eh?*

Willow had decided to broach the subject of getting hitched whilst out celebrating her birthday with Charlie.

Finishing her lamb, Willow had put her knife and fork together. At that moment, Charlie had leant across the table and romantically taken her hand in his. As he'd smiled at her, the soft candlelight had flickered across his handsome face, lending a golden glow. It had seemed like the perfect moment.

'So,' she'd beamed, aware that birthday champagne had made everything deliciously fuzzy as well as emboldening her. 'Can I ask you a question?'

Charlie's smile had expanded. The last time Willow had used that very suggestive tone of voice, she'd been faintly drunk – like now – and feeling randy. She'd later gone on to initiate some mind-blowing sex which had been amazing, especially as most of the time their love life was not an earthmoving experience. He supposed they'd been together too long for her to stir his loins more than a perfunctory once-a-week coupling. Charlie allowed himself a little daydream. Perhaps his girlfriend was going to suggest something outrageous, like… having a threesome. Wasn't that every man's fantasy? He knew that Willow's bestie was back on the dating market. Perhaps the girls had been gossiping behind his back whilst sharing a bottle of wine between them. Maybe Emma had tipsily confided that she'd always fancied Charlie, and what about they shared him for one night of no-strings passion? Charlie wouldn't mind that at all. Her boobs weren't as big as Willow's, but her lean and wiry body indicated a capacity to crawl all over a man's body like a spider on amphetamines. Willow was now squeezing his hand, her tongue flicking over her lips to wet them. How suggestive and delightful.

'What is it?' he'd murmured huskily. 'Tell me, darling.'

'How do you feel–?'

Willow had paused, suddenly looking awkward.

'Go on!' he'd smiled encouragingly.

'About getting married?' Willow had blurted.

Charlie had frozen. There'd been a moment of stunned silence and then he'd whipped his hand away from hers.

'Married?' he'd yelped, loud enough to have the couple at the next table turning to look at them speculatively.

'Y-Yes,' Willow had quavered, her bravado popping as quickly as the champagne bubbles in the ice-bucket on the table.

'I thought you were going to ask–'

'Yes?'

'If I fancied… dessert,' Charlie had blustered.

'I do,' Willow had said.

Those two words had further unnerved Charlie. Help. Was she saying her wedding vows already?

'I don't.'

'Don't want dessert, or don't want to get married?'

'Neither,' he'd said, aghast.

Willow had promptly burst into tears. The ear-wigging couple at the next table had looked upset on her behalf.

'Give him time, love,' the lady had said, leaning across and patting Willow's arm.

'I've already given him well over nine years,' Willow had sobbed.

She'd pushed back her chair and stood up, leaving Charlie frantically summoning the waitress for the bill.

Willow had cried all the way home. Charlie had sat silently beside her as he'd steered the car. Once home, he'd feigned a headache and disappeared upstairs. Willow had stayed downstairs and popped the cork on a birthday bottle of Prosecco. She'd drowned her sorrows while watching old re-runs of *Friends*. Willow had known exactly how Rachel had felt about wanting to marry Ross, but not being able to have him.

At some point Willow had fallen asleep. Upon waking, cold and stiff on a Sunday morning, she'd discovered Charlie had gone out. There was a note beside her.

Sorry about last night. I've gone to Mum's. She's feeling down. See you later xx

Charlie's mum had recently been widowed. Grace was, understandably, grieving and sad. When Charlie didn't come home Sunday evening, Willow tried not to mind. Nor did she text Charlie to ask if his mum was okay. Better to wrap her dignity around her like the duvet she was later huddled under, alone.

When Monday morning rolled around, she was surprised to discover that at some point Charlie had come home, showered and gone to work. She must have been out cold not to have heard him. Willow had duly crawled out of bed and into the shower before setting off to work at Mosley Library.

And now, as she stirred her first coffee of the day in the library's tiny kitchen, she briefly wished she was colleague

Jean's daughter, recovering in plaster from a broken wrist. Because a broken wrist would heal far more swiftly than a broken heart.

Chapter Two

Charlie was behind his London desk long before any other staff began filtering into the trendy open-plan office block that overlooked the River Thames. A desire to distance himself from Willow before she was properly up and about had been his number one priority. The last thing he wanted was twenty questions on why he didn't want to get married.

He'd spent some of the remainder of the weekend at his childhood home where his widowed mother now lived alone. Grace had expressed surprise upon seeing her son on the doorstep without Willow. She knew it had been Willow's birthday, but Charlie had made an excuse about his girlfriend having a migraine and needing to be left alone to quietly sleep it off. On Sunday, he'd taken his mother out to lunch at a local carvery. Over coffee, he said that Willow had texted saying she was fine now, so he'd better get back.

As soon as Grace had waved him off, Charlie had taken advantage of his car's Bluetooth and rung a number saved on his mobile simply as "Kev". However, Kev wasn't a man. Moments later a female answered. It was the same woman he'd spent two hours with *prior* to turning up on his mother's doorstep to establish a cast-iron alibi.

As he waited for the number to connect, Charlie told himself it was unlikely Willow would check up on his movements, but it was best not to take chances, hence using his unsuspecting mother as a means of cover. The number began to ring, and was answered almost immediately.

'Hey, sexy lady,' he said, making his voice deliberately husky.

'Hey yourself,' said the woman, clearly pleased to hear from him.

'Fancy a re-run of last night?'

'If you insist,' the woman giggled.

'I do, I do,' Charlie murmured, and then blanched.

God, those two hideous words again.

'The coast is clear for the rest of the day and all of tonight,' she said.

'In that case, I'll stay over – as long as you don't mind me disappearing before the sun comes up. I'll try not to wake you in the morning.'

'Can't you go to work from mine?'

Charlie could imagine her lovely mouth pouting at the other end of the line, and he smiled.

'You are very demanding. In more ways than one.'

'I can't help it where you're concerned,' she said, voice teasing again.

'Good,' said Charlie smugly. 'Unfortunately I don't have a suit with me, so have no choice but to get up with the dawn chorus.'

'Never mind. I'll take what I can of you,' she said happily.

'See you in ten minutes.'

Charlie had hung up and floored the accelerator.

He hadn't meant to start an affair. He hadn't meant to start *anything*. Their paths had, from time to time, crossed over the years. And yes, there had always been banter. But Charlie bantered with all the ladies. Some women called it flirting. But most of the time it really was meaningless in Charlie's case. After all, he bantered with the old girl who cleaned the office and vacuumed around his legs if he was still working on a report. Just because he made risqué comments about the sucking power of her nozzle didn't mean he was hinting at a blow job, for goodness sake.

That was the trouble with females. They had a propensity to misunderstand things. If Charlie meant business with a woman, then he would leave her in no doubt of his intention. All it needed was a raised eyebrow, a loaded silence, and a few smoulders. There was no need to muck about wasting precious shagging time on meaningless banter if he was planning on going in for the kill.

Charlie had always been careful not to do the dirty on his own doorstep. Any extra-curricular sexual activity on his part had always been well away from the home base… stag weekends abroad, hens looking for one last fling before saying "I do" – God, those words again – or business meetings at the sister company in Birmingham where the totty was hot even if the accent was not. But this thing with Kev was a bit too close for comfort. It was playing with fire. It was also the longest he'd ever had another woman on the go. Usually he loved them and left them. One-night stands with no strings had been the rule. Except he'd broken his own rule. Somehow he'd let this woman become a lover. Charlie had been in her bed more times than he could now remember, and he didn't like that. It made him feel uneasy. It also thrilled him.

If someone had asked Charlie whether he'd cheated on Willow a lot, he'd have looked incredulous and said, "Most definitely not". The reality was that for every year he'd been with Willow, there had been as many women. It wasn't a good track record. Charlie told himself that it was purely because he'd not had enough time to sow wild oats before buying a house with Willow and "sort of" settling down.

He'd met Willow on a lad's holiday in Ibiza where the boys' collective plan had been to booze and bonk the night away, then recover under a sunshade on the beach during the day. Charlie had spotted Willow two sun loungers along from his, laying on her back. Her Rapunzel-gold hair was fanned out around her head before spilling down on to the wet sand. She'd looked almost like a mermaid with her shell-coloured bikini struggling to contain two magnificent breasts that gently rose and fell as she snoozed. A pretty but not-so-ample brunette had been on the sun bed next to the blonde vision. The brunette had caught Charlie looking. He'd smiled helplessly and the girl had got up and come over.

'I'll get straight to the point,' she'd said, doing exactly that. 'Is it me or my friend you're interested in?'

Charlie had been mildly amused at the brunette's frankness.

'You're very lovely,' he'd said, smiling disarmingly. 'But I do rather favour curvy girls.'

'What you really mean is that you're a boob man,' she'd tutted.

'Yes,' he'd grinned. 'But you're definitely Stuart's type' – he'd pointed to his mate crashed out under the sunbrella to his right – 'so go and wake him up and tell him to buy us all some ice-cold beers.'

Charlie had later found out that the brunette was called Emma. As he'd predicted, Stuart had immediately hit it off with Emma and they'd ended up inseparable for the remainder of the holiday, just like Charlie and Willow. But, in Charlie's case, instead of the holiday romance coming to a natural end, he'd reconnected with Willow once home and been with her ever since. He should have taken a leaf out of Stu's book and waved good-bye to her at the airport but, at the time, Willow's golden hair and shapely figure had mesmerised him. Apart from anything else, he couldn't bring himself to hurt her. Willow was like a puppy. Very, very sweet.

Charlie wasn't prepared to risk his car being spotted by anyone who might – no matter how unlikely – know him, so he parked two streets away. Walking towards the house, he found the door on the latch.

'Darling,' she purred, pulling him into the hallway. 'You came.'

'Not yet, but I will shortly,' he quipped, scooping her into his arms.

And the rest was kiss-tory.

A lack of sleep had cast a pallor over Charlie's usually glowing complexion. Poring over a merger and acquisitions report, he heard rather than saw Ben – a longstanding colleague and now long-time friend – pulling out his chair at the next cubicle along.

'Hello, hello,' said Ben with a grin as he flicked on his screen. 'You're in very early. Trouble at home?'

'Course not,' said Charlie, looking up.

He made sure his expression conveyed innocence. Ben might be one of his best buddies, but there were some secrets you kept to yourself. Especially when they were so close to home.

'I should've done this wretched report on Brown & Humphrey before going home on Friday,' Charlie explained. 'Consequently, I spent the whole weekend worrying about it. I decided to set the alarm for five and get in before the phones started ringing.'

Charlie added some figures to the on-screen spreadsheet.

'What's your excuse to be in so early with such enviably white eyeballs?'

Charlie was aware that a marathon sexy stint and lack of sleep had left his pretty blue eyes shot through with pink lines. Early night tonight. He'd give Willow a ring in a bit and make placatory noises and suggest spag bol in front of the telly. It would give him the chance to assess her mood, make peace if required, and practice dodging the "M" word if she brought it up again. Calling her at work also meant she wouldn't be able to have hysterics of the unfunny kind.

'Ditto,' said Ben, interrupting Charlie's thoughts. 'I've got a report of my own to finish. Incidentally, my eyeballs are always white. Even if I get bladdered.'

'It's not natural.'

'What, getting bladdered?'

'No, having such white eyeballs.'

'Here,' said Ben, reaching into his jacket pocket.

He extracted a small oblong box and lobbed it in Charlie's direction.

'Eyedrops. White eyeballs guaranteed. Have them on me. I have more at home.'

'Cheers,' said Charlie.

He pocketed the box with a grin, then leant back and stretched.

'Go and make us both a coffee.'

'Blimey, I've been here two minutes and already you've whipped my eyedrops and started giving orders.'

'Yeah, but I've had a heavy weekend,' said Charlie, yawning.

'Thought so,' Ben murmured. 'Hope she's worth it.'

Charlie tutted, feigning annoyance. He watched Ben go off to the fancy kitchen at the far end of the floor where Beryl, coffee-maker extraordinaire, usually presided between the hours of nine and five. The hour was still too early for Beryl to make an appearance.

Charlie turned back to his screen with Ben's words echoing in his head. *Hope she's worth it.* The truth of it was, she wasn't. Not really. She wasn't even his type, dammit! So why did he find himself repeatedly risking everything he had with Willow? Did he subconsciously want Willow to find out and be the one to do the dumping, saving him the trouble? Not really, because he didn't want to end it with Willow. He might not wish to marry her, but he didn't want to let her go either. So why did he behave like this?

Because… because…

His mind struggled to find reasons why.

Willow was pretty. She turned heads. *He* knew that, even if she didn't. His girlfriend was kind. She was also very efficient on the home front. The house always looked nice, she was a good cook *and* she ironed his shirts. Ben's girlfriend didn't do that. Usually it was Ben ironing *her* stuff. Was Charlie, perhaps, staying with Willow out of habit? Maybe. But, then again, he couldn't imagine life without her. His thoughts looped in circles. He was too young to remember Prince Charles's embarrassingly awkward moment when asked if he was in love with Princess Diana, or the famous reply of "Whatever *in love* means", but like the future king, Charlie presumed that whatever love was it was *that* that kept him by Willow's side. He comforted himself with the thought whilst squirting eyedrops in his tired eyes, then thanked Ben for the coffee.

He took a noisy slurp as he mentally ran through what he'd say when he called Willow… preferably without Ben overhearing.

Chapter Three

'For goodness sake, Willow,' snapped Jean. 'Whatever is the matter with you this this morning? That's the third time you've misdirected a member of the public. That lady was asking you to help with IT access. Not a tooth abscess.'

'Sorry,' Willow mumbled.

'We have an author due in shortly. She's giving a talk to the public. Perhaps you could help her set up her display table without losing concentration.'

'Okay.'

'And try and look enthusiastic and smile.'

'Okay,' Willow repeated.

She must pull herself together. But it was hard when you'd wrecked your own birthday mentioning the M word to a boyfriend with a bachelor mindset.

Willow had devoted hours to privately analysing the whole thing. She'd been too forward. She should have let Charlie do the talking. She'd emasculated him… been too presumptuous… frightened him… scared him off… made him feel trapped. And then she'd got angry and berated herself. She hadn't been forward enough… she should have grimly hung on to Charlie's hand thereby denying him escape… then concisely listed reasons to get hitched. Like proving they were committed to each other… publicly celebrating their devotion in front of their family, friends and loved ones… because, dammit, it was also romantic and wonderful and gorgeous, and surely every girl's dream to feel – just for one day – like a fairy-tale princess in her Cinderella dress, a tiara glittering away in her hair as her very own Prince Charming promised to love her for ever.

Oh. My. God, sneered the little voice in her head. *You don't truly believe all that sexist rubbish, do you?*

'Excuse me–'

Do you think women burned their bras and fought for independence so that the likes of you could carry on playing the little woman? What century are you living in?

'Hello? Er, I wonder if–'

Geez, Willow, if Charlie wore slippers, you're the sort of idiotic female who'd have warmed them by the fire ready for him to step into when he was home from work. Man up, girl! Be indignant! Be strong! He turned you down. How DARE he!

'Um, can you hear me–?'

If he doesn't want to marry you, that's his loss, BUT for heaven's sake start having some respect for both yourself and the sisterhood and get HIM to iron YOUR stuff, occasionally walk the vacuum around the house, put a wash on, oversee the online shop, ask if he can run YOUR bath, and generally scamper after YOU! Do you hear me?

'Can you hear me–?'

'Oh give me a flipping break,' Willow snapped.

'O-Oh, I'm so sorry, I didn't mean–'

Willow turned scarlet as she realised that a little old lady had been trying to get her attention.

'Omigod, I'm so sorry,' she gabbled. 'I wasn't talking to you, I was talking to–'

A pair of cloudy blue eyes bored into hers, waiting for an answer.

'Myself,' said Willow, nodding away. 'I'm in… amateur dramatics. Just rehearsing my lines.'

'You're very believable,' said the little old lady.

'Good.'

Willow gave a shaky laugh. Thank goodness Jean was busy talking to Fiona and Theresa, the other two members of staff. If Jean had overheard Willow snapping at a library visitor, there would have been hell to pay.

'How can I help?'

'I want to give a talk about my latest book. I can do it now, if that's okay.'

Ah. This must be the author Jean had mentioned.

'Fantastic,' said Willow, dredging up a smile. 'What's it called.'

'Free Willy.'

'Really? Hasn't that already been done? I'm sure a guy wrote it. What was his name?' – she clicked her fingers, waiting for the info to drop into her brain – 'got it. Keith Walker.'

'Oh no, dear' – the little old lady shook her head – 'that became a movie and was about a whale. *My* book is about how to have a successful and rewarding sex life in your eighties. Perhaps your partner can't perform. Or you're widowed and don't have anyone to perform. Or you don't have enough pension to *pay* for someone to perform. Free willy. Literally.'

Willow blinked. Was this conversation actually happening?

'I self-published the book,' said the little old lady proudly.

'W-Wow. Amazing,' said Willow faintly.

What the hell was Jean playing at not properly vetting an author promotion?

'Where are your paperbacks?'

'It's one of those new-fangled e-books. My granddaughter sorted out the techie side, but I have plenty of visual props.'

She shook a grocery bag, and Willow caught a glimpse of cucumbers, courgettes and aubergines.

'Um, could you wait here a minute? I need a word with my superior.'

'Of course, dear,' said the little old lady cosily.

Willow shot over to Jean who was manning the enquiries desk.

'Jean, can I have a quick word? You know that author you were talk–?'

The phone rang. Like a traffic cop, Jean's palm shot up.

'A member of the public is ringing this library,' she said reverently, for all the world as if it was Her Majesty on the line. 'Therefore, that member of the public takes priority.'

She picked up the handset, chest swelling importantly.

'Mosley Library, good morning. How can I help you?'

'Excuse me?' said a voice.

Willow turned to see a pleasant looking middle-aged woman standing next to her.

'My name is Mary Rogers. I'm a writer and here to talk about my book.'

Willow looked at the woman blankly. How many authors had Jean booked?

'Um, could you to take a seat over there,' said Willow, pointing to a row of hard-backed chairs. 'My colleague will be with you shortly.'

Willow turned back in time to see Jean's face darkening with displeasure.

'This call is for you. It's Charlie.'

'Oh,' squeaked Willow, in both fear and delight.

'One moment, please,' said Jean to Charlie.

She put down the handset and turned to Willow.

'Can I remind you' – she hissed – 'that personal calls are not permitted during working hours, especially on the library's phone.

'I-I'm sorry,' Willow stuttered.

She really wasn't having a great Monday morning.

'It must be an emergency.'

'Let's hope so, otherwise I might have to consider giving you a verbal warning. Now what was the problem with the visiting author?'

'We seem to have two of them. The first is over there.'

Willow pointed to the little old lady who was now busily making a vegetable display on a side table. Jean's face instantly morphed into a bulldog chewing a wasp.

'What on earth–?'

She marched off leaving Willow to grab the handset and take Charlie's call.

'Hello?' she quavered.

What could possibly be so important for Charlie to call her in *his* working hours *and* at the library? Her blood ran cold. Perhaps there had been a family emergency. Or… now her blood was turning to ice… perhaps he couldn't stand the thought of going home to her tonight and wanted to give fair warning? Could today get any worse? Maybe, in the next five minutes, she'd have been sacked by both her boss and her boyfriend.

'Darling,' said Charlie.

Willow was so relieved at the endearment she almost slumped over the enquiry desk's upper counter.

'I've behaved like a dick. Will you accept my apology?'

'Yes,' she said, without hesitation.

'Good.'

Charlie lowered his voice.

'Can we have kiss-and-make-up-sex tonight?'

'Yes,' Willow repeated.

She briefly wished her boyfriend was more romantic and had instead said he'd like to *make love* to her. But she mustn't complain. A squawk from Jean fragmented her thoughts. Turning, Willow saw her boss marching the little old lady towards the exit, vegetable props back in the shopping bag.

'I shall look forward to ravishing you later, angel,'

whispered Charlie.

'Me too,' Willow murmured.

She'd pull out all the stops tonight and think of an added ingredient to spice things up.

As if on cue, the little old lady let out a shriek.

'What am I going to do with all these cucumbers?'

Chapter Four

Willow spent the rest of the day in a manic mood. Charlie wanted to make things right!

Perhaps the little cogs in his brain had been turning over and over since Saturday night's fiasco. Maybe Charlie had thought, "Why am I behaving like a wuss? I'm thirty-five years old and have been with the girl of my dreams for years. Let's do this!"

You just don't learn, do you? sneered the little voice.

I can live in hope, can't I? she retorted.

The little voice didn't deign to reply.

Willow couldn't wait for the hands of the clock to signal it was time to go home.

When Jean finally gave the all clear to leave, Willow was out of the library like Lewis Hamilton screeching off the starting line in the Grand Prix.

On the drive home, her mobile rang. The name "Emma Everest" flashed up on the caller display. Unlike Charlie's super-duper flashy BMW, Willow's little Citroen had neither Bluetooth nor hands-free apparatus. As she was now frustratingly stuck in rush-hour traffic, she committed the cardinal sin of discreetly answering her mobile. Holding the phone against the base of the passenger seat, she switched it to loudspeaker. Now she was able to put both hands on the steering wheel and stay on the right side of the law, should a police car cruise up beside her.

'Hi, Ems!'

Willow had to raise her voice so her bestie could hear.

'Are you driving?'

'Yeah. I'm on my way home.'

'You're so lucky having a local job and avoiding the London commute. I've had to let my usual train go off without me. Getting a seat these days is rarer than my mother not nicking my clothes, but today there wasn't even standing room. It's ridiculous.'

'Poor you,' said Willow sympathetically. 'Why not get a job nearer home?'

'Because the pay is rubbish. There's no choice in the matter. If I want more dosh, I must commute to the City. Anyway, now that I'm saving for a deposit to buy a place, every penny counts. As much as I love my mum, being back home with her is more challenging than when I was living with Jon.'

Emma and her ex-boyfriend Jon had parted acrimoniously. She'd helped pay the mortgage but, as her name hadn't been on the deeds and they'd never married, there was nothing Emma could do about claiming a percentage of a house she'd never legally owned. Willow heard her friend give a gusty sigh.

'The sooner I have my own space, the better. My mother is driving me mad.'

Willow suppressed a giggle as a picture of the very

glamorous Karen Everest popped into her head. Karen wasn't like the average middle-aged mother. At forty-six, she'd only calmed down a smidgen since her teenage years. Back then she'd been something of a wild child but preferred to use the term "free spirit". But whether a wild child or a free spirit, her wings had been clipped upon discovering she was expecting twins at the tender age of fifteen.

At sixteen, Karen had become mum to Emma and Noah. At seventeen, she'd married the twins' dad, Andy. By eighteen, both Andy and Karen had separated. Shortly after their divorce, Andy and his parents had moved to Australia. However, before they'd emigrated, there had been a bitter custody argument. This had been resolved by Karen keeping Emma, and Andy taking Noah.

Over the years Emma had reluctantly declined invitations to visit Australia and stay with her father and brother. Karen had discouraged Emma in getting to know her Oz family. Karen didn't like being reminded she'd messed up in her teens and had struggled with motherhood because she'd still been a child herself. She tried not to think about the little boy she'd given up to a teenaged ex-husband's family. Karen's parents had featured heavily in raising Emma. Consequently, she tended to treat Emma like a kid sister rather than a daughter.

'Do you know what Mum did?' said Emma, sounding outraged.

'Tell me.'

'I bought a fantastic pair of shoes for work. This morning I went to put them on, and there was no sign of them.'

'Ah.'

Willow had a feeling what was coming next.

'Mum had already left for work at the pub, and I was running late. So I rammed my feet into a pair of old flatties and belted off to the station. Once on the train, I texted her asking if she'd seen my new shoes. She replied almost immediately. "Oh darling, I couldn't resist borrowing them. Aren't they gorgeous! Do you mind if I wear them this weekend? I might have a date." I was livid. No doubt the shoes will be returned covered in beer slop.'

'That is naughty of her,' Willow agreed. 'But, on the upside, it must be fun having a mum who's young enough to share your stuff.'

Willow couldn't imagine sharing anything with her own mother. Anita, at sixty-two, had lost her waistline completely, and whilst she might have once had lovely legs, these days they were criss-crossed with purple veins. Willow had never seen her mother in high heels. In summer, Anita wore open-toed Birkenstocks and, in winter, sensible pumps. She was the opposite of Karen in every way, from her short unvarnished nails and pepper-grey hair, to her make-up-free face. Despite not bothering with herself, Willow could see her mother had once been a beauty, whereas Emma's mum bought her glamour. Karen's wavy brown hair was highlighted with expensive golden streaks. Her polished nails were immaculate thanks to the nail bar in Mosley, and she never ventured out of the house without make-up. Willow hoped she would look as good as Emma's mum when she one day turned forty-six. She wouldn't mind her figure either. Karen had a silhouette that most twenty-year-olds would envy.

'Make sure you reclaim your shoes this evening, then hide them,' Willow suggested.

'Flipping right,' Emma tutted. 'And stuff Mum's date this weekend because I have one myself.'

'Really? You kept that quiet. What's he like?'

'I'm not telling you.'

'What?' Willow was taken aback. 'Why ever not?'

'Because you won't approve.'

'Oh no. Not another guy who is twenty years older than you. I know you like these father-figure types, Ems, but don't saddle yourself with another Jon.'

'No, no, no. He's nothing like that. Actually, he's–'

'Don't tell me. He's loads younger. Is that it? You've gone the other way and now you're cradle snatching.'

'No!'

'What is it then?'

'Just, well, um…'

Willow sighed as the penny dropped.

'He's been round the block six million times. Am I right or am I right?'

'No, nothing like that. He's okay.'

'So what's the issue? Come on. Spit it out.'

'Look, leave it. Nothing will likely come of it. It's just a bit of fun.'

'He's not married, is he?'

When Emma didn't reply, Willow tutted.

'I hope you know what you're getting yourself into.'

'He's not married,' said Emma miserably. 'He's just not, you know, entirely free.'

'So he's living with someone.'

Another silence.

'Okay, let's change the subject.'

Willow didn't wish to upset her friend with a lecture.

'Good idea,' said Emma.

She was keen to get off the topic of her never-straightforward love life.

'Anyway, the reason I phoned was to see if you had a lovely birthday.'

Willow wanted to tell Emma about how she'd wrecked her own celebration because of the M word, but decided against it. If Emma wasn't keen to confide about her new boyfriend, then Willow didn't feel obliged in talking about her botched proposal. And anyway, Emma often made little digs about Charlie being a commitment-phobe, so even if Willow *did* mention it, Emma would probably roll her eyes and say, "Well, what did you expect?".

'I had a nice birthday,' said Willow carefully.

After all, it had been perfectly pleasant until she'd put her knife and fork together and mentioned the unmentionable.

'What did Charlie buy you?'

'A handbag.'

'Oooh, lovely. Was it that designer one you were recently salivating over?'

'No. I changed my mind about that one after spotting a

leather bag in M&S.'

'Really?' said Emma in surprise.

Willow had been nuts about the designer bag and dropped heavy hints to Charlie.

'This one is far more practical. It has lots of zips and pockets.'

'Oh, well, good. If you love it, that's all that matters.'

'Yes, I do,' said Willow, feeling depressed.

Her mother would have been thrilled with the bag. Like Anita, it was very sensible.

'Did Charlie buy you anything else?'

'Mm. A really pretty pair of earrings.'

'Oooh, lovely. Us girls like our baubles, eh! What did he surprise you with? Sapphires to match your eyes?'

'Er, no. They're cubic zirconia. But I love them,' said Willow loyally.

She omitted mentioning that the earrings hadn't come from a jeweller, but also been bought at Marks.

Willow had tried not to dwell upon Charlie's choice of birthday presents. She suspected he'd left present buying until the last minute, then panicked and asked his mother to dash out on his behalf. Both gifts were exactly the sort of thing Grace would buy for herself.

'Charlie also took me to a fabulous restaurant.'

There was a gasp at the other end of the line.

'Omigod! Was it that fancy restaurant in Covent Garden? The one you couldn't stop talking about? You lucky thing! What was it like?'

'Er, no. We went to the local pub.'

'Oh.'

'The, er, restaurant in Covent Garden was booked solid. For the next six months.'

'Ah.'

Willow stared through the windscreen at the traffic, aware that her mouth had turned down at the corners. Heavens, she mustn't feel like this. She was soooo lucky having a boyfriend who'd made a fuss of her. The bag, whilst not designer, certainly wasn't a cheapie, even though the earrings had probably cost no more than a fiver. And the pub grub had been delicious. She mustn't feel short-changed.

Well, I think you SHOULD feel short-changed, said the little voice.

Willow rolled her eyes.

Oh, here we go.

Yes, here I go. You spent a fortune on HIS birthday. You put a lot of thought into it. Charlie was whisked off by high speed rail to the London Eye. You both had your own pod complete with champagne. Then on to The Shard for dinner. And let's not forget that exquisite shirt you bought him. The price tag was two hundred pounds. You scrimped and scraped to pay for it all, and your salary is a FIFTH of his.

'Anyway,' – Willow was keen to get off the subject of her birthday – 'you're only a week younger than me. So how will *you* be celebrating this Saturday?'

'Well, I'm keeping my fingers and toes tightly crossed I'll be taken out, but, just in case he can't get away–'

'Oh, Ems, I'm so sorry. I didn't mean to be insensitive asking that question.'

'It's all right.'

Willow could imagine Emma shrugging at the other end of the line.

'I'm sure he'll leave his girlfriend eventually, with or without me in the equation. And anyway, it's not like it's serious between us. It's still quite new.'

'So, just in case your date night doesn't happen, shall we celebrate together?'

'Of course,' Emma chirped. 'I was hoping to spend Saturday with you anyway.'

'Great! What have you got in mind? Some shopping?'

'Noooo,' Emma laughed. 'I'm thinking of something far more fun than that.'

'What?'

'Visiting a tattoo parlour. I fancy getting inked.'

'Really?'

'Yeah! What do you say we both have one?'

Willow blanched. Somehow, she didn't see herself with tattoos.

'I'm not sure it's me.'

'Of *course* it's you! I can see you now sporting an explosion of stars across one shoulder.'

'I-I'll give it some thought,' Willow stammered.

'Or – I know – what about us having something small on the top of one leg? Then, if we don't like it, it's out of sight.'

'I suppose.'

'Brilliant! Be sure to put it in your diary.'

'Fab,' said Willow weakly.

What had she committed to?

Chapter Five

Letting herself into their neat semi, Willow dumped her handbag in the hall, whizzed up the stairs and had a super-fast shower.

Towelling herself off, she sprayed perfume over her wrists before slipping into soft fleecy loungewear – perfect for chilling and, later, snuggling up to Charlie.

Dashing back downstairs, she went into the kitchen and began prepping dinner. Charlie loved spag bol. As she set about chopping onions and sprinkling herbs over sizzling meat, she hummed away to herself. Charlie might not want to marry her – yet – but he now knew he'd behaved like a moron *and* apologised too. Progress!

Leaving the mince to brown, Willow set about making a tomato and basil sauce, all the while contemplating her future with Charlie. She was quietly confident that the entire weekend fiasco was turning itself around. Firstly, she'd planted the seed of the M word. All she had to do now was water it. Making Charlie his favourite dinner after a hard day at work was the start of that little seed sprouting a root. Having make-up sex would provide a second root. Before long the seed would put out a shoot, hurtling upwards, seeking the light that would surely now dawn on Charlie. It just needed time.

If Willow had been a gambling person, she'd have bet a tenner that in another twelve months Charlie would have proposed. After all, he was five years older than her, and many of his mates had married. He'd been to more stag stitch-ups in the last two years than an events company. He surely had no bachelor friends left. Many were now busy helping wives prepare the spare room as a nursery. The days of Friday nights in trendy wine bars were over. Very occasionally one or two of Charlie's friends were let off the marital leash for a pint at the local pub. Lately Charlie had lamented, "At this rate there will be no one left to have a drink with. They all rush home to have quality time bathing baby Bianca or little Logan." Indeed, it was only colleague Ben who remained unmarried. Like Charlie, Ben lived with his girlfriend. However, Anna wasn't bothered about marriage. She'd also told Ben she would never wreck her tummy muscles having his kids.

Willow transferred the sauce into the pan of browned mince. While she stirred, her thoughts remained on Anna. Willow didn't like to admit it, but she didn't resonate with Ben's girlfriend. Whenever they occasionally made up a foursome for a Saturday night curry, it was always Ben and Charlie who did most of the talking. If Anna did make conversation, it would only ever be about her latest promotion or her next marketing campaign. Invariably such meetings took place in the boardrooms of glamorous European cities. On the one occasion Anna had thought to ask Willow how her job at the library was going, she'd stifled a yawn and then started scrolling through her mobile. Anna had made it obvious she wasn't remotely interested in hearing about bossy Jean or how Willow sometimes had to stay late to finish cataloguing.

Shaking dried spaghetti into a saucepan, Willow decided not to boil it up just yet. She didn't want the pasta to be a soggy mess by the time Charlie arrived home. Hopefully he'd only be another half hour or so. The commute from London was a swift one thanks to living fifteen minutes from Ebbsfleet International and its highspeed railway.

Suddenly there was the sound of a key in the door.

'I'm home,' yodelled a familiar voice.

'Charlie!'

Willow abandoned her cooking and bounded into the hallway.

'You're early. How lovely.'

'Come here,' he said, kicking off his shoes and pulling her into his arms. 'I couldn't stand another moment at the office. Getting home to you suddenly seemed far more important.'

He kissed her full on the mouth, making her squirm with pleasure.

'Am I forgiven?'

'Of course.'

'Good.'

He sniffed the air appreciatively.

'Mm. Something smells good.'

'Your favourite.'

'Let me get out of this suit.'

'I'll go and put the pasta on.'

As Charlie took the stairs two at a time, Willow heard the faint ping of a text message on her boyfriend's mobile. Seconds later he was in their bedroom and out of sight.

Upstairs, Charlie reached for the phone in his jacket pocket. A text. He smirked. Nice one. It was good to be wanted. But he really did need to cool it with the sender. This was never meant to have happened. Apart from anything else, the lady was getting a bit needy. Better to concentrate on Willow and mending bridges, especially before he went away this weekend. His work department had to go to a boring convention in Birmingham. Regrettably it was compulsory attendance. On the upside, if temptation should come his way, at least it wouldn't be on his doorstep – unlike the sender of this text.

Charlie sighed. At some point he'd have to break things off. Gently of course. No doubt there would be tears. He would be a gentleman and let her cry on his shoulder. He'd pass her a tissue to dab her pretty eyes all the while murmuring it was better this way, and of *course* she wouldn't want to hurt Willow by ever blurting out what they'd done, would she?

Charlie was fairly certain she wouldn't let the cat out of the bag. After all, she said she loved Willow too. If she really meant that – and Charlie thought she did – then his secret was safe.

He chose to ignore the nagging voice in his head that, lately, had started to taunt him.

The truth will always out…

Chapter Six

Charlie had barely sat down at the kitchen table when he was on his feet again.

'What's the matter?' Willow asked in alarm.

'We've forgotten something.'

'The Parmesan is on the table.'

'No, not that.'

Charlie was now rummaging around in the cupboard under the sink. A moment later and he'd extracted a tealight from Willow's emergency "power cut pack".

'There,' he said, setting the candle down on the table between them.

Moments later a flaming match had been put to its wick.

'That's more like it.'

Willow nearly fell off her chair. What a romantic touch, and Charlie had done that with no prompting whatsoever.

'Cheers,' he said, clinking his glass of red against hers. 'Now tell me all about your day at the library. I trust no members of the public upset anyone. The last thing Mosley needs is a sighting of Jean in a strop. Is she aware that anger makes her mammoth bosoms quiver like unset jelly?'

Willow gave a snort of laughter, then told Charlie all about the little old lady and her carrier bag of cucumbers. Charlie let her waffle on. It allowed him to eat without interruption and my goodness he was hungry. Ben had popped out at lunchtime to get himself a sandwich. Charlie had asked if he'd get him a couple too. He'd asked for a peanut butter and tuna. When Ben had dropped the paper bag in front of him, Charlie hadn't bothered to check inside, instead taking a huge mouthful of wholemeal. Seconds later he'd nearly spat it across his keyboard.

'What the hell is this?' he'd spluttered, trying not to gag.

'Peanut butter and tuna,' Ben had said. 'That's what you asked for. That's what you've got.'

'Yes, but not *together*,' Charlie had replied, rolling his eyes. '*One* peanut butter. *One* tuna.'

He'd chucked the disgusting sandwiches in the bin.

'What's the matter with you? Your concentration has been off all morning.'

'Nothing,' Ben had replied moodily.

But Charlie had known otherwise. Something was up. Ben would tell him in his own time. He always did. No doubt he'd confide what was wrong this weekend when they were in Birmingham, relaxing over a drink or two.

'That reminds me,' said Charlie, interrupting Willow's flow about a display of courgettes.

What the hell was that all about?

'Don't forget I'm away this weekend.'

'Oh,' said Willow in disappointment. 'Why's that?'

'Another boring work convention,' said Charlie, winding

spaghetti around his fork. 'I'm sure I told you.'

'I must have forgotten. What a shame. Ah well, in that case I might as well spend Saturday with Emma.'

Charlie's fork froze mid-air.

'Why?'

'Why what?'

'Why spend Saturday with Emma?'

'Because it will be her thirtieth birthday.'

'Oh yes, that's right.'

'Wow, you actually knew that?'

Willow looked at Charlie in amazement. Most of the time he couldn't remember her own birthday, never mind her bestie's.

'Yeah' – he shrugged casually – 'I'm sure you mentioned it recently.'

'Ðid I?' Willow frowned. 'Anyway, Emma wants me to go to a tattoo parlour with her.'

'Whatever for?'

'To get a tattoo, silly.'

She rolled her eyes.

'Rather her than me,' said Charlie, pulling a face. 'As long as she realises that thirty years from now it might not suit her. Are you having one?'

'Emma wants me to, but I'm not sure. Would you still fancy me with a tattoo?'

'Only if you have my name on the inside of your wrist.'

Willow flushed with pleasure. The seed's first root had sprouted. Why else would Charlie suggest she have his name inked on her body if he wasn't planning on spending the rest of his life with her! Willow thought she might indeed have Charlie's name on the inside of her wrist. But not yet. Only after he'd put a ring on her finger. To do so beforehand might jinx the chance of a proposal.

Charlie forked up the last of his spaghetti before draining his glass of wine.

'Have you finished?' he said.

For a moment Willow was thrown. Finished what? Chatting about her day at Mosley Library, or talking about Emma's impending tattoo?

'Your dinner?' he prompted.

Due to her doing most of the talking, Willow's meal was virtually untouched. All the heat had gone out of it. She'd have to put it in the microwave.

'Only I want my dessert,' said Charlie.

'It's only tinned peaches and whippy cream,' said Willow apologetically.

'You're the peach' – he pulled her to her feet – 'and I'll definitely have you with the whippy cream.'

He cupped her face in his hands before lowering his mouth to hers. Willow's legs nearly gave way from the sudden desire that whooshed through her body. Charlie hadn't behaved like this since… since… well, she couldn't remember.

'Go upstairs,' he murmured. 'I'll bring the cream.'

'You're kidding,' she gasped.

What on earth had got into him?

'We're going to have some fun,' he promised.

And he meant it. It had been very pleasurable licking chocolate body paint off his lover, and she'd done some amazing things with her tongue when it had been spread over his erection. But she wasn't around to give a repeat performance. And anyway, all that had to stop. His lover had taught him inspiration. Just because that chapter was coming to an end, it didn't mean creativity had to stop.

Stifling a giggle, Willow scampered up the stairs peeling her clothes off along the way. Whatever was Charlie going to do with the whippy cream? Spray a foamy bikini on her body, then lick it off? This was unchartered territory. Seconds later, Charlie appeared behind her, shedding his office clothes over the landing floor.

'Two seconds,' he said hoarsely, before disappearing into the bathroom.

A moment later, the shower had burst into life.

Willow resisted the urge to rub her hands together and cackle with glee. Instead she busied herself switching on the bedroom lamps which immediately turned her white skin to pale gold.

Peeling back the duvet, she flopped down on the mattress, star-fishing out her arms and legs in anticipation. Then she shot upright again. Whippy cream would make a mess. Perhaps she should lay a towel over the flat sheet? But that wouldn't be so romantic. On the other hand, she'd only just laundered all the bedding. Without a towel, the sheets would have to be washed again.

Her sense of practicality rose to the fore, but as Willow

made for the hot cupboard to fetch the towel, Charlie appeared in the doorway. He'd taken the liberty of already creaming up – and it wasn't with Factor Fifty.

Seconds later, Willow had forgotten all about how to prevent the duvet turning into a trifle.

Chapter Seven

The following morning, Willow awoke to the touch of Charlie's lips against her forehead. He always got up an hour before her because of his commute.

'See you later,' he whispered.

'Bye, darling,' she replied sleepily.

'Oh, and you might want to strip the bed before you go to work. It's a bit sour in here.'

'Okay.'

Willow's eyes pinged open. Nothing like a bit of reality interrupting your rose-tinted dreams. Still, they'd had a lot of fun last night. Messing up the bedding had been worth it, although Willow suspected she'd never look at whippy cream in quite the same way again. Emma had once told her that she and Jon had regularly enjoyed spreading chocolate body paint over themselves. Willow couldn't begin to imagine the mess *that* would make.

Willow waited until Charlie had let himself out of the house, then swung her legs out of bed. Reaching for her mobile, she sent Emma a quick text.

I completely forgot. Charlie is away this weekend in Birmingham. A boring work convention (his words). If you're still getting a tattoo on Saturday, I'll def come with you. Whatever time you like xx

Half an hour later, Willow had showered, and the smelly bedding was whizzing around in the washing machine. Making up the bed with fresh linen, she hummed to herself. She and Charlie were back on track, and she'd never felt so content.

★★★

Charlie's train shot out of the last tunnel before London and zoomed towards King's Cross International. The 4G coverage reconnected and a flurry of texts landed on his mobile with a stuttering *ding-ding-dingggg*. Everybody scrambled to their feet, waiting impatiently for the train to roll to a standstill. The carriage aisle was now like human lasagne.

Remaining in his seat, Charlie used the extra minute before disembarking to scroll through his messages. The first was from Willow.

Love you xx

The second was from Ben:

Mate, Anna's been a right bloody bitch this morning and made me late. Cover my back until I'm in. Please can you print out Bryson's exit planning report for me and put it on Drummond's desk. If Drummond comes looking for me, tell him you don't know where I am. Oh, and hang your jacket over the back of my chair so it looks like I'm in, eh? Cheers. I owe you one.

The third was from Kev:

Yay for telling Willow you're going to a work convention! So happy! I was thinking about having a tattoo, but can skip it. So where shall we go? An Indian summer is forecast for the weekend. How about Brighton? I fancy paddling in the sea, walking along the beach, eating fish and chips under the stars, followed by some al-fresco sex. Can't wait!!! Xxxxxxxxxxx

Charlie sighed and turned his attention back to the first text. He wasn't up for returning Willow's declaration of love. Not yet. He didn't want his girlfriend misinterpreting things and believing he was weakening about the M word. Equally, he didn't want her thinking he was a total bastard. His fingers tapped out a reply:

You're such a babe xx

He re-read the second text and wondered what was going on between Ben and Anna. Every month, regular as clockwork, she gave Ben hell. Ben claimed Anna suffered rampant PMT. Last time around Ben had dared to change the channel in the middle of *Strictly.* Anna had gone berserk, snatched the remote control and threatened to bludgeon him with it. Ben had responded with a weak joke that his favourite cops from the Seventies would rescue him. Star Key and Hash. Anna hadn't laughed.

Charlie tutted. Anna was a handful. Thank God Willow didn't behave like that. He knew Willow's hormones played her up from time to time, but usually they made her weepy rather than bad-tempered. He could still remember the time he'd come home from work and found her in floods of tears. She'd been so distraught he'd presumed someone had died.

There had indeed been a death. Of a daddy long-legs. Willow had attempted scooping the creature up but accidentally knocked off one wing and a couple of legs. Horrified at inadvertently causing harm, she'd put the insect out of misery by squashing it. Cue intense bawling. Charlie had comforted Willow and kissed away her tears. He'd ended up gently making love to her. When Charlie had suggested to Ben that he try deflecting Anna's PMT with some old-fashioned rumpy-pumpy, his friend had looked horrified. "When Anna is in that sort of mood," he'd cried, "I'm not letting her anywhere near my willy."

The train doors had opened and people were now surging forward. Charlie quickly replied to Ben's text:

Will cover your back at the office!

He then added a thumbs-up emoji.

Slipping the mobile into his jacket pocket, Charlie grabbed his briefcase from the overhead shelf. A moment later and he was bringing up the rear of the crowd stepping on to the platform. Head down, he headed towards the ticket barrier with his travel card at the ready.

Kev's text had gone unanswered. For now, Kev could wait.

Chapter Eight

Halfway through the morning, Charlie started to feel irritated. There was only so long you could cover for a missing colleague. Drummond hadn't been happy with the report Charlie had printed out on Ben's behalf and had already been out once looking for Ben and… uh-oh… speak of the devil… their boss was once again stomping this way.

'He can't *still* be in the toilet,' Drummond snapped.

'His stomach feels upset,' said Charlie.

'*I* feel upset,' Drummond roared. 'You'll have to deal with this report on Ben's behalf. I want it back on my desk, making full sense, in half an hour.'

Charlie was sorely tempted to remind Drummond about his own deadlines, not to mention preparing for a meeting with a major client this afternoon. However, he knew better than to argue with Drummond who, when breathing fire, could make a dragon look inadequate. Instead, he picked up Ben's report, smiled at Drummond and said that of *course* he'd deal with it, whilst mentally jabbing two fingers in the air. Blasted man jack-booting around.

On top of everything else, his mobile was pinging a series of messages from Kev. It was starting to jar. His phone was positioned next to his keyboard, the screen visible and now displaying yet another WhatsApp message. Picking up the mobile and flicking the volume to silent, he was outraged when it began vibrating in his hand. One word lit up the screen. Kev.

'Hello?' he hissed.

'What's going on?'

'Nothing's going on. I'm at work.'

'But you've not replied to my messages.'

'Because I'm at work.'

'But you've read them, so why not reply?'

'I haven't read them!'

'Two blue ticks tell me you have.'

'What I mean is' – Charlie blustered – 'I haven't read them properly.'

He felt annoyed at being put on the spot. What was this? Twenty questions? He didn't get this sort of interrogation from Willow. At the other end of the line, the voice softened. A change of tack.

'Sorry. I'm missing you, Charlie Bear,' she cooed.

'I'm missing you too,' he said, then instantly cursed himself.

He wasn't missing *her*. The only thing he missed was their wild sex.

'I can't wait to have you all to myself this weekend,' she persisted. 'Shall I book a B&B?'

'No,' he said irritably.

Oh God. Drummond was hovering. Why was Kev calling him at the office? Willow never called him at work.

'Why not?'

There was a pout in her voice.

'Because this weekend I really *do* have to go away on business.'

There was a pause while she digested this.

'To Birmingham?'

'Yes. To Birmingham.'

'Right.'

Another pause.

'And we all know what happens in Birmingham, eh?'

Charlie gnashed his teeth. Why had he confided to her about the high jinks he'd previously got up to when away. Well, he knew the answer to that. It had turned her on. Or so she'd said, anyway.

'Nothing will be happening in Birmingham other than a boring work convention.'

At the other end of the office Drummond swung round and glared at Charlie. Damn. Had he overheard? He gave his boss a weak smile.

'Listen, I can't talk. Ben's not in. I'm trying to do the job of two people and my boss is giving me the evil eye.'

'But what about this weekend?' she persisted, ignoring Charlie's plea to end the call. 'You know perfectly well that after the convention you'll be out with your mates. Since when did you pass up being entertained on a Saturday night? You'll be ogling table dancers, signalling to your favourite, then wining and dining her before taking her back to your hotel for a night of passion.'

'That only happened once.'

'That's not what you told me. You said it happened every time you went away.'

'I was exaggerating.'

'Why?'

'Because I thought that was what you wanted to hear.'

'Well I've changed my mind.'

'Right. Glad we've sorted that out. Now I really do need to go.'

'How do I know you won't cheat on me, Charlie?'

'You're carrying on like a jealous wife.'

'I'm not.'

'Yes, you are.'

'Oh, does that annoy you then?'

'Frankly, yes. It does. Willow doesn't behave like this.'

'That's because Willow has no idea that you're an unfaithful bastard,' she snarled. 'And don't you *dare* compare me to that lump. I can understand why you started playing away when it comes to Willow. After all, you've told me yourself that you don't fancy her any more and there's no action between the sheets. But I'm not as drippy as Willow. Nor am I up for being lied to, Charlie. Do you understand?'

Charlie put the report down. He closed his eyes and pinched the bridge of his nose between thumb and forefinger, as if trying to block out pain. This was ridiculous. How the heck had a bit of flirty fun turned into being hassled at work with an accusation about being cheated upon?

He had a sudden recollection of that old film he'd once

watched with Willow. What was it called? Ah yes, *Fatal Attraction*. It had starred Glenn Close and Michael Douglas. Glenn had fluttered her eyelashes at Michael who'd fluttered his own back. The next thing was his kid's pet rabbit being casseroled. Was that what was happening here? Charlie mentally batted the thought away and berated himself for the path his mind had skittered along.

You're overreacting. Of course she's not a bunny boiler. Moron! But this moment serves as a reminder that you need to extricate yourself. Might as well do it now, eh?

'Hello?' she said. 'Why aren't you saying anything?'

'I'm thinking, sweetie,' he soothed.

'What are you thinking?' she said sulkily.

'I'm thinking that–'

In the nick of time he stopped himself from saying, "We need to talk.". Those words would unleash wrath.

'I'm thinking that I'd like to see you tonight,' he said instead.

Hell, he'd have to bite the bullet and tell Willow he had to work late.

'Can I see you this evening?'

'Yes. Leave it with me. I'll make sure the coast is clear for a few hours.'

'Fine,' he said. 'See you later.'

'That you will,' she giggled, all smiles again. 'You'll see *all* of me later.'

Sighing, Charlie ended the call.

Chapter Nine

Charlie spent the next thirty minutes revising Ben's report. After returning it to Drummond, he sent a hasty text to Willow.

Sorry, babe. Going to have to work late. Ben hasn't arrived at the office. Something about him and Anna having a blazing row. Currently doing his work and mine. Don't cook for me. Will grab a burger from the drive-thru xx

Ben slunk in just before noon. He quietly slid into his chair and, within seconds, made it seem as if he'd been about, if not visible.

'What the heck's been going on?' Charlie demanded.

'I don't want to discuss it,' said Ben.

He tapped his keyboard, then pretended to be studying a spreadsheet.

'Mate, you owe me,' said Charlie in annoyance. 'I've had a crap time redoing your report and an even crappier time dealing with Drummond. So come on, spit it out.'

'Ah, you know. Women trouble.'

'You mean *woman* trouble.'

'No, women. In the plural. You see, there's two of them.'

'What?' said Charlie in confusion. 'Are you trying to tell

me you're seeing someone else?'

'Sort of.'

'Sort of?'

'Ah, you know. It just happened.'

Charlie knew only too well how something "sort of" became "just happened".

'Does Anna know? Is that why you had a row?'

'Noooooo!' said Ben with a shudder. 'No way does she know. I'm not up for having the groin cut out of my suits, thank you very much.'

'Okay, so if Anna doesn't know about this other woman, why are you late to work? What was going on at home?'

'The usual monthly nonsense. Full-blown PMT. Every flipping month she goes off her head with rage. This morning she was snarling like a Pitbull because I'd failed to put the lid on the coffee jar. She was absolutely gunning to turn a minor irritation into a major argument. When I refused to react, she snatched my toast and flung it across the kitchen. Seconds later the china plate had followed. It hit the ground and cracked the floor tile. She screamed, "Now look what you made me do". I told her to calm down and said I'd clear up the mess, but she stalked off. By the time I'd put the broken china in the bin and mopped the floor, she was back looking wild about the eyes. She said she'd rung her office and told them she wouldn't be in because she had an upset tummy. Then she said I had to stay at home with her to comfort her. I told her not to be daft and said I was going to work. I put on my jacket but couldn't find my shoes. It turned out she'd hidden them.'

'Well, why didn't you put on a different pair of shoes?' said Charlie.

He thought about his side of the wardrobe at home, the base of which was stuffed with footwear.

'Surely you have loads of shoes?'

'Mate, she'd hidden them all' – Ben flung his arms wide – 'even my flip-flops.'

'You're wearing shoes now. How did you get them off her?'

'No, Charlie, you don't understand. I grabbed my car keys and left the house in my socks. I drove to the local shopping mall and visited one of the shoe shops. I felt a right berk walking in with nothing on my feet.'

'And this is all because Anna has PMT?'

'Yes!'

'Why hasn't she visited her GP?'

'Oh but she has. Ages ago. The doctor wanted to prescribe anti-depressants.'

'Truthfully?'

Charlie arched an eyebrow.

'Yeah. Well I believe so. I didn't go with Anna to the appointment.'

'Why anti-depressants?'

'The quack thought they might stop the mood swinging. Except Anna went bananas at the doctor. "You want to add another statistic to our Prozac nation?" she screamed, before storming out. Mate, she makes my life a misery. Sometimes I wonder if the PMT is just an excuse for her to pick, pick, pick.

She's like a bird with a particularly sharp beak attacking me over anything and everything. Is it any wonder that I responded to the smile of another woman?'

'A smile?' Charlie quizzed. 'A smile is one thing. Letting it become something else is another matter.'

Hark at him. If only Ben knew what *he'd* been up to.

'Yeah, I know,' Ben sighed.

'Where did you meet her?'

'In the local Chinese of all places. On that particular night, the trains had been playing up. We'd both got home from work late. Anna was in a mood. As ever. To placate her, I said I'd nip out to Ming's and get a takeaway. When I got to the restaurant, all hell was breaking loose. One of the chefs was having a strop. He walked out leaving the kitchen staff struggling with the orders. The manager gave everybody drinks on the house as an apology for the extra wait time. I sat down with a beer and struck up conversation with this sweet-faced woman. We just clicked. It's amazing how much you can find out about someone in half an hour. She told me she'd recently broken up with her boyfriend and was treating herself to some comfort food. And I said… well, I said…'

Ben trailed off, his expression sheepish.

'You said what?' Charlie prompted.

'I said that I was in the middle of separating from my live-in partner and had also come out for comfort food.'

'So you lied.'

'Bent the truth.'

'But you're *not* in the process of separating from Anna,'

Charlie pointed out.

'I am now,' said Ben determinedly. 'I've made up my mind.'

'What, as of this second?'

'Yes. I shall tell Anna this evening. Well, maybe not *this* evening. After all, I don't want her chucking more plates about. I'll have to pick my moment. But I can't carry on like this, Charlie. Even if Anna didn't turn into a wild woman every few weeks, the bottom line is she's not my soulmate. She is *so* self-obsessed. I want a woman who's soft and smiley. Someone who welcomes me when I get home. Someone like your Willow.'

'Willow?' said Charlie, startled.

He'd never really thought of Willow like that before. But Ben was right. Willow was indeed soft, smiley and welcoming. It made Charlie feel even more confused about why he played away behind his girlfriend's back.

'I can't understand why you play away behind your girlfriend's back,' said Ben.

Flipping heck. Was Ben turning into a mind reader?

'She's such a smashing girl.'

'Yes, I know,' said Charlie lightly. 'But I haven't quite finished sowing all my wild oats. You remember that saying? What the eye doesn't see, the heart doesn't grieve.'

Ben rolled his eyes. He was about to answer when a shadow fell across both desks.

'How's your stomach?' boomed Drummond.

'Much better, thank you,' said Ben quaking.

He prayed his day wouldn't get any worse. The last thing he needed was Drummond bawling him out.

'Sorry about earlier. Think I ate some dodgy prawns last night.'

'No worries, lad,' said Drummond. He suddenly grinned. 'In fact, I have good news. Thanks to the feelers you put out, we've landed the Carpenter & Co account. They're a very big fish' – Drummond was now sounding like a cat who'd been given salmon instead of kibble – 'so it's only right you should handle their account. Do a good job and there will be a big fat bonus.'

'That's… that's great.'

Oh the sweet relief for not being yelled at.

'Pop along to my office after lunch. We'll go over the details.'

'Right. Will do,' Ben nodded.

Drummond walked off, whistling loudly. Ben exhaled weakly. He looked at Charlie.

'Thanks for sorting out that report, mate. Listen, shall we go for a drink after work? I'm not in any hurry to get home.'

'Ah,' said Charlie. 'I'd love to, but I promised Willow I wouldn't be late.'

Wow, sneered the little voice in Charlie's head. *The lies just trip off your tongue, don't they? Now you're not just telling Willow porkies, you're also being untruthful to your best friend.*

Charlie ignored the little voice.

'Tell you what. How about we have some fun this

weekend instead? After the convention? We can have a few drinks, then check out the girlies at that club.'

'I'm up for a few drinks, but no thanks to the girlies. I don't want any additional complications in my personal life. Anyway, I think I've fallen in love.'

'Don't be daft,' Charlie laughed.

'I mean it. I've never felt this before.'

'What's her name?'

'I'm not telling you. I'd rather not discuss her. She's special. *We're* special. I don't want you pouring scorn on it.'

'It's not special,' said Charlie derisively. 'It's called *rebounding*. The best thing you can do is chat up someone else this weekend and have some no-strings sex.'

'Like you do?' said Ben irritably. 'You have a lovely girl at home, yet you mess her about.'

'I don't mess Willow about,' Charlie protested. 'If she knows nothing about it, she's not being messed about, is she!'

Ben shook his head.

'No offence, mate, but I just don't get you.'

Charlie gave Ben an injured look.

'I'm not married, for goodness sake!'

'As good as,' Ben countered.

'I don't agree. Marriage is complicated, whereas living together isn't. Willow and I could walk away from each other tomorrow, and there would be no problems. There wouldn't be any need to consult a solicitor or spend a fortune on legal fees. We wouldn't have to provide affidavits in some court of law stating why we wanted to divorce. Simple.'

‘You bought a house together,’ said Ben. ‘It’s jointly owned. That’s a commitment in itself.’

‘Ah, but not the same as a having a marriage certificate,’ said Charlie, wagging a finger at Ben. ‘In the conveyancing contract there was definitely no clause that said, “Till death us do part.” I know, because I read it from start to finish. And anyway, enough about me and Willow because this conversation is about you and… you and…’

Charlie prompted Ben to provide the girl’s name.

‘Oh no you don’t. You’re not catching me out. Her name is my secret.’

‘You’re being ridiculous.’

‘No, I’m not. Anyway, you’re right about the rebound thing. If Anna and I split – and I really think we need to – then I want some emotional space before pursuing another relationship. I want to be sure it’s the real deal.’

‘Excellent’ – Charlie clapped his hands together – ‘which is even more reason to get your leg over this weekend.’

‘Oh bog off, Charlie,’ said Ben, but without rancour. ‘I will never understand why you are so duplicitous to Willow.’

Which was precisely why Charlie had never confided in Ben about Kev. It was one thing to have the occasional one-night stand in Birmingham and for Ben to judge Charlie as a bit of a lad now and again. It was quite another to have a regular lover on your doorstep. Charlie wasn’t up for his best mate diminishing him from likely lad to contemptible cad.

‘Just saying,’ Charlie shrugged.

‘Well don’t. You worry about your own love life, and I’ll

worry about mine.'

'I don't have any worries about my love life,' said Charlie glibly. 'None at all.'

Which wasn't strictly true. Because even as he uttered those words, a part of his brain was already pondering how to extricate himself from Kev's manicured claws.

Chapter Ten

At a little after five thirty, Charlie grabbed his jacket, left the office and, like an ant re-joining its army, entered ranks with the swift-moving crowd striding towards Kings Cross station.

Jogging past those who'd chosen to stand on the right, he took the steps of the escalator two at a time. Brandishing his travel card, he pushed through the turnstile and ran along the platform just as a guard blew his whistle. Charlie hurtled through the train's open doors with all the exuberance of a marathon runner crossing the finishing line. Perfect timing! The doors shut with a soft hiss. Seconds later the carriage began to gently rock as the 17:34 headed south towards Ebbsfleet International.

Moving along the aisle, Charlie flopped down on a vacant seat. Resting his briefcase on his thighs, he closed his eyes. He needed to concentrate on what he was going to say to Kev.

He was reluctant to go inside her house because it put him at a psychological disadvantage. After all, it was *her* territory. However, he could hardly conduct the conversation he wanted to have in his own home. Not with Willow around. Or even *not* with Willow around. He just couldn't risk it. The very thought of that made him feel twitchy and, if another commuter had chosen that moment to look at Charlie, they would have seen his body give an involuntary jerk.

The train shot into a tunnel, and Charlie's thoughts began to drift as he entered that half-way place between wakefulness and nodding off. In his mind's eye he saw himself ringing Kev's doorbell. A moment later and she was standing before him. Suddenly everything was like an old black-and-white movie.

Her: Charlie Bear!

Him: Heyyy.

Her: Come in.

(Door gently click shuts. Charlie remains standing in hallway.)

Him: I'll come straight to the point. This has got to stop.

Her: Oh.

Him: It's not going anywhere. It *can't* go anywhere.

Her: (*Sad but understanding.*) You're right.

Him: (*Gives her full benefit of his baby blues which convey perfect mix of sympathy and regret.)* What we had was wonderful.

Her: (*Tearful but not enough to wreck mascara.*) I will never forget you.

Him: Likewise. You will always be here. (*Touches heart.*)

Her: Oh Charlie Bear. You're so romantic.

Him: I know.

Her: Thank God Willow never found out. (*Snatches hand back and presses fingers to temples.*) I love her like a sister.

Him: Our secret is safe. (*Embraces her tightly.)* What we

did was wrong, but by ending it now we're making everything right.

Her: That's so true, Charlie Bear. You are very wise.

Him: I know. (*Arranges features into expression of innate wisdom.)*

Her: Leave, Charlie Bear. I cannot stand another moment of this torture. (*Opens the door and pushes Charlie out of house.)*

Him: Au revoir, my darling.

(Blows a kiss, turns away, and tries not to shout "YIPPEEEE".)

The overhead speaker fragmented Charlie's inner showreel with the announcement that the train was arriving at Ebbsfleet.

Opening his eyes, Charlie stifled a yawn, content that he had a rough plan in his head on how to finish things between him and Kev.

Walking out of the station, a sudden chill wind whipped his hair about. Cold spits of rain began to pelt his face. Turning up the collar of his jacket, Charlie put his head down and began jogging towards the car park. He realised the nights were now drawing in. The sun was already low in the sky, its brightness restricted by a bank of dark clouds which were huddled together like witches around a cauldron. He shivered and felt a spray of goose bumps erupt across his skin. Trotting up to his car, he popped the button on the key fob and sank down gratefully behind the steering wheel, glad to be out of the elements.

As the engine turned over it gave a throaty *vrrroom.* Pointing the bonnet towards Mosley, Charlie offered up a small prayer of thanks that Kev's house was on the other side of the village, well away from Willow and the eyes of any prying neighbours.

The initial patter of rain had now turned into a teeming cloudburst. Usually Charlie parked two streets away from Kev's house but, because it was now chucking down, he decided to pull up outside her house. After all, he'd only be five minutes. In the unlikely event of a friend of Willow's spotting Charlie's car and later questioning it, he'd say… he'd say… yes!... he'd say that he'd mistakenly thought Willow was here having a cup of tea, and he'd decided to join them both.

Perfect reasoning, Charlie. Don't over-complicate things. Keep excuses simple.

Leaping out of the car, he ran up the garden path and took refuge in the open porch, almost squashing himself against the wooden panels of the front door in order to avoid the downpour. His hand, already frozen and now running with tiny rivers of water, went up to the doorbell. His index finger was so wet it slid off the button, and he couldn't make it ring until the second attempt.

The door opened a fraction.

'Charlie Bear!'

Kev's head bobbed into view while the rest of her remained out of sight, shielded by the doorframe.

'Heyyy,' he said with a smile.

'Come in.'

The door clicked shut behind him, but Charlie's mentally rehearsed opening line died on his lips. Kev was wearing nothing but a fire-engine red lipstick and matching high heels. The only sound that escaped his lips was a gasp. All intention to stick to the script he'd concocted on the train fluttered away like the autumn leaves littering outside's wet pavements.

Charlie felt powerless to resist. And Kev knew it.

She took him by the hand and led him up to her room.

Chapter Eleven

Kev didn't let go of Charlie's hand until he was in her bedroom. Exactly where she wanted him.

He was now shedding clothes faster than a menopausal woman having a hot-flush. This was the only time Kev ever had any power over Charlie, and she wanted to make the most of it. Off went the shirt. Down went the trousers. A pair of socks were balled up and tossed through the air, narrowly missing one of the many candles she'd lit earlier and placed around the room.

'Careful, darling,' she cautioned. 'We don't want a fire.'

'I'm already on fire,' said Charlie hoarsely.

Now his boxers were whizzing past her left ear. They landed on the curtain rail, dangling for any passer-by to see.

Kev smirked. Wouldn't it be wonderful if – by some crazy Law of Sod – Willow was in the area right now. Perhaps she might even be walking up to Kev's front door this very moment! After believing Charlie's excuse about working late, wouldn't it be ironic if Willow had decided to pop over and spend the evening here? She'd arrive anticipating a cuppa and natter. Instead she'd clock Charlie's car outside. Do a double take. Her brain would start whirring. Why was her boyfriend *here* of all places? He was meant to be at work.

Kev sighed. How convenient it would be if this were so, because then Willow would start to put two and two together. Her eyes might at this very moment be looking up at the bedroom window where – gasp – Charlie's boxer shorts were waving from the curtain rail. Might Willow's voice at any second foghorn through the letterbox?

"I know you're in there, Charlie Goodman. I've rumbled what's going on. Consider yourself dumped!"

Charlie pulled Kev down on top of him and she gasped – partly from pleasure, partly from the madness of this whole situation. For it *was* a mad situation. Crazy. She wasn't even sure how this whole thing had started. Wait. It was coming back to her. It had been that coffee morning… the one that Willow had bullied everyone she knew into attending. A fund-raising event at the village hall. Some worthy cause that Willow had been involved in, alongside her self-righteous old bag of a boss. What was her name? Jen? No, Jean. That's right. A domineering woman who'd evidently never heard of waxing strips. You could have plaited the hair on Jean's quivering upper lip.

Charlie had been in the background, trying to look supportive. He'd been bored stiff. She'd gone over to him. They'd chatted – just like they'd done a thousand times before. Except *this* time something between them had shifted. A look from her. A quizzical raising of an eyebrow from him. Then a testing of the metaphorical waters.

'I'd rather be anywhere than here, wouldn't you?', he'd

asked.

She'd smiled suggestively.

'I can think of one place.'

His eyes had widened slightly.

'Does it feature a bed?'

She'd nodded slowly, her pupils dilating to the size of the charity cakes Willow had been trying to flog.

Charlie hadn't wasted a moment. Casually passing over his phone, in a low voice he'd instructed her to put in her number. She'd done so in full view of everyone in the hall, before saving the entry under the codename "Kev". From that moment on, whenever they'd been alone together, that was what Charlie called her. She regarded it as a secret affectionate name, and he'd become her Charlie Bear. She'd handed the phone back with a shiver of delight, relishing the promise of what was to come.

When they'd had their first assignation, she'd assumed it would be a one-off. However, they'd had such a frisson of excitement from their rendezvous, they'd repeated it. But, just like the drug, she'd found herself hopelessly hooked on Charlie.

Lately he'd been dropping hints about ending the affair. She wasn't stupid. She'd picked up the recent vibes. She was also deliberately ignoring them. Until Charlie said those three little words, *it is over*, she was playing dumb. Why? She'd asked herself that question a thousand times. The only answer she could come up with was because she was enjoying herself. Certainly too much to let him end it. She wanted more. *Much* more. Every now and again she fantasised that Charlie might have fallen in love with her. Wouldn't that be fantastic? Although, deep down, she knew they weren't really suited to each other. But, then again, didn't they say that opposites attracted?

If only Charlie would come to his senses and realise that he needed to end his relationship not with *her*, but with his live-in girlfriend. And yes, it *would* make things awkward between her and Willow. After all, they'd known each other for a long time. But… Willow would get over it. Eventually. She was still young enough to meet someone else. Willow wasn't compatible for Charlie on so many levels. She probably wanted babies, and Kev knew that Charlie didn't. Which suited *her* fine. In her opinion, motherhood was so overrated. How many times had she and Willow been in a café, gossiping, only to have their conversation wrecked by someone's kid letting out ear-piercing wails? It was the same in restaurants. And aeroplanes. *She* was the one who always ended up with a fractious toddler sitting behind her. It was no joy listening to a kid screaming about cabin pressure playing havoc with its eardrums, especially when that kid's racket upset everyone else's eardrums.

Kev collapsed onto the mattress beside Charlie, breathing hard. He sighed contentedly, then pulled her into the crook of his arm. She snuggled into him, wishing this was something they could do every day, not just in snatched moments. Two minutes later, she realised the rise and fall of Charlie's chest had taken on a slow and steady rhythm. Glancing up under her eyelashes, she realised he'd dozed off. She smiled. Poor darling. But how fortuitous for her. Despite having known Charlie for several years, she had no pictures of him. Well, not personal ones. Images on her phone of Charlie and Willow didn't count, whereas pictures of Charlie in her bed most definitely did.

Her mobile was on the bedside table. Kev made a long arm and grabbed it. Seconds later, she had a treasured shot of Charlie's handsome features against the backdrop of her Cath Kidston pillowcases. She then reached into her underwear drawer. Seconds later, like a shower cap, she'd placed a fishnet thong over his head. She took another picture. Just for fun. It would be something to occasionally look back upon and giggle.

After all, it wasn't like anyone else would ever see it, was it?

Chapter Twelve

'What are you doing?' said Charlie, coming to.

He pulled the thong off his head.

'Just messing about,' said Kev with a giggle.

'Ha bloody ha,' he tutted, lobbing the thong at her.

Kev ducked and the itsy-bitsy piece of underwear landed on the carpet, as did the mobile which she let slip from her hand. She didn't want Charlie knowing about her secret pictures. She would look at them later. After he'd gone. A shadow passed over her face.

'What's the matter?' he asked, propping himself up on one elbow to properly look at her.

'Oh… you know,' she said with a sigh.

'No, I don't know, otherwise I wouldn't ask. Go on. Spit it out.'

Her mouth turned downwards.

'Your forthcoming trip to Birmingham. I honestly thought you'd made that up to get away from Willow for the weekend and be with me.'

Charlie was silent for a moment. Oh God. He should never have allowed Kev to lead him upstairs to her bedroom. But what red-blooded male could resist scarlet lipstick and matching high heels worn by an otherwise naked woman? Certainly not him. He should have stayed in Kev's hallway and stuck to the script he'd formulated on the train. Now wasn't the moment to do a "it's-not-you-it's-me" speech. Not when he couldn't make a quick getaway due to his clothes being scattered around the bedroom and–

Where were his boxers?

'What are you thinking?' she prompted.

Why did women always want to know what men were thinking?

'That I ought to be going.'

'When will I next see you?'

'I'll text.'

To say that you won't be seeing me.

Hell. Only wimps dumped by text. Okay. Fine. He'd be a wimp. Whatever. He just needed this to end.

'Can I ask you a question?' she said.

'About?'

'Your trip to Birmingham.'

Why did she keep harping on about Birmingham?

Charlie tried not to look shifty.

'What about it?'

'I want to know what *really* goes on when you're away.'

'It's a work convention. What do you think happens? That we put whoopee cushions on the CEO's seat and ping elastic bands at him as we snigger behind our notepads?'

'Now you're being silly,' she tutted. 'You know perfectly well what I'm talking about. You've told me all about the dodgy lap dance places you've visited, not forgetting the seedy nightclubs that you and your colleagues have frequented. And let's not omit the number of girls you've picked up.'

'Look, we discussed this when you rang my office. I went to a club once' – Charlie lied – 'and that was long before anything was going on between us. Yes, hands up' – he made a gesture of surrender – 'I was persuaded to go along after shipping too much booze and being the worse for wear. But, as the Hollywood legend Paul Newman once famously said, "Why would I go out for a hamburger when I have *filet mignon* at home?"'

'At home?' said Kev sharply. 'Are you telling me Willow is your *filet mignon*?'

'No, you big silly,' he said, deliberately softening his voice to appease her. 'I'm talking about *you*. Nothing goes on between me and Willow. I've told you repeatedly. She's like my kid sister.'

Now that Willow's name had been mentioned in a platonic context, Kev decided to pursue this line of questioning, even though it was a taboo subject. She wanted answers.

'If Willow is like your kid sister, why are you still living together?'

Charlie shrugged.

'I guess it's the easy option. We have a house together. She pays her share of the mortgage, which makes things cheaper for me. And she looks after me. It's nice having my shirts ironed and having a meal put on the table.'

He gave an embarrassed laugh to acknowledge he was using Willow.

'Plus I'm fond of the old girl,' he added, just to prove he wasn't a total shit.

'Old? She's *thirty*, Charlie. Not ninety.'

'Just a figure of speech.'

'Huh.' Kev pursed her lips. 'You're older than Willow by five years.'

'Okay, let's not point score.'

'So what exactly are you going to do about her?'

'Do?'

'Yes, *do*, Charlie.'

Kev knew she was pursuing a dangerous subject, but she couldn't resist.

'Do I have to *do* anything?' said Charlie, looking confused.

'Yes! What about us?'

Charlie was starting to resent this line of questioning.

He flopped back against the pillows and stared up at the ceiling. This was the perfect moment to bow out. To say, "Listen, confession time. I'm a bastard. A *big* bastard. And once a bastard, always a bastard. I can't possibly continue foisting my bastardness on you for another second. So I'm going to do the honourable thing and let you go." What would she say to that? Probably, "You BASTARD," and then he could say, "Exactly!".

'Charlie?' she prompted.

'Yes?'

He didn't look at her. Instead he kept his eyes on the

ceiling. Tiny cracks fretted the plasterwork around the light pendant. He silently harrumphed. What a parallel to this relationship. It was full of cracks.

'We get along so well, and the sex is great,' she gabbled. 'Why don't you tell Willow the truth about us? In time, she'll get over it.'

Charlie wasn't so sure. In his mind's eye he could see Willow staring at him in disbelief, the terrible hurt in those puppy-dog eyes. "You don't want to be with me any more? You want to be with *her?* But why, Charlie? What did I do wrong?"

'And anyway, she must know things aren't okay between you both.'

'Really?' said Charlie frowning. 'And why would that be?'

'Derrrrrr,' she said, her voice laden with sarcasm. 'You said yourself that the pair of you don't have a sex life.'

'Ah, well, that's… that's down to Willow. Not me.'

'You mean it's her *choice* not to have sex?'

'Yeah, yeah,' Charlie nodded. 'Willow never had a huge sex drive.'

'I thought you said the two of you were like rabbits when you met in Ibiza.'

'That was then. This is now. She's no longer like a rabbit.'

'What, more like a jellyfish?'

'Eh?'

'You know, one of those creatures that don't need a male in their life. Did you know that jellyfish can even breed without a male? Isn't that amazing!'

'Um, I didn't know that. And anyway, I wouldn't say Willow was like a jellyfish.'

'What is she like then?'

'More like a teddy bear,' said Charlie thoughtfully.

'In what way?' she asked, hackles rising.

Charlie had failed to detect the hostility in Kev's voice.

'Willow is like a teddy bear because she's cuddly.'

'Cuddly?' she growled. 'Do you still have cuddles?'

'Noooo,' said Charlie hastily. 'Not like that. Not in the way you're thinking. I meant she's cuddly as in–'

'Fat?'

'She's not fat!'

'Yes she is,' Kev snarled. 'She hasn't got a figure like mine.'

'No, no, she hasn't,' Charlie soothed.

Kev didn't have a spare ounce of flesh on her body. Embracing her was like hugging an ironing board, whereas Willow was soft and voluptuous. It was a joy to rest his head on her pillow-like boobs. He groaned. What was he doing? He should be at home with Willow, not here with Kev having this manipulative conversation.

'So when are you going to end your relationship with her?' Kev persisted.

Charlie wriggled against the mattress. He didn't want this discussion. There was only one obvious escape route, and he took it. Shifting his body, he pressed his mouth against hers. That would stop her talking. Kev instantly yielded, putty in his hands. Thank God for that. He'd just have to try and rise to the occasion, even if it did mean getting home even later.

Chapter Thirteen

At home, alone, Willow had missed Charlie's company. On the upside, it had been nice watching the telly with the remote control in *her* hand rather than being subject to Charlie's constant flicking.

As Charlie had agreed to grabbing a burger from the drive-thru, she'd not bothered cooking properly for herself. Instead she'd opted to eat a tottering pagoda of toast. The plate had been piled high with golden triangles topped with melted cheese. For a second Willow had hesitated, thinking that perhaps she should have put together a salad. She was always coveting Emma's tiny waistline. But then she'd told herself that all the diets in the world would never give her Emma's lean frame, so Willow had dismissed all thoughts of eating rabbit food. Life was too short.

Plate in one hand, a mug of tea in the other, she'd snuggled against the sofa's many layers of cushions and had a lovely time watching old re-runs of *Only Fools and Horses*.

The hands of the clock were now edging towards ten. My goodness, Charlie was going to be knackered. Poor love. He worked so hard. Willow pointed the remote at the telly. A moment later and the screen went black. Standing up, she stretched, listening to her spine crack as the vertebrae unkinked. She hadn't bothered to draw the curtains. Outside the sky was as dark as a demon's heart. Rain had lashed the windows all evening.

Wandering into the gloom of the kitchen, she dumped her cup and plate in the sink. She'd wash them up in the morning. A rumble sounded overhead, and Willow cringed. Of all the things that frightened her, a storm was top of the list. Her fear of thunder and lightning was even greater than spiders.

Moments later, the kitchen was bathed in a harsh, bright glow. Whimpering, she pressed the flat of her hand against the light switch. Instantly the shadows fell away. Another grumble reverberated through the heavens. When Willow had been a child, her mum had tried to lessen her storm phobia by laughing it off. Anita West had cheerfully told her daughter that the noise was only God moving his furniture around in Heaven. But five-year-old Willow hadn't believed the story. If God had a house in the sky, how come she couldn't see it?

Another streaky zigzag forked through the atmosphere, lighting up the garden beyond the kitchen window. Willow lunged for the cord to the kitchen blind, wrenching it downwards. She knew she wouldn't be happy until the curtains in every single room had been closed, keeping the flashing in abeyance. If she put in her earbuds and listened to some loud music, it would drown out the sound of the storm. Between the house's black-out blinds and Harry Styles' latest album, she might just be able to kid herself the outside weather was nothing more than a bit of drizzle. The buds were on her bedside table.

Willow made to leave the kitchen but, just as she was about to turn off the light, the room was plunged into darkness. She gave a squeak of alarm. Oh no. A power cut. She wasn't particularly scared of the dark, but thanks to drawing the downstairs curtains, she now couldn't see a thing. Another crash came from above. Dear God. Never mind Him upstairs moving his furniture about, right now it sounded like a bunch of explosive experts demolishing a high-rise block of flats.

Trying to ignore the fear prickling her scalp, she stuck her hands out in front of her. Negotiating the kitchen doorway, Willow edged through the gap and then felt her way along the hall. Had she left her mobile in the lounge? It had a built-in torch. Willow debated whether to look for it. She couldn't be certain it wasn't tucked into one of the sofa's cushions, or even somewhere on the floor. In fact, was it in the lounge at all?

A fresh rumble was building momentum and Willow gave another squeal of fear. All she wanted was to slide under the duvet, pull it over her head and quietly shake. But to do that, she needed to get up the stairs. She gulped at the prospect of blindly negotiating a staircase.

Fumbling her way along the hall, she tried to keep her mind calm, but her brain was having none of it. It kept projecting huge images of monsters lurking round corners, goblins hiding in cupboards, and demons waiting to pounce.

There was another crash, as if a huge oak were being felled. Squeaking like a mouse with a cat after it, Willow edged forward only to painfully stub her toe against the bottom stair tread. Dropping to all fours, she began to climb slowly and carefully upward. By the time she'd reached the landing, her heart was thumping erratically and a slick of perspiration was beading her upper lip.

'Come on, Willow,' she muttered to herself. 'Pull yourself together.'

Keeping down on all fours, she shuffled towards her bedroom.

'You're nearly there. Well done. That's it. Keep going, keep… *owwwww!*'

She yelped as her head thumped against something. The blasted door was shut. Feeling her way upright, she leant against the doorframe, taking a moment for the pain in her forehead to subside. Steadying herself, she lowered the door handle. Inching her way into the room, another flash of lightning lit up her surroundings and she was relieved to quickly glimpse both her earbuds and mobile by the bed. As the room plunged back into darkness, Willow negotiated her way around the bed, then quickly pulled the curtains together.

Rubbing the sore spot on her brow, she sank down on the bed with relief. In a minute, she'd get undressed and curl up in a ball under the duvet. She just needed to take some deep breaths and wait for her heart to stop galloping. And then she froze. Because, despite the noise going on outside, her ears had detected a sound within. There it was again. She held her breath and listened to a loud creak beyond the bedroom. It was the loose floorboard on the landing. It only ever made that noise when stood upon. Dear Lord. There was someone in the house with her.

Her mind began to race with possibilities. Was it a burglar? Had it not been a power cut after all? Rather, had the lights going out been part of the burglar's grand plan, using the storm to disguise him stealthily cutting wires, blanketing the house in darkness, in order to steal all her worldly goods?

An icy finger of fear stroked its way down her spine as her aortic valves sped up to deal with a fresh adrenalin-dump. She half-expected her heart to burst out from under her ribcage and bounce off the bedroom walls like a rubber ball. The floorboard gave another squeak indicating the intruder's foot had moved – which meant he was coming into her bedroom.

Willow had no available weapon to hand. Maybe she could grab one of the pillows and give the intruder's head a surprise wallop? Now she could hear breathing. There wasn't a moment to lose. Groping in the darkness, her fingers curled around one pillow, holding it secure in a vice-like grip. She needed to work out where the unwanted visitor was standing so that her blow made accurate contact. She'd have to get him to speak. She gulped, swallowing down a lump the size of a ping-pong ball.

'Who's there?' she croaked, poised for action with the pillow.

Ahead of her, a mobile's torchlight suddenly shone directly at her. The thin white beam immediately blinded her, rendering any pillow-bludgeoning useless. A scream was starting to rise in her throat. Her eyes squinted against the light as Willow struggled to make out the shape looming in the bedroom doorway… a shape that was now coming towards her.

Willow's scream exploded into the air just as two hands roughly grabbed her shoulders, but her cry was instantly drowned out by another clap of thunder. She briefly wondered if it was possible to die of fright.

'Shhh,' said a man's voice. 'It's okay.'

'Charlie?' she whimpered. 'Oh my God' – she dropped the pillow and collapsed against his rain-soaked jacket – 'I was so frightened. I thought–'

'Don't be scared,' he said, as she hugged him hard. 'I'm home now.'

If Willow hadn't been so relieved, she might have noticed that mingling with the smell of wet clothing was another scent. Like a fine spider's thread, it was clinging between the fold of Charlie's shirt collar and skin. Not aftershave. Rather, perfume. If Willow hadn't been so distracted by another thunderbolt cracking overhead, she might have wondered at the perfume's familiarity, and demanded to know why her boyfriend reeked of another woman.

Chapter Fourteen

'Coffee,' said Ben, placing a steaming mug alongside Charlie's keyboard.

'Cheers.'

It was Wednesday morning and both men were once again early to the office. Ben's reasons for logging on an hour before anyone else were two-fold. Firstly, he wanted to get to work on the new Carpenter account before the phones started ringing. But secondly – and more importantly – he'd wanted to get away from Anna.

However, Charlie's reasons for flopping down on his executive chair a little after 8 a.m. had nothing to do with the profit and loss columns of Humphrey & Co but everything to do with speaking to Kev, preferably without any flapping ears. He hadn't been thrilled to see his best buddy already at his desk.

Charlie was getting desperate about ending this affair. He'd been unable to telephone his lover on the drive to the station due to black spots interrupting the signal. Nor had it been practical to ring her on the commute to King's Cross. Now it was tunnels that played havoc with the signal. Apart from anything else, he hadn't wanted an entire carriage overhearing him ending a relationship. Charlie could imagine only too well what sort of reaction he'd have got from his fellow ear-wigging commuters. Mrs Duffel Coat for example. She always sighed a lot as she scowled at her reflection in the window. She'd likely have swivelled her eyes to Charlie, then given him a death stare. Then there was Mr Tutter. He always eavesdropped on anyone trying to have a discreet chat. Only this morning a young man had been quietly telling his wife what he'd later like for dinner. Mr Tutter had clicked his tongue loudly at the suggestion of pizza and chips. Nor had Charlie wanted to sound like a horrible heartbreaker in front of Miss Pretty Face. She often exchanged a shy smile with Charlie over the rim of her kindle. Charlie could imagine only too well Miss Pretty Face replacing her smile with a look of disgust.

Ringing Kev from home was also out of the question due to Willow being around. Nor could Charlie absent himself to make a call from the garden without his girlfriend wondering what he was up to. He could envisage it now.

'Why are you hiding in the bushes, Charlie?'

'I'm not hiding. I'm... er... talking to the plants.'

'Talking to the plants? Are you doing a Prince Charles?'

'That's it!'

'I don't think Prince Charles would approve of you telling our roses that you want to nip things in the bud. It might kill them.'

Charlie took a sip of coffee and sighed. Ben was sitting only feet away. He would be able to hear everything. Nor could Charlie hole up in the loo – anyone could walk in. Even if it were possible to hijack the lift and keep his finger firmly on the "Doors Close" button, there was no signal once in the lift. The stairwell was out of the question because it echoed and amplified conversation. There was no way he wanted everyone on the floors above and below picking up what he was saying. In fact, where the hell *could* he talk to Kev without being overheard? If only he'd done it face to face last night. But wisdom was easier with hindsight. Charlie really didn't want to do the dirty by text. It wasn't kind. However, it was starting to look like the most practical option. He sighed again.

'A penny for them,' said Ben.

'Eh?'

Charlie looked up.

'Your thoughts. You're doing an awful lot of huffing and puffing.'

'Oh. Sorry.'

'What's up?'

Ben picked up his own coffee, sipped and then cradled the mug. His posture indicted he was taking a break and was all ears.

'Nothing's up,' said Charlie.

His mind inexplicably veered back to last night where a certain part of his anatomy had been more up than down.

'I thought I saw your car yesterday evening,' said Ben conversationally.

Charlie froze.

'What are you talking about?'

'Your car. In Mosley.'

'Well that's hardly surprising. I live in Mosley,' said

Charlie, giving a half-laugh.

'No, I mean I could have sworn I saw your car parked in a residential road on the south side of Mosley. You live on the north side.'

'And you don't live in Mosley at all, so how would you know if you saw my car?'

For a moment Ben looked furtive. Then his expression cleared and he gave a non-committal shrug.

'I didn't want to go home to Anna. So when I got off the train at Borough Green, I went for a drive instead. I found myself heading towards Mosley. I pulled into one of the side roads and spotted your car outside a house.'

'There are a lot of houses in Mosley' – Charlie gave Ben a withering look – 'and no doubt a lot of Beamers too.'

'So it wasn't your car?'

'Of *course* it wasn't my car,' said Charlie.

He arranged his features into an expression that indicated Ben's suggestion was preposterous. Charlie also made a mental note to keep Ben away from Willow for a bit. At least if Ben and Anna were going through a rocky patch, there wouldn't be any foursome dinner dates in the diary for a while.

'Strange,' Ben persisted. 'It looked exactly like your car too.'

He puffed out his cheeks and looked at Charlie speculatively.

'Yesterday you had eyes pinker than an albino rabbit. You also mentioned you'd had a heavy weekend. Are you being honest about not doing a dirty on your own doorstep?'

'Ben, your line of questioning is getting more and more ludicrous,' Charlie tutted. 'It's one thing to chat up the ladies on a jaunt to Birmingham. It's quite another to mess around with someone in Mosley.'

Charlie was impressed with the way he delivered his lines. He'd sounded so believable he was almost convincing himself. Perhaps he'd missed his vocation? He should have been an actor.

Ben set down his mug and, leaning on his elbows, steepled his fingers. His expression became thoughtful.

'I hear what you're saying, but the funny thing is' – he gave a little chortle – 'I stopped to look at the house where this Beamer was parked.'

'Whatever for?' said Charlie.

'Because I spotted something really bizarre.'

'My goodness, I wonder what it was?' said Charlie, hamming it up and piling on the sarcasm. '*Another* house next door? *Another* Beamer parked alongside the first Beamer? Or – wait for it – a supermarket van delivering Number Fourteen's weekly shop?'

'Nothing like that,' said Ben, shaking his head. 'I saw a pair of boxer shorts.'

'Being delivered to Number Fourteen?' Charlie joshed. 'Not *Freshly clicked* but *freshly dicked.'*

He laughed at his own joke. Ben didn't laugh back.

'These boxer shorts were hanging off a curtain rail.'

Ben's eyes didn't leave Charlie's face.

'They were just dangling there, as if their owner had

whipped them off in one hell of a hurry. By coincidence, they were the same make as that poncy brand you always insist on wearing. You know, the ones with the big writing on the elastic. I could read the lettering from the pavement.'

Charlie could feel the colour draining from his face. He hoped Ben wouldn't notice. It was one thing to deliver a few lines with the aplomb of Sir Laurence Olivier, it was quite another controlling one's complexion.

'How amazing,' said Charlie, attempting nonchalance. 'So, let me get this straight. You went for a drive to get away from Anna but ended up parking in a residential road and behaved like a Peeping Tom.'

Now it was Ben's turn to pale.

'Steady on. I'm not a pervert.'

Charlie was delighted at his friend's sudden discomfort. Good. Nothing like turning the tables on someone.

'Sounds distinctly pervy to me, mate.'

Now Charlie was sounding like a judge preparing to give his summary in a court of law.

'If I were you, I wouldn't let on to Anna that you were driving round the back streets studying people's underwear. What was the name of the road again?'

Ben blinked.

'I… I didn't mention the name of the road.'

'Didn't you?'

'No.'

'But what *was* the name, out of interest?'

'I don't recall,' said Ben, his eyes sliding away from

Charlie's gaze.

Charlie noted his friend's body language. He was lying. Interesting. Charlie wondered what the real reason was for Ben being outside Kev's house. It was too much of a coincidence. And then a light bulb went off in his head. Granted, it was only a dim light bulb, but it filled Charlie with hope. Was it possible that Kev was also Ben's lover? Had Ben driven to Kev's house on the off-chance to let her know that he was dumping Anna for *her,* but then clocked those boxers framed in her bedroom window and realised that loyalty might not be Kev's best character trait? Charlie cleared his throat.

'You told me yesterday that – rows with Anna aside – you had recently met another woman. That you were seeing someone else. Were you, by any chance, outside her house when you spotted those boxer shorts?'

'No!' Ben protested.

His body flinched, so much so that some of his coffee slopped across the desk.

'I've already told you. I was just driving around while trying to clear my head about Anna.'

But it was debatable who, out of the two men, was now looking the shiftiest.

Chapter Fifteen

'So how are things with you and Anna now?' asked Charlie.

He presumed that Ben had gone home to face the music at some point last night.

'We're finished.'

'Really?'

'Yes. I told Anna that I don't want to be with her any more.'

'How did she take it?'

'Weirdly. Initially she looked delighted. Then she smashed some ornaments and told me to go to hell.'

'Quite well then. For Anna,' Charlie added. 'So have you told your new girlfriend that you're now technically single?'

'I don't have a new "girlfriend".'

Ben looked annoyed.

'You do! You *told* me you'd met someone special.'

'Yes, she is special. But nothing has ever gone on between us. I mean, we haven't slept together. We won't. Not while I'm under the same roof as Anna. Instead we've gone for walks. Held hands. That sort of thing. It's all been very old-fashioned.'

'How romantic,' said Charlie mockingly.

No wonder Kev couldn't get enough of *him* if Ben wasn't

putting out.

'Mate, are you sure this woman is special?' he asked gently.

Ben was a nice guy. And whilst Charlie had nothing against Kev personally, he didn't want to see his best friend being shabbily treated. He knew Kev could have moments of being two-faced. He'd seen her over the years saying one thing but doing something else. And look at her now… sleeping with him while smiling into Willow's face. Nor was Charlie all together surprised at the possibility of Kev entertaining him between her sheets whilst, at the same time, having romantic strolls with Ben. But no way was Kev a suitable partner. Hell, she made Anna look like Mary Poppins. However, if Charlie's hunch was right about Ben's "special lady", it meant he now had the perfect escape clause from his own relationship with Kev. Hooray!

'I really like her,' said Ben, finally answering Charlie's question. 'But I haven't yet told her that I'm leaving Anna. I was going to last night but–'

'But she had another man's boxer shorts hanging in her window,' said Charlie, finishing Ben's sentence.

'I did *not* visit anyone's house last night,' Ben insisted.

But his ears had gone bright red. A sure sign he wasn't being truthful.

'I just think' – he continued – 'that for now I need to be on my own. To… you know… take a deep breath. I told you before, I don't want this lady to be some sort of rebound. I want it to come to something. But there's a time and a place. Know what I mean?'

'I suppose. And is Anna still in the dark about… what did you say her name was?'

Ben rolled his eyes.

'Nice try. But as I said before, I'm telling you nothing. Not yet.'

Charlie shook his head.

'I have no idea why you're being so secretive. Are you dating a celebrity? Is that it? You want to keep her name out of the press. Is it Lady Gaga? She's meant to like ordinary guys,' Charlie teased.

'I'm not "dating" anyone.'

'I disagree. If Willow knew I was going for clandestine walks with another woman and exchanging starry-eyed looks, she wouldn't be impressed.'

'I think Willow would be even less impressed if she found out about your Birmingham bonks,' Ben rebuked.

'But they don't mean anything.' Charlie gave a dismissive shrug. 'So what's happening next in the saga of Anna and Ben? Will you get home tonight to find your clothes in a suitcase on the doorstep, and the locks changed? Or will you open the door and need to dodge another flying ornament? Or might Anna have cunningly wired up the electric mains to the door's lock so that you are propelled into the next world by a zillion volts?'

'Anna said she will buy me out.'

'Will she now?'

Charlie gave a low whistle. Not for the first time was he reminded that Anna was a high-flyer and earnt a fortune. If

Charlie and Willow ever split, no way could Willow even begin to entertain the idea of buying him out.

'Anna is organising a valuation of the house later today. Meanwhile, I'll ring a solicitor in my lunch hour. Might as well get the legal side rolling.'

'Wow. Looks like you mean business. When are you going to move out?'

'Anna wants me to leave as soon as possible. She says she's not prepared to live with the loo seat left up until her funds clear into my account.'

'So where will you go?'

Charlie knew that Ben couldn't move in with his parents. Last year they'd taken early retirement and moved to Cornwall. Commuting was out of the question.

'Ah. Interesting you should ask me that,' said Ben.

'Oh?'

Ben hesitated for a moment.

'I was hoping I could move in with you and Willow.'

Chapter Sixteen

'Move in with me and Willow?' Charlie repeated, his eyebrows shooting upwards.

'It would only be for a few weeks,' Ben reasoned. 'I want to buy one of those swanky apartments being built at Ebbsfleet Valley. You know what it's like with newbuilds. The salespeople want the paperwork done and dusted in twenty-eight days. Given the speed of the conveyancing, I'll have moved out of your place before you'd even got used to having me around. Obviously I'll pay rent.'

'Sure,' said Charlie without hesitation.

Money was always a persuasive factor.

'Don't you want to square it first with Willow?'

'She'll be fine about it,' said Charlie dismissively.

'Well, if you're sure she won't mind, then brilliant! Thanks, mate. If it's all right with you, I'll pack my gear after work and bring it over tonight. Shall I transfer you the rent money in advance?'

'Yeah, that would be great.'

'Is a thousand okay, meals included?'

'Sounds good to me.'

Charlie was practically purring. No need to tell Willow.

'Thanks, matey,' said Ben, looking relieved. 'It's amazing isn't it?'

'What is?'

'How your life can alter in a moment. I mean, this time last month, I was living with Anna and had no idea that a trip to a Chinese takeaway would be the catalyst for my life changing.'

'Amazing,' said Charlie dryly.

He didn't really believe in all that nonsense about Fate taking a hand in things. Charlie was the first to scroll past inspirational posts on Facebook. Kev had posted such a status only last night, and he'd rolled his eyes. She'd written:

You never know what's around the corner. It might be everything. It might be nothing. You keep moving… one foot in front of the other… and then, one day, you look back and realise you've climbed a mountain.

Which was ironic coming from her. The only thing Kev had ever climbed was him when spread-eagled upon her mattress.

'I'd better get on with some work,' said Ben. 'I feel so relieved knowing I'll be sleeping at yours tonight, and not have to listen to Anna ripping the arse out of all my failings.'

'I feel happy too,' said Charlie. 'For you,' he quickly added.

But the reality was that Charlie was overjoyed to know Ben was planning on buying his own pad. This meant that, soon, Kev would likely move in with Ben. No more Kev and Charlie. Hurrah, hurrah, hurrah! Which meant he no longer had to fret about how to end things with Kev thanks to Ben romantically pursuing her. Charlie wanted to raise his arm and punch the air. This also meant he could immediately dispense with any guilt about being an unfeeling bastard. After all, Kev hadn't given *him* any consideration when she'd been out walking with Ben, looking at him with goo-goo eyes and making out she was Miss Virtuous.

Feeling happier than he had in a very long time, Charlie reached for his phone. Given that there was no longer any need to tippy toe about, he tapped out a text:

Heyyy! I have it on very good authority – well, a very good hunch – that you are having an old-fashioned romance with another guy. It's never been my style to cramp somebody else's, so I'll bow out leaving the field properly clear for him. Wishing you all the best with B! Xx

Charlie hit the send button, congratulating himself on a no-fuss extrication from Kev. He'd barely tossed the mobile across his desk when it began to ding like an impatient guest ringing Basil Fawlty's desk bell.

'Blimey, you're popular,' said Ben. 'Who's that?'

'No one important,' Charlie grinned.

He felt so liberated.

'Sounds like you're important to them,' said Ben. 'Mate, if you're not going to reply, switch your phone to silent. I need to crack on with my report, and that endless dinging will drive me dotty.'

'Sorry.'

Still grinning, Charlie picked up the phone again and

switched it to silent. The WhatsApp messages were still coming in. One sentence at a time. They were all from Kev. Obviously. He had no intention of reading them. He didn't want two blue ticks letting her know he'd acknowledged them. However, the texts were flitting through the screen and, as the last chat bubble appeared, his eyes snagged on Kev's last words.

If you don't reply to my messages, I will tell Willow EVERYTHING.

Charlie's grin disappeared as if he'd wiped it with a double dose of vanishing cream.

Chapter Seventeen

Charlie clicked on Kev's texts and read them properly.

There were six in total. The emotion in her messages had gone, in seconds, from a speed of nought to ninety. She'd started texting in stunned disbelief, but concluded with full-blown anger:

Charlie Bear??? You must be pranking me!

Who the heck is 'B'?

Wait… you seriously think I'm in TWO relationships?

How dare you accuse me of going with another guy.

And how DARE you dump me by text.

If you don't reply to my messages, I will tell Willow EVERYTHING.

Charlie gulped as he re-read that last text. His Adam's apple bobbed up and down his windpipe. He had to resist a sudden urge to dash to the loo and empty his bowels. How had he got this so wrong? But he hadn't. Surely. Ben had mentioned wanting to speak to his new lady last night, so why else would Ben have been outside Kev's house?

Because Ben was doing exactly what he TOLD you he was doing, said Charlie's inner voice. *Clearing his head as he drove aimlessly about, before coming up with a master plan to buy a swanky bachelor pad in Ebbsfleet. Landing up outside Kev's house was simply a coincidence. Mosley isn't exactly the size of America, you moron!*

Charlie groaned. He'd now done exactly what he'd previously hoped to avoid… dumped Kev by text and majorly pissed her off. He couldn't risk Kev carrying out her threat and telling Willow. Charlie wouldn't put it past her to now do that. She was the sort of woman you didn't scorn. Not unless you wanted your life wrecked.

You're the one who's single-handedly wrecking his life, said his inner voice. *Why did you ever get involved with Kev in the first place? Of all the females on the planet, why her?*

Charlie couldn't answer that question. Kev had more faults than the cracks in Earth's crusts, and could be feistier than a racehorse waiting for the off at the Grand National. But combine the two together, and somehow it gave a heady sexual chemistry. What the heck was he going to do? But… Kev *had* to be Ben's new love interest. It was too much of a coincidence that Ben had been outside her house last night. Kev must be pretending not to know who 'B' was. Perhaps she was faking outrage because she didn't want to let Charlie go for the time being. He needed to get to the bottom of this. He glanced at Ben.

'Hey, I know you're knee-deep in the Carpenter account, but I'd really appreciate – I mean, like, *really* appreciate – you telling me the name of your new lady.'

Ben frowned.

'Whatever for?'

Charlie struggled to think of a quick answer.

'Well, I'm assuming she's local. Is it possible she might – I dunno – ever call at my house? You know, to see you after you've moved in with us?'

'She won't call at your house.'

'She might do.'

'She won't.'

'But what if she does?'

'Then I'll properly introduce her to you,' said Ben, looking mildly amused. 'But it's highly unlikely she'll come a-calling because I have no plans to tell her where I'll be temporarily living.'

Charlie changed tack.

'I think I know who she is,' Charlie blurted in a desperate bid to goad Ben into revealing this woman's name.

'Really?' said Ben, suddenly wary. 'Go on, then. Who is it?'

Charlie fixed Ben with a look designed to make him crumble and confess all.

'It's Kev.'

'Come again?' Ben scowled. 'Are you implying I want to leave Anna because I've fallen for a bloke?'

'Wait… I mean… you see… what I *meant* is Kev is the name that *I*–'

'If you think this is a huge joke and start a rumour about me changing sides, then I swear I'll–'

Both men were cut short by the sound of Charlie's phone ringing.

‘Saved by the bell,’ said Ben coldly.

He glanced across at Charlie’s mobile, squinting in order to read the caller’s id.

‘Well, fancy that. You have a call from this Kev person! Are you sure it’s not *you*, Charlie, who’s changed sides?’

Chapter Eighteen

Charlie snatched up his phone. Before he could even say anything, Kev's squawking battered his eardrum.

'Don't you dare hang up,' she yelled.

'I'm at work,' Charlie hissed.

He was aware that Ben's ears were almost visibly wiggling in order to hear what Charlie was saying. It was also clear that any attempt to placate Kev was going to fall on stony ground. He had no choice but to let her run with her rant until she'd finished.

Charlie leant back in his chair and listened to Kev expressing both disbelief and anger over his text. Within seconds he had a pounding headache and had to hold the phone away, although he was still able to catch the odd expletive.

'…uck's sake… don't know what the hell you're playing at… thought you cared… who do you think you are… just using me… no idea who B is… demand you talk to me face to face…'

He put the phone back against his head just in time to hear Kev deliver her ultimatum.

'…tempted to tell Willow precisely what sort of man her

boyfriend really is.'

It was going to take some exceptional grovelling to undo the upset he'd caused.

'I'm sorry,' he whispered into the phone. 'I honestly thought you were seeing someone else.'

'Whatever gave you that idea?' she demanded.

'It was something I overheard,' he said, madly improvising. 'When I was in the Spar at the bottom of your road. A guy was chatting to his mate about a woman he was seeing. She had the same name as you,' he finished weakly.

'My name isn't unique,' she said, still annoyed, but thawing slightly.

'I know. I guess it's that old cliché of putting two and two together and coming up with more nonsense than one of Teresa May's old Brexit deals.'

There was silence at the end of the line indicating Kev was digesting this. It prompted Charlie to plough on and deliver a trump card.

'And… and I was jealous.'

'Were you?' she said, melting quicker than a block of butter in a microwave.

'I was.'

He crossed his fingers.

'Jealousy is a whole new experience for me.'

'I'm not sure I believe you.'

Charlie slumped over his keyboard. He wasn't out of the woods yet.

'Let me prove it to you,' he whispered.

'When?'

'This evening. I'll pop round after work. We'll have a quick–'

'No, not quick,' she said, cutting across him.

'I was going to say a quick bite to eat.'

He contrived to sound wounded.

'You mean… as in going to a restaurant?' she asked in delight.

'Um, well, I was thinking more along the lines of me bringing something in.'

'Oh.' Her voice went flat. 'I guess we mustn't let the good people of Mosley see you and I holding hands across a candlelit table in a public place. Village gossip would never do, eh?'

'I think we could both do without village gossip muddying the waters. After all, look how easy it was for me to get the wrong end of the stick,' he pointed out. 'I want to see you but–'

'But what?' she said sharply.

Charlie took a deep breath. There were no two ways about this. It was one thing to flatter Kev and make out he'd felt jealous. But the crux of this matter was that this relationship was going nowhere. *Could* go nowhere. Nor did he want it to. The only thing he wanted was to end it.

'We do need to talk,' he said frankly.

'I can't see you at home. Not tonight. We'd be interrupted, and then you'd have some serious explaining to do.'

Charlie began to drum his fingers in irritation. Fine. He

was left with no other choice.

'Tell you what. I'll book us a room somewhere. For tonight. Do you know *The Beagle and Bugle*?'

'Oh my goodness.' Kev gave a shriek of delight. 'Is it that dear little pub restaurant on the High Street in Seal?'

She'd been there once with some girlfriends a couple of years ago. The inside had been full of knotty-beamed charm, golden floorboards, and cosy sit-soft areas dotted around a vast open fire. The menu had been sublime too.

'That's the one,' said Charlie.

Seal wasn't a million miles away, but it was far enough not to bump into anyone from Mosley.

'I didn't know you could book a room there.'

'One of its best kept secrets,' said Charlie.

Bugger. The effort involved in gently dumping Kev was going to cost him dear. But it had to be done.

'I'll get on to them now and sort out the booking. You pack an overnight bag. I'll see you there later.'

'If I arrive before you, what name shall I say you've booked under?'

'Mr and Mrs Kev,' said Charlie, without thinking.

'How romantic,' she purred.

Charlie slapped his forehead. Why had he said "Mr and Mrs" Kev? Or "Mr and Mrs" anything? The last thing he wanted was to give Kev the wrong idea, especially after lying and telling her he'd felt jealous about her supposedly having another man.

'I'll have to pop home first and grab my own overnight

stuff,' he said. 'If you do get there before me, grab yourself a gin and tonic and stay toasty by the fire.'

'Gin and tonic?' she mocked. 'I don't think so. I'll be sipping champagne. The bottle will be keeping cool in an ice-bucket until you join me.'

'Sounds great.'

He forced a note of pleasure into his voice, although he felt sick to his stomach. However, the rendezvous with Kev was essential. It was all about ending the relationship on a high note for her, limiting hurt or anger. He liked to think it would guarantee Kev looking back on their time together fondly, knowing it had been nothing more than a bit of fun.

'Oooh, I can't wait,' she said, giggling like a teenager. 'See you later, Charlie Bear.'

Charlie hung up and wiped his brow.

'I think I got the gist of that,' said Ben.

'Don't. Say. One. Word,' Charlie growled.

He viciously rubbed the heels of his hands over his face.

'Sorry, but I'm going to say several,' said Ben. 'You've clearly got yourself into a monumental mess, and' – he put up one hand like a traffic cop – 'I do not want to know the details.'

'Can you cover for me tonight at home?' Charlie implored.

'Cover for you?'

Ben raised his eyebrows so high, for a moment they disappeared in his hairline.

'Mate, do you know something? I love you like a brother, but by God I'm starting to dislike you too. You haven't even told that wonderful girl of yours I'm moving in this evening, and now you're not even going to be around? When the residents of Mosley discover you're not home and another guy is staying with Willow, curtains will be twitching faster than Miley Cyrus on a twerking spree.'

'Don't go on at me,' Charlie implored. 'I've got myself in a bit of bother. I promise that after tonight it will be sorted.'

'I hope so, for your sake,' said Ben, turning back to his computer.

Charlie took another deep breath. At this rate he'd be hyperventilating.

Colleagues were now trickling into the office. From the wary looks on their faces, Drummond was around. Damn. But it couldn't be helped. Charlie needed to make a reservation at *The Beagle and Bugle.* Then he needed to phone Willow. The first was easy. He could do that online. The second would be a little trickier.

Chapter Nineteen

Willow was having a busy morning cataloguing. She didn't particularly mind gathering metadata, but it would have been nice to have had some help. However, Theresa and Fiona were assisting elsewhere, and Jean was doing what she liked doing best… presiding over the front desk.

Willow discreetly checked Jean out. Currently she looked like Queen Elizabeth ensconced in the Throne Room at Windsor Castle. Jean hadn't quite mastered Her Majesty's accent, but she always gave it her best shot. She was doing it now. Answering the phone in an overly elocuted voice.

'Hellair. Mosley Li-brair. Can I help yew?'

From her seat a few feet away, Willow observed her boss and tried not to giggle as Jean's bosom swelled with self-importance. But seconds later Willow knew something was wrong because her boss's complexion had changed from pearly-pink to plum-puce. One could almost see the steam coming out of her ears. Clearly the caller wasn't a member of the public enquiring if JK Rowling had a new book out.

'I thought I told yer last time, Charlie,' – Jean's posh accent had done a bunk – 'that personal calls in *my* library aren't allowed.'

Willow felt her stomach contract with fear from the rebuke that would no doubt follow. At the same time her heart leapt with joy. Charlie had defied Jean in order to speak to her. How amazing! She pretended not to notice Jean staring at her. Out of her peripheral vision Willow caught a glimpse of her superior's expression. She looked like a walrus who'd anticipated a fish supper but been given tofu. Willow let some hair fall across her cheek to hide her discomfort.

'Young lady,' said Jean sternly.

Willow looked up, feigning surprise.

'That chap of yours is on the phone. Again. He says it's imperative he speaks to you. I'm telling you now, after this, no more personal calls. And you can tell Charlie from me that if he disobeys, it will end in a verbal warning for you. Understood?'

'Sorry,' said Willow looking contrite. 'It must be an emergency.'

'Emergencies go to 999. Not Mosley Library,' Jean sniffed.

Willow pushed back her chair and scuttled over to the telephone. God forbid that Jean should transfer the call to Willow's desk. Oh no. Instead Jean would want to eavesdrop on Willow's conversation to determine what crisis was interfering with her staff's duties whilst talking to a man too handsome for his own good.

'Hello?' said Willow.

She watched as Jean flumped back down on her chair, pretending to fiddle with some papers.

'Hey,' said Charlie.

'Is everything all right?' Willow asked, managing to convey just the right amount of worry.

Jean made a harrumphing sound.

'I just called…' said Charlie, before trailing off.

Those three words instantly had Willow holding her breath in anticipation of something wonderful. Before she knew it, she was having a mini daydream with Charlie singing, "I just called to say I love you," as a familiar soundtrack played in the background.

'Yes?' she prompted.

Jean picked up all her papers, shuffled them furiously and then slapped them back down again.

'I just want to…'

'What?' she whispered, still in la-la land.

Was Charlie going to add "kiss you"? Like that song by Soulja Boy about kissing through the phone? It was one of her favourite tunes, even though she knew Charlie couldn't stand it.

So he's hardly likely to serenade you down the wires with lyrics he loathes, right? said the little voice in her head.

Willow pinged back to the present, trying and failing not to notice Jean scowling.

'There's no easy way to say this,' said Charlie ominously.

Willow's blood ran cold. Something must have flickered in her expression because, for a fleeting moment, Jean looked concerned.

'Two things,' Charlie continued. 'Firstly, I have to go away on unexpected business. A major client is being difficult and we're in danger of losing the account. Drummond wants me to placate him. I'll be home later to pack an overnight bag.'

'Oh,' said Willow, swallowing disappointment.

What with the imminent Birmingham convention and now this, Charlie's work seemed to be contriving to keep them apart.

'Also, Ben and Anna have busted up.'

'No way! That's awful.'

'Even worse. Ben is now homeless. Anna is being a right bitch and has chucked Ben out,' said Charlie, bending the truth.

'Anna shouldn't have done that. After all, Ben owns half the house. He should stand his ground.'

'He doesn't want the aggro. I've said he can move in with us.'

Willow closed her eyes, forcing herself to count to ten.

'Charlie, I don't think–'

'Too late. He looked so pathetic... so desperate... I'm afraid I just couldn't turn him down.'

Charlie was now sounding more sincere than an MP telling his constituency he was campaigning to abolish Council Tax.

Willow was aghast. It wasn't that she didn't like Charlie's friend, but she knew exactly what was going to happen. Not one but *two* men with the remote control. *Two* men to clear up after. *Two* men belching, picking their noses and scratching their privates as they lolled around in front of the television.

And how would Ben's presence impact upon her private

life with Charlie? Would Ben be slumped on the sofa at midnight, sobbing into man-sized tissues while she and Charlie tried to edge their way upstairs to bed. She could imagine it now... her keeping her fingers crossed for some action, but Charlie shaking his head.

'We can't leave him downstairs, babe. He's crying his eyes out. Surely you understand?'

'But I'm desperate for you to make love to me, Charlie.'

Whereupon her boyfriend would recoil in horror.

'Good heavens, absolutely not. I couldn't possibly perform knowing Ben is crying all over our cushions.'

Or, even worse, when Ben finally *did* make it to bed, his presence would encroach upon her and Charlie. She could see it now... Charlie's lovemaking noises accompanied by the sound of Ben trumpeting into his second box of jumbo tissues. And then, when Charlie gave his customary "Oo-oh-oooh" upon climaxing, Ben would duet with sobs of "Ah-ah-ahhh".

Willow wasn't happy about Charlie's bombshell news. However, she was a sweet girl and couldn't bear for anybody to be having a rotten time – and Charlie knew that.

'It won't be for long, sweetie,' he implored. 'Just while he sorts himself out.'

Willow caught Jean glaring at her. She was tapping one finger against her watch.

'Definitely only a few days?'

'Promise,' said Charlie, crossing his fingers for the second time that day.

Jean was now stabbing her watch so hard, Willow half

expected the glass to break.

‘I have to go,’ she said. ‘Will I see you later?’

‘Briefly.’

‘Okay. Don’t leave without saying good–’

But Charlie had already hung up.

Chapter Twenty

Jean deliberately kept Willow late at the library insisting she make up the time spent talking on the phone to Charlie. Willow didn't argue. She'd much rather work an extra hour for five lost minutes than have a verbal warning on her personal file.

As a result of leaving the library later than usual, by the time she got home Charlie had already packed and was ready to be on his way. He came down the stairs clutching an overnight bag, just as Ben arrived with an alarming number of suitcases and black sacks.

'Hey,' said Ben greeting them both.

He dumped the last of his belongings at Willow's feet.

'I really appreciate this. It means so much having good friends like you and Charlie.'

'Our pleasure,' said Willow, instantly feeling guilty at her earlier reluctance to put Ben up.

She glanced at Charlie and gave him a smile of commiseration.

'Where's Drummond sending you?'

The question took Charlie by surprise. He'd been so pre-occupied with Kev's ultimatum and the importance of placating her, he hadn't given any thought to the name of his make-believe destination.

'Where am I off to?' he repeated, stalling for time.

'Cambridge,' said Ben, leaping to Charlie's rescue, just as Charlie said the first thing that popped into his head.

'Brighton.'

'Cambridge first,' said Ben hastily. 'Then Brighton.'

'That's right.'

Charlie nodded frantically.

'The client has two offices and... er... I have to go to both.'

'Couldn't Drummond have let you go first thing in the morning?' asked Willow.

'Um, not really,' said Charlie vaguely.

'Why ever not?'

'Why not?' Charlie repeated, floundering for a plausible excuse.

'Yes, why not?'

'The client wants a breakfast meeting,' said Ben, coming to the rescue.

'Yes,' Charlie agreed. 'Six o'clock sharp.'

'Well you can't be in Brighton *and* Cambridge for breakfast, can you?' said Willow with a laugh.

'No, no, you're right. Which is why I'm having a breakfast meeting at six o'clock in Brighton and then a working lunch with the client in Cambridge. He shifts location faster than a speeding ticket.'

Charlie forced himself to laugh.

'The guy's an utter nightmare.'

'I see,' said Willow.

She didn't really see at all. She stepped over one of Ben's suitcases and set her handbag down on the hall table.

'Well surely you have time for dinner before you go?'

'Sadly not.'

Charlie was desperate to get out the door before Kev started calling his mobile. The last thing he needed was demands to know why he wasn't yet at *The Beagle and Bugle*. He was already running later than he would have liked.

'The client hinted at…'

He racked his brain for an appropriate answer.

'A supper meeting,' said Ben helpfully.

'That's it!' said Charlie, offering up a silent prayer of thanks for Ben being quicker off the mark than he was right now.

He couldn't cope with all these lies. He needed to scarper before any more whoppers were told. Despite Willow looking baffled, she wasn't challenging anything that had been said. If she did, Charlie would just have to blame Drummond for everything.

'And now I really do need to dash.'

He gave Willow a perfunctory peck on the cheek. Turning, he tripped over a pile of Ben's stuff, then stumbled out. As the door slammed behind him, there was a moment's awkward silence between Willow and Ben. They'd never been alone together before. Without the glue of either Anna or Charlie, neither was quite sure what to say to the other.

'Sorry about all this,' said Ben.

He gestured at all his gear filling the hallway.

'And I'm sorry about you and Anna,' said Willow.

'These things happen,' Ben shrugged.

'If you don't mind me saying' – Willow ventured – 'you don't seem terribly upset.'

Ben decided to come clean.

'I'm not. To be honest, the whole thing is just a massive relief.'

'Oh.'

Willow was heartened to know she wouldn't be listening to Ben working his way through the vast box of tissues she'd discreetly placed by the spare bed.

'And… is Anna upset?'

'I'm not sure. If anything, she's simply dismissive. I think she wishes I was more like her. You know, feisty. Someone who joins in with the crockery throwing, instead of ducking. She told me I have all the passion of a pensioner at a rave.'

'Right.'

She didn't really know what to say. Anna was the chalk to Willow's cheese. She had nothing against Ben's ex-girlfriend, but Anna wasn't the sort to call up for a cosy natter. In fact, Willow couldn't imagine Anna pouring her heart out to anyone. Unlike Emma, Willow's best friend. Indeed, Willow couldn't wait to ring and offload to *her*. That's what besties were for. Willow knew Emma would totally sympathise at Willow's current predicament, from hearing about jackbooting Jean to domineering Drummond. And as for Ben… Willow could almost hear Emma gasping "Noooo" at being landed with Charlie's best mate.

Feeling a smidgen happier, Willow decided she'd make the best of things with Ben for now.

'I guess I'd better make a start on some dinner while you put your belongings away.'

'Sure.'

Ben returned Willow's smile but struggled to look her in the eye. He was bloody annoyed with Charlie. He'd been dragged into being an accomplice for Charlie over whatsername. Kev. Huh! What woman was called *Kev*?

Not for the first time did Ben realise just how trusting Willow was. Anna would have shone lights in his eyes to get to the truth. She'd always been able to sniff out a porky-pie.

He picked up one of his cases, then abruptly put it down again.

'Do you want me to help you prepare dinner? I'm very domesticated. Anna trained me well,' he said with a deprecating laugh.

Ben didn't add that he'd nearly always been the one to prep their evening meal. As far as Anna was concerned, her job was *far* more exhausting than Ben's, which was reason enough for him to do the cooking. And the clearing up. And anything else she'd ordered him to do. Thank goodness he'd extricated himself. That was partly why he'd reluctantly agreed to go along with whatever Charlie was up to right now… because Ben knew Charlie was desperate to disentangle himself from a woman who was sticking like Velcro and wouldn't take no for an answer.

At some point he was going to sit Charlie down and do some straight talking. It was one thing to help a mate out of a tricky situation, but not when he had a gorgeous girl like Willow at home. She had "Perfect Partner" stamped all over her. Ben also wanted to make it crystal clear to Charlie never to take advantage of him again. His conscience was giving him hell over the whole thing.

'Help?' Willow queried, interrupting Ben's thoughts.

'Yeah. I could peel the veg or…' he trailed off.

Willow was so flabbergasted at Ben's offer of assistance, for a moment she could only gape at him. Blimey. When was the last time Charlie had ever done such a thing? She couldn't remember. Actually, she could. It was never.

'Really, it's fine. You sort your stuff out.'

'Well, if you're sure,' said Ben, now feeling a bit gauche.

'I'm sure.'

'Right, then I'll… '

He pointed at the staircase.

'Yes,' she said, and this time gave him a proper smile.

Half an hour later, delicious smells were wafting up the staircase to Ben in his new bedroom. His stomach let out a growl of hunger. He'd managed to fit most of his clothes in the small wardrobe but had now run out of room. Lifting the frilly valance around the bed, he discovered it was a divan with two empty draws. Thank goodness. He was just folding the last of his belongings away, when Willow yodelled that dinner was ready.

She had opted to lay the small table in the kitchen, rather

than the one in the dining room where she and Charlie usually ate. Willow liked to court romance which – whippy cream aside – was usually thin on the ground. She often lit a pretty candle centrepiece to add some ambience. Consequently she didn't feel comfortable with the idea of eating in there with Ben. However, the kitchen's bistro table was very casual. It was often used as an additional prep surface, and regularly covered in flour and pastry trimmings.

'Something smells good,' said Ben, coming into the kitchen and rubbing his hands together.

His voice was over-jocular, and Willow could tell he felt as uncomfortable as her about their eating together.

'Listen,' she said, placing her hands against the work top and giving him a frank look. 'Don't feel you have to sit here making conversation with me.'

'O-Oh,' said Ben, looking both surprised and relieved.

'If you want to read the newspaper while eating or watch the telly' – she indicated the small flat screen on the other side of the kitchen – 'then I really don't mind.'

'Is that because you want to disappear into the pages of a romance?'

He nodded at the Kindle languishing near the hob. She'd obviously been reading while stirring the gravy.

She hesitated.

'Only if you're reading too.'

'I don't read romances,' he teased. 'But I do like scrolling through the news on my phone.'

He removed his mobile from his back pocket and set it

down by his knife and fork.

'My habit used to drive Anna mad.'

Willow laughed.

'Well it won't drive me mad and, yes, I'd like to do nothing more than read my Kindle whilst mindlessly eating.'

'Feel free then,' said Ben in delight.

Willow gave a small sigh of relief and placed her Kindle on the table.

'Glad we've sorted that out,' she grinned.

They ate their dinner companionably. Ben read an article about Prince Harry's fury with the press and the way they were treating wife Meghan, while Willow imagined that she was the heroine in the sizzling hot romance she was currently enthralled with. In her mind's eye she could picture Charlie as the bad boy billionaire who – despite his incredible looks, charming personality and stonking wealth – had only just realised he was madly in love with his personal assistant. Willow had no trouble letting her imagination put *her* in this character's shoes. Now Charlie was saying he couldn't dictate another letter until he'd dictated exactly what he was going to do to her. On his desk. Which was huge. Like a certain part of his anatomy.

'I feel sorry for Harry and Meghan,' said Ben.

Willow tore herself away from the billionaire who was panting harder than a randy mongrel pursuing a Crufts' winner.

'Why's that?'

'Well, they don't have it easy, do they?'

'What, you mean, with all their wealth, servants, and

luxurious accommodation?' she teased.

'I think Harry's pretty down to earth. He was living in a very twee cottage before he married Meghan. It didn't even have air conditioning.'

'Ben, the average homeowner in Britain doesn't *need* air-conditioning,' Willow pointed out.

'We will in the future,' said Ben darkly. 'Global warming will see to that. I don't know about you, but I hardly slept during our last summer.'

'It was a sticky one,' Willow agreed.

'You're not kidding. Thirty-seven degrees in Mosley, and that was in the shade. It's ridiculous. Since when did England *ever* reach that sort of temperature? And apparently this is the shape of things to come. My new place has air-con,' he said happily.

'Your new place? Have you found somewhere to rent already?'

Charlie had promised Ben would only be with them for a few days, so this line of conversation was as welcome as the word on the doormat in Willow's hall.

'Oh, I won't be renting,' said Ben shaking his head. 'There's no point. Not when I have plenty of equity and the means to get a mortgage.'

Willow's mind began to whirr. If Ben was buying a property, he wouldn't be staying for "just a few days". More like several weeks. She gulped at the thought of just how many weeks. When she and Charlie had bought their house, the conveyancing had dragged on for nearly five months.

‘So… ah… where are you looking to buy?’

‘Over at Ebbsfleet. They have some amazing high-spec apartments. It’s a newbuild.’

Willow exhaled discreetly. Okay. Not too bad. Builders of brand-new properties always put their buyers under immense pressure to complete in twenty-eight days. As Ben wouldn’t be in a conveyancing chain, the time target was achievable.

‘That’s brilliant,’ she enthused. ‘The location is every commuter’s dream. Which Phase have you set your sights on? One or two?’

Phase One had been built ages ago but was close to towering pylons. Phase Two was more pleasing on the eye but… hang on. When she’d recently driven past the development, there had been a socking great banner on display. Two words had blazed across it. Sold Out.

‘I’m not buying from either,’ said Ben.

Willow’s stomach lurched. If Ben wasn’t buying an apartment on Phase One or Two, then–

‘Phase Three?’ she quavered.

‘Got it in one,’ said Ben delightedly.

Willow tried and failed to match his enthusiasm. Phase Three wasn’t even underway. Ben might be living with her and Charlie for up to a year.

Oh boy. She couldn’t *wait* to ring Emma and offload about THIS.

Chapter Twenty-One

'You're a really good cook,' said Ben, putting his knife and fork together.

'It was only a fish pie,' Willow shrugged.

'*Only* a fish pie? Listen, if Anna had cooked this, I'd never have heard the end of it. She'd have expected praise to the rafters.'

'Doesn't Anna like cooking?'

'No. Her idea of providing a meal is sticking some fishfingers under the grill and shaking out some oven-ready chips on a baking tray – and still expecting praise to the rafters. I was the one who did the cooking.'

'You?'

'Yes,' Ben nodded. 'Why are you looking so surprised?'

'Sorry, I didn't know I was. I shouldn't really be astonished. After all, there are loads of men out there who love to mess about in the kitchen. Look at Gordon Ramsey and Jamie Oliver. They've made millions showing us what to do with a frying pan, as if cracking the code to a mystery.'

'Oooh, isn't that a borderline sexist comment?' Ben teased. 'I'm sure there were heaps of men chopping chives or plaiting pastry long before Gordon and Jamie turned up on the box.

Anyway, I quite like cooking. I find it relaxing.'

'Really? One day you'll make some lucky lady a wonderful husband.'

'Not sure about that.'

'Oh. Aren't you into marriage either?'

Ben looked at Willow warily.

'What do you mean by *either*? Are you comparing me to Charlie?'

Willow flushed to her roots.

'I… no. Not at all. I just assumed…'

How had their conversation – so neutral up until now – suddenly taken such a personal turn?

'What I meant was…'

Help. What had she meant?

'Hang on a minute,' said Ben.

He shifted in his seat.

'Has Charlie broached the M word?'

Perhaps this was why his best mate was so desperate to get shot of that Kev woman. Could it be that Charlie was considering proposing to Willow? In which case, how amazing. The guy was finally growing up!

Willow's face was still flaming.

'Um, no. No, Charlie hasn't mentioned marriage.'

'That's a shame,' said Ben, looking disappointed. 'So how do you know he's not keen? Oh… wait…'

He trailed off as realisation dawned.

Willow was now so red from embarrassment she was making a tomato look anaemic.

'Got it in one,' she murmured. '*I* broached the M word with *him*.'

'Ah.'

'And made a prize prat of myself.'

'Bad reaction?'

Willow screwed up her nose.

'Let's just say that Charlie's response was like asking the Pope if he'd ever consider converting to atheism.'

'So Charlie turned you down.'

'Yup. I felt beyond foolish for mentioning it,' said Willow miserably.

Her mouth drooped like an upside-down moon crescent, and Ben's heart squeezed. He reached across the small divide, folding one of her hands into his.

'You mustn't feel foolish,' he said, squeezing her fingers absent-mindedly. 'It's only natural to think about making your commitment a formality. After all, you've been together long enough.'

Willow glanced down at her hand enveloped in Ben's. An onlooker would have been forgiven for thinking they were having a romantic moment. His touch was firm. Reassuring. She liked him even more for his kindness, and wanting to lessen her obvious embarrassment.

'The question I would ask is…' – Ben gave her a frank look – 'do you believe Charlie is the right man for *you*?'

Her response was immediate.

'Definitely.'

Ben looked at Willow's expression. She'd lit up like the

shops along Oxford Street at Christmastime. She really didn't have a clue about her boyfriend's shenanigans.

'Charlie is my world,' she added.

'You've never stopped and thought you could… well… do better?'

Ben knew he was wandering down a perilous path. One where Charlie might rapidly become a tricky topic. He didn't want to diss his best mate, but he felt duty-bound to drop Willow some gentle hints. She needed to know that Charlie wasn't a gorgeous golden god, even if the lucky bastard did physically resemble one.

'Do better?' said Willow, looking amused. 'You mean, why didn't I bag Prince Harry before Meghan Markle wowed him?'

'Well why not?' said Ben seriously.

'I'm nothing special. No prize catch. Just an ordinary girl with an average IQ working at the local library and living her boring life. I can't pore over spreadsheets full of figures like you and Charlie, or raise finance from investors, nor oversee mergers and acquisitions whilst juggling a management buy-out. You and Charlie are brainy, brawny and total babe magnets.'

Now it was Ben's turn to blush. Anna had never called him a "babe magnet".

'Well thanks for all those compliments, but actually Charlie and I just happen to be good at what we do. Just like *you* are good at what you do. And no *way* are you ordinary. My mother would be thrilled to bits if I turned up on her doorstep with a girl like you.'

'Like me? Why?'

'Because you're steady.'

'Which also translates as dull,' she countered. 'Whereas you and Charlie are what *my* mum would call "a good catch".'

'You're doing yourself down, plus you clearly have no idea how attractive you are.'

Ben quickly let go of her hand, just in case Willow thought… well, he didn't know what Willow might think.

'I think you're too good for Charlie,' he blurted.

He needed to shut up. Before this line of conversation took a dangerous turn and became a thorny subject revealing Charlie for what he was. Not quite a thorn, but definitely a prick.

Willow was flattered that Ben thought her both attractive and too good for Charlie. Nonetheless she couldn't take his words seriously. He was just being kind. It was women like Anna who were life's beauties with success stamped all over their on-trend power suits. She could see Anna in the board room, her tumbling hair full of salon-highlights, lips enhanced to bee-stung perfection as she addressed the directors.

Willow sighed.

'On the plus side, one advantage of having such a middle-of-the-road job is that I never have to go away overnight or massage the egos of irate clients. I feel tremendously sorry for Charlie. He works so hard.'

'Yeah.'

Suddenly Ben couldn't look Willow in the eye.

'Is this client really so awful?' she persisted.

'Yeah, yeah. Practically wants nursemaiding over everything.

Please, God, don't give me bad karma for telling lies. I'm just trying to protect the sweet lady sitting opposite me.

'But Mr Montgomery is an important customer,' he added.

'I thought his name was Mr Humphrey?' said Willow, looking puzzled.

'Oh… er… yes, Mr Humphrey. Mr Montgomery is… um… Mr Humphrey's sidekick.'

Ben could feel himself getting flustered. The subject needed changing.

'Tell you what. Let me help you clear up, and then I'll make us both a cup of after-dinner coffee.'

He stood up, desperate to busy himself. He didn't want to think about Charlie or where the guy was right now.

Willow stood up too, pleasantly surprised at Ben's offer of help. She was ninety percent sure he wasn't just being polite. She privately bet he never left the loo seat up either. Charlie never did anything domestic. Unless you included assuming a horizontal position on the sofa in front of the television.

The two of them pottered about companionably. As Willow washed and Ben wiped, she allowed herself a little daydream. How nice would it be if it were Charlie beside her right now? She imagined that, instead of Ben in the kitchen, it was her boyfriend. Charlie was the one putting that clean plate into the overhead cupboard. Now he was reaching for two mugs. Spooning instant coffee into them. Adding boiling water. Then milk. Now turning to face her. Raising an enquiring eyebrow as he showed the colour of the coffee.

'Strong enough?'

'Lovely, darling,' she sighed.

Too late Willow realised this wasn't Charlie handing her a drink. One glance at Ben revealed he was highly amused at the endearment.

'I mean…'

She trailed off, blushing furiously.

'Slip of the tongue,' Ben smiled. 'I get it. Hopefully I won't call you my pet name for Anna, or you might feel upset.'

'Should I ask what it is, or is it too personal?'

'I'm not sure she was even aware of it' – Ben laughed – 'because I didn't dare say it to her face. But whenever she was stropping about – which was most nights – I used to mutter, "There she goes again… Anna Pir-anna." A play on the word "piranha".'

Willow gave a snort of laughter.

'I guess that pet name isn't very flattering.'

There was a pause as they both stood together in the kitchen, clutching their coffees.

'Would you mind–?' they said at exactly the same time.

'Ladies first,' said Ben.

'Would you think me rude abandoning you? It's only for a bit. Only I'd quite like to have a chat with my bestie.'

'And by "chat" I suppose you mean an hour-long chin-wag,' Ben laughed.

'Something like that.'

'Of course. Don't feel you have to keep me company. I'm a fully-fledged grown-up. I can even cross the road without a chaperone,' he joked.

'Well, if you really don't mind, then I'll take my coffee upstairs with my phone. If you want to watch the telly then…'

'Brilliant!'

Grinning happily, he headed off to the lounge.

Willow smiled. Cradling her coffee in one hand and her mobile in the other, she made her way up to her bedroom. Sighing happily at the anticipation of a long girly gossip with Emma, she sank down on the bed and waited for the call to connect. Emma's line started to ring. And ring. After the tenth ring, her voicemail clicked in.

'*Hi, I can't take your call right now but if you're ringing about PPI, my recent car crash, or failure to pay British Telecom, do yourself a favour and…*'

BEEEEEEP

Willow cleared her throat.

'Hey, Ems. I was hoping to have a natter. Charlie's away tonight and… wait for this… there's another man in my house,' she giggled. 'Call me back and I'll tell all!'

But Emma didn't call back. It was only much later, when Willow was snuggling down under the duvet alone, that she found herself wondering why her bestie hadn't breathlessly returned her call demanding to know what man – if not Charlie – was under Willow's roof.

As her eyes shuttered down, Willow decided it was out of

character for Emma not to be around on a midweek evening. Before sleep claimed her, Willow's last thought was puzzling where Emma could be.

Chapter Twenty-Two

Meanwhile, when Charlie had arrived at *The Beagle and Bugle*, he'd felt somewhat calmer and more positive about the evening ahead. He'd successfully fobbed off Willow's questions regarding his short-notice fictitious business trip, and Ben had backed up Charlie's whereabouts – albeit reluctantly.

Charlie was aware that Ben was an unwilling alibi but, following his split with Anna, the desperation to have a roof over his head made Ben malleable.

The stage was now set for dealing with Kev. Charlie had googled the dos and don'ts of how to dump a woman, and so far his plan had ticked several appropriate boxes:

DON'T do it on her birthday

DON'T do it at Christmas

DO do it to her face

DO do it kindly

He'd fulfilled the first three rules, but the last box still had to be dealt with. However, he would definitely do it kindly. Well, to the best of his ability. The question was… how? *How* to do it kindly? On the drive to Seal, Charlie had rehearsed aloud three versions of what he might say to Kev.

Darling, you deserve so much better.

If Kev demanded to know why she deserved so much better, than Charlie would take the next step:

Babe, I've cheated on you.

Okay, that wasn't very kind. But he needed a trigger to make Kev dump *him* so that she took control which – by his reasoning – was kinder than him dumping her. However, there was always the possibility that Kev might cry but say she'd forgive him. In which case Charlie needed an absolute fail-safe reason for Kev to never want to see him again. The only excuse he'd managed to come up with so far was:

Sweetie honey lollipops, I'm gay.

Okay, playing the camp card did make Charlie slightly panicky. It would take some serious acting skills. He'd need to convince Kev that all the time she'd been naked apart from her sexy scarlet stilettos, he'd been privately fantasising about a strapping six-footer wearing nothing but a pair of rugby boots. Hm. He might have to wing it and see what mood she was in. Not long to find out either. He gulped. Ahead loomed *The Beagle and Bugle.*

Indicating left, Charlie's car bounced over the ramp into the pub's private car park. Seconds later he'd reversed the BMW into the shadows of the far corner. The pub's security light didn't quite reach over there, rendering the number plate invisible. He wasn't anticipating encountering anyone he knew in this part of Kent, but it was best to err on the side of caution. Sometimes the world was a small place, as he'd discovered so very recently when Ben had wandered into Kev's road and spotted Charlie's boxers flying at full mast off Kev's curtain rail.

The pub didn't have a separate reception area. Instead, the main bar doubled as the check-in point for a booking. As Charlie ducked under a low beam, the landlord greeted him.

'Good evening, sir.'

'Hi,' said Charlie, adopting a businesslike tone. 'You have a room for me and my…'

He trailed off. No way was he saying the "wife" word. Uh-uh.

'Ah, yes. Here we are,' said the landlord, tapping a pencil against an A4 book. 'Mr and Mrs Kev.'

Charlie almost groaned aloud as he recalled his flip remark to Kev about what name to use. He'd stopped at a cash machine en-route. When it came to check-out time, Charlie didn't want to use his visa card. The last thing he needed was the landlord saying, "Mr Kev? Sorry, Sir, but this visa card belongs to Mr Charles Goodman. Whilst you were tucking into your bacon and eggs, I took the liberty of telephoning the Fraud Squad. They're sitting over there on table two. But please, do finish your breakfast before they interrogate you."

'Here's your key.'

The landlord handed Charlie a brass fob.

'I do believe the lovely Mrs Kev is over there' – he pointed – 'in our snug.'

'Thanks,' said Charlie, pocketing the key and picking up his overnight bag.

Kev was sitting next to a roaring fire. He could hear the cosy crackles and pops from here. She was holding a flute of pale gold bubbles. Champagne was chilling in an ice-bucket on a table beside her. Despite the warmth inside the pub, Kev hadn't removed her overcoat. She was buttoned and belted in something that made her look like a sexy detective.

Charlie felt a faint surge of hope. Perhaps Kev hadn't taken off her coat because she wouldn't be staying? Maybe she'd been sitting there, nursing her drink for the last ten minutes and rehearsing what *she* would say to *him*?

"Charlie Bear. I've re-read your earlier text and come to two conclusions. Firstly, you're a bastard. Secondly, you can go to hell. Have this on me."

And then she'd go berserk, chucking champagne and ice-cubes about. It would cause that old boy shuffling past to slip over. He'd likely crack his head open on that hearth… causing instant death… the landlord would call the police… Kev would be arrested… go to prison for a hundred million years… leaving Charlie free to breathe without hyperventilating and…

'Charlie,' Kev yodelled. 'Over here!'

He took a deep breath and tried to steady himself.

Come on, rally. You can do this. Square your shoulders. She's just a woman, not a lion about to rip you apart. She might not like the outcome of tonight, but you've taken trouble to do the task thoughtfully… to her face… in a pleasant setting… spoiling her – that's champagne she's drinking! No doubt she'll order the most expensive dish on the menu too. Just remember that you're paying for it, matey – along with the sumptuous four-poster bed waiting upstairs. All this so she can have one last bitter-sweet good-bye to look back upon and cherish.

Pep talk over, Charlie stuck up a hand and waved back.

‘Charlie Bear,’ Kev purred as she stood up to greet him.

A lingering kiss was planted on his lips. Anyone looking would have been left in no doubt that the handsome blond guy by the fire belonged to the pretty brunette in the raincoat.

‘I’m so happy,’ said Kev as she sank back down in her chair.

‘That’s nice,’ said Charlie, mustering up a smile.

‘Nice?’ she queried. ‘Such a bland word, darling.’

Charlie flopped down in a wing chair beside her.

‘I’m glad you’re happy,’ he said. ‘You deserve it.’

‘Let’s make a toast to our happiness.’

Charlie visibly flinched at Kev’s words, but fortunately she was busy pouring his champagne and didn’t see.

‘Here you are,’ she said, passing him the glass. ‘To us.’

Charlie smiled weakly.

‘To us.’

Those two words hadn’t been in his script.

Chapter Twenty-Three

Charlie let the golden bubbles roll over his tongue before swallowing. Mm. Nice. He had an overwhelming urge to use alcohol as a crutch. Perhaps he could get bladdered and make a public disgrace of himself, so much so that Kev would be provoked into ending their relationship on the spot. Brilliant idea! And then he wouldn't have to make up porkies about being gay.

He necked the champagne, then held out his glass for a refill.

'Steady, Charlie Bear,' said Kev with a tinkle of laughter.

'I'm thirsty,' he said, allowing petulance to creep into his voice.

Brilliant! He congratulated himself. *Another superb touch, Charlie.*

Yes, maybe this was the way forward? Behave like a prat and irritate Kev and… yes, that was it!... create an argument. Why hadn't he thought of this before? Fantastic idea.

'Thirsty?' Kev queried. 'Shall I order some water?'

'No. I want champagne.'

That's it! Demand. Be rude. Don't say "please".

'Well in that case,' she smiled, 'I'll join in too!'

Kev set the two glasses down on the table, side by side, and refreshed them.

'Awfully generous of you, Charlie Bear,' she murmured, pausing to check the level in the bottle. 'However, what's left won't last five minutes. I'll order another.'

Kev stuck up her hand, catching the eye of the passing landlord just as Charlie began to down his second glass.

'Another one of these, please,' Kev beamed, waggling the bottle.

'Certainly, madam. Another Bolly coming up.'

Charlie nearly choked. Bloody hell. He hadn't bothered checking the label and failed to realise Kev had ordered Bollinger. No wonder it tasted good.

'Perhaps we should cancel the champagne and go straight to dinner,' he said, recovering himself.

'Oh, but I've ordered it now,' Kev protested.

The landlord hovered.

'Yes? No?'

'Yes,' said Kev firmly.

'The lady says yes.' The landlord gave Charlie a sympathetic smile. 'I've learnt that if the lady gets what she wants, then the lady is always happy. Which means you'll be happy too.'

'Great,' said Charlie, looking slightly sick.

'Celebrating?' asked the landlord chummily.

'Yes,' Kev beamed. 'It's our anniversary.'

Charlie nearly dropped his glass. Anniversary? God, he couldn't stand the word. It was almost as bad as "wedding".

'In that case, let me extend my good wishes,' said the landlord, smiling. 'How many years have you been wed?'

Charlie could feel himself turning green. He knew Kev was only teasing, but Charlie wasn't comfortable with larking about. Especially as tonight was about blowing Kev out. It wasn't appropriate to play-act hubby-and-wifey soppiness.

'Oh it's been weeks, not years,' Kev grinned mischievously. 'We're so in *lurve* we celebrate every Wednesday. That's the day we first got together.'

Charlie was changing from green to grey. Had Kev really just said the words "so in love"? Just like the M word, the L word rarely cropped up in Charlie's vocabulary.

'A weekiversary,' said the landlord, looking amused. 'That's so cute. Let me get that champagne and' – he checked his wristwatch – 'I'll take it through to your table in the restaurant. It's getting on for eight o'clock and Chef likes orders in before half past.'

'Wonderful,' said Kev getting to her feet.

Charlie noticed she was wearing another pair of skyscraper heels, this time in black. She teetered off towards the restaurant leaving him to trail after her.

'Don't forget your bag,' said the landlord, grabbing the canvas handles and passing the holdall to Charlie.

'Ta,' he said meekly.

He should have taken the bag upstairs earlier. Ah well.

'What shall we have?' said Kev, sitting down and taking a menu from a hovering waitress.

Charlie's swiftly picked out the cheapest dish on the menu.

Thanks to Kev ordering two bottles of Bolly, he was worried about not having enough cash to settle up tomorrow morning. Damage limitation was necessary.

'The pasta looks nice.'

He looked up at the waitress.

'I'll have the tortellini, please.'

'Would you like a starter, sir?'

'No, thank you.'

Kev lowered her menu and raised one eyebrow at Charlie.

'No starter?'

'I'm good, thanks.'

He patted his stomach, as if to indicate he was weight-watching.

Kev turned to the waitress.

'I'll have the quail's eggs to begin with, followed by a medium rare fillet steak, triple-cooked chips, peppercorn sauce and' – her eyes perused the side dishes – 'the green beans.'

Charlie could feel his lips pursing. Kev had chosen the most expensive things on the menu. Flipping heck, this woman was no cheap date. His mind wandered back to Willow's recent birthday where she'd ecstatically hoovered up a dish that had been a third of the price.

'Excellent choice,' said the waitress, retrieving the menus. 'Would you like me to hang up your coat?' she said to Kev.

'No, I'm feeling a bit chilly,' said Kev dismissively.

She waited for the waitress to leave before giving Charlie her full attention.

'So,' she said, looking at him speculatively. 'I'm still

flabbergasted that my lover got all worked up believing I was seeing another guy.'

'Sorry?' said Charlie, momentarily thrown.

Kev's voice hardened.

'I'm talking about your dump text.'

'Oh… that. Yes… yes. I overheard a guy talking to another fella in the local Spar about his hot date with–'

'A woman who had the same name as me,' said Kev, finishing his sentence. 'Yes, you did say.'

'Yes, I did,' Charlie nodded.

He picked up his glass and drained it. He'd need a cellar-full of this stuff to get him through what really needed saying.

'Silly Charlie-Bear,' Kev teased. 'But we're good now, aren't we?'

'Well' – Charlie took a deep breath – 'as I said on the phone earlier, we need to talk.'

'Of course we need to talk, darling,' Kev cooed. 'But first I want to reassure you that there is no need to ever be jealous about anyone else.'

She leant in and took his hand across the table.

'You're my man, and I'm your woman. Right?'

Charlie squirmed in his seat. It was now or never.

'Darling, you're lovely.'

'Thank you.'

'But, baby angel-pie…'

No, that wasn't quite right. He coughed and tried again.

'You deserve someone so much better,' he said, mentally reaching for his pre-rehearsed script.

'Nonsense,' said Kev, her smile slipping. 'Are you trying to give me the brush off?'

Charlie wished he could be as direct as Kev. His next line was meant to be a confession. To say he'd cheated. Seeing her set expression, he instead found himself in the grip of cowardice and the words weren't forthcoming. He'd have to leapfrog over option two and go straight to number three, declaring he was a closet homosexual.

'Sweetie honey lollipops…'

'What did you just call me?' said Kev, her eyes widening.

'I'm g-g-g–'

'Are you having some sort of l-l-laugh?' Kev parodied, although Charlie could tell she wasn't remotely amused.

Instead he found himself saying something entirely different.

'Willow is suspicious about me seeing someone, so I think we should cool it.'

There. He'd said it. Kev's expression had changed from one of faint annoyance to murderous outrage.

'What?' she snapped.

'Just for a bit,' he quaked.

Oh well, two steps forward and one back.

'Cool it for a bit?' Kev repeated. 'How long is "a bit"? I don't want to stop seeing you.'

Charlie was now wriggling in his seat like a naughty schoolboy caught in the glare of an uncompromising headmistress.

'A bit as in… a little while.'

'You're not answering my question.'

'Right… you see… the thing is…'

Charlie licked his lips nervously.

'Willow has suggested getting hitched,' he blurted.

A picture of his girlfriend's face, happy and slightly flushed from birthday alcohol, popped into his mind's eye. Her words reverberated in his head: "How do you feel about getting married?"

'Married?' said Kev in surprise. 'Hang on a minute. You just said that Willow was suspicious about you seeing someone. Now you're telling me she wants to get married. That doesn't stack up. What exactly is the story here, Charlie?'

'Er… both,' he lied. 'She asked me outright if I was seeing someone. I said no. But she said' – he cast about for an excuse – 'that I needed to prove I was being faithful to her, and that the only way to prove it was by marrying her.'

'To which you said, "Willow, it's about time we had a frank talk. You don't put out, whereas your friend does, so I'd rather be with her."'

'Ah… well… the thing is' – Charlie picked up his napkin and began twisting it over and over in his hands – 'I wondered if I should give the idea some serious thought. After all' – he was gabbling now – 'if I marry Willow, then she won't suspect I'm playing around and then… then…er… then…'

'Then we can carry on as previously,' said Kev, finishing Charlie's sentence for him. 'Is that what you're trying to say?'

'Erm… something like that,' Charlie twittered. 'I mean, ha ha' – he tried to make a hasty joke – 'it's not like *you* want to marry me, is it?'

'Don't I?' said Kev, arching one eyebrow.

Oh crap. How the heck had he just walked into *that*?

Charlie stared at Kev, aghast, while his mind detached, zoomed off to the local church, crashed through the heavy arch doors, and then skidded to a standstill at the altar.

Dear God in Heaven. I know I don't pray very often... okay, I never pray at all... but there's a first time for everything, eh? And I'm in deep poo here. We're talking shit loads, if you'll excuse the pun. God, please get me out of this. I'm begging you. If you get me out of this, then I promise I'll–

'No, I don't want to marry you.'

Charlie's mind screeched out of the church and thudded back into his body. For a few seconds he was speechless – which was long enough for his ego to rear its head. Before he could stop himself, his mouth was speaking without his brain's permission.

'You wouldn't marry me?' he spluttered. 'Why ever not?'

'Hm, let me see,' said Kev pretending to take a moment to consider. 'Because, as a husband, I'm not sure I could trust you, Charlie Bear. I believe that when a man marries his mistress, it creates a vacancy.'

She regarded Charlie sadly. Despite him repeatedly saying he only ever slept with her, she wasn't convinced. Deep down, Kev knew Charlie wasn't the right person for her. However, when she'd started this crazy relationship, she hadn't meant for him to crawl under her skin and burrow deep within her heart.

When the waitress delivered Kev's starter and, later, their

mains, the two of them concentrated on eating rather than chatting. Both were preoccupied with their own thoughts.

Kev couldn't stop thinking about Willow wanting to marry Charlie. Privately she was aghast. Nor could she permit it. Okay, she'd committed the sin of breaking the rules of friendship and trust, but it didn't stop her from having a love for Willow. Somehow Kev needed to warn Willow that getting hitched to Charlie would be a very bad idea. But how to do it without giving herself away? Right now, she didn't know. But, then again, Willow had only suggested marriage. It hadn't been an out-and-out proposal. Perhaps it wouldn't happen? After all, there was no engagement ring in the equation. Kev decided she'd cross that particular bit of the matrimonial bridge if and when she came to it.

Charlie's armpits were pouring with sweat. All his lies and scrabbling about for excuses to cool it with Kev had made him very hot under the collar. Kev was under the impression that taking a break would only be for a little while. Currently he was off the hook. But for how long? Charlie wondered if he could persuade Willow to emigrate to Australia with him. That way he'd never have to see Kev again. He was sure there were libraries in Oz. Willow would find a job eventually. Meanwhile he could transfer from the London office to the Sydney branch. He put his knife and fork together and glanced up at Kev.

'Fancy a pudding?' he asked, forcing joviality.

'No. I fancy you.'

'Good,' he said, relieved at the change of subject.

He stood up, stooping briefly to grab his holdall before turning back to Kev.

'Didn't you bring an overnight bag?'

'I have everything in here,' she smiled, patting her handbag. 'Shower cap, toothbrush and a clean pair of knickers.'

'I love a lady who travels light,' Charlie quipped.

If ever he and Willow went away, her suitcase always ended up being sat on in order to do up the zip.

Charlie led the way out of the restaurant. Upon reaching the staircase in the foyer, he took Kev by the hand.

She allowed him to fold her palm in his and started to quiver with excitement at what was going to happen next. Charlie might be a bastard, but he was extremely satisfying between the sheets.

Once on the landing, they began kissing, and continued all the way to the door of their room. Charlie's lips worked their way down Kev's neck while his hands fumbled at getting the key in the lock. Falling into the room, he immediately set about undoing her coat's belt and buttons. As the garment slid to the floor in a rustling heap, he realised in a flash why Kev had refused to take the coat off in the restaurant. Underneath she was wearing nothing other than an eye-popping bra with matching thong and suspenders. *This* was what he wanted. No strings sex. It was a shame they were going to cool it down, especially when, right now, things were hotting up. But it was for the best.

Two hours later he was both spent and knackered. Kev lay beside him looking sated, although she was much quieter than usual. That suited Charlie fine. He didn't want any pillow talk. The last thing he needed was Kev rehashing their "take-a-break" conversation. She'd accepted things better than expected, but for some reason he felt twitchy.

'I think I'll have a shower,' he said.

For a lark, and to keep the mood light, he picked up Kev's shower cap and plonked it on his head. It was pale blue and covered in bright pink unicorns. It made him look both comical and ridiculous. Kev took one look at him and convulsed.

'Back in a bit,' he grinned.

Kev watched Charlie pad off, then reached for her mobile. Within seconds, steam had filled the bathroom and Charlie was singing away. She swung her legs out of bed, briefly pausing to click on the phone's camera icon. Tiptoeing forward and keeping her body out of sight, she slid the phone around the doorframe. Charlie instantly appeared in the viewfinder, his back to her. A large mole over his left butt cheek was clearly visible. There was no mistaking his identity to any woman who knew him intimately.

Kev pressed the camera button and watched Charlie's moving image convert to a still shot. Seconds later, it was saved to her phone's memory. Unlike before, this picture wasn't something to later mull over with a smile. Oh no. She didn't like the words "emotional blackmail". Rather, Kev thought of the saved photograph as a kind of insurance. It was the least she could do after sleeping with her friend's partner. Kev didn't want to use the picture to hurt Willow. Instead, she saw it more as a way of protecting her.

Kev just hoped she would never have to use it.

Chapter Twenty-Four

Willow was awoken a little after six in the morning by the landline ringing. Thinking it might be Charlie calling to say good morning before he beetled off to Cambridge, or Brighton – or whatever location his demanding client wanted him to be at next – she made a long arm and grabbed the receiver before its shrillness disturbed Ben on the other side of the wall. Her eyes were too sleep-bleary to make out the number displayed in the handset's window.

'Hello?' she said groggily.

'Hi,' said a female voice.

'Who's this?' said Willow, stifling a yawn.

There was a pause before the voice responded.

'Is Charlie there?'

Willow blinked.

'Who shall I say is calling?'

'It's Anna.'

'Anna? *Ben's* Anna?'

'Yes, except I'm no longer Ben's Anna,' she said dryly.

'Sorry, I'm not properly awake. Did you say you wanted to speak to Charlie, or did you mean you'd like to speak to Ben?'

‘Actually, neither,’ said Anna. ‘Sorry to be calling you so early, Willow. I had a burning desire to offload before I head into work.’

‘Um… you want to offload to me?’ said Willow in surprise.

She’d never considered herself to be close to Anna, so why was Ben’s ex ringing *her*?

‘Ben told me he’s temporarily moved in with you. No doubt he’s making me out to be a right bitch, but I wanted to tell Charlie not to believe a word of it. But as he’s not around, I’ll tell you instead.’

‘Er… right,’ said Willow uncertainly. ‘But really, Anna, it’s none of our business what’s gone wrong between you and Ben. You don’t need to tell–’

‘On the contrary,’ Anna snapped. ‘*You* of all people need to be aware what’s gone wrong between us.’

‘Why?’

‘Because men are shits. That’s why. And I might as well tell you. I’ve met someone else. It’s not relevant who he is. But I want you to know I’m not the sort of woman to fall into another man’s arms. Not unless the guy is more interested in looking at his phone over dinner than making conversation with his gorgeous partner.’

Willow marvelled at Anna’s self-confidence, not only over her looks, but her candour in declaring it.

‘Maybe I was a bitch at times’ – Anna continued – ‘but, hey, so what? Women like me don’t thrive with a complacent partner. I need a man with edge. Someone who can be a bit tricky. Keep me on my toes. And I think I've found that person. Do you see?'

'Er… I'm not sure.'

Willow was privately thinking that in the sixty seconds of conversation they'd had so far, this was the longest Anna had ever spoken to her.

'It's really important you understand what I'm saying' – Anna's tone took an earnest turn – 'because I want to give you the heads-up.'

'About what?'

Willow flopped back against her pillow. She wished Anna had chosen to offload about her love life to someone else. She'd been denied an hour's sleep. After all, her alarm wasn't due to go off until seven.

'About what?' Anna repeated. 'About men, of course!'

'Sorry, you've lost me.'

'Okay, let me explain. Firstly, I suspect Ben has met someone else, so you can hardly blame me for doing the same thing.'

'Anna, it's none of my business.'

'Secondly,' – Anna ignored Willow and swept on – 'have you ever stopped to question your relationship with Charlie?'

Willow was bemused. What on earth was Anna burbling about? She must try and concentrate on what was being said, because so far this conversation had made no sense whatsoever. Willow propped herself up on one elbow, rubbed the sleep from her eyes and then flicked on the bedside lamp.

'What has my relationship with Charlie got to do with

you?'

'More than you realise. I *know* things about Charlie,' she said meaningfully. 'Things you wouldn't be happy about.'

Willow was starting to get annoyed. Okay, so Charlie and Ben were sometimes as thick as thieves. Willow knew that. She wasn't daft. But she had a similar relationship with her own bestie. Emma knew things about Willow that Charlie didn't. Like the time they'd both got plastered and Willow had lied and said she'd only had one vodka and tonic. Everyone did that. Went on an occasional bender but made out they hadn't. Charlie included. It didn't make either of them dodgy people.

'I want to protect you,' said Anna changing tack.

'From what?' Willow huffed.

She knew Anna had a propensity to be wacky at times, but this conversation was getting cosmic.

'Where is your boyfriend right now?'

'In Cambridge. And Brighton,' Willow added as an afterthought.

'Two places at once, eh? Boy, he certainly gets around.'

'It's business.'

'Are you sure?'

'Yes, of course I'm sure,' said Willow indignantly. 'What sort of question is that?'

'A legitimate one. I've known you for a long time and, believe it or not, I'm very fond of you.'

Willow's eyes widened. Anna was fond of her? Was this the same woman she'd shared numerous social occasions with only to be ignored while Anna cosied up to the men? From the other end of the line came a heavy sigh.

'Listen, I need to leave for a breakfast meeting at the office. Before I go, can you promise me something?'

'It depends what it is,' said Willow cautiously.

'I want you to promise me that you'll never marry Charlie.'

Chapter Twenty-Five

Willow was so taken aback at Anna's question, at first she couldn't find the words to reply.

'Promise me,' Anna repeated.

'Marriage isn't on the cards, Anna' – Willow eventually spluttered – 'but even if it was, I'm not making such a promise.'

'Well if the subject ever arises, think on. I've heard all about Charlie's antics. Straight from the horse's best mate's mouth,' Anna added.

'W-What?' Willow stuttered.

This couldn't be happening. In a minute she'd wake up and think, "That was a peculiar dream, and featuring Anna of all people. How bizarre."

'Ask the man sharing your spare bedroom. And don't say you weren't warned. Anyway, I must go. Give me a call when you have some free time. We'll do drinks. Toodle-oo.'

For a moment Willow didn't know what to do. She lay there, staring into the gloom, her mouth hanging open like a dental patient who'd had one numbing injection too many. Her bemusement subsided and gave way to fury. How *dare* Anna cast doubts about Charlie's character. He was good man, and a conscientious employee. Just look how loyal he was to his cantankerous boss. Heavens, if Drummond ordered Charlie to jump, Charlie's response was, "How high?". Her boyfriend was a grafter. The events of this week proved that. Home late for two nights in a row, then dropping everything to dash off and appease a tetchy client.

The more Willow thought about it, the more outraged she began to feel. Anna was bang out of order. Willow knew what this was all about. Anna had busted up with Ben and now she was feeling bitter. Oh, she might have casually mentioned there was a new man in her life, but Willow wasn't sure she believed it. Why else would the woman try and cause trouble? Anna was festering over Ben not wanting to be with her. In turn, this had made her jealous of Willow's enduring relationship with Charlie. There could be no other explanation.

Flinging back the covers, Willow stomped off to the bathroom only to find the door locked.

'Won't be long,' Ben called from within. 'Oh, and I'd leave it for five minutes if I were you.'

Great! And when Charlie was home, Willow would have not one, but two men ponging out the bathroom.

It wasn't Willow's nature to be grumpy. However, what with Anna's feather-ruffling wake-up call coupled with a burgeoning bladder, she was starting to feel irritable. All Willow needed was a bad time at the library with Jean, and her mood would be set for the day – and it wasn't even yet seven in the morning.

'Sorry!' Ben trilled against a backdrop of frenzied toilet flushing.

'No worries,' Willow sighed. 'I'll go and put the kettle on.'

Downstairs, she flicked on lights and drew curtains before filling the kettle. Her stomach rumbled. Finding the bread, she slotted a couple of slices into the toaster, then added another two for Ben. She had no idea if he was a marmalade-on-toast type of person or whether, like Charlie, he preferred to grab a cappuccino and croissant from the station café en route to work. Time would no doubt tell. After all, it looked like Ben would be under her roof for months, which made her feel even more annoyed. Willow wasn't aware she was banging cupboard doors as she reached for cups and plates, until Ben came into the kitchen.

'You're cross,' he said, just as the temperamental toaster catapulted its contents on to the worktop.

'No, no, honest, I'm not,' Willow lied, as Ben relieved her of the plates.

'I'll butter the toast,' he said. 'You make the tea. I'm really sorry you couldn't get in the bathroom' – he opened the fridge and reached for a tub of spread – 'especially as I set my alarm earlier than usual. I thought I'd have showered and shaved long before you were up.'

'It's fine,' said Willow, dropping teabags in mugs. 'I'm not usually awake at this hour, so ordinarily a bathroom situation wouldn't be a problem. The phone woke me up.'

'Yeah, I heard it. Was it Charlie?'

'No.'

There was a pause as Willow slopped boiling water into

the mugs. A second later and a teaspoon clanked vigorously against the china as milk was added.

'Something tells me the caller rattled you as much as you're rattling those mugs,' said Ben, trying to make light of Willow's jerky movements.

'Yes, she definitely did that,' Willow muttered.

The teaspoon clattered down on the worktop.

'She?'

'I might as well tell you. It was Anna.'

Ben's buttery knife paused mid-air. He looked astonished.

'Whatever did she want?'

'To warn me off.'

Ben's mouth dropped open.

'Does she think you and me…' he trailed off.

'No, nothing like that.' Willow shook her head. 'She wanted to know if I had any plans to marry Charlie and, if so, to think long and hard before saying "I do".'

'You're joking, right?' Ben looked flabbergasted. 'Actually, scrap that. I can see you're serious. Why on earth would Anna do such a thing?'

Willow passed Ben his tea.

'You tell me,' she said in annoyance.

'What do you mean?'

'According to Anna, I should ask *you* why Charlie isn't a safe bet to marry.'

'Eh?'

Suddenly Ben couldn't look Willow in the eye. He took the tea from her and, head down, returned to buttering the toast.

'Is there something I should know, Ben? Anna indicated that Charlie' – she blew out her cheeks and imperceptibly shook her head – 'I don't know… gets up to no good. I'm assuming she's dropping heavy hints about him chasing other women. But I'd know if he did something like that, wouldn't I?'

'Course you would,' said Ben stoically, frantically buttering away.

At this rate there would be no spread left in the tub.

'Got any jam?' he asked, desperate to change the subject.

'Cupboard to your right.'

'Thanks.'

He peered inside the cupboard, anxious to hide his flaming face.

'Why are your ears bright red?'

'Are they?' said Ben vaguely.

He grabbed hold of a jar.

'Oh, look. Strawberry. My favourite. Is that all right for you?' he gabbled.

'Fine.'

Willow made a "whatever" gesture with one hand.

'Spill the beans, Ben. What do you know about Charlie that I don't?'

'Shall we sit or stand?' asked Ben, handing Willow her plate of toast.

'I really don't care,' she said in exasperation. 'I just want to know why your ex-girlfriend finds it necessary to ring me at the crack of dawn with a bizarre request to never marry Charlie, when the man in question hasn't even proposed.'

Ben pulled out a chair and sat down heavily. He resisted the urge to lay his forehead against the table's surface. God, here he was, in another house, Anna nowhere in sight, and yet the blasted woman was still causing him problems. What the hell was she playing at?

'My ex-girlfriend can be a bit of a nutter.'

'She sounded pretty sane to me,' Willow countered, sitting down opposite.

'Look, if you're questioning Charlie's loyalty, then surely you should speak to him yourself?'

'I've never had cause to doubt Charlie,' Willow reasoned. 'But you have to agree, it's not very pleasant having someone you know lob a verbal missile at your relationship.'

'Of course,' Ben agreed.

How he wished he didn't know about blasted Kev, or the real reason for Charlie being away right now. He liked Willow too much to lie.

'So what do you know that I don't?' Willow persisted.

'Okay,' said Ben slowly as his mind scrabbled for a plausible explanation. 'Well, there have been times when Charlie has said he's working a teeny bit late and...'

'Yes?'

Ben could hear the sudden anxiety in Willow's voice.

'We've gone to the pub after work. Just for a quick drink,' he added.

He was telling the truth. The pair of them had done that

on one or two occasions.

'Right.'

'Nothing too bad, eh?' he said, smiling weakly.

He was damned if he was going to tell Willow anything else. Bugger Charlie for putting him in this situation. He would be having a few stern words when he next saw him. Or… hang on. What about manipulating this situation so that *Willow* scared Charlie? Brilliant idea! He took a deep breath.

'Maybe you should also ask Charlie about Kev.'

'Kev?' said Willow, looking puzzled.

She'd never heard Charlie mention anyone from the office with that name.

'Yes,' said Ben, forcing a jovial chortle. 'Kev can be a bit naughty, ah ha ha ha! Never happy with a swift half. Always wants the full pint.'

'I see,' said Willow. 'So you're saying this person is a bad influence?'

'Totally,' said Ben, nodding his head vigorously. 'I've told Charlie to put his foot down. Unfortunately Kev can be very persuasive. However, I'm sure a few words from you will sort it out. But Mum's the word, eh?' Ben tapped the side of his nose. 'You didn't hear that name from me.'

'Okay. And thanks,' said Willow looking both relieved and grateful.

'Good. I'm glad we've got that sorted.'

He shoved some toast in his mouth and tried not to gag. Thanks to his ex-girlfriend stirring things, he felt sick to his stomach.

Chapter Twenty-Six

Charlie settled the bill for his and Kev's overnight stay at *The Beagle and Bugle*, handing over cash to avoid any recorded transaction on his bank statement. Willow wasn't a snooper, but he was playing it safe.

Stuffing his wallet into his back trouser pocket, Charlie took Kev by the elbow to guide her through the foyer towards the exit. But Kev wouldn't budge.

'Can't we have a final coffee by the log fire?' she asked.

'No, or I'll be late to work.'

'Just ten minutes,' Kev pleaded.

Charlie was eager to be on his way, but he didn't want to annoy Kev. An angry woman was a dangerous woman.

'Sweetie, we've already had breakfast in bed together,' he pointed out.

'And very nice it was too. Did you like what I did with your sausage?' she said playfully.

'Of course. But now I need to go.'

'To Willow.'

Charlie noted the sudden change in Kev's tone. Truculence.

'No,' he said patiently. 'To the office.'

'When will I see you again?'

Charlie gazed at her incredulously.

'But… you're not. I mean… we're not seeing each other again.'

'Pardon?'

Her eyes flashed with anger.

'We discussed this,' Charlie cajoled.

He again tried steering Kev towards the exit, but she wasn't having any of it.

'You said we wouldn't see each other – and I quote – *just for a bit.*'

'Er, that's right,' Charlie nodded.

Oh for goodness sake. Fine. Let her think they'd resume things in a month or two. If that was what it took to make his escape, then so be it. He'd just fob her off if she rang or texted. Tell her that Willow was in the room. That he couldn't talk. Or, even better, he wouldn't answer her calls. Yes, fantastic idea. And then Kev wouldn't be able to talk to him at all.

'So let's make a date,' said Kev, fishing in her bag for her phone.

Charlie couldn't believe he was hearing this. He'd given Kev a wonderful night to look back upon as a precious rose-tinted memory. The restaurant bill alone had almost brought him out in hives, not forgetting the price of the Bollinger. The pub's mark-up had been astronomical. Then, this morning, Kev had demanded room service. A cooked breakfast *and* Bucks Fizz. Charlie had gulped down his food, mindful of the time and need to get to work. He'd barely put his knife and fork together when Kev had pushed him back against the mattress and writhed all over him. Whilst that had been nice enough, he'd been unable to stop himself checking the digital clock beside him. He'd silently willed Kev to hurry up and climax so he could get on with checking out. And now, after spoiling her rotten, here she was delaying him further in the foyer of this flipping pub with a well-manicured finger hovering over her electronic diary.

'Tell you what' – she chewed her lip thoughtfully – 'let's leave things for a fortnight to appease Willow's suspicions. In which case… how about the twenty-sixth?' She entered Charlie's name in the diary. 'You know, Charlie Bear, I really enjoyed coming here. Perhaps we should make this our regular place to meet up. Then there will never be any worries about being disturbed. I'll book us in now.'

She made to move towards the reception desk, but Charlie grabbed her arm and spun her round.

'*Darl*-ing,' he whispered, just as the landlord appeared.

'Still here?' he beamed.

'We thought we'd have a quick coffee,' said Kev, taking Charlie's hand.

Suddenly he was the one being guided, but in the opposite direction to where he wanted to go.

'Sure,' said the landlord. 'Go in and I'll be right with you.'

'Wonderful,' she beamed. 'We'll have two cappuccinos.'

She propelled Charlie towards the sofa by the fire.

'There,' she said, sinking down into the sofa's squashy depths. 'Isn't this nice?'

Her eyes bored into his, daring him to defy her.

'No, not really. I'm going to be late to work.'

'Nonsense. Just say the train was cancelled. Ten minutes won't matter. Now then, where were we?'

Kev consulted her electronic diary.

'Ah yes. Two weeks today. Another overnight stay here.'

'It's too soon,' Charlie hissed.

'Then when?' said Kev, glaring at him.

'A couple of months.'

'But that's *eight weeks*,' she shrieked, just as the landlord appeared with their cappuccinos.

'Here we are,' he said, setting the coffees down on the table in front of them. 'Enjoy.'

'I fully intend to,' said Kev, looking at Charlie meaningfully.

The moment the landlord was out of earshot, she swivelled round to face Charlie.

'I'm *not* going without sex for two months,' she said adamantly.

'Can't you use–'

'Don't even suggest it,' Kev interrupted.

Charlie shrank back against the sofa. Kev was starting to look a bit wild about the eyes. He needed to try a different tack.

'Look, angel. I really did mean it when I said we needed to cool it.'

'And your point is?'

'Exactly that. Now please don't pin me down.'

'I thought you liked being pinned down,' she fired back.

Charlie reached for his cup. He made himself take a slow sip while his brain scrabbled like a frantic hamster. He needed to come up with something to say to Kev once and for all.

'Please, try and see things from my point of view, darling. I have a heavy work schedule at the moment. Also, my best mate has just busted up with his girlfriend. He's temporarily moved in with us and is really needy' – Charlie lied – 'and constantly wants a shoulder to sob all over. What with Willow asking twenty questions about my whereabouts plus demanding I marry her, frankly I'm exhausted. Can we just leave things for a few weeks?' he wheedled.

Charlie gave Kev his best puppy-dog-eyes look. Her own were like two flints.

'I'll compromise with you,' she snapped. 'One month, not two.'

'Okay,' said Charlie wearily.

Picking up his cup, he drained it. Mentally he felt shattered. He'd dodge out of seeing Kev when the time came. At least for now he had a month's grace. He told himself that a lot could happen in the space of four weeks.

Little did Charlie know how prophetic that thought would be.

Chapter Twenty-Seven

Charlie belted into work half an hour late. He was dismayed to see Drummond hovering by Ben's desk.

Thankfully, Ben had switched Charlie's monitor on. A calculator and pen sat on top of some artfully scattered papers. Ben had even placed a half-drunk cup of coffee next to everything, although Charlie reckoned the drink was likely now tepid.

Stealthily, Charlie slid his briefcase under the desk and slipped into his chair. Seconds later he was poring over the report as if he'd been in the office for hours.

'Sterling work,' Drummond was saying to Ben. 'You know what this means, don't you?'

Drummond sniffed the air, as if inhaling a heavenly smell rather than the sour whiff of Charlie's armpits which were infiltrating the office. After his diabolical morning with Kev his deodorant had badly let him down.

'It means money,' said Drummond, clapping Ben on the back.

Their boss was smiling like a Cheshire cat whose saucer of semi-skimmed milk had turned out to be double cream.

'Or, to be more precise, a big fat bonus,' Drummond

added.

'Thank you.'

Ben was flushed with pleasure. He looked like he'd been presented with a Euro Millions cheque.

'Good morning, Charlie,' said Drummond, now looking over at him.

Charlie pretended to be startled out of deep concentration.

'Ah, hello there, Mr Drummond.'

He straightened up. His spine gave a series of cracks, as if he'd been bent over paperwork for hours, rather than pulverised by Kev's earlier bedroom workout.

'Your dedication hasn't escaped me either,' said Drummond, beaming away.

'Thank you, Mr Drummond, but' – Charlie decided a bit of bum-licking would be beneficial since the "bonus" word had been mentioned – 'it's easy to be dedicated. After all, I love my job and it's a pleasure to work for you.'

Out of the corner of his eye, Charlie spotted Ben rolling his eyes and making puke-in-a-bag gestures.

'That's what I like to hear.' Drummond chuckled appreciatively. 'Carry on, lads.'

Their boss swaggered off, a smug smile on his face.

Charlie grinned and picked up the mug on his desk. Taking a large gulp, he immediately regretted it. The coffee wasn't just stone cold, it was disgustingly scummy too.

'Bleurgh,' he said, wiping the back of his hand across his mouth.

'Almost as "bleurgh" as your little speech,' said Ben.

'He's in a good mood,' said Charlie, nodding at Drummond's departing back. 'Do you think Mrs D let him get his leg over last night?'

'Shh,' Ben shushed. 'Definitely not. I've heard his wife has left him. Rumours are rife. Apparently Mrs D has served Drummond with divorce papers. According to the office grapevine, old Drummers isn't remotely upset because he has a new woman, *and* she's almost half his age.'

Charlie gave a theatrical shudder.

'Well whoever she is, she must be desperate. I mean, the guy isn't exactly a stunner.'

'Ah, but he has something else that makes him attractive,' said Ben knowingly.

'Please don't tell me you've seen Drummond naked in the office showers, and his todger is bigger than the boardroom table.'

Ben tutted.

'No. And anyway, Drummond doesn't ever use the office gym. He has no need to worry about workouts when he's attractive to the opposite sex for entirely different reasons.'

Charlie looked puzzled.

'Like what?'

'Money, of course. He's flipping loaded. And his position in a company like this means he oozes power. It's a total babe magnet. And talking of babes' – Ben lowered his voice – 'how did last night go? Have you extricated yourself from whatsername… Kev?'

'Sort of,' said Charlie.

'I don't want to know the details.'

'I've managed to get rid of her for a month.'

'I said I don't want to know the details.'

'Blasted woman won't leave me alone.'

'Mate, I said–'

'Yeah, I know. You don't want the details. And that's fine.'

Charlie picked up his pen, and then put it down again.

'You know, I can't carry on living like this.'

'What, getting into the office late and me covering your backside, or drinking coffee that the cleaner forgot to clear away? That wasn't a prop put there by me. It was yesterday afternoon's leftovers that you swigged.'

Charlie shuddered.

'I don't want to know the details,' he said, parodying Ben.

'Well nobody is forcing you to carry on the way you do.'

Ben was now gearing himself up to lecture Charlie.

'I spent a very pleasant evening with Willow. And a very pleasant morning too,' he added as an afterthought.

'Good to hear. Just so long as you didn't spend a very pleasant night with her,' Charlie quipped.

'I wouldn't say no if the offer was there,' said Ben slyly.

'Hands off, mate. She's mine.'

'Really?'

'Yes, really. You know, now that I've finally extricated myself from she-who-shall-not-be-named–'

'For a month,' Ben scoffed.

'That's all I need,' Charlie retorted. 'I think I've had an

epiphany.'

'Do you even know what that word means?' said Ben sarcastically.

'Yes, it's a light-bulb moment,' said Charlie triumphantly.

'Make sure you don't bang your head on it,' Ben muttered.

'I've decided to enjoy this weekend's convention in Birmingham and, er, you know' – Charlie winked – 'make the most of being far away from home.'

'Oh God,' Ben sighed.

'And then I shall hang up my condom and return to the bosom of my home… and Willow's bosom too…'

Ben rolled his eyes.

'And become a reformed man,' Charlie added.

'Yeah, right.'

'I mean it,' Charlie nodded. 'Well, I think I mean it. I mean it for now. Enough to do a monumental U-turn and seriously think about asking Willow to marry me.'

'You WHAT?' Ben gasped.

'Well, it's just a thought,' Charlie shrugged.

'Is that your grand plan to finally get this Kev woman out of your hair?'

'Sort of,' Charlie grimaced. 'I think it is actually going to take a marriage certificate to penetrate her brain that I'm not interested in pursuing things long-term.'

'Wow, what a romantic reason to get married,' Ben tutted.

'Hey, I can be romantic when required,' Charlie protested. 'You should have seen me last night letting Kev loose in the restaurant with a fillet steak and two bottles of Bollinger and–'

'I said I didn't want to know the details.'

'Okay, okay,' said Charlie putting his palms up.

'And what about Willow? Do you think she would accept your proposal?'

'Of *course*,' Charlie laughed, as if the very idea of Willow turning him down was preposterous.

'Right. Fab.'

'Hey, try not to sound too enthusiastic.'

Charlie leant over and gave Ben a good-natured slap on the back.

But Ben reckoned his best mate wouldn't be laughing if Willow asked who Kev was.

Chapter Twenty-Eight

When Willow arrived at work, Jean was already in and fussing about with the noticeboard.

'If you're making yourself coffee, do me one too.'

Please, Willow silently added, although she didn't dare voice the word aloud.

'Sure,' she nodded.

Shrugging off her coat, Willow headed over to her locker. She slipped her jacket and bag inside. Willow was just about to shut the door when her handbag vibrated. Reaching inside, she pulled out her mobile which had been switched to silent so as not to annoy Jean. Glancing at the screen, she was pleased to see she had a text from Emma.

Sorry not to pick up when you rang last night. Wasn't in a great place. Suspect my fella is dumping me. He wants to cool things for a bit. Spent the whole night crying. But never mind me and my meltdown. What's all this about Charlie being elsewhere and you having another man in the house? Want details! Call me when you haven't got battle-axe Jean watching your every move. Xxx

Her boss's voice made Willow jump so violently, she banged her head on the open locker door.

'Battle-axe Jean would like to know how long it takes to make coffee?'

Furious at having a private message read over her shoulder, Willow lobbed the phone into the locker and slammed the door.

'Coffee coming right up,' said Willow ignoring Jean's "battle-axe" reference.

She walked off to the kitchenette feeling her superior's eyes like twin laser beams upon her back. Blasted woman. Who did she think she was creeping up on her like that and, even worse, sneakily reading a personal message? It served the old biddy right spotting a disparaging comment about herself.

Filling the kettle, Willow set about making the drinks. She might as well do coffees for Theresa and Fiona too. Thankfully, the library was currently quiet, with only a couple of people using the IT resources. As Willow poured scalding water into the mugs, the library phone rang. Seconds later, Jean's over-elocuted telephone voice could be heard.

'Mosley Librair, hellair?'

Transferring the mugs to a tray, Willow headed towards reception. She found Jean clutching the handset to her vast bosom and doing an impression of an angry bullfrog. Willow instantly had a sinking feeling in her stomach. What now? She didn't have long to find out.

'I thought I told you' – Jean hissed – 'that it's forbidden to have personal calls at the library?'

'You did,' said Willow, setting Jean's coffee down on the personalised coaster next to her keyboard.

'Then why have you got a personal call?' Jean demanded.

'Maybe it's because the caller doesn't know the library rules,' said Willow calmly.

'Then perhaps' – Jean wasn't prepared to be outdone – 'you'd like to enlighten the lady who is asking for you?'

Glaring at Willow, Jean thrust the handset at her.

'I would like to point out' – Willow's tone was quiet but firm as she looked Jean in the eye – 'that I'm taking this call because you've instructed me to advise the lady accordingly, and not because I wish to engage in a personal call.'

Jean's eyes bulged and her mouth dropped open. She wasn't used to being answered back. Especially from Willow, who was usually like a little mouse. How dare she cheek her.

'When you've finished your *personal* call' – Jean's eyes flashed with anger – 'I'll see you in my office.'

'Gladly,' said Willow.

She'd had enough of Jean's bullying. If Willow had deliberately behaved in such a way as to justify the endless digs and rebukes, then fair enough. But friends and family generally didn't call her at work. Okay, Charlie had phoned at the start of the week, but that had been a one-off. If Jean wanted to see Willow in her office to issue another verbal warning, then Willow would just have to stand up for herself. Enough was enough.

Turning her back on Jean, she put the handset to one ear.

'Can I help you?'

Silence.

'Hello?'

Silence.

'Is anybody there?' said Willow in annoyance.

Well wasn't today turning out to be peachy. First, she'd been rudely awoken by the phone a whole hour before she needed to get up. Second, she'd had to listen to Anna bizarrely demanding a promise that Willow never marry Charlie. Third, Jean was clearly gunning for a row, and now, fourth, she had a silent caller.

'I don't know who you are' – Willow sounded far more authoritative than she felt – 'but please don't ring me at my workplace, especially if you have nothing to say.'

Willow was about to hand the phone back to an eavesdropping Jean, when the caller finally spoke. It was a woman. She whispered two words which left Willow shocked. The emotion must have registered on Willow's face, because Jean's own expression changed from fury to curiosity.

'I b-beg your pardon?' Willow stuttered.

The caller repeated herself.

'Leave Charlie.'

And then the line went dead.

Chapter Twenty-Nine

'Bad news?' asked Jean.

She eyed Willow speculatively. The muscles in Willow's face were moving so much, they appeared to be doing a work-out.

'I-I've just had an anonymous phone call,' said Willow shrilly.

'What did she want?' said Jean curiously.

'I'd rather not say,' said Willow, as two red marks suddenly stained her cheeks.

The shock was blurring into rising anger.

'And now you're going to order me into your office to give a second disciplinary over some unknown idiot calling me. There's nothing to say this woman won't ring again. And again and again and again. No doubt you'll then take the greatest pleasure in firing me.'

Willow was aware that her voice was rising, but she didn't seem able to stop. A huge outpouring of frustration at the injustice of it all was rising up and spilling out in a wordy jumbly mess. People were now looking her way. A young mother with two pre-school children was listening with interest, as were the two people using the library's computers.

Theresa and Fiona were both trying and failing not to hang on to every word of Willow's rant.

'Come into my office,' said Jean abruptly.

She stood up, pausing for a moment to grab the coffees Willow had made only moments earlier.

Here goes, thought Willow as she followed Jean's swaying backside.

Suddenly she didn't care about her job. All she was concerned about was Charlie. Or, more particularly, what might be going on in her relationship that she didn't know about. It was too much of a coincidence that, only hours earlier, Anna had telephoned with a ridiculous request that Willow promise to never marry Charlie. And now another female had got in touch, this time telling her to leave him. Or was it the same woman? Was it Anna who had just made that call?

Willow's mind whirred. No. The caller had sounded nothing like Anna. Perhaps Anna had got a friend to make the call? Unlikely. After all, Anna could have simply incorporated "leave Charlie" into her early morning speech of "don't marry Charlie". So, if it wasn't Anna who'd whispered in her ear, who the heck *had* it been? Willow didn't have the foggiest.

'Sit down,' said Jean, indicating the chair by her desk.

So this was it. Willow could only guess at how Jean's sermon was going to roll out. Perhaps she should give as good as she got? Maybe she could make an allegation against Jean? Say that her boss was a bully? As Willow flopped down heavily on the chair, all the fight went out of her.

'I'm not going to give you a verbal warning,' said Jean, although her upper lip was quivering ominously. 'Anonymous calls don't count. The caller was mindful and withheld her number, more's the pity. But just to set the record straight, the only reason I'm hard on you, Willow, is because I think you're a great little worker. I believe you have the potential to one day run Mosley Library yourself.'

Willow blinked. Was she hearing things?

'R-Really?'

'Yes, really,' said Jean, not quite managing to smile, but at least no longer grimacing disdainfully. 'Now I don't know what was said in that call, but it clearly upset you. What about you have the rest of the day off, just to demonstrate what a sympathetic, magnanimous person your battle-axe boss can be, eh?'

Jean's mouth gave the smallest of twitches.

'Oh, but there's no need for…'

Willow trailed off.

She wasn't a flake by any means but, if the offer was there, why not take advantage? After all, Ben was at work. Charlie too. Neither of them would be home for hours. Leaving the library early would give Willow an opportunity to carry out what she suddenly had an overwhelming urge to do.

'Actually, I do have a bit of a headache,' she said. 'It's probably all the nervous energy I've just expended. Especially when I thought you were revving up to give me another verbal warning or, even worse, the bullet.'

'Go home,' said Jean, picking up her coffee. 'But have

your drink first. Shame to waste it.'

'Okay. Thank you,' said Willow, picking up her mug.

Her mind raced ahead. As she sipped on autopilot, her brain had already jumped in her car, started up the engine, let out the clutch too soon and kangarooed off down the High Street, heading out towards North Mosley.

She had the germ of an idea, but the thought of carrying it out made her heart pound unpleasantly. It was a preposterous plan. Well, certainly for her. The concept filled her with revulsion. And then she found herself mentally back-pedalling. Nope, she couldn't do it. Better to stay at work after all. It simply wasn't in her nature to carry out such a thing.

Willow gave a strangled whimper causing Jean to peer over the rim of her cup in consternation.

But then again, if she *didn't* do this, she might never get the opportunity again. Right, okay, she *would* go home. She *could* do this. And if her fears proved to be unfounded then... then... psychologically speaking, for the rest of her life she'd wear a hair shirt and give herself twenty lashes every day.

Willow shook her head imperceptibly. Last night, if someone had said – just before she'd turned out the light – that in less than twelve hours she'd be back home and on a mission, she'd have laughed in their face. However, the anonymous caller had planted a nagging doubt in her brain which wouldn't go away. Not until she'd done this thing that she would never, ever, tell another soul about. Not even her best friend Emma.

Chapter Thirty

Willow shoved the key into the lock. As the front door swung open, she paused for a moment, surveying the hallway. Even though this was her home, she felt like a burglar. After all, she was going to behave just like one. The only difference was, she wouldn't leave a mess.

Cautiously, she stepped inside.

'Hello?' she called out, and immediately felt foolish. Nobody was home.

Shutting the door behind her, on impulse Willow drew the safety chain. She didn't want to tempt the Law of Sod and have Charlie or Ben turn up claiming sudden man flu and an urgent need to crawl under the bedcovers so they could die in peace. Even though she knew in her heart that the likelihood of this was remote, Willow didn't trust the Law of Sod one little bit. She stood uncertainly on the doormat, listening to the thick silence. You could have heard the proverbial pin drop.

The doorbell ripped apart the stillness, zigzagging into her brain like a shrieking pneumatic drill. She screamed and leapt off the doormat as if it were suddenly a dangerous animal. Heart thumping, she turned and peered through the spyhole. A courier was standing on the other side. Keeping the chain on, she inched the door open and peered suspiciously at the man.

'Hello, love,' he said cheerfully, addressing Willow's one visible eyeball. 'Your neighbour's out. Any chance you could take this?'

He presented a small box for her eyeball to inspect.

'I guess so,' she said, reluctantly peeling back the chain.

'Cheers,' said the courier, thrusting the box into her arms. 'Sign here, please.'

He produced a plastic box with a screen, and Willow squiggled her signature.

'Fantastic,' the courier beamed. 'You have a nice day now.'

'Thanks, although it's been flipping awful so far.'

'Oh... er... sorry to hear that, love,' he said, dropping his smile and appearing uncomfortable.

He wasn't used to dealing with females who, now that he could see both of this lady's eyeballs, looked slightly unhinged. He backed away, desperate to return to the sanctuary of his van.

Willow sighed and shut the door. Putting the box to one side, she took a deep breath. If she was going to behave like a thief, she ought to get on with the burglary... metaphorically speaking.

Moving upstairs, she stood on the landing and peered into the bedroom she shared with Charlie. The hot water tank in the cupboard to her left suddenly gurgled like a rumbling stomach. Willow found her tummy replying. But she dismissed her mid-morning hunger pangs. They were no respecter of the seriousness of this matter. She was about to cross not just a line of trust, but to abuse that trust too.

Stepping into the bedroom, she flung open the wardrobe and surveyed the contents within. There was a central area with a high-placed rail from which jeans and trousers dangled from pegged hangers. Either side were twin rails, one high, one low. The left side accommodated Willow's clothing. She ignored her skirts, blouses, cardigans and coats, and instead turned her attention to the right side. This area contained Charlie's suit jackets and shirts. These were the garments that interested her. Willow pulled up her sleeves and, like a pickpocket, got to work.

Her fingers moved like spindly spider's legs, quickly dipping into pocket after pocket as she worked her way along the rail of shirts. She wasn't expecting to find anything in the breast pockets, and she didn't.

Moving down to the lower rail, she began to search more thoroughly. Suit jackets had all manner of hidden places to conceal things. But what exactly was she looking for? A telephone number? A woman's name? A photograph? She didn't really know. Presumably if she found something, her intuition would shriek, "Unfaithful Bastard Alert!"

She gulped and took a deep breath as she dug into an inside pocket. One side. Now the other. Moving outward. Past the lapels. Downward. Now frisking the fabric like a security checker at an airport, just in case the very lining was hiding secrets. Swooping up. Another outside pocket, but… oh, it was stitched up. Okay. Move on. Next jacket. And the next. Now the other sort of jackets. The ones that Charlie teamed with jeans.

Willow's fingers delved in and out. Her pulse accelerated when she came across a small piece of paper. Pulling it out, she gazed in relief at a dry-cleaning ticket that hadn't been thrown away. Carefully replacing it – nothing must look as if it had been violated – she moved on to a short coat with a fleecy collar. She loved this on Charlie. Indeed, she'd borrowed it once or twice, enjoying snuggling into its cosy, too-big depths.

Her heart skipped a beat as her hand encountered something small, hard and cylindrical in shape. What the heck was this? Withdrawing the object, she felt a shockwave ripple through her. Oh my God. A lipstick.

Suddenly Willow felt nauseous. Her legs were no longer capable of holding her up. She sank down on the carpet, her mind reeling. Who did it belong to? She unfurled her hand, letting the tube roll backwards and forwards across her palm. The case was gold. She twisted it apart, so the colour was fully revealed. It was exactly the sort of shade she liked to wear. A peek at the tiny sticker on the base informed her the shade was called *Bad Bitch*. A piece of Willow's mind peeled away as she wondered how many people had blown a marketing budget coming up with such an awful name. And then a lightbulb lit up a different part of her brain.

'You bloody idiot,' she said aloud, letting out a snort at the same time.

The snort became a giggle. Then a laugh. Two minutes

later she was still convulsing, tears pouring down her face. Willow realised she was in the grip of hysteria borne from relief. The lipstick was hers. She must have put it in there the last time she'd borrowed Charlie's jacket and failed to take it out. Not so much *Bad Bitch,* more *Silly Bitch.*

Pocketing the lipstick, she rocked back on her heels. The worst was over. She was sure of it. Even so, best to check everything. Just to be on the safe side.

Willow continued peering into everything. Even Charlie's shoes. She also slipped her hand inside every sock in his bedside drawer. There were no love notes, nor receipts for meals in unfamiliar restaurants. There now remained only one thing left to do. And it was a biggie.

Quivering like a fox cornered by a hunting hound, she went into the box room that doubled as Charlie's study. There, on the desk, was his laptop. He'd never made any secret of his password. He used the same letters and numbers for everything. From paying a gas bill or accessing his gym membership, to viewing his on-line bank statements. It was the latter that Willow was interested in.

Her heart was now hammering like a woodpecker on amphetamines. She'd gone well and truly past the point of no return. Snooping on Charlie's finances was just the pits. But she couldn't help herself. Both Anna's words and those of this morning's anonymous caller kept reverberating in her brain.

I want you to promise me that you'll never marry Charlie… promise me… promise me… promise me… leave Charlie… leave Charlie…

Her eyes flit from one side of the screen to the other, taking in a couple of direct debits, a standing order to their joint account which took care of the monthly bills, numerous purchases at the station café, and the restaurant that Charlie had taken her to last weekend for her birthday.

Everything was in apple-pie order. The only thing that puzzled her was a large cash withdrawal from an ATM. The transaction date was yesterday. Charlie wasn't one to carry cash on him, much preferring the ease of contactless purchasing. Strange. She chewed her lip thoughtfully. And then it came to her. Of course. It was to do with the tetchy client. Charlie would have withdrawn that money to provide the wretched man with a butter-him-up breakfast and, later, a lavish dinner liberally garnished with flattery. Charlie would keep all the receipts incurred and later claim it back as expenses.

She logged out and snapped the lid down. What a fool she'd been to allow the likes of Anna and an anonymous madwoman to put the wind up her. There was no need to look for complications or sub-plots when there were none. She'd found nothing, because there was nothing to find.

Willow let out a huge sigh of relief. Charlie might be allergic to the M word, but that didn't make him a bad person, and certainly not an unfaithful one.

Feeling both disgusted and ashamed of what she'd just done, Willow went downstairs to make a cup of tea.

Chapter Thirty-One

Armed with a cuppa, Willow glanced at the clock on the kitchen wall. It was getting on for lunchtime. Now that her despicable act was behind her, she felt able to think about food.

Rustling up a quick cheese sandwich, she scoffed it greedily. Realising that she currently had the luxury of time to respond to Emma's earlier text, she picked up the phone. Her bestie had asked for details about the man in Willow's house while Charlie was away. Never had Willow been so ready to get so many things off her chest… although she'd be omitting the details of going through Charlie's belongings and especially his bank statement.

Willow tapped out Emma's number. With a bit of luck, her friend would be on her lunchbreak and available to talk. Willow was delighted when Emma picked up said she was free to gossip.

'I've had a right morning,' Willow moaned. 'It was so bad that Jean sent me home.'

'Battle-axe Jean sent you home? My goodness, whatever's been going on?'

'What hasn't?' Willow countered.

'You'd better bring me up to date. And what's all this

about another man in your house?' said Emma in astonishment. 'I couldn't believe what I was hearing when listening to your voicemail. Are you going to lob a bombshell at me and say you've met someone else?'

Willow wasn't sure, but just for one moment she could have sworn Emma had sounded hopeful about Willow having another man. But before the thought could even take root, she dismissed it as having an over-active imagination, no doubt brought on by the events of the last few hours.

'No, I haven't met another man' – Willow gave an astonished laugh, as if the very idea of her two-timing Charlie was absurd – 'but you go first, Ems. I was really concerned when I read your text this morning. What's all this about you not being in a great place, and this guy you've been tentatively seeing suddenly wanting to cool things?'

'Oh, isn't it always the way with men?' Emma grumbled. 'They love you and then flaming well leave you.'

'Is that what's happened then? He's cleared off?'

'Not totally' – Willow could sense Emma shrugging – 'but he might as well have done. After all, he wants us to take a break. Just for a bit. But how long is "a bit?"' Emma complained.

'I don't know,' said Willow sympathetically. 'But you're worth far more than taking a back seat whilst waiting for some guy to make up his mind about whether he wants to be with you or not. He sounds like a mind-messer. And didn't you say he was already in a relationship?'

'A relationship in the throes of dying,' said Emma

defensively.

'Nonetheless, it does sound' – Willow picked her words carefully – 'a teensy bit complicated.'

When Emma didn't reply, Willow was worried she'd offended her.

'I mean, the likely reason for him wanting a break–'

'Yes?' said Emma eagerly.

'Is to extricate himself from his current relationship, and then have a bit of time to himself. Just to, you know, catch his breath.'

'Do you think?'

At the other end of the line, Emma's voice had whooshed like a high-speed elevator from deep despair to sky-high hope.

'Yes, I do think. In fact, I'm positive,' said Willow, crossing her fingers. 'But it doesn't stop me from worrying about you, Ems. I don't want you getting hurt.'

'Too late for that.'

Gloominess whipped away Emma's previously positive tone.

'But don't fret about me. I'll get over it.' She gave a derisive laugh. 'After all, I've had plenty of practice over the years.'

'I just know that there's someone out there waiting for you,' said Willow encouragingly. 'You'll see.'

'Yeah, well I wish he'd hurry up and come along and help me get over this guy. Why are all men dickheads?'

'I don't know.'

Willow didn't believe *her* man was a dickhead but decided

to go along with Emma's opinion given her blue mood.

'Anyway, enough about me and my failed relationships,' said Emma. 'So do tell. If you're not secretly giving Charlie the run-around, how come you've had another guy in your house? Has he gone?'

'No, he's still there,' said Willow mischievously.

'And Charlie knows about him?' asked Emma, mystified.

'He does. In fact, it was his suggestion.'

'Okay, now you're really blowing my mind. Let me get this straight. Your boyfriend wasn't around last night, but this other guy was?'

'Yes.'

'And he stayed the night?'

'Yes,' Willow giggled.

'And Charlie condoned this man sleeping with you?' said Emma in astonishment.

Willow burst out laughing.

'Okay, I'll come clean. So, when I tried calling you, it was with the intention of having a bit of a bitch-fit rant. I was really fed up. Last night Charlie had to unexpectedly go away on business, which was disappointing enough – lately, I've hardly seen my boyfriend – but to cap it all off, Charlie's allowed his mate from work to move in. Ben. I felt miffed actually, because Charlie didn't even think to ask me how I felt about the arrangement. Typical man. Anyway, it transpires Ben hasn't been happy with Anna – that's his girlfriend – for ages, so now they've gone their separate ways. However, they've got to sort out selling their house, and as neither of them wish to suffer each other's company before the house is sold, Charlie told Ben he could move into our spare room. I came home last night to find the hallway stuffed with plastic sacks and suitcases, and was far from impressed. But I could hardly tell Ben to sling his hook. Nor could I have a private row with Charlie about it because he was hastily stepping over everything and fighting his way towards the front door. He had an overnight bag in one hand, and said he was off to see a demanding client who'd threatened to take business elsewhere. So there I was, still in my coat, saying a rushed good-bye to my boyfriend, and expected to cook dinner for another man. Anyway, Ben and I shared a companionable meal together. Obviously mad-arse Anna came up in the conversation, and before you tell me off for being rude about her' – Willow lowered her voice confidentially – 'she is most *definitely* mad-arse because, do you know what that woman did?'

Willow paused dramatically but didn't wait for Emma to reply and swept on.

'Anna phoned me at the crack of dawn. Can you believe it? It was still *dark* outside, that's how early it was. Anna said she was really fond of me – ha, can you believe that! – so much so that she was most concerned about my own relationship, and said I must never marry Charlie. Indeed, she wanted me to *promise* her. Can you imagine? How flipping mad-arse is that? The woman is clearly bonkers. Meanwhile I have Ben on the other side of a paper-thin bedroom wall, which I'm far from happy about. I mean, can you imagine what it's going to be like trying to have quiet sex knowing that Ben will be able to hear everything? But that's not all.'

Willow paused but only to take a deep breath.

'When I arrived at work this morning, I'd barely been there two minutes when Jean answered the phone and there was yet *another* mad-arse woman asking to speak to me. So I took the call – which infuriated Jean *big* time – but was greeted with long silence. So I got a bit stroppy which prompted the woman to hiss two words. "Leave Charlie." It really freaked me out. Ooooh, my flesh has erupted in goose bumps just thinking about it. I mean, what the hell was *that* all about, eh? And who would even do such a thing?'

Willow rattled to a standstill and waited for Emma to reply. The subsequent lengthy pause had Willow assuming her friend was too gobsmacked to speak.

'Ems? Hello? Are you still there?'

'Yes… I'm here,' said Emma faintly. 'I was, er, just trying to get my head around everything you've said. I mean… wow! How barmy. I don't speak to you for one night and in less than twenty-four hours your private life has gone nuts. Have you told Charlie?'

'No, not yet. But I will. I guess I'll have to pick my moment when he's back home and Ben isn't around. Flipping heck, I can't even have a private conversation with my own boyfriend now that someone else is living with us.'

'Do you know how long this guy is going to be with you?'

'Ben said he wants to buy a newbuild over at Ebbsfleet, but the site is still wasteland. It looks like he's going to be with us for a while.'

'Poor you,' said Emma.

However, her tone lacked sympathy, and Willow noted this. She was surprised. And puzzled. In fact, Willow could have sworn her friend was now sounding quite jolly.

'I must get back to work,' Emma chirped. 'Are you still on for Saturday?'

'Yes. Definitely. I'm looking forward to it. Charlie and Ben are in Birmingham for the weekend – another work convention – so I can hang out with you for as long as you like.'

'Great!'

There it was again. A definite note of cheerfulness in her friend's voice. Was she imagining it or… surely Emma wasn't *pleased* that Ben was living with them and cramping not just their style but also their sex life? Willow shook her head, as if dismissing the thought. Emma's emotions were all over the place right now. Of *course* she'd be down one minute and chipper the next. And then Willow tutted. Why was she overthinking everything?

'I'll come round to yours on Saturday morning and pick you up,' said Emma. 'Parking is always hell in town on the weekend, so it's pointless taking two cars.'

'That's kind, but are you sure you don't mind being the driver?'

'Not at all. See you about ten'ish. And I hope you're up for getting a tattoo with me.'

'Hm, we'll see. Although' – now it was Willow's turn to be chirpy – 'Charlie did suggest me having his name put on my wrist.'

Emma's tone instantly switched to the voice of doom.

'I wouldn't.'

'Why ever not?'

'Tattoos last forever, but sometimes relationships don't.'

Chapter Thirty-Two

Charlie arrived home from work while Willow was chopping veg for dinner.

From her position by the kitchen window, Willow observed her boyfriend coming through the garden gate. Her heart sank at the sight of Ben bringing up the rear.

Willow was certain Ben wouldn't have told Charlie about Anna's weird phone call. Telling Charlie served no purpose. Ben had made no secret of the fact that Anna was a hothead. Even if Charlie was told, he'd likely dismiss Anna's action as that of a woman with an axe to grind… and not bothered about who got in the way of that axe.

Willow deliberated whether to tell Charlie herself about Anna. Hm. Maybe. However, Willow *did* want to tell Charlie about the anonymous phone call at the library. After all, that had been unpleasant. She would tell Charlie in a quiet moment… whenever that might be.

'Babe, I'm home,' yodelled Charlie.

He came into the kitchen with a big grin on his handsome face.

Charlie had given himself a pep talk and decided he had every reason to smile. After all, he'd engineered a month's space from Kev. Throughout his day at work, with each passing hour, he'd become more confident that the time apart from Kev would transition to one of permanence. He'd reasoned that Kev was an attractive woman. She'd soon get chatted up by other guys. Also, as Kev was a borderline sex-addict, it likely wouldn't take long for one of those guys to become a bed mate. And when that happened… bingo! Charlie would be completely free of the blasted woman.

If Willow ever brought Kev home in the future, he'd be able to look her in the eye and say, "Heyyy! Willow tells me you have a new man. I'm *so* thrilled for you." And he would genuinely mean it.

Willow put down the chopping knife and let Charlie give her a brief hug.

'I missed you,' she said.

'Me too,' said Charlie automatically.

It wasn't true. Quite apart from being put through a sexual marathon with Kev, he'd also been too busy tying himself up in knots trying to end their relationship. During that final cappuccino in the pub's lounge, he'd had to bargain hard for a month's breathing space. Kev had almost defeated him. The landlord had definitely been giving the pair of them sidelong glances trying to work out their relationship. A flipping tiring one, Charlie told himself. God, even his nuts felt knackered.

'Back in a sec,' said Charlie. 'Ben and I need to get out of these suits.'

'Sure,' said Willow.

She caught Ben's eye. He was standing in the kitchen

doorway looking awkward.

'Hi, Ben.'

'Hey.'

'Come on, matey,' said Charlie, giving Ben a prod. 'Stop hanging around like a spare part.'

'Sorry,' said Ben, moving out the way.

As he followed Charlie up the stairs, she heard him apologise again.

'I feel like I'm third-wheeling with you and Willow.'

She also heard Charlie's reply.

'Don't be daft. Willow is absolutely fine with it.'

But over dinner, Willow felt like *she* was the one third-wheeling. Charlie was only interested in talking to Ben. He wanted to speculate about Drummond's new girlfriend, know the progress of the Carpenter account, and bitch about Mr Humphrey who – in Charlie's opinion – was a five-star prat. When Charlie finally paused for breath, Ben turned to Willow and courteously asked if she was okay.

'You look a bit pale,' he said.

'I did feel a bit peculiar earlier,' she said. 'In fact, I came home from work early.'

She omitted saying exactly how early.

Ben immediately looked concerned.

'Are you feeling better now?'

Charlie put down his knife and fork and peered at her.

'You look fine to me, although' – he gave a bark of laughter – 'if anything I'd say you look guilty about something. Have you been up to no good?' he teased.

Willow instantly flushed to her roots.

'No,' she said hastily.

Her body twitched. She looked like a person half expecting a tannoy to crackle into life announcing she'd frisked her boyfriend's entire wardrobe and knew his bank balance to the exact decimal point.

Both men were looking at her. Charlie speculatively. Ben uncomfortably.

'You *have* been up to something,' Charlie crowed. 'Come on. Spit it out!'

'I haven't,' Willow protested, but her face was now redder than a bottle of Merlot.

'Course she hasn't,' said Ben, coming to the rescue.

Ben was wrongly presuming that Willow had allowed Anna's early morning call to get to her. That maybe Anna was the reason why she'd come home early, but that she didn't want to tell Charlie about it. Poor Willow. She had absolutely nothing to hide. It was Charlie who was the guilty one with all his ducking and diving around Kev.

Willow was desperate to get the spotlight of attention off her and change the subject, even if it was still work-related in order for Ben not to feel excluded.

'Anyway, never mind me,' she said brightly. 'Tell me all about your business trip to Brighton and Cambridge, Charlie. How did you get on with the tetchy client?'

There was a moment's silence where neither Charlie nor Ben said anything.

Both men did a quick, guarded eye-meet. Ben then began

attacking his dinner like a stray dog going through restaurant bins, while Charlie's expression morphed into a replica of how Willow had been looking only seconds ago. He immediately stuffed an enormous potato in his mouth, rendering him incapable of speaking.

Peculiar, thought Willow as her eyes flit from Ben to Charlie, then back to Ben again.

'Do *you* know this client?' she asked, when Charlie didn't reply.

'No,' said Ben quietly.

Charlie swallowed down the potato and put his knife and fork together.

'No more talk about work,' he said firmly. 'Let's just say that my client meeting was successful. All I want to do now is relax.'

He turned to Ben.

'Come on, matey. Let's grab a beer from the fridge and watch some footie.'

'Ah, but shouldn't we first help Willow with–?'

'No, she's a big girl. She doesn't need any help.'

Charlie was almost dragging Ben away from the table in order to avoid further questions from his girlfriend.

Willow remained seated, her meal not quite finished. She wondered if she'd imagined the undercurrent when Ben and Charlie had exchanged looks. Everybody seemed to be behaving a bit… well, oddly. First Anna… then Emma… now Ben and Charlie.

Moments later she heard Charlie applaud the ref blowing

the whistle before issuing a red card. Sighing, she stood up and flicked on the little telly in the kitchen. She'd watch a bit of soap nonsense whilst clearing away the dishes. Scraping some dried-up potato off a pan, she tried not to feel resentful at Charlie clearing off with Ben and not sticking around to chat to her. Hopefully they would catch up with each other when they were in bed.

Charlie was still glued to the television long after Willow had cleared up the kitchen, watched *Coronation Street* and then three back-to-back episodes of *Friends*. She'd also munched her way through an entire packet of Jaffa cakes. Feeling slightly sick from overdosing on orange jelly and dark chocolate, she made her way upstairs and decided to have a bath. Perhaps it would be better to have a soak at night rather than a shower in the morning in order to reduce bathroom congestion.

When Charlie finally came into their bedroom, it was getting on for midnight.

'Still awake?' he said in surprise.

Willow put down her kindle.

'Of course. I've been waiting for you.'

'Ah,' said Charlie, trying not to look horrified. 'Not tonight. I'm bushed.'

The last thing he needed was a sexy romp. His willy might drop off from exhaustion.

'I haven't had a chance to talk to you all evening,' Willow complained. 'I wanted to tell you about my day. Well, specifically, my morning. It wasn't exactly run-of-the-mill.'

‘Sorry, darling,’ said Charlie, sounding far more contrite than he felt.

He didn’t mind what his girlfriend wittered on about so long as it didn’t involve twenty questions regarding a fictitious trip to Brighton and Cambridge.

‘Let me quickly clean my teeth and then you can chat to me in bed.’

Willow picked up her kindle again and read another two pages against a backdrop of spitting, rinsing and gargling, and then Charlie loudly peeing.

‘That’s better.’

He slid under the duvet and flopped back against the pillows.

‘What did you want to talk about?’

Willow set aside the kindle and lay back too.

‘I want to tell you the real reason why I came home early from work,’ she said.

In the background Willow could now hear Ben spitting, rinsing, gargling and then loudly peeing. Was this what she was going to have to listen to every night?

She ploughed on, keeping her voice low so that Ben couldn’t overhear, and quickly told Charlie all about Anna’s weird phone call.

‘But you must promise not to discuss it with Ben. I don’t want him thinking it’s his responsibility about how his mixed-up ex-girlfriend behaves.’

Without waiting for Charlie to reply, Willow swiftly moved on to the anonymous phone call at the library.

'It was a woman, and she told me to leave you,' Willow gasped. 'So what do you make of all that?'

She stared up at the shadows on the ceiling.

'Crazy or what?'

But Charlie didn't reply. He was fast asleep.

Chapter Thirty-Three

'Morning,' said Ben cheerfully, as he passed Willow on the landing.

He was waiting for Charlie to come out of the bathroom, and Willow was very glad she'd opted to have a bath the previous night.

'Hi,' she replied. 'Do you want some breakfast, or will you grab something at the station café with Charlie?'

'I'll go to the café. Might as well live dangerously,' Ben joked weakly.

'Not too dangerously I hope' – Willow bantered – 'after all, today is Friday the thirteenth.'

Ben suddenly looked anxious.

'I wish you hadn't said that. Something awful always happens when it's Friday the thirteenth.'

'I heard that,' said Charlie, coming out of the bathroom with a towel slung around his hips. 'I've never heard so much superstitious claptrap in my life. If something disastrous comes your way, it would have happened anyway. Bad luck doesn't store itself up and wait for the calendar to roll around to Friday the thirteenth.'

Willow was inclined to agree, but she gave Ben a

sympathetic smile as he disappeared into the bathroom.

'Shall we get a take-away tonight?' she asked Charlie, following him back into their bedroom. 'I quite fancy a chicken korma.'

'I'd rather not,' he said, vigorously rubbing down his body before dropping the wet towel on the floor.

The last thing Charlie wanted was his pores oozing garlic when he arrived in Birmingham tomorrow. Willow regarded him in disappointment.

'What about a Chinese then?'

'No thanks.'

Charlie had high hopes of pulling. No way could he kiss a girl through the night if his mouth still harboured traces of ginger, star anise and spices. Mouthwash was as good as useless after such meals.

'Can I not have a night off from cooking' – Willow stooped to pick up the towel –'or am I perceived as some sort of housekeeper who trots out meals for you and unexpected house guests, along with being a personal wet-towel-picker-upper.'

She balled up the offending towel and flung it at Charlie. It slapped him square in the face. Charlie stared at her in astonishment. Good heavens. What on earth had got into Willow? She was behaving in a very un-Willow-like way. He retrieved the wet towel and placed it on the bed instead.

'Of *course* you can have a takeaway, sweetie,' he said, adopting a pacifying tone. 'What about a nice pizza?'

A cheese and tomato jobbie wouldn't wreck his breath,

would it? He'd ask chef to leave out the onions. Just in case.

'Okay,' said Willow, but her expression told Charlie she hadn't been placated.

'Is something wrong?'

He began putting on socks and boxers at lightning speed before rifling through his shirt rail.

'Yes!' Willow exclaimed, removing the wet towel off the duvet. 'I was talking to you last night about something fairly monumental and–'

There was a knock on their bedroom door.

'Come in,' said Charlie.

Having speedily buttoned up his shirt and slung a tie round his neck, he was now zipping up his flies.

'Am I interrupting?' said Ben apologetically.

'Of course not,' said Charlie, grabbing his suit jacket. 'Willow was just saying that she fancies a pizza later. We'll grab some on the way back from the station tonight.'

'Lovely,' said Ben, smiling at Willow. 'Good choice.'

'See you later, babe,' said Charlie.

He gave her a fleeting kiss on the cheek. A second later and he was out of the bedroom and dashing down the stairs. Ben hovered for a moment.

'I hope your day is better than yesterday.'

'Thanks. Me too.'

Ben lowered his voice.

'What did Charlie say about–?'

'Ben!' Charlie shouted from the hallway. 'Come on, matey, or we'll miss the train.'

'I'd better go,' he said, giving a helpless shrug.

'Have a good day, and don't worry about it being Friday the thirteenth.'

'Thanks.'

He gave a rueful smile then made after Charlie, leaving Willow to go into the bathroom and hang her boyfriend's wet towel over the heated rail. In that moment she felt more like Charlie's mum than girlfriend and lover.

As it happened, Willow did have a good day. Jean was courteous and polite. Theresa had made a cake and brought it in to share, and Fiona made everyone coffee to go with the Victoria sponge. No members of the public were rude or surly. Nor did the library receive any anonymous phone calls. By the time Willow was back home, she'd perked up hugely and was looking forward to the pizza takeaway. She had even convinced herself that she might be in for a little romance before Charlie went away for the weekend.

But later, as she snuggled into Charlie, he quickly let her know that he wasn't up for any lovemaking or pillow talk.

'I'm tired, babe,' he said, turning over and flipping the cover over his head.

And he genuinely was. The week had been mentally exhausting. Thankfully everything had worked out well for him. Kev hadn't rung or bombarded him with texts. Ha! Friday the thirteenth hadn't thrown any curved balls at him! He drifted off to sleep with a smile on his face.

Charlie had certainly been right about one thing. Bad luck didn't just happen on Friday the thirteenth. Sometimes – as in

Charlie's case – it came along on Saturday the fourteenth instead.

Chapter Thirty-Four

Charlie rolled out of bed on Saturday morning with a sense of anticipation.

Hurrah! He was off to Birmingham for a work convention. Everybody knew those last two words were a code name for something that didn't feature in the office manual. If you were one of the newbies fresh out of uni, a work convention also meant "getting juiced". If you were of a similar age to Charlie, it was "getting tanked". And if you were over fifty, it was "getting wasted".

Charlie's good spirits continued to soar as he set about packing. Leaving his overnight bag open, he went to the wardrobe and selected his most expensive shirt. Once the boring business part was over and done with, there would be a formal gathering which was always very pleasant. But it was the bit that followed that Charlie liked best, namely heading out with a few mates for a night on the town.

Charlie wondered if Ron would be joining them. Ron was one of the office oldies. Last time around he'd had his heart set on going to a club, but not made it due to drinking too much too soon. Off the marital leash, Ron had wasted no time ordering lime-coloured cocktails before drunkenly making eye contact with a female newbie by the name of Suzie. Looking not unlike the character Owen Newitt from *The Vicar of Dibley,* he'd complimented Suzie on her "splendid pair of knockers" and told her to visit his room if she fancied a performance that would leave her gasping.

Unfortunately Ron had been the one left gasping when Drummond had tapped him on the shoulder and pointed out that Mrs Ron might not approve of such antics, and Drummond most definitely didn't… because Suzie was his niece. Ron had turned as green as his cocktail.

Charlie snorted with laughter at the memory, just as Willow came into the bedroom with cups of tea for them both.

'Share the joke,' she said, handing him one of the mugs.

Charlie took a sip, then set the tea down so he could get on with folding his pristine white shirt.

'I was just thinking about the time one of the guys made a dick of himself in front of the big boss.'

'What did he do?'

'Got spectacularly sozzled, then made an atrocious pass at a woman who turned out to be one of Drummond's relations.'

'Oh dear.'

Charlie shrugged.

'The guy's an idiot. He's always getting into trouble.'

'Why?'

'He can't hold his drink and doesn't know when to stop.'

Ah, thought Willow, this must be the colleague that Ben had mentioned. The one who was a bad influence. What was his name? Trev? No, Kev.

'He sounds like a liability.'

'Oh he's all right really.'

'Well don't let Kev lead *you* astray.'

Charlie jerked and his head snapped up.

'Wh-What did you just say?'

Willow frowned. Her boyfriend had gone as white as the shirt he was clutching.

'I said–'

'Yes, I heard you,' said Charlie abruptly. 'What do you know of Kev?'

The last thing Willow wanted was to land Ben in trouble for revealing the name of the work colleague who sometimes persuaded Charlie to go for a drink.

Maybe it had been a blessing in disguise that Charlie had fallen asleep last night when she'd been moaning about Anna and the mysterious anonymous caller. It meant she could bend the truth. However, she didn't want Charlie tackling Ben. The poor guy could hardly be blamed for mentioning this irresponsible Kev person, or prevent the actions of his mad-arse girlfriend. Correction, *ex* mad-arse girlfriend. Willow decided to madly improvise.

'Okay, well, yesterday I had a peculiar phone call at the library.'

'From whom?'

Charlie was now so pale he was making his shirt look as though it had spent a fortnight in the Bahamas.

'From an anonymous person who told me that sometimes you aren't really working late at the office… that sometimes you've been out with Kev.'

Charlie looked like he was going to puke.

'What did this person sound like?' he growled.

'Female. Well spoken.'

Willow took a sip of tea and regarded Charlie's reaction over the rim of her cup. Blimey. Her boyfriend almost looked ill.

'And that's not all,' she added.

Having mentioned the anonymous phone call and got Charlie's full attention, now was as good a time as any to tell him what the mystery woman had said.

'She told me to leave you.'

'Leave me?' he repeated incredulously.

Charlie had to resist the urge not to slump down on the floor and crease his precious shirt.

Flipping hell. It was all kicking off, wasn't it? Bloody Kev wasn't going to let him go. All his efforts to distance himself were turning to ashes. He'd have to see her and have it out. How *dare* Kev think she could coerce him into resuming their relationship. It was tantamount to, well, emotional blackmail. Yes, that was exactly what it was. The woman was obviously a bunny boiler. Thank God they hadn't got a rabbit. Although Kev had a different sort of rabbit. He had a horrible vision of coming home from work and finding Willow by the stove, peering into a pot of boiling water and saying, "But what *is* it, Charlie?" and him, slightly hysterical, saying, "A sexy present, darling. I wanted to sterilise it before you tried it out. You can't trust anything that's made in China these days."

Oh God. Now he was having ridiculous thoughts about vibrators.

'Did this person say anything else?' he gasped.

'No.' Willow shook her head. 'Do you have any idea why I received such a call?'

Charlie felt his stomach contract with tension. Was Willow challenging him?

'No idea at all,' he said faintly. 'It's probably just some saddo who's jealous of our relationship.'

'I did wonder that,' said Willow thoughtfully.

'What a bloody cheek,' said Charlie, glad that Willow was being led down this line of thought. 'Don't take any notice.'

'The only thing is–'

'What?'

'Well, if this woman is jealous of our relationship–'

'Yes?'

'Then it would stand to reason that we know her.'

Charlie gaped at Willow. Why had he ever thought she was a bit of an airhead? Right now, she was on a trail. Joining up the dots. Sooner or later she'd put them all together and see the full picture. A portrait of Kev.

'I'm not sure about that,' he blustered. 'It's more likely to be someone who has seen you out and about with me and recognised you from the library. They probably thought we looked deliriously happy and now they want to cause trouble. You get people like that.'

'But this person mentioned you by name.'

Charlie gave a casual shrug while his mind raced to come

up with a plausible answer.

'Perhaps this person overheard you saying my name while talking to me?'

He wanted to end this conversation, so he set about doing it in exactly the way he always did when a woman boxed him into a corner. Charlie abandoned the shirt, removed the mug of tea from Willow's hand, then swept her into his arms and held her tight.

'Forget about this stupid person who called you at the library.'

'But–'

'No, I mean it. Don't let it bother you. Whoever this woman is, she's nothing. No one. Okay?'

Willow rested her head on Charlie's shoulder, luxuriating in his embrace. She felt his lips kiss the top of her head. Seconds later, his mouth was on hers.

'Charlie?' called Ben, from the next room. 'I've run out of razors. Can I nick one of yours?'

Charlie pulled away from Willow and grinned.

'Bad timing, eh?'

'Never mind,' she sighed. 'I can wait until you're home again.'

'That's a promise,' he smiled.

As he went off to find razors for Ben, Charlie mentally made another promise.

To pay Kev a visit when he was back from Birmingham.

Chapter Thirty-Five

'Heyyy,' said Willow in delight as she opened the front door to her bestie. 'Happy birthday, Ems!'

She pulled a grinning Emma into the hallway and hugged her tight, just as Charlie and Ben clattered down the stairs clutching their overnight bags.

'Look who's here!' Willow beamed at Charlie. 'Wish Emma many happy returns.'

Willow was quick to notice that her friend's smile had frozen.

'Happy birthday,' said Charlie politely.

'Happy birthday from me, too,' said Ben, hopping from one foot to the other and looking incredibly gauche.

'Thank you,' said Emma quietly.

'Ah, Ben,' said Willow. 'I'm not sure if you two have met before?'

'Um...' said Emma vaguely.

Willow was aware of a sudden tension in the small hallway. Everyone seemed to be behaving strangely.

'Anyway' – she turned back to Emma – 'this is Ben, Charlie's mate from work. He's between properties at the moment, and staying with us for a few weeks.'

Willow hoped Ben had caught that last word. *Weeks.* Not *months.* Or, God forbid, *years.* But Emma wasn't looking at Ben. She seemed to be avoiding eye contact with him. Or, hang on, was it Charlie she was avoiding eye contact with?

Willow's gaze flit from Emma to Charlie. Her boyfriend had his head down and seemed to be deliberately busying himself by fussing with the handles of his holdall.

'We'd better be off,' said Ben.

'Yes,' Charlie agreed.

His tone was suddenly brisk. He gave Willow a quick peck on the cheek, then almost flattened himself against the hall wall in order to pass Emma.

'Bye,' said Ben.

He was still looking awkward. Willow didn't know if it was because he wasn't sure whether to kiss *her* good-bye too. She took a small step backwards, her body language immediately signalling that it wasn't necessary.

'Have a successful work convention' – Willow held open the front door as both men stepped outside – 'and I do hope the conference isn't too dull.'

Ben opened his mouth to say something, but Charlie appeared to nudge him in the ribs.

'It will be boring as hell,' said Charlie firmly.

Willow waved, then shut the door after them. She turned back to Emma.

'Are you okay?'

'Yeah, great. Why wouldn't I be?'

Emma was smiling again, but Willow felt it was forced.

Her friend had arrived lit up like a hundred-watt lightbulb, but within seconds the sparkle had dimmed.

'You look like someone who has just had a ton weight dumped on their shoulders.'

'Oh, it's something and nothing,' Emma shrugged. 'Are you ready to go?'

'Almost. I just need to change handbags.'

Emma followed Willow upstairs to her bedroom.

'So define "something and nothing",' said Willow.

She scattered the contents of a formal black bag used for work across her duvet. Today she would use her tan satchel. It would look perfect teamed with her jeans and brown leather boots. For a moment Willow's fingers hovered mid-air as she contemplated which bits of paraphernalia she required.

'Well' – Emma plonked herself down on one corner of the bed – 'I'm now thirty years old.'

'And what's wrong with that?' asked Willow, shoving a lipstick into the satchel's inner zip pocket. 'You're talking to a woman who had the same birthday herself last week. I survived.'

'Yeah.' Emma gave Willow a wan grin. 'But it's not so much the age thing as–'

'What?'

'Well, look at me.' Emma spread her arms wide. 'Single and alone.'

'There's nothing wrong with being single and alone,' Willow protested.

'And back home with her mum,' Emma added

mutinously.

'Fair comment,' said Willow.

Much as she loved her own mother, Willow really wouldn't want to be under the parental roof again.

'At least your mum is still young and trendy,' Willow pointed out.

'Which means she nicks all my clothes and make-up,' Emma countered.

'Ah. Point taken.'

Willow's own mother was much older than Emma's. Unlike Karen Everest, Willow's mum had long succumbed to the menopause and middle-age spread, whereas Karen still had a whippet-thin body and could even have another baby if she so desired.

'I guess swiping your stuff is the downside to having such a youthful mother. She did, after all, start a family very early in life.'

'Too early.' Emma's lip curled. 'She was still a kid herself. And that's why I'm feeling a bit fed up. Today I've reached a "big" birthday… and so has Noah.'

Willow paused in buckling up the satchel and regarded Emma for a moment.

'You know, sometimes I forget you have a twin.'

'So does Mum.'

'Oh come on, Ems. I'm sure Karen hasn't forgotten about Noah. After all, she gave birth to him.'

'Huh. She kept her baby boy for all of five minutes, before allowing my father's family to take Noah away.'

'But that's how your parents worked things out,' said Willow gently. 'You know all this. Their quarrels about custody. How they compromised with each other to resolve arguments.'

'Yeah.'

Emma gazed at the carpet for a moment.

'My mum's family raised me, and Dad's family raised Noah. But everyone on my dad's side emigrated. What sort of relationship have I had with any of them? Sporadic, that's what. And Noah isn't just my brother. He's my *twin*. Twins are meant to have such a special relationship. But ours has been long-distance. We've lived nine-and-a-half thousand miles apart and I've been denied that special bond.' She blinked furiously. 'My relationship with both my father and brother has been *very* patchy.'

'Hardly surprising, given the distance,' Willow carefully pointed out.

'But it's more than that,' Emma sniffed. 'Mum has positively encouraged me not to have too much contact. I've turned down numerous invitations to Australia, and all to appease Mum. You see, she doesn't like being reminded of Noah. It flags up her past which, before she got pregnant, was full of wild parties. She'd rather forget the years that culminated in her giving up one of her children.'

'Perhaps it's Karen's coping mechanism,' Willow pointed out. 'After all, it can't have been easy giving her little boy up.'

'Yes, and I get that. But it's still hard to deal with. It's on significant days like today – *our birthdays* – that I struggle with keeping the resentment buried.'

Emma's eyes shone with unshed tears and she hastily blinked.

'This morning I received a lovely card from Noah.'

She opened her handbag and rootled within.

'He also sent this.'

Emma passed a piece of paper to Willow.

Taking it, Willow immediately saw it was a photograph. Her eyes widened at the image. A man. And a drop-dead-gorgeous one at that. Her brain let out a sigh of approval that sounded very much like "phwoarrrrr".

Noah was standing against the backdrop of an Australian sunset. He looked absolutely nothing like his sister. Emma was a brunette, but Noah's hair was much darker. Almost black. As was the stubble grazing his cheeks. His skin was tanned, and his body was both lean and well-muscled. He reminded Willow of someone. She chewed her lip, trying to think who it could be. And then it came to her. Emma's brother wasn't unlike one of Madonna's ex-lovers. What was his name? Willow couldn't remember. But he'd once been one of the iconic pop star's dancers and had caused a huge sensation dating a woman thirty years his senior. Willow gazed into the brown eyes looking back at her. Noah was hot.

'Turn it over,' said Emma.

Willow flipped the photograph round and saw a handwritten message.

Happy birthday, little sis (I'm allowed to say that because I'm five minutes older than you!). I'm taking time out for some long-overdue travelling including catching up with my English family. I'm doing a three-month trip covering some of Australia's North Territories before flying over to China for an explore, then to France, on to Amsterdam, a wander through Europe, finally finishing in good old Blighty (as I believe you Brits say). The timing will take me to roughly the third week of December. It would be GREAT to spend Christmas with you and Mum xxx

'What a wonderful message,' said Willow. 'Just think, after all these years you're going to be reunited with your brother. That's amazing!'

'I know.' Emma gave a watery smile. 'Unfortunately Mum isn't so enthusiastic.'

'What?' Willow's eyebrows shot upwards. 'Don't be daft.'

'She really isn't keen.' Emma shook her head. 'She's worried about Noah asking a ton of questions. The third degree, and all that. She thinks seeing him again will open a sore. Currently Mum's blanking the subject. It's almost like she's pretending that Noah hasn't got in touch.'

'I'm sure she'll come around. Karen has over two months to get used to the idea. You know, Ems, try and see it from your mum's side. Noah is planning on walking back into both your lives. Maybe your mum is apprehensive because the reality is that she doesn't want him leaving her all over again.'

Emma sighed.

'Yeah, maybe. I never thought of that.'

'Is Noah travelling alone, or is he bringing a girlfriend, or even a wife?'

'He's doing the trip alone. There was a girlfriend. Caitlin. But apparently they wanted different things from life, whatever that means. She called it a day.'

Passing the photograph back to Emma, Willow marvelled at her slightly trembling hand. She also wondered why she felt so ridiculously pleased to hear that Emma's brother was single.

Chapter Thirty-Six

Willow looped the satchel's strap across her body, then grabbed her coat.

'Right then,' she said to Emma. 'Let's get this tattoo of yours sorted. And no, I'm not having one.'

'Oh come on,' Emma wheedled. 'You promised.'

'I promised to hold your hand, not to share your pain.'

As the two women made their way downstairs, the doorbell rang.

'Wonder who that is?' said Willow.

She wasn't expecting anyone. Perhaps Charlie had forgotten some vital item – a toothbrush or change of underpants – and had dashed back home. But then again, he'd surely use his housekeys. Unless, of course, it was his keys he'd forgotten.

But when Willow opened the door, instead of Charlie standing there, it was Anna. For a moment the two women simply stared at each other. Willow felt a wave of annoyance. What the heck was Ben's ex doing here? First the woman had the audacity to wake her up at a ridiculous hour insisting Willow promise to never marry Charlie, and now she was here in person. Would more crazy demands follow? Did Anna want

Willow to make a promise in writing?

'Hello,' said Willow coolly.

She would have preferred to rudely demand, "And what the flaming heck do *you* want?". But she'd never been one to be intentionally ill-mannered. It simply wasn't in her nature.

'Ah. I can tell from your tone you're still sore at me.'

Emma stood a little behind Willow and stared at Anna in astonishment. The friction between this visitor and her friend was almost tangible. Emma could feel herself tensing too.

Her eyes swooped over the woman on the doorstep. Tall'ish. Attractive, but a definite hardness around the mouth. She was stylishly dressed in a cropped leather jacket teamed with distressed jeans. The material was so slashed Emma presumed it to be deliberate because it was artfully framing an enviable tattoo. A pretty butterfly danced across Anna's left thigh.

'If you're after Ben,' said Willow, 'I'm afraid he's not here. He and Charlie have gone to a work convention.'

'Oh yes. Charlie's beloved Birmingham,' said Anna sarcastically.

'Hardly,' Willow tutted. 'He can't stand the place.'

'Really? Then perhaps he is gallivanting closer to home these days.'

Anna paused to glare at Emma.

'Gallivanting?' Willow questioned. 'I'm not sure I understand your choice of word.'

'Would *you* know what I mean?' said Anna, challenging Emma.

'Most definitely not,' Emma protested.

She could feel her cheeks colouring but held Anna's gaze, which was like a searchlight seeking out lies.

'Can I ask *you* a question instead?' Willow interrupted.

Anna tore her eyes away from Emma and looked at Willow.

'Sure. Ask away.'

'Did you ring me at the library on Thursday morning?'

Anna blinked.

'That's a strange question. If I'd rung you at your library, I would have said it was me calling.'

'So you didn't call?' Willow persisted.

'No.'

'You're sure?'

'Hm, let me see,' said Anna.

She shifted her weight to her left leg and put her right hand to her chin in a parody of someone thinking.

'Did I ring you on Thursday morning?' she drawled. 'Yes. You know I did. At your house. But did I call you at the library? No.'

Anna's eyes swivelled to Emma again, but this time her gaze wasn't met. Emma appeared to be enthralled with Willow's hall floor.

'Why do you ask?' said Anna.

Willow hesitated before speaking.

'Someone rang, but we got cut off. The caller sounded like you.'

Anna shrugged.

'Not me.'

She opened her handbag and removed some envelopes.

'The reason I've popped over is to give Ben his post. As I've missed him, would you be kind enough to give him these?'

'Sure,' said Willow, taking the mail. 'Was there anything else? Only we were on our way out.'

She wanted Anna to know her visit wasn't going to be turned into a social occasion. There would be no invitation for coffee.

'No, nothing else' – Anna gave a brittle smile – 'other than reminding you of what I said in the phone call that I *did* make. See you.'

She turned on her heel and walked off leaving Willow gaping after her.

'Flaming cheek,' she spluttered. 'Did you hear that, Ems?'

'Yes,' said Emma, finally tearing her eyes away from the hall floor.

She watched Anna walking along the pavement, before turning a corner and disappearing out of sight.

'If you ask me, she's a bit of a cow.'

'That's an understatement,' Willow seethed. 'And in her telephone call she had the cheek to say she was fond of me. I mean, really?'

'Ignore her,' said Emma stoically. 'I liked her tattoo. Did you notice it?'

'Yes. It must be new. She never had it when she was with Ben. Maybe it's symbolic. You know, marking her break from Ben. Freedom. Transformation. That sort of thing.'

'Mm,' said Emma thoughtfully. 'Think I'm going to nick it. After all, I'm on a break from my man – *if* he was ever my man,' she added sadly. 'But for now I'm a free agent, and I shall express it. Just like Anna. C'mon, let's go. I'm going to get a butterfly tattoo.'

Chapter Thirty-Seven

Emma spotted an empty parking space directly outside the tattoo parlour. Whizzing into it, she cut the engine, then took a deep breath.

'Wow,' she murmured, peering up at the shop's boutique-styled window. 'Seems like a cool place.'

She was doing her best not to sound fazed, but the quiver in her voice indicated otherwise.

'Are you nervous?' asked Willow, following her friend's gaze.

'No,' Emma lied.

The glass-and-steel frontage permitted a clear view to the interior within. It appeared to be devoid of both staff and customers. The girls could see a cosy waiting area furnished with oversized comfortable chairs. To the right was a chiller stocked with complimentary drinks. A chrome coffee table, smothered in glossy mags, rested upon a deliberately scuffed-up floor. Centre stage was a vast reception desk-cum-display-cabinet, the inside of which was brightly lit with tiny spotlights. From their vantage point they could see beams of light cleverly showcasing jewellery, from barbells and body spirals to ear shields and navel gems.

Willow tried to imagine someone putting a needle through her tongue and suddenly felt a bit odd. She hoped she didn't go woozy when the artist was poised over Emma's chosen body part. The last thing she wanted was to make a fool of herself.

Emma unfastened her seat belt. Disguising her nerves with briskness, she gathered up her handbag.

'Today is my birthday. The number ends in a zero, so it's considered a landmark. Therefore, I'm celebrating with a matching life event.'

Willow didn't know if Emma was saying this as an observation or an affirmation. She watched her friend push open the passenger door and get out. She was definitely unsteady on her feet.

'Are you okay?' Willow called anxiously.

'Yes.'

Which wasn't quite true. Emma decided her legs were indeed a little wobbly.

Willow unhooked her own seatbelt and joined Emma on the pavement.

'Never mind me,' said Emma, clocking Willow's pallor. 'How are you?'

'Yeah, I just feel a bit… you know… strange.'

'Oh for goodness sake, what are we like?'

Emma grabbed Willow by the arm and propelled her towards the studio door.

'It's *me* having a tattoo. Not you. Let's get inside and then you can sit down.'

An old-fashioned bell jangled overhead announcing their arrival. Willow immediately tottered over to one of the huge leather chairs. Flopping down, she leant forward and lowered her head between her ankles. She was feeling seriously strange. Willow heard the light thwacking noise of Emma setting down her handbag on the glass desk-cum-cabinet, followed by the sound of an internal door opening. The pad of footsteps signalled a member of staff had joined them.

'Hey,' said a male voice.

'Hiya,' said Emma. 'We're here for–'

'A tattoo. Yup. I've got a lady called Emma Everest in the diary.'

Willow thought the man's voice sounded very smiley and pleasant. She sensed him looking in her direction.

'Hey, don't worry, Emma.' He addressed the crown of Willow's head. 'It's quite normal for you to feel like this, especially if it's the first time.'

'Oh, but she's not…'

Emma trailed off as the man hastened over to the chiller.

Willow heard its door open, then items within being selected. A moment later and footsteps were hastening over to Willow. She eyeballed a pair of feet clad in desert boots.

'Get this in you,' said the boots. 'You need to get those sugar levels up.'

A chocolate bar and can of cola were thrust into her hands. Willow clutched the goodies and gently eased herself upright. Suddenly she was looking into a pair of amused grey eyes.

'Sorry,' she whispered. 'I don't know what came over me.'

She broke into the chocolate and put a chunk in her mouth.

'It's just nerves,' the man smiled. 'I'm Jezz. Your artist.'

'No, you're not,' said Emma, sounding peeved. 'You're *my* artist. *I'm* Emma Everest. The swooning damsel here is Willow. My bestie. She's come along to give me support, but somehow the roles have been reversed.'

Jezz looked from Willow to Emma and then back to Willow again.

'You're not the one having a tattoo?'

Willow shoved another lump of chocolate in her mouth before shaking her head vehemently.

'No. And any thoughts I ever had of maybe getting one have now slipped straight through that narrow gap under your shop door and legged it up the high street.'

Jezz laughed.

'Fair enough. Are you feeling better?'

'Much.'

Willow popped the ring on the can of cola and took a swig.

'I didn't think you looked familiar' – Jezz peered at her – 'although, to be fair, I don't remember you either,' he said, glancing back at Emma.

'My initial appointment was with Tash,' said Emma. 'I think it was your day off when I visited the shop. I looked at various portfolios, but it was yours I liked best.'

'Good to hear,' he said, walking back to the desk. 'Did you find a design you liked?'

He regarded Emma from the other side of the counter.

'Well, initially I was thinking of something in black and grey, but this morning I saw someone with a butterfly and it just…' – Emma shrugged – '*spoke* to me. If that makes sense.'

Jezz stooped to reach for something under the desk. When he straightened up, he was clutching a large portfolio.

'Here.' He flipped the folder open. 'This section shows the tattoos that I particularly love. They're drenched in spiritual symbolism. Your butterfly certainly falls within that category.'

Emma began turning the pages, her eyes greedily devouring the designs. And there it was. A blue lacy butterfly. The very one that had danced across Anna's thigh. Her fingers tremulously traced its outline.

'This is the one,' she said reverently.

'Sure?'

'Never been more certain. I want it here.'

She touched the top of her leg.

'Come on then.' He snapped the portfolio shut. 'Let's take you through to the studio.'

At that moment the shop's old-fashioned bell jangled again, and everyone automatically looked to see who it was.

'Oh no,' Emma muttered. 'What's she doing here?'

Jezz's grey eyes flickered with interest as a slim brunette entered. She waved at Willow before walking over to join Emma. Jezz treated the woman to a dazzling smile.

'You are so like my client' – he addressed the newcomer – 'you simply must be Emma's sister.'

'No,' said an irked Emma, cutting across him. 'This is my

mum.'

'Your mother?' said Jezz, clearly astonished. 'Well, it's lovely to meet you, Mrs Everest. I was about to take Emma through to the studio.'

'Please, do call me Karen,' she said coquettishly.

She stuck out a hand which Jezz shook, holding on to it slightly longer than was necessary.

'I've never met a tattoo artist before,' Karen simpered. 'Delighted to meet you.'

'I'm Jezz, and the pleasure's all mine,' he said huskily.

Emma rolled her eyes. Here we go. Just when she thought her rather sexy tattoo artist might be up for a bit of flirty banter throughout her inking, along came her mother all set to steal the show.

Chapter Thirty-Eight

'Come on through, girls,' said Jezz.

He opened a door which led into a large studio. The room was bathed in bright light spilling through large sash windows. In the background, two other artists were busy at work.

'Why are you here, Mum?' Emma hissed.

'Because I was feeling fed up,' Karen whispered back. 'I simply *had* to get out the house or I'd have gone bonkers.'

'I thought you were seeing your fella today?'

'Huh,' Karen tutted. 'Chance would be a fine thing. I'm being messed about.'

'I know that feeling,' Emma muttered.

'Why, what's going on with your boyfriend?' Karen asked.

'Not a lot,' said Emma snippily.

'When am I going to meet him?'

'You're not. What about yours?'

'Ditto,' said Karen, pursing her lips.

'Don't do that.'

'What?'

'That thing with your mouth. Makes it look like a cat's bum.'

Jezz stifled a snort. He was clearly ear-wigging.

'Emma, if you'd like to go in there' – he pointed to a cubicle – 'and remove your jeans. Help yourself to a clean towel. Pop it around your hips, and then I'll see you over there.'

He pointed to a couch that resembled a dentist's chair.

A netful of butterflies immediately took off in Emma's stomach. She tried to ignore the sensation and instead concentrate on the butterfly that she *did* want… two lacy blue wings. But she was struggling to hold the picture. Emma glanced at the lookalike dentist's chair. It reminded her of Mosley Dental Practice which she didn't like visiting at the best of times. The numbing injection always made her flinch. And here she was about to have a tattoo gun with up to seven needles pierce her flesh again and again and again and–

For a moment the room swam.

'Ah, not you too,' said Jezz, grabbing hold of Emma's arm. 'Lie down.'

He bundled her over to the lookalike dentist's chair. Suddenly Emma's head was reclining backwards whilst her lower body was elevating, so that her ankles were now higher than her stomach.

'That's better,' said Jezz. 'Now we're getting some blood to your head.'

'I just need distracting,' Emma whimpered. 'Tell me why you became a tattoo artist.'

'Well, I started my career as a photographer and, despite hugely enjoying it, there was a feeling that something was missing. Whenever I was travelling about, I found myself doodling on anything and everything, so much so that it became a bit of an obsession. To cut a long story short, those hundreds of squiggly sketches lead me to explore the world of tattooing. It's taken years to perfect a fusion of realism, sacred geometry, mandalas and dot work.'

'Fascinating,' said Karen, crowbarring her way into the conversation.

'Thanks,' he smiled at her. 'But I also love anything that nods at magical or uplifting imagery – like Emma's butterfly for instance.'

'Do you know any tattoo jokes?' asked Karen.

Jezz chuckled.

'None that are repeatable.'

'Oh don't be shy' – Karen swiped him playfully on the arm – 'after all, everyone here is over eighteen.'

'Some of us more than others,' muttered Emma.

'Aw, c'mon, Jezz,' Karen wheedled.

'Okay, don't say I didn't warn you,' he twinkled. 'Well, a young American guy, madly in love with his girl, decided to get her name tattooed on his private parts. Her name was Wendy. The tattoo had to be done while his you-know-what was erect but, when it wasn't hard, all you could see was the W and Y. Shortly after having this tattoo, the guy married his girl and they honeymooned in Jamaica. One evening the man was using a public toilet and, standing next to him, was a Jamaican guy who also had the letters W and Y on his whatsit. The American said, "Hey, is your girl called Wendy too?", and the Jamaican laughed and said, "No. That says: *Welcome to*

Jamaica and Have a Nice Day".'

Karen immediately creased up with laughter. Emma regarded her mother sourly. Her mum had been here for all of ten minutes but had somehow instigated a situation where it was perfectly acceptable to talk about the size of men's todgers.

'Are you feeling better now?' Jezz asked Emma.

'Not particularly,' she growled.

'In which case' – he turned to Karen – 'can you fetch me some chocolate from the chiller?'

'Sure,' said Karen. 'Um, is it okay if I have some too? I can never say no to chocolate.'

'Help yourself,' said Jezz. 'And while you're out there, would you mind checking on your friend Willow too? I don't want a shop full of fainting females.'

'Certainly,' said Karen, flashing Jezz a smile. 'Thankfully I'm made of tougher stuff. I won't be fainting when you do *my* tattoo.'

'*Your* tattoo?' said Emma, frowning at her mother.

What was her mum playing at?

'Since when were you getting a tattoo?'

'Since now. If you must know, I came out today to avoid the landline ringing. First it was your father calling from Australia, and then your brother. And not just once. Several times over. Noah is hassling about staying in December. He's even talking about spending Christmas in England.'

'And what's wrong with that?' said Emma.

'Everything,' said Karen in annoyance. 'I don't need any additional reminders about the past. Seeing all this body art' –

she waved a hand at the other two artists on the far side of the studio – 'has made me realise that something substantial has been missing from my life.'

'What, like a gigantic tattoo?' said Emma sarcastically.

'Yes, maybe,' Karen cried. 'Perhaps I'll have a butterfly on my thigh too.'

'Oh don't copy me, Mum,' said Emma in exasperation.

'Can I suggest' – Jezz said to Karen – 'that you put some thought into this. After all, it's a momentous occasion. And anyway, I don't have time to do you as well today. You need an appointment.'

'Okay, that's a date,' said Karen winking at him. 'I'll come back and let you give me lots of pricks another day.'

'Great,' said Emma, determined to break up her mother's flirtatious innuendo once and for all. 'So, back to me. Let's get this done.'

Chapter Thirty-Nine

Charlie let out a gusty sigh that earned him a curious look from Ben.

'That sounds like a man breathing out a shedload of stress.'

'Yeah,' Charlie nodded. 'Something like that.'

The two men were seated at a small table in a pub next door to their hotel. They were having a pre-dinner drink before meeting up with some colleagues who'd also been at the work convention.

Earlier, when they'd all filed out of the business auditorium, there had been an almost carnival mood. Charlie knew he wasn't the only one looking forward to a night of unwinding without wives, girlfriends, or secret mistresses keeping tabs on their men's whereabouts.

'Do you mind me asking' – Ben leant in close to avoid being overheard by anyone – 'what the heck is going on in your private life?'

'I could ask the same of you,' said Charlie, dodging Ben's question. 'You told me you'd met someone but won't tell me anything about her.'

'Touché,' said Ben. 'But, unlike you, I'm now a single guy.'

'I'm single too,' Charlie protested.

'No, you're not. You have a partner. Her name is Willow. Ring any bells?' he said sarcastically.

'It's certainly not dinging any wedding bells, because she hasn't got a ring on it.'

'Bloody hell, mate,' Ben spluttered. 'Don't you have a conscience? Willow is a sweet girl. An absolute diamond. You've been playing away, and even if you won't give me all the details, nothing can change the truth of the matter. How do you imagine Willow would feel if she discovered what you get up to behind her back?'

'Look,' said Charlie, spreading his palms wide. A gesture of coming clean. 'Believe it or not, this week has been a defining one for me.'

'What does that mean?' said Ben, looking confused.

'It means – and don't ridicule me when I say this – I'm actually thinking of settling down.'

'Mate, you already are "settled down",' Ben pointed out. 'You have a joint mortgage with a beautiful lady who's been sharing not just your bed these past few years, but also your life.'

'Yeah, yeah' – Charlie waved one hand dismissively – 'but when I say "settle down" I really do mean that I'm seriously considering foregoing anyone else.'

Charlie momentarily contemplated his pint of lager.

'I think I might have finally grown up.'

Ben snorted.

'About flipping time. After all, it's well over a decade since you left your teens behind.'

'However' – Charlie held up one finger – 'whilst away from home it would be madness not to have one final fling… one last dropping of the boxers in order to indulge in some frantic no-strings steamy sex with someone I never have to see again.'

Ben tutted.

'So you're planning on pulling tonight?'

'Of course. And so, my friend, are you.'

'Oh no I'm not,' said Ben resolutely.

'Oh yes you are,' said Charlie in a pantomime voice. 'As you just pointed out, you're single. Footloose and fancy free, mate. Make the most of it.'

'I don't want to. I'm using this time to reflect. To put an appropriate distance between Anna and–'

He abruptly shut up.

'Who?' Charlie pounced.

'Never mind. You'll find out. In another two or three months. I want to be sure nobody can ever point the finger and say, "Oh dear, that woman is Ben's rebound."'

'Well until you're officially hooked up with she-who-shall-not-be-named, can I suggest you pop into the men's toilets, stick some money in the machine on the wall and treat yourself to a packet of rainbow condoms. You need to indulge in some uncomplicated pleasure.'

'Like you?'

'Like me,' Charlie nodded, picking up his glass and draining it. 'Fancy another?'

'Go on then. You've twisted my arm.'

'Back in a tick.'

Charlie walked over to the bar where a small group of women had congregated. One of them gave him the once over. Clearly she liked what she saw because Charlie clocked her nudging a little blonde number who had her back to him. As the woman whispered in her friend's ear, Charlie smirked. God had bestowed him with both good looks and the gift of the gab. Maybe, in a bit, he'd chat this female up and see where it led. It would save him the bother of going on to the club in order to pull.

Whilst waiting for the barman, out of his peripheral vision Charlie watched, amused, as the woman finished whispering to her blonde girlfriend. She'd no doubt told her gal pal to subtly turn around and check out the handsome Adonis standing behind her. Three… two… one. Yup! As he'd suspected, Blondie was now swivelling her head to casually regard Charlie. He had trouble not laughing out loud. Women thought they were so discreet, but sometimes they couldn't be more obvious.

Charlie let his gaze wander back to the woman who'd initially checked him out, and then lazily move on to Blondie. He wanted her to know he'd been studied and was perfectly up for taking it further. But before he could say anything, Blondie let out a squawk.

'Charlie!'

Charlie jumped. Flipping heck. He'd seen this woman before. In fact, he'd seen *all* of her before. He'd picked her up the last time he'd been in Birmingham, what… two months ago? Yes. It was definitely her. He'd met her in the very club he'd been planning on going to later this evening. What was her name? Sandra? Sarah?'

'Oh my God,' Blondie shrieked. 'I'm so glad to see you again.'

She tottered towards him and flung her arms around his waist.

'Darling,' said Charlie, returning the hug, while his brain scrambled for Blondie's name.

The woman who'd given him the once-over was looking incredibly put out that Blondie had claimed Charlie for herself.

'Aren't you going to introduce us, Sophie?' she grumbled.

Sophie! That's right. If Charlie remembered correctly, Sophie was a recently separated secretary who'd temporarily moved in with her sister following a dispute over the marital home.

'Listen, girls' – Sophie turned to her group of friends – 'me and this gorgeous guy have some serious catching up to do. You'll have to carry on without me.'

Sophie turned back to Charlie.

'Come on, handsome. Whatever plans you've made for this evening, cancel them. You're taking me out to dinner.'

She looped an arm through his and led him towards the pub's exit.

'A night with you will be my pleasure,' Charlie murmured.

Passing Ben, he gave a discreet shrug. Ben rolled his eyes

and stood up. He'd have to get his own pint. Never mind, thought Charlie. Perhaps Ben would get lucky with Sophie's pissed-off mate. He should at least try. Ben seriously needed to loosen up. Since meeting this secret woman, he'd turned into a boring old fart. I mean, who exactly was this female he kept referring to, and why was she so special? Whilst Ben hadn't exactly been around the block like Charlie, there *had* been a time when his mate had been less stuffy. He'd been up for the occasional pub crawl and – in Charlie's pre-Willow days – had convulsed when Charlie had told him a story about one little minx writing her phone number on his willy. What a hoot that had been.

Back then Ben had laughed along with Charlie, and been fun with a capital F. These days he was more like a nun with a capital N. Charlie let his thoughts return to the present and tuned in to Sophie who was chatting away.

'...and I'm just so relieved to see you again...' she was saying.

'Me too, sweetie,' he said huskily, giving her arm a squeeze.

She really was quite a looker and, if he recalled correctly, she'd been pretty hot between the sheets.

'...because we need to talk.'

If Charlie hadn't been so distracted with thoughts about later taking Sophie back to his hotel bedroom and undoing all those tantalising buttons on her little black dress, he might have paid more attention to the ominous note in her voice.

Chapter Forty

'How was it for you?' said Jezz to Emma.

He had a wicked twinkle in his eye.

'Excruciating,' she snapped.

She wasn't sure if Jezz was mocking her or being flirty. He'd bantered with both her and her mum throughout the procedure, although it had been Karen who'd hung on to Jezz's every word whilst endlessly flicking her hair, sticking out her chest, and making comments full of smutty innuendo.

'You'll be a returning customer,' said Jezz confidently.

'Unlikely. Apart from anything else I'd had no idea it would take so long. It was daylight when I came in. Now it's dark. Poor Willow. She must be bored out of her skull waiting for me.'

'She's fine,' said Karen. 'I told her to go shopping.'

'Oh,' said Emma, looking put out.

She had hoped to go shopping with Willow herself, but hadn't realised how time-consuming this appointment would be.

'This is a sizeable tattoo and was never going to be a quick job,' said Jezz. 'Anyway, it's always the ones who protest the most that come back for more. They're the ones who secretly enjoy the pain.'

'Not me,' said Emma firmly.

'I can't wait to have my tattoo,' said Karen, batting her eyelids at Jezz. 'Pain causes the central nervous system to release endorphins, which generate an opiate-like response in the body.'

'You're right,' said Jezz. 'The role of endorphins is to block pain, but it can also produce a feeling of euphoria. Athletes, for example, know this. They refer to it as "the runners' high."'

'I don't run' – Karen let her eyes snag on Jezz's – 'but I do enjoy a good massage. I love it when the masseur finds the sore spot on my back and kneads right into the muscles. It makes me cry out with the absolute joy of it all.'

She picked up a tendril of hair and began slowly twisting it around one finger, her gaze not leaving his face.

'A classic example of the thin line between pleasure and pain,' said Jezz, holding Karen's gaze.

Emma's eyes flicked between Jezz and her mum, like a spectator at Wimbledon. Her mother was clearly staking her claim on Jezz. Pulling all the flirty stops out. But exactly where the heck was this new line of conversation going? She didn't have long to find out.

'Yes, I agree,' said Karen, speeding up the hair twiddling. 'Some pain is exquisite – like those massages I adore – whereas other pain is just awful. Isn't it strange that I wince when my daughter treads on my foot, but I'm quite happy paying a small, robust woman to make me moan?'

Emma rolled her eyes. Only her mother could use the word "moan" and make it sound like she was having an orgasm. Frankly it was embarrassing. Willow's mum didn't carry on like this.

A mental picture of Anita, Willow's sensible and practical mother, sprang to Emma's mind. There she was, pinny on and standing alongside Jerry, Willow's mild-mannered father, letting him massage her tired shoulders. "That's it, Jerry. Right there. Oooh, perfect. You can stop now. Shall I put the kettle on?" But her *own* mother was something else. Emma's mouth fell open as Karen dared to push the conversation boundaries further.

'I suppose, the pain of a massage is enjoyable because one can relax into it.'

'You're right,' Jezz nodded. 'And therein lies the key to enjoying pain. It's about trust and control. You trust the masseur to keep your best interests at heart.'

'Yes,' said Karen, giving him a dazzling smile. 'It's that same sense of trust and control that makes sadomasochistic sex… the giving and receiving of pain… so pleasurable. Er, so I hear.'

'Ah… erotic spanking. Yes, you're right. Er, so I hear too. Perhaps, after all, I *can* find the time to do your tattoo today.'

Karen stopped twiddling her hair and looked at Jezz under her lashes.

'Perfect,' she purred. 'I shall look forward to the delightful sting… and delightful warmth… and delightful vibrations.'

'Delightful,' said Jezz, nodding away.

'I suppose the bottom line is' – Karen frowned theatrically – 'that there is no bottom line when it comes to spanking.'

'Except the bottom line,' Jezz murmured.

'I think you're both talking out of your bottoms,' said Emma, swinging her legs over the side of the couch.

Heaven only knew what this tattoo artist and her mother would be getting up to later. Yuck.

Emma peered down at her tattoo. Despite the whole experience hurting like mad, it had been worth it. She was thrilled with her butterfly. Emma wondered if she'd ever get to show the tattoo to her lover. Oh dear, she must stop thinking of him in that way. She also wondered what he was doing right now… miles away in Birmingham.

Chapter Forty-One

Charlie was having a frustrating evening with Sophie. Having abandoned Ben in the pub, he'd walked Sophie across the road to a restaurant.

She seemed to be stringing out the dinner they were having, taking way too much time over choosing a starter. Why couldn't she just skip straight to mains? It would speed up getting them out of here. He wanted to get Sophie back to his hotel room and maximise recreational time under the duvet.

'I can't decide whether to go for the curried parsnip soup or settle for the goat's cheese tartlet with velouté. Do you fancy a starter, Charlie?'

'Only if there's something on the menu called "Sophie".'

Sophie giggled. 'I'm starving. Aren't you hungry?'

'Just for you,' he murmured huskily.

'Oh Charlie, you are naughty' – she giggled again – 'but I do love my food.'

Charlie, on flirty autopilot, only just managed to stop himself saying, "and I love *you*". From the look on Sophie's face, she'd been half-expecting him to say those very words.

Instead Charlie said, 'So you love food. Does that mean

you enjoy cooking too?'

'I do,' she beamed. 'What about you?'

'Now and again.'

He loathed it.

'What's your speciality?' she asked.

Charlie appeared to give this a moment's thought.

'Chocolate brownies,' he said eventually.

'Oooh, I *love* chocolate brownies,' Sophie squealed. 'Will you make them for me one day?'

'Of course, darling. Although I might get seriously distracted if you're around me while I'm making them.'

Sophie smirked upon hearing this.

'You mean you might incinerate them?'

'Exactly. But on the upside, it would be the quickest way to burn two thousand calories.'

'You are funny, Charlie.'

'And you're sexy. Are you sure you want dinner? I'd much prefer to be ravishing you than sitting in this restaurant. Shall we go back to my hotel right now? I can always order room service later.'

Sophie opened her mouth to say something but was interrupted by Charlie's phone, which had been resting next to his side plate. It let out a merry tinkle signalling Willow was ringing. Charlie snatched it up before Sophie could see his girlfriend's name on the caller display.

'Hey,' he said into the mouthpiece.

'Hi, darling. I was just calling to see how you are. How did the convention go–?'

'It's a shocking line,' Charlie lied, cutting across Willow. 'I can hardly hear you. Let me give you a call back later.'

Without further preamble, Charlie hung up. He then switched the phone off.

'Who was that?' asked Sophie.

'My mother.'

The waitress appeared with a notepad and pen. Her request to take their orders thankfully stopped Sophie from asking any awkward questions about Charlie's mother. He couldn't quite remember what line he'd spun Sophie when he'd last seen her. It was important not to contradict himself. At least not before he'd got her between the sheets.

The waitress melted away and Sophie reached across the table. She enfolded Charlie's hand in hers.

'Isn't this nice?' she beamed. 'I can't tell you how pleased I am to see you again. I was in such a panic after discovering I'd lost your number.'

Charlie was puzzled. He wasn't aware he'd given Sophie his contact details. He must have had far too much to drink to have done such a thing. How careless. It was one of his rules… always take the girl's number. Never the other way around. Okay, he'd broken that rule with Kev, and to his detriment. Just look at how that had turned out. The blasted woman hadn't left him alone. He'd had some very sweaty moments with Kev texting him at home, badgering for sex, even with Willow sitting right next to him as they'd watched telly together.

'You lost my number?' said Charlie, pretending to be

outraged.

'Yes, but that's probably because you wrote it on a really tiny scrap of paper. It must have fluttered to the floor in our moment of passion and, later, been accidentally vacuumed up. It was only when I'd finished hunting high and low, that I realised what had probably happened. By that point the vacuum cleaner had long been emptied, and I'd resigned myself to believing I'd never see you again.'

'And that would have been terrible,' said Charlie disarmingly.

Hopefully, after tonight, he never would see Sophie again.

'So give me your number, but this time we'll do it properly.'

She withdrew her hand from his and reached into her handbag for her mobile.

'This time' – she waggled the phone at him – 'I'll put it in here.'

'Later, darling. There's plenty of time for exchanging numbers.'

'No, I want to do it now,' she persisted.

There was something in her tone which warned Charlie she was having a moment of doubting him. That would never do. Not before he'd got her into bed.

'And then I want to ring your phone to double-check I programmed the number correctly,' she added.

O-*kay*. She was definitely having a moment of doubt. Fine. He'd give her his contact details. After they'd been to bed, he'd block her number. Simple.

The time at the restaurant passed too slowly for Charlie's liking but he played the game and flattered Sophie. She lapped up his compliments until she was glowing brighter than Kev's collection of aromatherapy candles. Finally, after listening to her interminable waffle about her yoga hobby, how much she loved her goldfish George, and what a bastard her ex-husband was for threatening to flush George down the toilet, Charlie was able to settle the bill. And now they were standing up, and she was linking her arm through his. Hurrah.

Sophie allowed Charlie to walk her back to his hotel, through the foyer, into the lift, down the corridor, inside his room and – he mentally punched the air – flop down on the bed where he finally got to work undoing all those tiny buttons on her little black dress. But… what was she doing?

'Stop that,' she said, slapping his hand away.

'Why?' he gasped.

Had he just spent all that money wining and dining her only to have her turn him down at the last minute?

'Because they're not real, silly.' She gave a tinkle of laughter. 'Look. There's a hidden zip. See?' She pointed.

'Even better,' he murmured, as desire flooded through him. 'It will be like undoing a beautiful present.'

For the next hour neither of them said a word, for which Charlie was particularly grateful. He'd already decided that Sophie's voice wasn't so much sugar sweet as saccharine sour. It jarred him. And if he heard one more time how George loved swimming under his ornamental bridge and wagging his fishy tail like a dog, he might say something regretful. Like understanding why Sophie's husband had accused her of loving George more than him.

Finally spent, they sank back against the mattress. Sophie snuggled into Charlie's armpit.

'How's your sister?'

Charlie's brain reeled. His sister? He immediately adopted a vague tone.

'Which one?'

'The sister you live with. Willow?'

'Oh… *that* sister.'

'Is she still awful to put up with?'

'Yes, dreadful. Drives me mad. Natters on and on about her boring job at the library. Tells me off for not being more involved with the community or helping with local fund-raising. She's ancient before her time, poor dear.'

'Are you still looking to move out?'

'Yes. In time. I need to pick my moment. Willow relies heavily on the rent I pay for my room. She'd expect me to have a very good reason for finding somewhere else to live.'

'I can give you a perfect reason,' said Sophie silkily.

For a moment Charlie didn't respond. Where was this conversation going?

'Do you remember me saying earlier' – Sophie stroked Charlie's arm – 'how relieved I was to see you?'

'Er, yes.'

'And do you recall me saying there was something I wanted to talk about?'

Charlie rewound the earlier conversation in his head.

'Um, vaguely.'

'Well you can tell your sister there is now an excellent reason for her to find someone else to rent the spare bedroom.'

'And what reason might that be?'

'Because you've met me, and now we're getting a place together.'

'What?' said Charlie, half laughing at Sophie's impudence. 'Steady on, darling. This is only our second time together.'

'That as may be,' she said, a steely note entering her voice. 'But it only needed the first time for you to make me pregnant.'

Chapter Forty-Two

Willow's Saturday had played out far less stressfully than Charlie's.

While Emma had been laying on Jezz's lookalike dentist chair getting inked, Willow had visited all the shops along the local high street.

She now dumped her shopping bags in the boot of Emma's car, before sinking into the passenger seat with a contented sigh. Willow hadn't spent money on a tattoo, but she'd had a heavenly time blowing the cash gifts from her recent birthday.

'Sorry you didn't get to come with me,' she said, glancing across the handbrake at Emma.

'Don't be daft. Far better to shop than sit in a studio twiddling your thumbs. I had no idea tattoos took so long, or that you'd turn into a Fainting Flora the minute Jezz whipped out his big gun.'

'Not that the two are related' – Willow giggled – 'but where is your mum?'

Emma started the car up, at the same time rolling her eyes at Willow's question.

'My mother is getting a tat.'

'She's not really going through with it, is she?'

'Oh but she is. If you'd have heard her and Jezz chatting – actually, substitute that last word for "flirting" – you'd have died of embarrassment. That's the trouble with my mum. She forgets that she gave birth to me. Instead she treats me like I'm her best buddy, which is nice sometimes, but not always. If you'd *heard* her in there, Willow, you'd have been shocked. Imagine watching your own mother fluttering her eyelashes at a guy *waaaay* younger than her. She made a complete fool of herself.'

'Are you sure?'

'Sure of what?' said Emma, accelerating out of the parking bay. 'Shall we head into town? I fancy a huge glass of wine with a birthday pizza.'

'Are you sure she was making a fool of herself? It sounds to me like Jezz was encouraging her. And yes to the wine and pizza.'

Emma blew out her cheeks as she changed gear.

'Okay, perhaps she was just making a fool of herself to me. Not him. You're right. He seemed to like the attention she was giving him, but the innuendo was awful. They were discussing erotic spanking at one point.'

'What?' Willow laughed. 'How did they get on to that subject?'

'Somehow it followed on from a string of lewd tattoo jokes.'

Willow snorted.

'Tell me.'

'Must I? It's so embarrassing. Your mother wouldn't

dream of being outrageous.'

'My mother wouldn't dream of wearing a bikini. That doesn't mean to say it would be wrong if she did. Just tell me the jokes.'

'I can only remember one.'

'One joke will do,' Willow assured.

'Mum told Jezz that she'd heard about someone's husband having "I love you" tattooed on his willy. However, when he went home and proudly showed his wife, she was really cross and said, "There you go again. Trying to put words in my mouth."'

Willow laughed.

'It's not funny,' said Emma, scowling. 'My mother is forty-six years old but carries on like she's sixteen. It makes me cringe. She's so uptight about her past, no doubt her new tattoo will be worded accordingly. And Jezz was hugely distracted when I left. What if his spelling goes to pieces? Knowing my mum, she'll leave the tattoo parlour with her wrist incorrectly inked. *I have no regerts.*'

'Well she can always get it removed,' Willow soothed. 'And anyway, never mind your mum's tattoo. How's yours? Are you pleased?'

'I am,' Emma beamed.

'Then that's all that matters. Now let's enjoy the rest of the evening. I have no one to rush home to and can stay out as late as I like.'

'Me too,' said Emma ruefully.

She envied Willow having a partner to go home to rather

than a deluded mother. However, she was under no illusions about Charlie. She knew exactly what he got up to behind Willow's back. Her friend deserved so much better. Emma chose to ignore the little voice that suddenly piped up.

And doesn't she deserve so much better in the friendship stakes too?

Emma shook her head, as if her brain were a bowling ball that was now scattering the words of the sneering jibe. She hoped that if Willow ever found out about Charlie's shenanigans, she would forgive Emma her duplicity.

Chapter Forty-Three

Emma and Willow were half-way through their pizza when a mobile signalled an incoming FaceTime call.

'Is that you or me?' said Emma, fork hovering mid-air.

'Not sure,' said Willow, reaching into her handbag.

Her heart did a little somersault followed by a series of skippy beats. Perhaps it was Charlie calling. Maybe he wanted to tell her he was missing her like crazy. She imagined his golden good looks filling the screen as he flashed a smile worthy of a toothpaste commercial. And then maybe he'd say, "Darling! I had this overwhelming urge to say I love you. The work convention has been awful. The usual plebs sucking up to Drummond. All I could think about was my gorgeous girl. I wish I was with you right now… snuggling up… having a snogging sesh… then getting carried away… me ripping off my–" and then he'd abruptly break off and give an apologetic little laugh and say, "Oops! Didn't realise you were out in public, darling. Ah, hi there, Emma! Yes fine, thanks, and you?"

But, disappointingly, it wasn't Willow's mobile bleeping.

'It's yours,' she said.

Emma hastily swallowed a mouthful of pizza before

scrabbling inside her handbag.

'Oh, wow. It's Noah,' she said, flashing the caller display at Willow. 'Excuse me a mo.'

'Go right ahead.'

Emma swiped the screen. Moments later, she was greeting her twin.

'Hiya, bro!' she grinned.

Willow was pleased that her bestie was so obviously thrilled to speak to her sibling. It was evident she had great affection for Noah, despite circumstances keeping them apart. Willow was pretty sure that Emma would have toned down her exuberance if Karen had been in the restaurant with them. Much as Willow was fond of Karen, she did secretly sympathise with Emma having a mother who – it had to be said – was a handful. Sometimes Karen behaved like a teenager having a tantrum, which was absurd given that the "teenager" was actually forty-six years old.

'Hey, Ems! I know you're probably still out celebrating your birthday, but I wanted you to be the first to know that I've booked my ticket to England. I decided to tweak my time-out tour and shall now spend the entirety of December in the UK. This means I'll definitely be having a very overdue Christmas with you and Mum.'

Willow couldn't help overhearing Noah talking. Never had the Australian accent sounded so sexy. There was no denying that Emma's brother had a gorgeous voice. It reminded Willow of both gravel and velvet.

'That's fantastic!'

Emma's face had lit up.

However, although Emma was delighted to hear Noah's news update, she wasn't sure how her mother was going to take it. It was a bit strange hearing Noah referring to Karen as "Mum", because he'd never had a proper maternal relationship with her. Emma knew that Noah also called his stepmother "Mum", which was only right given that her father's second wife had been the one to raise Noah as her own.

But now wasn't the time to think about Karen, or how she would protest about Noah's visit. For now, Emma wanted to be selfish. She'd pleased her mother for long enough. Now it was time to please herself, especially where Noah was concerned. And who knew, maybe in the New Year Emma *would* finally go to Australia. It would be wonderful to properly meet her half-sister and get reacquainted with her father. She was thirty years old for goodness sake. She should be able to do these things without worrying about her mother's approval. And maybe, in the New Year, she might have a boyfriend to take with her.

Emma's thoughts automatically swerved off to Birmingham, but she swiftly reined them in again. No. She mustn't think about *him*. For now, the pause button had been pressed. She must concentrate on the present instead, and Noah's wonderful news.

'Hearing this has made my birthday extra special,' said beamed.

'Ha!' said Noah. 'You might still be enjoying your birthday, but mine finished eight hours ago. Today *here* is actually *your* tomorrow.'

'Oh my goodness, that sounds so weird. I keep forgetting that you are hours and hours ahead in Oz.'

Noah chuckled. 'Indeed. I've just had my breakfast. Where are you right now?'

'Having my dinner,' Emma laughed. 'I'm out with my bestie. We're having a pizza. Hey, you can say hello to her. This is Willow.'

Emma swung the screen around just as Willow was cramming a huge piece of margherita in her mouth. As Noah's face came into view, Willow thought she might choke. The guy was even better looking than in the photograph Emma had shown her earlier.

'Hi,' Willow croaked, spraying crumbs everywhere.

Noah was having a major knee-jerk effect on her, which was ridiculous because, well, she was madly in love with Charlie for starters! But then again, feeling occasionally attracted to another member of the opposite sex wasn't against the law, was it? She'd probably feel the same if, say, she met her favourite popstar crush. Yes, that was it. She was simply reacting to Noah's good looks in a similar way. That was why she now felt like a tongue-tied schoolgirl and couldn't think of a single thing to say. Instead she stuck up some greasy fingers and waggled them by way of greeting.

'Lovely to meet you, Willow,' Noah grinned.

'And you,' Willow gushed.

She gave Noah an idiotic grin and hoped she didn't have a bit of oregano stuck between her front teeth.

'Without sounding corny, if all my sister's friends are as good looking as you, then I have even more reason to visit England.'

Willow blushed with both embarrassment and pleasure. Was he flirting?

Oh, don't be so ridiculous, Willow. The man is simply being charming. Perhaps all Australians are like it.

But despite sitting there and glowing pinkly like a raspberry-ripple sunset, Willow was secretly thrilled. It was always nice to be paid a compliment, especially when it was being given by such a heavenly looking guy. And that accent! Phew… she could almost feel her nerve-endings sighing. Thank goodness they were only FaceTiming. Heaven knows what effect this man might have on her if they ever met. She gulped. For surely at some point they *would* meet.

'Before you get carried away with your flirty banter, Noah' – Emma swung the screen back to her – 'Willow is taken.'

'Shame,' said Noah lightly.

Emma carried on chatting to her brother, privately noting that her bestie was looking very flustered. Willow's body language smacked of attraction on her part. And then a lightbulb went off in Emma's head. What if she could later orchestrate a romantic situation between Willow and Noah?

What if indeed…

Chapter Forty-Four

Charlie's romantic night with Sophie was rapidly turning to ashes.

'Pregnant?' he yelped, sitting bolt upright in his bed.

Sophie's head, previously tucked into Charlie's armpit, fell backwards causing some vertebrae to crack from the sudden movement.

'Ow!' she grumbled, rubbing her neck.

'You can't possibly be pregnant,' Charlie protested.

'Well I am.'

She propped herself up on one elbow and regarded him crossly.

'Don't look so surprised. I didn't manage it all by myself. You had something to do with it too.'

'No, no, no, no, no,' Charlie gabbled. 'Don't put that number on me.'

He shrank away from Sophie, scooting across the mattress in a desperate bid to put distance between her and himself.

Moments ago, she'd seemed so attractive. Now she was looking more and more like the wicked fairy in *Sleeping Beauty*. Except Sophie was no sleeping beauty. She was wide awake and continuing to morph before his very eyes. Now she was Snow White's stepmum, the Evil Queen. He realised his thoughts were looping. Thinking of Snow White automatically made him think of Willow, except she had blonde hair rather than black hair and–

Christ, what was his brain doing exploding with all this mental imagery of Disney characters?

Because, Charlie, your sub-conscious is flagging up to you that Willow is sweet and kind and the obvious candidate as a life partner, whereas lately you've been fooling around with Kev, and now Sophie, who in their own way want to trap you, just like those Disney baddies.

Charlie groaned. Of all the times to have an epiphany. And actually, wasn't this the second one? Heck, who was counting? He certainly wasn't. Sweat was starting to bead across his upper lip. He cowered in the corner, his back jammed against the wardrobe as he stared at Sophie in horror. She languidly returned his gaze.

'I don't know what the problem is,' she was drawling. 'The first time we met you told me you loved me.'

'No, I didn't,' Charlie objected.

'Yes, you did. It was just before you got me into bed. I wouldn't have gone with you otherwise. I guess it's something of a blip getting pregnant quite so early in a relationship but–'

'This isn't a relationship,' Charlie interrupted.

Sophie was pulling the oldest trick in the book.

'If it isn't a relationship' – she frowned – 'then what the hell is it?'

'It was only ever a bit of fun,' Charlie protested.

He grabbed his boxers and put them on inside-out. God he couldn't wait to get out of here. Except… except this was *his* room. He needed *her* to get out.

'Fun?' Sophie squawked. Her face blotched with anger. 'How dare you.'

Charlie began rapidly dressing, shaking his head in disbelief. She couldn't be pregnant. He'd worn a condom for goodness sake. Or had he? He had a nasty feeling he'd been rather the worse for wear when trying to put the wretched thing on. That he'd not quite managed to do it. Yes, it was coming back to him now. She'd slapped his hand away and said…

'You told me you were on the pill!' he accused.

'No, I never.'

'Yes, you did,' he spluttered. 'That's why I didn't use a condom just now.'

'Rubbish,' Sophie protested. 'You told me that *you'd* take care of protection. And when you didn't, I assumed…' she trailed off.

'Assumed what?' said Charlie, looking horrified.

'Assumed that I meant something to you.' Sophie glared at him. 'You kissed me all over and whispered that I was the most beautiful woman you'd ever been to bed with.'

He quavered at her words. Standard Charlie patter.

'You told me I was the sort of woman you'd like to settle down with.'

More Charlie patter. He'd heard enough. He knew the script and didn't need reminding of it.

'I'm not ready to settle down,' he said, stuffing his feet into his shoes.

Grabbing his overnight bag, he began chucking stuff inside.

'Too bad,' she hissed, getting off the bed and coming towards him. 'You're going to be a daddy. So what are you going to do about it, eh?'

'Do?' Charlie repeated.

He'd failed to lace up his shoes and nearly tripped over in his haste to get away from her. Right now, he only had one advantage over Sophie. He was dressed and she wasn't.

'I'm going home. That's what I'm doing.'

Backing away from her, he darted towards the door. Seconds later Charlie was fleeing down the hotel corridor, then down the stairs two at a time, before crashing through the fire exit into the car park. He had no idea if he was still over the limit to drive, but at least Sophie didn't know which car was his. If nothing else, he'd hunker down out of sight until he *was* able to drive. And then he'd be off. Straight down the M40.

Charlie was aware that he'd be leaving Ben in the lurch. Ben would have to hitch a lift home with one of the other guys.

As Charlie rushed towards his vehicle, he thanked the universe, the moon, the stars, and God in his heaven that home was almost two hundred miles away, and that he'd never have to see Sophie again.

Chapter Forty-Five

Charlie ducked down in the driver's seat of his vehicle, heart pounding. He felt sick. Sick from the shock of Sophie's bombshell news, and sick from sobering up so rapidly.

Inside the car's temporary sanctuary, everything was dark and silent. There were no lamps in the hotel's car park. Subsequently the area looked somewhat eerie and uninviting. There wasn't even a courtesy light, like the sort that bobbed on for fifteen seconds when someone passed by.

Charlie didn't think Sophie would venture out in the night to peer into every vehicle. And anyway, she didn't know he'd travelled to Birmingham by car. It was far more likely that any search for him was taking place within the hotel. He imagined her hastily dressed and charging up and down the corridor calling out his name, or rushing into the foyer, heels clicking on the shiny polished floor, eyes stricken as she begged the night staff if they'd seen a blond man dash past. Perhaps she'd even ask if they would check the men's toilets on her behalf, to see if Charlie was hiding. Thank goodness he'd spotted that fire door and escaped.

Even so, Charlie couldn't relax. He hardly dared breathe in case the slightest movement gave him away. A part of him half-expected Sophie's face to appear at the windscreen, her nose squashed up against the glass, features distorted like a nightmare character from a horror movie.

Charlie began to tremble, partly from nerves, and partly from the cold. He longed to start the engine and get the heating on, but he didn't dare do that just yet. Fear was paralysing him. He squeezed his eyes tightly shut and focussed on listening. The fire door had been heavy. After he'd stumbled through it, the door had slammed after him with a crash loud enough to light up reception's switchboard with complaints. Therefore, if Sophie *did* dare to venture into the car park, surely he'd hear her coming?

His ears strained to catch any alien sounds. An empty can bounced across the tarmac causing Charlie's heart to shoot into his oesophagus. Had someone kicked it? Had that someone been Sophie? Had she exited the hotel via the *front* door, and crept round the building's perimeter to now search the car park? Perhaps she had tracked down her girlfriends and enlisted their help. Maybe they were arriving right now, en masse, ready to search together? After all, there was safety in numbers.

He heard the tin can roll again, and this time his heart relocated to his eardrums. Oh God, was that a voice he could hear? Or was his imagination playing tricks? A gust of wind whooshed against the vehicle, causing the chassis to sway. Charlie concentrated on breathing. In… out… in… that's better… and out.

He wondered what the time was. Reaching carefully for his mobile, Charlie held it low to the car's floor. The last thing he wanted was the screen lighting up the interior. He was surprised to see that it was only a little after ten o'clock. From his awkward position, he eyeballed the car's gearstick and pushed some stray hair out of his eyes. He couldn't stay like this for much longer. The handbrake was digging into his side. Apart from anything else, he was getting a backache.

Charlie pondered whether to start the car and make his getaway. Was he still over the limit? The more he thought about it, the more he decided it was okay to drive. There had been that earlier beer with Ben, but that was hours ago. He'd drunk some wine with Sophie, but considerable time had passed since his last glass, *and* he'd eaten a good meal. There had been plenty of "blotting paper", so to speak. So… his mind whirred… surely he was good to go? He'd chance it. He had to. Getting out of Birmingham was a priority.

Slowly inching himself upright, Charlie cautiously peered over the steering wheel. The car park was still empty. No marauding female gang was racing between parked vehicles baying for blood or, in this instance, Charlie's balls. The knot in his stomach eased slightly as he fully straightened up and snapped the seatbelt around his torso.

He stuck the key in the ignition. The engine coughed but didn't fire. Oh Lord, please don't let the car choose this moment to mess him about. Not now. Not in this crisis. Charlie applied pressure to the accelerator, and this time the engine turned over. He gave it a couple of revs, quietly appalled at the lack of strength in his legs. They felt like they'd been hijacked and replaced with cake mixture.

Charlie stared through the windscreen and, as he did so, a strangled cry escaped his lips. The fire escape door had flown back on its hinges. There, caught in his headlights and looking like an avenging angel, was Sophie. The wind swept her hair upwards where it rippled out like Medusa's snakes. Her lips peeled back as she snarled with rage.

'Come back here, you coward!' she cried.

Charlie was reminded of a joke Ben had told him earlier that evening. Good heavens. It seemed light years away. That had been when life was normal. Not this living nightmare. Ben had told him about a man who'd bought a book called *Cowards in History*, but all the pages had fallen out. Annoyed, he'd returned it to the shop only to be told, "*Cowards in History* is a spineless book."

As Charlie gunned the engine and the car lurched forward, in that moment he knew exactly what it felt like to be spineless.

Chapter Forty-Six

Kev was snuggled under her duvet, alone. Despite feeling tired, sleep was evading her.

She scratched her thigh absentmindedly, then winced. Her tattoo looked amazing, but it wouldn't stop itching. Trying to keep her fingers off it was proving challenging. She wished there was something to distract her. Kev's thoughts instantly flew to Charlie. If he was here right now, her attention would be instantly diverted.

Sighing, she flicked on the bedside lamp. The clock beside her showed the time as twenty past midnight. Earlier on, Kev had been reading a book. She'd borrowed it from Willow's library. It was one of those New Age reads about cosmic ordering. It had appealed to her partly out of curiosity and partly amusement. It now lay face down beside the clock. Perhaps she'd make herself a cup of tea and return to that last chapter. The one about manifesting your heart's desires. Huh! What a load of claptrap.

Five minutes later Kev was propped up in bed, sipping her tea and snorting with contempt at the advice within the pages.

Ask the universe to change your life. Begin with little things. For example, instead of requesting that the cosmos deliver a million-pound win on your Lotto ticket, start small. Focus on achieving, say, three numbers.

Kev tutted. Absolute rubbish. Although, hang on a minute, she hadn't checked last week's Lotto ticket. Okay, before she did that, how about doing what the book said? Right! Forget about hoping for the jackpot. Instead, concentrate on three numbers coming up trumps.

She closed her eyes and visualised the Lotto ticket. Now what? Wasn't there a magic word to utter? Abracadabra, or some such silliness? She opened her eyes again, skim-reading the page for advice.

One way of successfully ordering your heart's desire is to write it down in a letter. Address your letter to the universe and be very clear.

Oh, for goodness sake.

She rummaged in her bedside drawer for a bit of paper and a pen. Ah, *there* was her shopping list. She wondered where she'd put it. Kev smoothed out the creases, then turned the paper over. The other side was blank. Returning to the drawer, she found half a dozen defunct biros but – yay! – amidst the jumble was a reasonably sharp pencil.

Kev settled back against the pillows and drew her legs up to her chest. Using her knees as a table, she began to write:

Dear Universe.

That sounded very formal. She crossed it out and tried again.

Dearest Universe.

Hm. Should she perhaps make it more ingratiating? Would

it curry her better favour and leapfrog over all the other cosmic requests that were possibly being offered up to the heavens from locations all around the world? For the second time her pencil scratched out the words.

Beloved Universe.

Better. Now to make her desire both precise and concise.

Give me three winning numbers on last week's Lotto ticket.

Well, you couldn't get clearer than that. Okay, now to imagine posting this note into a letterbox that had an uninterrupted connection to a celestial sorting office.

Kev folded the note in half once, then twice. She focused on the small space between her knees. In her mind's eye, she imagined this space was the mouth of a cosmic mailbox. Without hesitating, Kev pushed the note through the gap. As the paper fluttered down to the mattress, she imagined it flying through zillions of miles of interplanetary space before being intercepted by a giant glowing hand. She visualised long fingers unfolding her note, and unseen eyes reading her request.

Right. Job done. Now to check that Lotto ticket.

Swinging her legs out of bed, Kev padded across the bedroom and grabbed her handbag from the dressing table. The Lotto ticket was in her purse. Not for one moment did she believe that three of its numbers would yield any financial reward, but it was an amusing experiment.

Extracting the ticket along with her mobile, she hopped back into bed. Now to go on the website and check last week's numbers.

Seconds later, Kev let out a gasp. Good heavens. She'd only gone and bagged thirty quid! Wow, how about that? She stared at the numbers in bemusement. Had she really just done her first bit of successful cosmic ordering?

Oh don't be absurd. It's a coincidence, that's all. You don't truly believe this book's bunkum, do you?

Kev blew out her cheeks. No. She didn't believe it. It was simply a happy fluke. On the upside, she was now thirty pounds better off. But her mind was already darting off and starting to play the "what if" game.

What if her command to the universe hadn't been a coincidence? What if she really had tapped into some sort of divine energy that had delivered those three lottery numbers? What if she could tap into it again? But this time with a different request. Something more challenging. Just to prove to herself that the mini lottery win was nothing more than one of life's freaky moments.

Kev took another sip of tea and cogitated. Okay. Time to up the stakes.

Setting her drink down on the bedside table, Kev retrieved both the shopping list and pencil, and once again set to work. Okay, cosmos. Try this for size!

Beloved Universe. Have Charlie ring my doorbell in the next sixty seconds.

Once again, Kev folded the paper upon itself and, closing her eyes tightly, posted the note through the gap between her legs. For the second time she heard the paper flutter briefly through the air whilst imagining her note zooming towards that glowing hand. There were those fingers again, opening her note, and those same unseen eyes were now scanning her request.

Kev flopped back against the pillows and stared at the ceiling. She felt wired and on edge. Perhaps she should've made herself cocoa instead of tea. Caffeine was a stimulant, not a sedative. She sighed. Ah well, there were all sorts of things she shouldn't have done in her life. Drinking tea at gone midnight was just one of them. Kev reached for the cup but, as her fingers curled around the china, her body gave an involuntary jerk of shock.

The doorbell was emitting a series of shrill rings.

Chapter Forty-Seven

Kev crept along the landing towards the stairs, mobile in one hand just in case she needed to call the police. The doorbell let out another urgent volley of bing-bongs. Who the heck was visiting at this time of night?

Not for one moment did Kev truly believe she'd manifested Charlie on her doorstep. Okay, she might have just won thirty quid on last week's Lotto ticket after writing a letter to the universe, but that was just a bit of quirkiness. No, the doorbell ringer must be some chancer out to rob her.

There had been a spate of burglaries in the village recently. One neighbour had forgotten to lock up before going to bed, and a prowler had simply strolled in and taken the keys to a brand-new BMW. And only last week, widower Mr Thompson had been victim to a scam. A well-spoken and presentable looking man had rattled Mr Thompson's doorknocker late at night claiming he didn't have a mobile and his car had broken down. Would Mr Thompson be a star and avail the use of his landline?

Poor Mr Thompson had let the stranger in, but then been manhandled and tied to a chair in his hallway while his house had been ransacked. Goodness knows how long Mr Thompson would have been in that pickle if his daughter hadn't popped by the following morning.

Kev tip-toed to the front door trying to ignore her heart which was thudding like the base guitar in a heavy metal band. Pressing her head against the wood panels, she peered through the spy hole. She had to suppress the urge to scream as a man's silhouette came into view. He was wearing a hoodie, but it completely shrouded his face.

The man raised his hand again, but this time made a fist which he hammered against the panels. When that didn't get any response from within, he pulled a mobile from his pocket. The screen eerily lit up his hood, but a dark void remained where his face should have been. It made him look like a ghoul. A rash of goose bumps erupted over Kev's arms. Who was the man phoning? Was he perhaps giving the thumbs-up to his gang?

"Harry? It's me. There's no one home. I've rung the bell umpteen times and bashed on the door too. Fetch the crowbar. We're going in."

Kev let out a squeak of fear. It was time to call the police. Better to be safe than sorry. Thank God she'd had the foresight to bring her mobile downstairs with her.

Shaking, she was about to tap out the number to Emergency Services when her phone exploded into life. Kev's nerves were already stretched to breaking point. She was in fight-or-flight mode. Consequently, before she could even think about what was happening, her reflexes had sprung into action and lobbed the mobile along the hallway.

Unfortunately, the jaunty ringtone of "Single Ladies" had been loud enough to alert Midnight Man to Kev's presence. He immediately began thumping on the door with renewed vigour.

It was all too much for Kev. Adrenalin had been whizzing around her body for the last few minutes, but now it had run its course and her legs buckled. Groaning with dismay she sank to the floor until her head was in line with the letterbox. The brass flap lifted and suddenly she was staring into a pair of piercing blue eyes.

'ARGHHH!' she cried.

'Kev!'

She stopped screaming. There was only one man who called her that. Charlie Goodman.

What the *hell* was going on here? First the lottery win. Now Charlie was on her doorstep when… hang on a minute… he was in Birmingham. At a work convention. He couldn't possibly be here. Either she was hallucinating or her cosmic ordering had plucked him from his Brummie hotel and plonked him here, in Mosley, at silly o'clock in the morning.

'Charlie?' she croaked.

'Open the door!'

'Is it really you?' she asked, staring hard at the eyes.

They were the same blue as Charlie's but looked very wild. A bit… deranged. But then again, if she'd just been beamed-up from Birmingham, she'd probably be feeling a bit peculiar too.

'Yes, it's really me,' said Charlie. 'Now *please* let me in.'

Wow, she'd have to keep reading that book. And she'd be sure to leave a five-star review on Amazon too.

Not only did I win some money on the lottery, but my lover was delivered to my doorstep by cloud courier.

Well, maybe she'd have to word it differently, otherwise Amazon might think she was a headcase.

'Hurry up, Kev,' Charlie urged. 'It's flipping freezing out here.'

His words galvanised her into action. Springing to her feet, she drew back the safety chain on the door and then released the catch.

Chapter Forty-Eight

'Oh my g-goodness,' Kev stammered. 'Are you okay?'

'I guess so,' said Charlie, looking bewildered.

He wasn't sure if he'd ever be okay again. Not after Sophie's revelation.

'But… what was the journey from Birmingham like?'

'I can honestly say it was something of a blur.'

'Yes, I can imagine,' said Kev, her eyes huge.

'In fact, tonight's been totally surreal,' said Charlie, shaking his head. 'One minute I was relaxing in my hotel room, the next–'

Kev cut across him, her voice anxious.

'But you're okay, yes?'

'I'm really not sure.' Charlie shook his head. 'It's been a crazy night.'

'You can say that again,' said Kev, with a giggle.

The sound carried a note of hysteria.

Charlie stared at Kev. Properly. She was behaving oddly. As if she'd had a shock or been weirded out by something. Perhaps his surprise visit at an unearthly hour had frightened her.

'Never mind me for a moment,' said Charlie, in a rare

moment of solicitousness. 'What about you? You seem out of sorts.'

'Ah ha ha ha,' Kev laughed shrilly. 'Yes. A bit. I mean–'

She broke off and launched into a rendition of the music from Dr Who.

'Dum-da-dum, dum-da-dum, dum-da-dum, dum-da-dum…'

'Eh?'

'Waa-OOOOOOOOOOOO!'

'Flaming Nora, my ears,' said Charlie, clapping his hands to his head.

What the heck had got into Kev? Her eyes were shining like a religious zealot who'd had a vision but couldn't put into words what she'd seen. She was eyeballing Charlie like he was some sort of supernatural entity.

'Bizarre or *what!*' she declared.

'Er, cosmic,' he agreed.

Charlie had no idea why Kev had wanted to sing Dr Who's theme tune, but decided to humour her. Perhaps it was her time of the month and she was feeling a bit hormonal or something. Willow had been known to take *Coronation Street* way too seriously when she was due on. He'd once caught her emulating the mournful notes of that frigging trumpet as she'd stood in the kitchen prepping dinner.

'But the main thing is' – Kev's face was wreathed in smiles – 'you're here!'

'I am,' said Charlie. And then an expression of horror came over his face. 'Oh my goodness, I completely forgot to check.

Are you alone?'

Help. He hadn't stopped to properly think this through. What if Kev wasn't alone? That would be the icing on the cake of this disastrous evening.

A sudden feeling of not being able to cope washed over him, and he rubbed the heels of his hands into his tired eyes. Was he having a nervous breakdown? Fancy not remembering to call Kev before turning up on her doorstep and ringing the life out of her doorbell.

'It's okay,' said Kev, squeezing his arm in reassurance. 'I'm alone.'

'Thank God,' Charlie whispered.

He really didn't know what he would have done had *another* female made a surprise appearance tonight, least of all one who would have demanded to know why he was here and not home with Willow. He had a mental image of that female angrily standing before him, putting two and two together, and then spilling the beans to Willow. If that ever happened, then the whole precarious pack of cards that was currently Charlie's world would come crashing down. As if he wasn't in enough trouble already with Sophie. Although… no… no… he wasn't in any trouble with Sophie… he'd done a runner on her. He was safe. Sophie hadn't a clue where he lived. Charlie mentally sighed with relief. He could forget all about Sophie.

'I'm alone,' Kev repeated, interrupting his thoughts. 'My housemate had a last-minute invitation for something better than staying at home. For goodness sake, Charlie. Relax!'

Relax? How could he! The whole reason he'd diverted his

homeward journey was to tackle Kev about her anonymous phone call to Willow at the library.

'She won't suddenly show up?' he asked, glancing nervously at the front door.

'Unlikely.' Kev moved closer to him. 'Have you missed me?' she asked throatily.

Charlie caught the tone in her voice and did a double take. He recognised that look in Kev's eyes. She was coming on to him. And yes, he had missed her, which annoyed him. But he wasn't going to fall back into the trap of being putty in her hands.

'Look, Kev–'

'Oh yes, do look,' Kev purred, letting her dressing gown slip off her shoulders and drop to the floor. 'Look all you like.'

Charlie tried not to be aroused. He was immediately let down by the one-eyed trouser snake writhing into action.

'That's new,' he said, trying to divert Kev's attention away from his erection.

He pointed to the blue butterfly on her left thigh.

'Do you like it?'

'Very pretty,' he said, as Kev stepped closer and pressed her body against his hardness.

He let out an involuntary groan before sternly telling himself that he needed to focus on the real reason why he was here.

'Kev, I need to ask you a question, but you might not like it.'

She reached for the buckle on his belt.

'What?'

He grabbed her hands, forcing her to stop what she was doing and listen to him.

'Did you anonymously phone Willow at the library and tell her to leave me?'

Kev shook Charlie's hands off and carried on unbuckling his belt.

'Did you?' he repeated.

'No.'

'I'm not sure I believe you.'

'Don't be ridiculous.'

'I can't have you playing silly buggers. It's not fair on Willow.'

'Nothing to do with me,' said Kev.

The belt came away from Charlie's trousers, and Kev slapped it playfully against the palm of her hand.

'Tell me the truth,' Charlie persisted.

'I have told you the truth. This conversation is starting to bore me, darling.'

A wicked gleam had appeared in her eyes. This time she slapped the belt against him.

Charlie decided to take Kev's denial with a pinch of salt. The important thing was he'd alerted her. She knew that *he* knew what she'd done. And now he'd warned her off. He didn't think Kev would be quite so brazen as to try a stunt like that again. But there was just one more thing he needed to point out.

'Even though I'm unexpectedly here, this doesn't change

things. You haven't forgotten that we're not really seeing each other, right?'

'Of course I haven't forgotten,' she said.

Hell, if she wanted to summon Charlie again, she'd simply post another letter to the universe. Easy-peasy. Slapping him again with the belt, Kev gave him her most seductive look.

'I have chocolate body paint in my bedroom. Remember how it was last time?'

Charlie did, and he nodded. This was what he loved about Kev. The slight kinkiness. Her willingness for sexy adventure. Even though Willow had been game with the whippy cream, it wasn't the sort of fun she'd instigate. But Kev... well, she was something else. Whippy cream, chocolate, belts, boots, champagne in the hollow of her stomach... she was up for anything and everything. And so was his treacherous todger.

'I need a shower first,' he said hoarsely.

'Not a problem,' said Kev, grinning in delight. 'I'll have one with you.'

Flicking him again with the belt, she shooed him up the stairs.

Oh, she was going to have *such* a lovely time tonight. Things had worked out perfectly. She had the house all to herself, and Charlie couldn't go home to Willow. Not at this hour. And whilst Charlie might have reminded her that their relationship was currently a non-relationship, Kev knew otherwise. She was *sooo* looking forward to Charlie properly snuggling down under her duvet. And this time she was going to take loads of photographs. Of him. Of her. And of the two of them together.

Just because she could.

Chapter Forty-Nine

Willow pushed the spatula around the frying pan, turning the rashers of bacon over before expertly flipping the eggs. She tossed some mushrooms and tomatoes into another pan and quietly hummed as she jiggled the contents about.

She'd anticipated Charlie and Ben being home Sunday evening. Consequently she'd planned on enjoying a quiet afternoon by herself, maybe giving herself a manicure and pedicure, before snuggling down on the sofa with a TV dinner. Instead Charlie had turned up at noon. He'd looked tired and seemed on edge. He'd also smelt faintly of chocolate.

'Darling!' she'd exclaimed. 'How lovely. I wasn't expecting you back until much later and… oh–'

She'd broken off as Charlie had shut the front door.

'Where's Ben?'

Charlie had shrugged and made vague noises about Ben popping over to see Anna.

'House discussions, or something,' he'd lied.

Willow hadn't questioned it because she knew that Ben and Anna's split would involve lots of necessary talks. But before she could even fling her arms around Charlie for a welcome home hug, he'd darted up the stairs and locked himself in the bathroom.

'I was just going to cook myself some bacon and egg,' Willow had called up. 'Would you like some too?'

'Please,' Charlie had replied.

Moments later, Willow had heard a bath being run. Strange. Usually Charlie had a morning shower. Perhaps he'd felt hot and sticky and wanted a warm soak after being cooped up in the car on the long drive back from Birmingham.

Stooping to pick up his abandoned holdall, Willow had been surprised when Charlie had erupted out of the bathroom, belted down the stairs and snatched the bag from her.

'I'll deal with that,' he'd yelped.

'I don't mind unpacking for you,' Willow had assured.

'Thanks, but I'll do it.'

And as he'd hurtled back up the stairs clutching the holdall to his chest, she'd caught another peculiar whiff of chocolate.

Dismissing it, she turned her attention to cooking the impromptu meal. The aroma of bacon filled the kitchen and, as the eggs gave a couple of spits and spats, she found her thoughts straying back to Noah.

Willow had got quite a shock when Emma had swivelled her mobile round so that Willow had come "virtually" face-to-face with her best friend's twin. She could hear Noah's voice now. Such a husky sexy Australian drawl. And those eyes! They'd definitely had the twinkle-factor and seemed to convey any number of possibilities for flirty mischief and fun. Or was she being fanciful?

If all my sister's friends are as good looking as you, I have even more reason to visit England.

She grinned stupidly at the hissing bacon. In three months, she'd meet Noah properly. How exciting.

And why is the prospect of meeting your bestie's twin so thrilling? asked the little voice in her head.

Well, because it's wonderful for Emma, of course – Willow hastily replied – *and I'm delighted for her. That's all.*

Hm, said the little voice.

Willow ignored it and instead turned her attention to the overhead cupboard. Baked beans. She was sure there was a tin in there somewhere. Ah, there it was.

Peeling back the lid, she concentrated on spooning the beans into a saucepan, doing her best to blot out the image of Noah's handsome face. Somehow his image had branded itself on her brain.

Meanwhile, as Willow absent-mindedly stirred the beans, Charlie immersed himself in a very deep bubble bath.

Despite showering at Kev's, he was convinced he still stank of chocolate. Heaven knows what was in that stuff, but it was pungent. He realised that in the space of eighteen hours he'd been to bed with two different women and lathered himself in soap four times. At this rate he'd wash all the natural oils out of his skin. Or his willy. Or both. God, he'd end up like a prune. Perhaps his willy would shrivel up like a raisin. At least if that happened, he'd never again be able to impregnate a woman.

He gulped and reached for Willow's sponge. The reverse side was an exfoliator. He had a sudden desire to scrub himself.

Hard. As if to wash away the events of last night.

And this morning, his brain added.

He closed his eyes, trying to blot out the memory. This morning, all he'd wanted was a cup of tea. But Kev, having used up the chocolate body paint the night before, had ransacked the kitchen larder.

'Ta-da!' she'd trilled, holding up a jar of hazelnut spread.

She'd then smeared the stuff over her breasts, draped her body across the kitchen table and demanded Charlie take her. He didn't think he'd ever again be able to look at a jar of hazelnut spread without thinking of Kev's nipples impersonating two gigantic chocolate buttons.

But Charlie hadn't been able to relax. Not properly. He'd been terrified of Kev's house companion turning up. It was all very well for Kev who, he suspected, no longer gave two hoots about Willow finding out. He also believed that getting caught gave the sex extra edge for Kev. She'd certainly made a racket upon climaxing. Charlie had shocked himself by faking it. He'd pulled out and, for the second time that weekend, hurriedly put on his boxers back to front all the while asking himself what the heck he was doing? Was he some sort of adrenalin junkie getting his rocks off in as short a time as possible with as many women up for it? Or was he a sex addict? He'd heard about such people. They couldn't get enough of it. Apparently they thought about sex all day long. While one part of their brain was busy at work plotting a million-pound deal, the other was planning a grapple in the board room with the CEO's personal assistant.

You're neither of those things, said the little voice in his head.

Oh – he replied – *in which case, what am I?*

A prat, said the voice.

Charlie put down the sponge and quietly acknowledged that the little voice was speaking the truth. After all, he'd already had two lightbulb moments. How many more wake-up calls did he need?

He sank beneath the bubbles, determined that from now on nothing and no one was going to come between him and Willow. It was time to settle down. Oh my God, he couldn't believe he was thinking such thoughts. But it was true. He really was. In which case – Charlie shot up out of the bubbles swiping bathwater from his eyes – it was time to do the unthinkable. Time to ask Willow to marry him.

Chapter Fifty

Charlie went down the stairs reeking of aftershave and anti-perspirant. He'd had a hefty squirt of the latter figuring it might be required when proposing. There was no time like the present, and the last thing he wanted was his pits turning into a gushing mess.

How should he put the question to Willow? Over the baked beans? Or now, before they ate? He could almost hear Ben shrieking, "Romance, matey! A woman wants romance!" Which was all well and good for someone like Ben who'd thought nothing of impulse-buying roses for Anna – when they'd been together – or whisking her off for a surprise weekend in Paris. But Charlie was different. He wasn't the soppy type. Willow would likely feel his forehead and produce a thermometer if Charlie presented her with a passport and bouquet of flowers.

A bouquet of flowers…

That's what every bride held in her hands upon walking down the aisle.

A bouquet of flowers…

Charlie felt a wave of heat wash over him. Instantly he felt hot, bothered and a little faint. He wondered if this was what peri-menopausal women felt like. Okay. He wasn't female, but he *was* going through a change of life. For everything would surely change if Willow accepted his proposal. For starters, her name would change. She would no longer be Willow West. She'd be Mrs Charlie Goodman. Willow Goodman. And she'd wear a shiny gold ring on her left hand. And he would too.

He had a sudden image of a matching band on his third finger. Of twisting it round and round. He could even see Ben in the background watching Charlie with amusement. "What are you doing?" Ben would ask. And Charlie would look at Ben in despair and say, "Working out the combination."

Oh God. He couldn't do it.

Willow looked up as he walked into the kitchen.

'Sit down and I'll dish up.'

She clocked the chocolate-smelling laundry tightly bundled in Charlie's arms.

'Give me that and I'll put a wash on.'

'I'll do it,' he cried, scuttling over to the washing machine.

The last thing he wanted was Willow's nose twitching like a police dog as she pulled everything apart. It was one thing ignoring brown marks on underpants, but quite another when it was all over one's shirt and trousers.

He stuffed everything inside the drum, shut the door, then opened it again and retrieved his mobile. Flipping heck. That had been close. He tucked the phone into his jeans' back pocket before pressing the washing machine's start button.

Willow paused, plates of bacon and egg held aloft as she eyed Charlie speculatively. She couldn't recall the last time he'd helped her with the laundry. If ever.

'You might want to put some soap in the dispenser.'

'Ha!' he laughed. 'Silly me.'

Charlie opened the little drawer and filled it with so much liquid it threatened to spill on the floor.

'Are you feeling all right?' said Willow, setting the plates down on the table.

'Never better,' Charlie beamed.

'Only you've put your work suit in there too.'

'Have I?'

'Yes. I'm sure the label says to dry clean only.'

'Doesn't matter.'

'But you'll wreck it, darling. Turn the machine off.'

'It's fine.'

'It isn't.'

'Oh yummy,' said Charlie, desperate to divert Willow's fussing about his suit. 'Bacon and eggs. My favourite. And baked beans. Wow.'

Charlie stared at the tiny haricots floating in orange sauce as if they were something he'd never seen before.

'And look, mushrooms! And here are some–'

'Tomatoes,' said Willow, frowning. 'Charlie, are you sure you're okay? Only you're behaving rather oddly.'

'I'm fine. Really. Just fine.'

He glanced anxiously at the washing machine. The drum had now filled with foaming water and everything was sloshing about. Willow was right about the suit. It would emerge six sizes too small but smell fantastic.

Pulling out a chair, he flopped down with a sigh of relief. Picking up his knife and fork, he was about to pop a mushroom in his mouth when he realised Willow was still staring at him.

'What?' he said.

Oh God. Had he missed a bit of hazelnut spread? Did he still have a tell-tale blob somewhere? Was Willow studying his left eyebrow? His hand automatically fluttered upwards, rubbing at the hairs. He glanced at his index finger. It was clean.

'You seem very tense,' said Willow, sitting down opposite him. 'Is something on your mind?'

'Yes,' Charlie nodded.

'Want to share it with me?'

'In a bit.'

Willow's brow puckered.

'Is it anything I should be concerned about? Only you look shaken up.'

'Nonsense,' said Charlie, forcing himself to laugh. 'No nasty shocks.'

Not if you didn't include a Brummie female announcing she was carrying your child, or standing in another woman's hallway in the early hours while she sang the theme tune to Dr Who.

'I'm just tired and feeling a little warm.'

'You look hot.'

'Thanks,' said Charlie, pretending Willow had paid him a compliment.

Sweat was now beading across his forehead and upper lip.

Perhaps he should also have sprayed deodorant across his face.

'Tuck in,' he said to Willow, nodding at her plate.

She picked up her knife and fork and, still regarding him curiously, began to eat.

'Delicious,' said Charlie, attacking his food.

If he kept his mouth full, he wouldn't be able to talk. And he really didn't want to make idle chit-chat. Not right now. The last thing he needed was Willow asking questions about the trip.

'How was Birmingham?' asked Willow.

Bugger.

'Mm mm,' said Charlie, chewing frantically and pretending it wasn't convenient to speak.

Instead he stuck his thumb up indicating the trip had gone okay, all the while keeping his jaws rotating long after he'd swallowed and his mouth was empty.

'I had a nice time yesterday with Emma and Karen,' said Willow.

Charlie mentally sighed with relief. Thank God. A different subject.

'What did you get up to?' he said, feigning interest.

'We went to the tattoo parlour. Emma got herself a gorgeous butterfly inked on her thigh. The tattoo artist was pretty fit. I think Emma had the hots for him.'

'Did she now?' said Charlie.

This was good news. Perhaps the guy would ask her out.

'Do you think they might hook up?'

Willow shrugged.

'Not sure. Emma is still hung up on some fella who, for reasons she won't divulge, remains an enigma. I didn't watch her having the tattoo because I came over faint and stayed in the waiting area. However, I have it on good authority that there was lots of sizzling chemistry going on in the back room.

'Good,' said Charlie, sounding pleased.

Sizzling chemistry, eh?

He failed to notice Willow looking momentarily stricken.

Sizzling chemistry.

Was that what *she'd* felt when she'd spoken to Noah on FaceTime?

His voice had sent multiple shivers and tingles zinging up and down her spine. Just like a song you hear on the radio and then can't get out of your head, Willow had been haunted ever since by Noah's twinkling eyes and handsome face.

Charlie scraped his plate, popping a final forkful of beans in his mouth. A second later, and he was starting to regret it. Perhaps he shouldn't have eaten so many. They didn't always agree with him. A schoolboy rhyme pinged into his head.

Beans, beans,
Good for the heart,
The more you eat,
The more you fart,
And the more you fart,
The better you feel,
So eat baked beans with every meal.

But he wasn't going to fart. He was going to propose. Bugger romance. It wasn't necessary. After all, the question itself was surely romantic enough. Wasn't it? Of course it was! Willow would be gobsmacked. Amazed. Delighted. She'd probably burst into tears. The time had come. Time to do it. Now. Yes, indeed. He fidgeted in anticipation. Ouch. His phone was digging into his bum. Best remove it from his back pocket, and *then* he'd go down on one knee. Wiggling the mobile out of his jeans, Charlie placed it face-up on the table, then cleared his throat.

'Ahem. Er, Willow. You asked me earlier if… ahem, ahem… something was on my… ahem… mind.'

'Did I?' said Willow, looking up in surprise.

'Yes. You did. And… ahem… there is… ahem…'

H-e-l-p.

'Do you want a glass of water?' said Willow, pushing back her chair.

'No, no,' Charlie protested, catching her wrist. 'Sit down. I'll be all right. Just… um… a bit nervous.'

His stomach gurgled in agreement as the baked beans travelled through his intestines.

'Nervous about what?'

Come on, Charlie. Man up.

'Well,' he said, getting slowly to his feet.

He grabbed the table's edge to steady himself.

'I do indeed have something on my mind.'

'Oh?'

'Something quite momentous.'

Charlie lowered himself down on one knee.

'Willow…'

Her eyes widened. Oh. My. Goodness. Her boyfriend was down on one knee. Was he… no, surely not… but then again, could he possibly be…?

'Yes?' she said tremulously.

Before Charlie could say anything, his mobile began to ring. Ben's name lit up the display. Oh no. What did his mate want? The timing couldn't be worse. He'd let it go to voicemail. A second later, and the phone went silent.

'Willow…' Charlie repeated, just as the phone once more exploded into life.

Ben. Again. Damn, it must be important.

'One moment,' he said to Willow, lunging for the mobile.

His stomach gave another gurgle. He couldn't stay down on one knee for much longer. Gravity was playing havoc with his bowels. He'd quickly take the call from Ben, propose to Willow, and then dash to the loo.

'Hello?' he barked.

'Mate, I'm hitching a lift back to Mosley with Drummond. But before we set off, I'm giving you the heads up.'

'About what?'

'That little blonde number you were with yesterday evening. Sophie. You cleared off, but she didn't.'

'What do you mean?' said Charlie, his guts twisting with anxiety.

'She's been doing some detective work and discovered Drummond is your boss. She's threatening to tell him everything in a bid to destroy your reputation and career. Sophie has already put me in the picture. I know about the baby. She's also told me that there are two brothers and a father baying for your blood. You've got your work cut out with this one, matey.'

'Oh God,' said Charlie, paling.

'I'll talk to you when I'm back. Sophie has made a list of demands. I can tell you now that unless you meet them, you're going to be in shit street. Right, I've got to go. Drummond's coming.'

The line went dead.

Charlie grasped the phone in anguish. He looked up at Willow helplessly. She was still staring at him, apparently spellbound.

'You were saying?' she prompted.

'Willow…' he tried again.

'Yes?'

But Ben's news had upset Charlie's equilibrium. Frazzled nerves, combined with the baked beans, were producing an aching need to fart.

'Darling, will you… will you… let me go to the toilet?'

And clutching both his phone and his stomach, Charlie belted off to the bathroom.

Chapter Fifty-One

Willow was perplexed. For a moment there, Charlie had set her heart racing. After all, why did a man ever go down on one knee? Well, to ask for a girl's hand in marriage, that's why.

Except Charlie hadn't proposed. He'd simply dropped to the floor, pulled some extraordinary faces and then legged it to the loo. But… he'd said there was something on his mind. Something momentous.

Willow wondered what Charlie had been going to ask. And although he'd said it was significant, it was more likely to be something dull and boring. She could imagine Charlie now saying, "As we've had bacon, eggs and all the trimmings for lunch, could we have something light for tea? Maybe a sandwich?" Food was a big deal for some men, and maybe Charlie had considered it important?

Or perhaps he'd wanted to tell her something awful. Her eyes widened with alarm. Oh my goodness. What if Charlie had been trying to say he wanted to break up? Willow was immediately reminded of Emma confiding how her mystery boyfriend had dumped her.

'He took both my hands in his, looked deep into my eyes, and then said we needed to take a break.'

Willow had thought it strange that the mystery man had taken Emma's hands in his. It was an action of affection, after all. But Emma had dismissed the notion.

'He probably held my hands so I couldn't whack him,' she'd quipped.

But maybe Charlie had gone down on one knee for neither of those reasons. Perhaps he'd done it to simply relieve some intestinal wind. Well, whatever the reason, it couldn't have been to propose. After all, it was only eight days ago – her birthday dinner no less – that she'd tentatively raised the subject of marriage to him. And look how that had turned out. Charlie had reversed away so quickly he could have beaten Usain Bolt in a running backwards race.

Bemused, Willow stood up. Dumping the lunch plates in the sink, she then set about cleaning the hob.

Upstairs in the bathroom, Charlie's bowels reflected the torment he was in. He wanted to know the full story about Sophie. How had she discovered that Drummond was Charlie's boss? He prayed Sophie wouldn't wreck his career. She couldn't really do that, could she? Charlie considered for a moment. Right now, Ben was probably with Drummond. However, Charlie didn't want to wait another second. He needed to know what the heck had been going on in Birmingham since his hasty departure. Even though Drummond would now be in the car with Ben, perhaps he could somehow speak to Ben in code. Charlie frowned. Maybe he could ask loads of questions aimed at whittling out the truth while Ben simply answered "yes" or "no". Right, good idea.

Ben answered his phone almost immediately.

'Hey, matey. How is Willow feeling?'

Ben was speaking in a very hearty manner. Overly hearty. Charlie instantly deduced that Ben was close to Drummond. Like… a handbrake's proximity. If the signal was good, Drummond might even be able to overhear what Charlie was saying. Charlie took his cue from Ben and played along.

'She's not so good,' Charlie replied, just as his bowels gave another noisy lurch.

Heavens, at this rate he'd be solely responsible for accelerating global warming.

'I'm with her now. You know, offering support and reassuring her. It's probably one of those nasty twenty-four-hour things, but Willow felt like she was dying last night. I had no choice but to rush home.'

'Mr Drummond says you did the right thing,' Ben assured. 'He also says he's sorry you were unable to attend this morning's meeting, but he's very impressed that you're so caring. I've told him that you're devoted to Willow, and that nothing can get in the way when it comes to her well-being. Not even an important work convention.'

Charlie could sense Ben nodding away in the passenger seat of Drummond's car.

'Oh absolutely, although I had to really wrestle with my conscience. After all, I love my job. And the company. I even love' – Charlie grimaced – 'Mr Drummond. I'll do everything I can to secure that next important client. That next target breakthrough. But Willow is my ultimate priority. I'd lay my life down for her. There's never been anyone else.'

Steady on, Charlie. Don't overdo it or Drummond might smell a rat.

'Mr Drummond asks me to convey his best wishes to Willow for a speedy recovery. Oh… hang on a moment, Charlie.'

There was a pause as Ben conferred with their boss. Charlie strained to hear what was happening. There came the sound of a car's engine stalling. No, wait. It had been switched off.

'A cappuccino to take away would be very nice, Mr Drummond. Thank you.'

Now a car door was opening. Seconds later it had clunked shut.

Ben let out a gusty sigh.

'I can talk, but probably only for five minutes max.'

'Where's Drummond gone?'

'We've pulled into a garage. The car needs diesel. Then he's going to grab us coffee to have on the go.'

'Then don't waste a second,' Charlie hissed.

He lowered his voice, just in case Willow was lurking on the other side of the bathroom door.

'Tell me what's been happening with Sophie.'

'Okay. There I was minding my own business and enjoying some breakfast at the hotel, when this woman crashed into the dining room. She was breathing heavily. Like she'd run a marathon or something. She was scanning the diners in such an intense way she reminded me of Arnie in *The*

Terminator. Her eyes locked on mine and suddenly she was striding over. Thankfully the others were in the buffet queue, so I was on my own. I recognised her instantly. It was the girl you went off with on Saturday night.'

'Shit,' said Charlie, as his bowels promptly obliged.

'She demanded to know where you were.'

'To which you said, "I have no idea what you're talking about,"' Charlie prompted.

'I told her the truth,' said Ben evenly. 'I said you'd gone home. She said, "To his sister? Willow?" And I said, "No, to his *partner*, Willow." And I can tell you now, matey, she looked so livid I thought her head was going to rotate three-hundred-and-sixty degrees. Either that or she'd start speaking in tongues.'

'Right. So that bit of news didn't go down well.'

'It most certainly didn't,' Ben agreed. 'And then she said she knew which company had been using the hotel's business facilities. Apparently her cousin has a friend who has an aunty who has a bestie who works at the hotel, and was happy to discreetly breach the Data Protection Act and supply Sophie with our company's details.'

'Bugger,' Charlie groaned.

'Even worse, she's also been given a list of every employee who has attended this weekend *and* every employee's address.'

'What?' Charlie yelped.

'Sophie also knows that Drummond is your boss.'

'Can't you tell her that I gave a false address. That I've moved. That you have no idea where I am because… I know… I've been fired from the company?'

'Mate, don't even jest about getting fired. She's threatening to tell Drummond everything. To bring your name into disrepute. She's already given him some chat-up.'

'You're kidding,' Charlie hissed.

'Sadly not. She sought Drummond out and told him she was a relative of yours.'

'Oh my God,' Charlie groaned.

'Don't panic. At least, not for now. However, Drummond thinks she's delightful and gave away loads of info about you. He told her all about Willow and what a lovely girl she was. Sophie made out she used to work with her.'

Charlie clutched his head in horror.

'Anyway, Sophie has told me to tell you that you need to cough up. She wants you to pay to fix her situation. She also wants a recuperation period. Somewhere hot and sunny. Dubai was mentioned. Oh, and not just for her, but also with her mother and sister. She says she needs them with her for support. She also said that if you don't meet her very reasonable demands, she won't hesitate to tell Drummond what a scumbag you are. Even worse, she'll turn up on your doorstep and tell Willow.'

'Do you think she's telling a pack of lies and trying to pull a fast one.'

'Mate, I have no idea. All I know is that she's got you by the short and curlies.'

'B-But,' Charlie stammered. 'This will cost me a small fortune.'

'Then don't give in to her demands.'

'But what if she carries out her threat and tells Willow?'

'It doesn't matter what she tells Willow, if *you* tell Willow first.'

'I can't do that,' said Charlie, appalled. 'Willow would dump me.'

'She'll dump you anyway if she finds out about this. Better to hear it from you, than some woman turning up in a billowing maternity dress.'

Charlie thought he might actually puke.

'N-No. I'm not telling Willow anything. I'll pay Sophie off. It will be worth every penny.'

'You're so caring,' said Ben sarcastically.

'Hey, don't be like that,' said Charlie in annoyance. 'What would you do in my position?'

'Mate, I'd have put a sock on it and been more responsible.'

'Yeah, okay. Says the man who was seeing another woman while he was still living with Anna.'

'Don't try and score cheap points,' said Ben in annoyance. 'At least I did the honourable thing and told the girl in question that I was living with someone else. It's not like we slept together. It was completely innocent in that sense. And anyway, I'm now apart from Anna, and I still haven't resumed things with the lady because I don't want it to be a rebound. So don't compare me to you, mate. I love you like a brother, Charlie, but sometimes you can be such an arsehole.'

'Okay, okay,' said Charlie placatingly. 'I asked for that.

Sorry.'

'Apology accepted,' said Ben.

He wasn't one to hold grudges.

'Did Sophie say anything else?' asked Charlie.

'She did.'

'What?'

'That you remind her of toilet paper.'

'Eh?'

'Because you're the sort of bloke who never appreciates what he's got until it's gone.'

'Right,' said Charlie, reaching for the toilet paper.

He tugged on the roll. It delivered two sheets before turning into an empty cardboard cylinder. Charlie stared at it. He'd run out of toilet paper. It eerily echoed Sophie's comment. But she hadn't been completely right with her mocking words. Okay, yes, maybe Charlie *had* been the sort of bloke who'd never appreciated what he'd got until it had gone, but *now* he was a reformed character. And he was going to prove it.

Just as soon as he managed to get off this damn toilet.

Chapter Fifty-Two

Unbeknownst to Willow, Charlie had a secret stash of money.

Throughout his years working for Drummond, Charlie had assisted many clients. He'd helped them thwart the Inland Revenue as much as was legally possible. Sometimes there were blurred lines between tax avoidance and tax evasion, but Charlie had always managed to create a middle ground. He was proud of the fact that not one of his clients had ever been investigated by HMRC. Whether advising sole traders to register as a corporation in order to reduce their tax bill, or whether concocting a legitimate inheritance tax plan, Charlie knew that where there was a financial will, there was a way. Apart from being rewarded with an excellent salary, he also enjoyed twice yearly bonuses. It was the latter that Willow knew nothing about.

Charlie had put the bonuses "in a safe place" and watched them grow. He had a vague notion about what he'd one day spend it on… a moment of madness blowing the whole lot in a Vegas casino. Or buying a sports car. Or even a desert island. They were more affordable than people thought. Although perhaps scrap that last idea. Desert islands didn't have Sky Sport. But never had Charlie anticipated spending a five-figure sum on a woman he'd only met twice.

In the days that followed *Sophiegate*, Charlie's head had been like an overstuffed washing machine threatening to blow the door off. He'd sought to relieve his stress by drinking too much, so much so that Willow had raised one eyebrow and asked Charlie if he'd received word that the grape harvest had failed.

Charlie's solicitor had produced a hastily drawn up document. In exchange for Sophie receiving a lump sum, she'd had to agree to three conditions. Firstly, she would never contact Charlie, Willow, or anyone at Charlie's workplace. Secondly, she would never reveal the financial arrangement, or the reasons for it, to anyone. Thirdly, any breach of the contract would cause the lump sum to be repaid with interest and compensation. She'd signed on the dotted line, taken the money, and told Charlie to go to hell. Ultimately, he was simply grateful to have gotten away with it by the skin of his very white teeth.

As time went by, Charlie had felt himself slowly relaxing. Life was peaceful again, and he was loving it. He considered himself a changed character. He didn't need man-trappers like Sophie, or sex-mad nutcases like Kev. He'd received some texts from Kev testing the water for resuming their affair.

Tonight. You and me. I have chocolate body paint. Let's get saucy!

He'd not replied.

Lick and tease! We'll work off those chocolate calories!

Charlie had hit the trash icon.

Sorry, sweetie. Sorry, sorry, sorry. I just miss you so much. I can't stop thinking about us together. I've never had this kind of connection before.

Charlie had replied to this last text somewhat curtly.

The connection is now a disconnection.

And then he'd blocked Kev's number.

The only woman Charlie wanted was the one who'd been by his side all along. He'd told Ben of his plans to propose to Willow and received a good reaction.

'At last!' Ben had whooped. 'You've finally come to your senses. Grown up. Admittedly it's taken a few decades for you to get there. But, as they say, better late than never. When are you going to ask her?'

'This weekend,' Charlie had smiled. 'Saturday night, to be precise. Do you think Willow will say yes?'

Ben had looked at his friend and been astonished to see the sudden anxiety in Charlie's eyes.

'Of course she'll say yes,' he'd assured. 'Just promise me two things.'

'What?'

'You'll never behave like a dog with six dicks again.'

'I promise. What's the second thing?'

'That you let me be your best man.'

'Agreed,' Charlie had said with a grin.

'When are you hoping to get hitched?'

'Soon.'

'How soon?'

And Charlie had grinned.

'I've been making discreet enquiries at one of the most romantic wedding venues outside London.'

'Not Goldhill Grange!'

Charlie had smirked.

'Yup. Sweeping entrance. Beautiful gardens. Lavish accommodation. Can't go wrong.'

'And when's it going to happen?'

'I was thinking of a Christmas wedding.'

'Nice. Gives you just over a year to plan it.'

'No, no, no, matey. I'm talking *this* Christmas. And they just happen to have had a cancellation for Saturday the seventh of December.'

'Oh my goodness. Have you reserved the date?'

And Charlie's smirk had turned into a full-blown grin as he'd high-fived Ben.

There had then followed lots of manly back clapping and congratulations, but Ben had suddenly clamped a hand to his mouth in horror. He'd protested that he couldn't possibly continue living under Charlie and Willow's roof when they'd be embarking on life as newlyweds. He'd then set about making alternative accommodation arrangements. But Fate had lent a hand.

The following day Ben had surprised Charlie with the news that Anna had successfully re-mortgaged in order to buy Ben out. Consequently, Ben was now able to proceed with his newbuild purchase *and* a whole year sooner than anticipated. Apparently the property sales team at Ebbsfleet Valley had been in touch. The sale of the last apartment on Phase 2 had fallen through. They'd told Ben it was his if he wanted it. Ben had said he did… and as soon as possible.

'So I'll be out of your hair long before you shake off the confetti,' Ben had laughed.

'Does this mean you'll be rekindling your romance with Mystery Woman?' Charlie had asked.

'Maybe,' Ben had said coyly.

Charlie had never felt happier. Sophie had gone. Kev was out of the equation. Ben would shortly be moving into his bachelor pad. Finally, Charlie's secret stash of money remained buoyant enough to pay for Willow's ring, a modest wedding and even a honeymoon in the Bahamas. Life was good.

For now.

Chapter Fifty-Three

Monday rolled around and, as the day got underway, Charlie was delighted that it was boring as hell. As was Tuesday and Wednesday. There was no summons to Drummond's office asking for an explanation about a tearful pregnant girl who'd rung his private line. Nor were there any messages from Kev.

Charlie had been twitchy about Kev making a second anonymous phone call to Willow at the library. He wouldn't have put it past her to whisper further commands that Willow dump him. Happily, the only memorable telephone call Willow had dealt with had been from an embarrassed OAP. Apparently the pensioner's puppy had destroyed a library book about dog training.

'I don't think my dog liked it,' the pensioner had laughed.

On Thursday, Ben took himself off to Cornwall telling Willow and Charlie he wanted a long weekend with his parents.

Friday was so non-eventful that Charlie could have kissed the ground.

Come Saturday, his mood had reached an all-time high. The working week was over, and he and Willow had the house all to themselves.

He'd caught her around the waist and pulled her back to bed for some impromptu sex. There had been no one to listen to them, no chocolate body paint had featured, and nothing out of the ordinary had occurred other than a text message from Charlie's mother asking if he could pop round when convenient as she had some lightbulbs that needed replacing.

'Shall I come with you?' Willow asked, still languishing under the duvet.

'No need,' said Charlie, heading off to the bathroom.

Willow lay back against the pillows and listened to her boyfriend cleaning his teeth. She hadn't seen Charlie's mum, Grace, for a little while. She also knew that Grace was finding widowhood lonely. Willow debated whether she should stop lazing under the cosy cover and visit Grace too. Her conscience won and she flung back the quilt.

'I feel so guilty,' she called to Charlie as she pushed her feet into her slippers. 'I'll come with you. Give me a moment and I'll quickly get dressed.'

'No!' said Charlie, reappearing in the bedroom doorway. 'Honestly, it's very thoughtful of you, but I… have some errands to do.'

'That's okay. I'll keep you company. Perhaps we can go for coffee when you've finished.'

'Actually' – Charlie was now looking shifty – 'the errands are… personal.'

Willow regarded her boyfriend in surprise. What could be so private that Charlie didn't want her around? Valentine's Day wasn't on the horizon, her birthday had been and gone, and there were still ninety-four shopping days to Christmas. Willow was perplexed.

'What are you up to?' she laughed, pulling on her dressing gown.

'Something nice,' Charlie replied as he started to dress. 'But it's a surprise.'

'What sort of surprise?'

'I told you. A nice one.'

'Give me a hint,' said Willow playfully. 'Just a teeny-tiny clue, eh?'

'Okay,' said Charlie, looking mighty pleased with himself as he buttoned up his shirt. 'It involves glamming up.'

'For what?' said Willow, her brows knitting together.

Even when Charlie had taken her out on her birthday, it had been low-key. Her boyfriend didn't take her to places that required *proper* dressing up. He never had. And likely never would.

Charlie zipped up his jeans and shrugged on a jacket. Bobbing forward, he kissed Willow on the nose.

'I'll be back at about seven this evening for a quick shower and change.'

'*Seven*?' said Willow in astonishment. 'But that's hours away. You can't be changing lightbulbs at your mum's all day long.'

'I told you. I have some other things to do.' He gave her a mischievous wink. 'All will be revealed later. So, when I come home, I expect you to be dressed in… oooh, I know, that little black number with the side splits that go all the way up to your armpits.'

'Okay,' said Willow in bemusement.

She'd only worn that dress once, and that had been on a girls' night out with Emma and Karen. She was amazed Charlie even remembered it.

After Charlie had sauntered out of the house, whistling merrily, Willow had some breakfast. Munching her way through some toast, she decided to give Emma a call.

'Hi,' said her bestie, a moment later. 'What are you up to?'

'Not a lot,' Willow replied. 'I suppose I could do some housework, but it can keep until tomorrow. Charlie's gone out but he won't tell me where.'

Emma's antenna pricked up and began quivering. What was Charlie up to?

'Is it a good thing he's gone out, or a bad thing?' she asked carefully.

'Oh, definitely a good thing,' Willow chirped. 'He told me he'll be back early evening and that I should be glammed up to go somewhere special. He said he has a surprise.'

Emma felt a stab of anxiety. She had a sneaking suspicion what this could be about. If she was right, a diamond solitaire would heavily feature. She *so* hoped her intuition was wrong.

'Well, rather a nice surprise than a nasty one,' said Emma, forcing herself to sound cheerful. 'Hey, if you're happy enough to leave the housework until tomorrow, how about we hang out together for a bit? I'm meeting Noah. You can say hello to him.'

'Noah?' said Willow in surprise. 'I thought he wasn't

coming to England until December.'

'Ah. When I say I'm *meeting* him, I mean a FaceTime session. We're hooking up in about an hour. I was heading into Mosley for a coffee anyway. The last thing I want is Mum overhearing me and Noah chatting. She's still blanking Noah on spending Christmas with us.'

'Really?'

'Yup.'

'But why?'

'Because she's a bitch,' Emma scowled.

Willow was shocked at the harshness of her friend's tone.

'I still don't understand your mum's problem over Noah.'

'There isn't a problem,' said Emma, frustration creeping into her tone. 'The "problem" is in Mum's head. She feels guilty for having nothing to do with Noah all these years.'

'Nobody is going to judge her. And surely not Noah! After all, he's making every effort to see Karen – I mean, your mum. So much so that he wants to spend Christmas in England with you both.'

'Much as I love my mother, I don't like her,' said Emma frankly. 'To be honest, I think she needs to see a counsellor and have a chat about it. Anyway, enough about her. Let's make today about us. Meet me in Franco's. We'll have a lovely gossip with Noah, without my flipping mother flouncing about in a strop.'

'Is your mum really that grumpy at the moment?'

'Dreadful. She'd probably snap out of it if she found herself a decent guy. Someone grounded. There must be a man somewhere on the planet who can help her forget a thirty-year guilt complex about giving away her son.'

'And what about you?' said Willow carefully. 'Any fresh developments on the romance scene?'

'Nope,' said Emma with a sigh. 'I guess I have to face the fact that my last man was a plonker.'

Willow suddenly felt awful. Here she was burbling about glamming up for Charlie and the anticipation of a nice surprise, when all Emma had to look forward to was chatting with Noah – and even that had to be done behind Karen's back.

'Okay, I'll see you soon in Franco's,' said Willow.

Ringing off, Willow realised her initial excitement over Charlie's surprise had dimmed. Instead she was feeling a different sort of thrill. A sense of anticipation. As she slipped off her dressing gown and went to her wardrobe, Willow rifled through the coat hangers looking for a pair of jeans. She was astonished to see that her hands were trembling as they fluttered along the clothes rail. Now why was that?

Plucking a pair of distressed denims from a hanger, she tried to ignore the fact that her earlier joy about Charlie's secret surprise had faded like a boat disappearing over the horizon. Instead Willow was filled with a sense of buzzy excitement.

She was going to speak to Noah.

Chapter Fifty-Four

Willow parked opposite Franco's coffee shop. The café had a huge bay-fronted picture window. Peering through her car's windscreen, Willow could see that Emma was already inside. Judging from her animated expression and extravagant hand gestures, Willow deduced Emma was already chatting with Noah.

Willow's stomach gave a delicious flutter of anticipation. Heavens, she felt like a teenager about to go on a date with her first love.

Get a grip, woman! the little voice in her head scolded. *This is Emma's brother. And as she's like a sister to you, it's practically incestuous having a crush on her twin.*

Willow inhaled sharply. Was that what she'd got then? A crush on Noah?

Oh, do stop trying to analyse your reaction. You've been down this path before. We've already had this conversation. It's just a bit of chemistry, right? People experience it all the time. It's nothing to get in a flap about.

Willow gathered up her handbag and got out the car. With her mind full of spine-tingling thoughts about Noah, she found a gap between parked vehicles to cross the road.

Yes, of course people experienced chemistry from time to time with another person. But should they really be quite so thrilled about talking to a person they'd never even met?

Stepping off the pavement, the sound of a lorry's squealing brakes duetting with a blaring horn, nearly had Willow rocketing out of her ankle boots. Now a window was buzzing down.

'Oi, Blondie!' yelled the apoplectic driver.

'W-What?' stammered Willow, clutching her chest.

She craned her neck upwards. A furious middle-aged man was glaring down at her.

'Did you know that I'm addicted to brake fluid?' he snarled. 'Fortunately I can stop whenever I want. That's a lame joke, but it's how I cope when a ditzy person like you decides to cross a road without looking.'

'I'm so s-sorry,' Willow stuttered.

Blimey. That had been a close one. She really must concentrate, or she'd have a premature arrival at the Pearly Gates.

'Look where you're going in future,' snapped the driver. 'You've just aged me ten years.'

'I'm truly very sor–'

But the lorry driver wasn't interested in her apology. Tutting, he roared off leaving Willow feeling very shaken. To her embarrassment, everyone inside the coffee shop had witnessed her near demise. All eyes were upon her as she wobbled across the road on jelly legs. By the time she'd pushed open Franco's door, her face was crimson with humiliation.

'Flipping heck,' squawked Emma, as Willow slumped down in the seat opposite. 'Are you all right? Wait. Stupid question. I can see you're not okay. You're shaking like washing pegged out in a hurricane. Here' – she pressed her phone into Willow's trembling hand – 'talk to Noah while I get you a cup of tea with lots of sugar.'

Willow was now vibrating so much from delayed shock, she wondered if she might judder right off her seat. As her eyes found Noah's, she just *knew* that her red face was deepening to magenta.

'What happened?' said Noah, looking concerned.

'I n-nearly g-got run over,' gasped Willow.

How embarrassing. She couldn't speak properly. Her teeth were chattering so much, she probably looked like she was wearing joke dentures that came out of a Christmas cracker.

'Was the driver not looking where he was going?' questioned Noah.

His initial look of alarm had changed to one of outrage.

'Er...'

Willow trailed off. She could hardly tell Noah that it had been *her* fault for being distracted due to her brain being stuffed with thoughts about *him*.

'Hey, look, the main thing is you're alive. It's not your time to go anywhere just yet. And thank goodness. Because I really *do* want to meet you, Willow.'

Once again she found herself enthralled with that sexy accent. And hearing Noah say her name made Willow think she might just keel right over. Her head was definitely getting closer to Franco's wooden tabletop. Perhaps her face would crash down on Emma's screen, and land squarely on Noah's image. And then, despite being thousands of miles apart, ironically they'd be cheek to cheek. A classic case of "so near and yet so far". She felt a giggle shoot out of her mouth. Oh God. She was losing the plot.

'Whoops-a-daisy,' said Emma.

She grabbed Willow's sagging shoulders with one hand as the other set down a cup of tea. Brown liquid slopped into the saucer.

'Let's get you sitting up properly. There we go. Sip. And another one. Good girl. How are you feeling now?'

Willow leant back in her seat as the sugary tea got to work.

'Better,' she nodded.

'Good,' said Emma, releasing her.

She slid into the seat opposite and retrieved her mobile.

'Drama over,' she said to Noah. 'Let me prop you against the condiments so both Willow and I can see you.'

'You've put me against the tomato sauce.' Noah protested. 'Oh well, I shall relish the fact that you've mustard up the courage to ketchup to my level,' he deadpanned.

Willow burst out laughing.

'That is a truly terrible joke,' she said, taking another slurp of sweet tea.

She was relieved that her hand was now completely steady even if, paradoxically, her aortic valves were in pandemonium. It felt like a trampolining gymnast had taken up residence in her ribcage.

'I do love a terrible joke,' said Noah winking. 'I can't wait to say hello properly and charm you with my Australian humour.'

'I shall look forward to it,' said Willow.

And she meant it. With a pang, she realised that December seemed light years away. How she wished she could do what Emma did, and just casually pick up her mobile and chat to Noah whenever she wanted. She gazed at the digital image before her, greedily drinking in his face. Those twinkling eyes. That slow, sexy smile. That mouth. Mm. She wondered what his lips might feel like against hers, and what he'd be like to kiss.

Ahem. Excuse me. I can't believe you just imagined kissing this guy. Outrageous!

Willow ignored the little voice in her head. There was nothing wrong in idly fantasising about kissing another man. It was just the chemistry thing. That had already been established.

Oh really? So if it's just a 'chemistry thing', why are you now eyeballing his shirt and admiring the dark hair peeking over the top of that button?

Willow could feel herself getting hot again, and it was nothing to do with the sweet tea and everything to do with her wretched conscience. Why were her thoughts suddenly skittering off and becoming erotic? Even as she asked herself this question, she couldn't tear her eyes away from Noah's shirt buttons.

Now she was imagining her fingers creeping into that tantalising opening and ripping the shirt apart, sending buttons scattering everywhere as she greedily feasted her gaze on Noah's bare chest… which would be sprinkled with *just* the right amount of hair… and pecs toned *just* the way she liked… his warm hands giving *just* the right touch… for *just* the perfect kiss and introduction to foreplay–

Foreplay? Geez, get a grip, woman.

'Willow?' said Emma, looking at her curiously.

'Fabulous,' she said brightly.

'Really?' said Emma, looking both surprised and pleased.

'I shall look forward to it,' said Noah.

He was looking delighted. Willow wondered why.

'Your guy won't mind, will he?' Noah asked.

'My guy?' Willow queried.

'Charlie,' Emma prompted. 'Your boyfriend.'

She was looking at Willow carefully.

'Remember him?'

'Oh, *that* Charlie,' said Willow, rolling her eyes theatrically and playing for time.

What had Emma and Noah been talking about?

'So Charlie definitely won't mind?' Emma prompted.

Willow looked at her friend in confusion. Oh dear. This was just typical of her. Zoning out. Having a little daydream… and a delicious daydream at that. Well, whatever they'd been discussing, it couldn't be an issue.

'Of course Charlie won't mind,' she said, giving a dismissive laugh, as if the very idea of Charlie minding about *anything* was preposterous.

'Then he must be a very magnanimous guy,' said Noah,

giving her such a blowtorch smile she thought her eyelashes might self-combust. Emma was now giving her a sly look. Willow ignored it.

'Bro, my battery is running low. We're going to have to end our FaceTime.'

'Catch you later, sis,' said Noah. He put up a hand in farewell. 'Lots of love.'

'Love right back,' said Emma.

Willow gave Noah a dinky wave. She only just managed to stop herself from saying, "Lots of love from me too."

The screen went blank.

'Well you're certainly full of surprises,' said Emma speculatively.

'What do you mean?'

Emma gave her a look that Willow couldn't quite work out. Pleased? Hopeful? No, more… triumphant. Yes. That was it. Definitely triumphant. Like she'd just played an ace card and was all set to steal the game.

'My brother said that when he gets to England, he'd like to take you out to dinner,' Emma winked. 'And you just agreed.'

Chapter Fifty-Five

Willow looked at Emma in shock.

'What? Are you sure?'

'Quite sure. I think your earlier flirtation with death has upset your marbles. Are you sure Charlie won't mind you having dinner with another man?'

Willow was so aghast at what she'd just let herself in for, she failed to see the way Emma was intently staring at her. If Willow had noticed, she would have spotted her friend looking like a world class chess player... one who'd just executed a move that put all her pieces in the right place.

Willow didn't know how to extricate herself from what she'd inadvertently agreed to. She didn't want to make Charlie out to be possessive. Because he wasn't. Well, she didn't *think* he was. He'd never been bothered by Willow dressing up and going out on a girls' night. If anything, he'd looked almost ecstatic each time he'd waved her off.

'Of course Charlie won't mind,' said Willow defensively. 'He'd probably love to come too.'

'I'm sure he wouldn't,' Emma mumbled.

'What did you say?'

Emma cleared her throat.

'Listen, Willow. I think Noah likes you.'

'Sure. And I like him. He seems very affable.'

'No, I mean, he *likes* you.'

Willow stared at Emma.

'Don't be ridiculous.'

'I'm not.'

Emma was closely studying Willow's body language.

'And, um, might I dare suggest that you like him too?'

Willow's mouth dropped open. Had her "chemistry" feelings been so obvious?

'Now you're being absurd,' she protested. 'I'm living with Charlie. And blissfully happy.'

'Are you?' said Emma, pouncing on Willow's last sentence.

She was aware that her heart had started to pound unpleasantly. This was unchartered territory. Emma had never dared to ask Willow outright if she was truly happy with Charlie, or whether she ever suspected him of playing away. But suddenly Emma couldn't bear not knowing any longer. Charlie hadn't yet walked away from Willow. Could it be that Noah might instead be the catalyst for Willow walking away from Charlie? Emma could only hope so as she continued watching Willow's reaction to her question.

'Well of course I'm happy,' said Willow, giving a strangled laugh.

'How's your sex life?' said Emma.

Oh, my goodness. Now she really was crossing a line.

Willow gaped at Emma.

'What sort of question is that?'

'A nosy one,' Emma admitted.

'My sex life is fine, thanks.'

'Honestly?'

This hadn't been the answer Emma had expected.

'I know we're best friends, Ems,' – Willow adopted a cautious tone – 'and that we share almost anything. I know we've laughed together at girly parties. The sort where dildos get passed around, and the best impression of sending a guy to heaven wins fluffy handcuffs. But I do draw the line at you prying into what goes on in my bedroom.'

Emma put her hands up in a gesture of surrender.

'Hey, I was only asking.'

'Why?' Willow persisted.

Emma realised her friend was rattled. Unusually so? Or was that just wishful thinking on her part?

'Because' – she shrugged helplessly – 'you accepted a date with my brother. It just got me thinking that maybe you weren't happy with Charlie.'

Even as she offered an explanation, Emma realised it sounded lame.

'I haven't' – Willow posted quotation marks in the air – '"accepted a date" with Noah. To be honest, I don't even remember him asking if I'd like to go for dinner. However, as you have already pointed out, I've not been myself since having a narrow escape with that lorry. But that doesn't mean I'm about to dump my *partner*' – Willow emphasised – 'and run off with a man I've never met. Apart from anything else, you're way off beam about Noah. He's coming to England to reconnect with you and your mum. An invitation to join him for dinner is just a platonic extension of easing himself into the community. I'm sure he'd be thrilled to meet Charlie. Hey, Charlie can introduce Ben too. I'm sure Noah would much prefer a night out with a couple of football-mad lads than some ditzy blonde who can't even cross a road without causing a drama.'

Willow rattled to a stop. Her cheeks felt pink with indignation and her breath was coming in short gasps.

The lady doth protest too much, methinks, sneered the little voice in her head.

And you can shut up, she crossly retorted.

'Well I'm glad we've sorted that out,' said Emma.

'There was nothing *to* sort out,' said Willow huffily. 'In fact, the next time you talk to Noah, give him my apologies and tell him I'm unable to accept his invitation. I don't want any misunderstandings.'

'Okay, okay,' Emma protested. 'I'll be sure to tell him, although there's really no need to be so prickly.' She decided to change tack. 'Anyway, I was only teasing you about Noah.'

Best to back down. She'd given matchmaking her best shot and it had backfired. Not only was Charlie *not* leaving Willow, but clearly Willow had no intention of leaving Charlie either. For a minute or so, the two women didn't say anything. Willow was the first to break the silence.

'Sorry, Ems,' she said. 'I didn't mean to bite your head off. I know you meant well.'

Emma gave Willow a weak smile. If only she knew the half of it.

Chapter Fifty-Six

As promised, Charlie returned home just before seven. Stepping into the hallway, he hummed the opening tunes to Vivaldi's *Four Seasons* and went upstairs looking extremely pleased with himself.

Pausing on the landing, he clocked Willow through the open bedroom door and let out a low wolf whistle.

'You look gorgeous, darling.'

And he meant it. Why was he only just appreciating how beautiful his girlfriend was? Every time he looked at Willow, Charlie realised how much he'd taken for granted what he'd had all along. His experience with Kev combined with the steep learning curve over Sophie had him constantly looking at Willow with fresh eyes. Everything that had gone before was irrelevant. The only thing that mattered now was the future.

'In fact' – Charlie stepped into the bedroom with a gleam in his eye – 'I think we have time for a quick sesh.'

'Oh no you don't,' said Willow, putting up her hands and creating an instant barrier between them. 'You're not wrecking my make-up just before we go out.'

'Okay, but I'm giving you fair warning now that I'll be wrecking it later. Starting with that luscious lipstick. I can't wait to kiss it all off.'

Willow giggled.

'Go and get in the shower. Perhaps you should make it a cold one.'

Charlie disappeared into the bathroom leaving Willow feeling bemused. She'd never known her boyfriend to be in such good humour. Whatever he'd arranged for tonight had clearly made him very happy. She just hoped it made her happy too, and that it wasn't a "buttering up" ploy in order to ask something of her that she wouldn't be too thrilled about.

The last time Charlie had been so attentive had been prior to telling her he was off on a stag weekend to Scotland. He'd assured Willow that he and the lads would be indulging in golf and a few innocent beers. The reality had been the stag drunkenly hooking up with a prostitute that someone had jokingly hired for the night, and Charlie nearly getting arrested for being naked from the waist down in public.

Willow had been unamused when Anna had accidentally let these details slip at one of her interminable dinner parties. Nor had she been able to get to the bottom of why Charlie had peeled off his boxers and trousers. At the time, Ben had given Anna a furious look as if to say, "Did you *really* have to tell Willow that?". Later, when home, Willow had pressed Charlie for details, but he'd feigned amnesia and airily said that none of it mattered because Ben had looked after him. As always. Good old Ben.

As Willow now reflected on the memory, she realised there'd been several occasions where Ben had stayed sober, but

Charlie had enjoyed one too many beverages and ended up in "situations". He'd always strenuously denied these situations being of his own making. Hm. Willow's curiosity deepened about what tonight was really about.

Charlie came out of the bathroom, a towel wound around his hips. A second later it had been dumped on the bed. Willow sighed and removed it, as she'd done a thousand times before. She left Charlie getting dressed and went to the bathroom. Folding the towel over the heated rail, she didn't linger to tidy up shampoo and conditioner bottles or wash away a puddle of toothpaste froth in the sink. The room was full of steam and she didn't want her carefully waved hair turning into a frizz-bomb.

Walking back to the bedroom, Willow selected a pair of high heels from the wardrobe.

'I'll be downstairs putting my shoes on,' she said.

Charlie looked up. Seeing the stilettoes, he nodded his approval.

'You can keep them on later,' he said with a wink.

'My pleasure,' she said, winking back.

He was definitely up to something. Ah well. Not much longer to find out. Turning on her heel, Willow went downstairs.

Slipping her feet into the strappy heels, Willow briefly admired her crimson toenails. She'd painted her fingernails in the same shade. Even her lipstick matched. It was colour-coded "Scarlet Woman". Not that Willow was a scarlet woman. She was a good girl. But right now, with the overhead light giving the illusion of a halo circling her hair, she looked like a very beautiful fallen angel. Charlie was almost visibly drooling when he came down the stairs.

'If I hadn't put so much effort into tonight, I'd drag you upstairs right now,' he said hoarsely.

My goodness, Willow was a stunner. Yet again Charlie was bewildered at how he'd failed to see what was under his nose all along. Compared to his girlfriend, Kev, Sophie and all the others were nothing more than a bunch of Plain Janes.

'I don't look that different,' Willow protested. 'It's just the dress.'

'And your lippy.'

'It's a new shade. Do you like it?'

'I love it,' he said. 'Your lips look like two rubies.'

Oh my God, *what* had he just said? That had to be the naffest compliment he'd ever paid a woman. Willow was looking at him like he'd turned into an alien who'd suggested beaming her up to Planet Knobhead.

'Are you feeling okay, Charlie?'

'Fine,' he said, clearing his throat. 'Let's go.'

He opened the front door and indicated she step outside first. Willow marvelled at Charlie's chivalry. When had he ever done that before? Never.

The cool evening air wrapped itself around her shoulders like a soft pashmina. She waited for Charlie to lock up and then accepted his proffered elbow. Wow. Nor could she remember the last time he'd invited her to link arms. Very gallant. And strange. And thoroughly out of character.

Willow was even more surprised when Charlie drove her to Goldhill Grange. She and Emma had often salivated about this jewel of a hotel promising themselves that, one day, they'd go there and treat themselves to a girly afternoon tea.

The huge old manor house was set in acres of manicured grounds against a backdrop of Kentish woodland. Renowned for its Michelin starred restaurant, Willow knew that tonight wasn't going to be a cheap date. She wasn't used to Charlie being extravagant or spoiling her. Goldhill Grange would have been the perfect place to have celebrated her recent thirtieth birthday. But that had been and gone. So why come here now?

The headlights arced across the gravel drive as Charlie selected a parking spot. As the engine died, they were momentarily plunged into gloom. He glanced across the handbrake at his girlfriend.

'Ready, sweetie?'

'Charlie, what is going on?' asked Willow in confusion. 'Is it your mum's birthday? A number with a zero on it? Or someone's special anniversary?'

'Nope,' Charlie shook his head.

'Is it someone's surprise party?'

'Yes,' said Charlie in delight.

'Whose?' asked Willow, looking panicky. 'I haven't bought a gift. Not even a card.'

'It's *our* surprise party,' Charlie beamed.

'You're making no sense.'

'Come on. Let's go in. All will be revealed.'

Willow allowed Charlie to help her out of the car, and

escort her up the ornate stone steps to the grand double-doored entrance. Inside the reception area, there were so many chandeliers that Willow momentarily felt like she was in the Lighting Department of John Lewis.

'Good evening, Mr Goodman,' greeted a uniformed man behind the desk. 'Miss West,' he nodded solicitously at her.

Willow nodded back.

'Your table awaits. Follow me to the dining room, please. I will pass you over to Miguel, your server this evening.'

Willow's high heels click-clicked across the polished floor but, seconds later, sank into a carpet so thick and plush she thought her stilettoes might peg.

She looked around the restaurant in wonder. *This* was eating out at its best. Diners' tables were spaced well apart so conversations remained private. It was very different to the local pub's rowdy babble where she'd celebrated her thirtieth. The only noise here was that of polished cutlery against china, and the soft murmur of couples conversing in hushed tones.

Willow's eyes did a quick sweep of the dining room. Yes, all couples. She couldn't see any evidence of trestle tables lumped together for Aunty Vera's seventieth birthday celebration, or beered-up lads moving from the bar to the restaurant and loudly belching as they perused drink-stained menus.

'My lady,' whispered Miguel as he directed Willow to sit down.

A white linen napkin was draped over her knees and, seconds later, a leather-bound menu pressed into her hands.

'Thank you,' mouthed Willow.

She daren't speak normally. This place was almost quieter than Mosley Library. She wasn't quite sure how she was going to chat to Charlie. It was all very beautiful, but not terribly practical if you wanted to let the wine loosen your tongue and have a moan about someone. Willow immediately thought of Emma. Not that she could moan to Charlie about what her bestie had said. And certainly not here. What would fellow diners make of the conversation?

"Hush, Fred. I'm earwigging on that young woman over there. Listen!"

"Lovely restaurant, Charlie. Now that I've shipped a few bevvies, can I tell you something? Earlier on today, Emma tried pairing me off with her twin brother. Now why would she want to do a thing like that? She also asked about our sex life. Outrageous. I was tempted to tell her that we do it forty times a week and recently caused a national shortage of whippy cream."

"Blimey, Fred. That must be why Miguel could only offer us custard with our dessert."

Charlie would probably wonder why Emma was asking such personal questions. He'd likely be annoyed too. Willow couldn't put her finger on it, but sometimes she detected frosty undercurrents between her boyfriend and her bestie. Mind you, Willow was now feeling a little frosty about Emma too. Perhaps she should have been more assertive and told Emma that she and Charlie had a fantastic sex life. She wondered what Emma would have said if she'd divulged the whippy cream details.

"Whippy cream? You mean you let Charlie squirt the stuff all over your nipples? Are you kinky? You'll be telling me he puts mayonnaise or tomato sauce on them next."

Thinking about tomato sauce immediately made Willow remember Noah's silly joke about ketchup. She grinned at the recent memory. But Willow's smile faded when she recalled Emma homing in like a heat-seeking missile with the suggestion that she have a date with her twin. Willow fidgeted uncomfortably. She'd have to watch herself in future. It was one thing feeling that *zinggg* of chemistry with someone, but quite another to let it show on your face.

Willow didn't like to admit to herself that Emma's nosey question had lodged in her brain. Even worse, it had started to fester. The reality was that Willow's sex life was mostly infrequent. She'd never dared complain to Charlie, because she knew he worked so hard and was invariably tired. Nor could Willow quite reconcile the Charlie she knew, to the Charlie in the last week or so. It was like someone had kidnapped her boyfriend, given him a massive testosterone injection, then returned him to her with a sky-high libido. Suddenly Charlie couldn't get enough of her. Why had he changed? She had no idea.

'Darling?' said Charlie.

'Sorry, I was miles away,' she whispered.

'I've ordered us champagne.'

'Lovely,' she mouthed.

'What?' Charlie leant in.

Willow didn't trust her voice to stay low, so she gave him a thumbs-up. Almost instantly she regretted doing so. This wasn't really the sort of place one did such gestures. It wasn't the right setting. It was a bit like witnessing Queen Elizabeth knight someone and then catch Her Majesty doing a high-five. Her musings were interrupted by Miguel returning with the champagne.

'My lady,' he murmured, pouring the chilled fizz into her glass.

Willow inclined her head. It was still too risky to speak. The last thing she wanted was her voice booming out and interrupting that couple over there who were so enthralled with each other. They were holding hands across the table and gazing deeply into each other's eyes. They had no need for words.

Miguel poured Charlie a flute of champagne and then, bowing and scraping, reversed away.

Charlie picked up his glass.

'To us,' he said softly.

Willow gently clinked her glass against his and nodded agreement.

Charlie cleared his throat.

'There's a reason I brought you here.'

'I can't hear you.'

Charlie leant in further.

'I said, there's a reason I brought you here.'

Willow found herself leaning in closer too.

'What have you caught?'

'What?' Charlie frowned.

'You said you'd caught something.'

'No, brought.'

'What have you bought?'

'Oh for goodness sake,' muttered Charlie.

'Cake?' Willow queried.

Charlie sighed and shook his head. It was no good. He was going to have to speak up. Loud and clear. Sod the other diners.

He fished in his jacket pocket for something, and then stood up. Moving round to Willow, he looked first at her and then at all the diners.

'Ladies and gentlemen,' he announced to the restaurant.

Everyone paused and regarded him curiously.

'Sorry to interrupt your evening, but there is something I need to ask my girlfriend, and I have to be absolutely certain that she hears me.'

And with that, Charlie dropped down on one knee. He looked up at Willow. She was staring at him with her mouth open.

'Darling Willow,' he said, producing a small jeweller's box.

It was open. Nestling against a black velvet cushion was a diamond ring.

'Will you marry me?'

There was a collective gasp as both Willow and the entire restaurant sharply inhaled.

'Oh!'

So *this* was the surprise Charlie had talked about. His proposal had completely floored her. Her mind careered backwards. Back to her birthday when she'd idly suggested marriage. Charlie had reacted so badly he'd disappeared for the entire weekend. Then there had been that bizarre moment in the kitchen the other day. He'd got down on one knee after she'd cooked brunch, but it had transpired he had tummy ache and wanted the toilet. But now, for reasons Willow couldn't fathom, her boyfriend had changed his mind. He wanted to get married. Indeed, he was so serious he'd booked Goldhill Grange to pop the question and produced a stunning sparkler in front of all these strangers.

'Darling?' Charlie prompted.

Willow stared at him, like a rabbit caught in car headlights. Why wasn't she feeling thrilled? Or wanting to whoop with happiness? Or even leaking a few tears of joy?

Her thoughts strayed to Noah… how he'd made her feel when they'd spoken on FaceTime. Excited. Fizzy. Like a shaken-up bottle of champagne that was just waiting to explode. And then her thoughts returned to Charlie. Here he was, finally down on one knee. Both he and the entire restaurant were holding their breath, waiting for the girl with the golden hair to answer the handsome man whose eyes were full of love. This was everything she'd ever wanted. Wasn't it? Well, it had been. On her birthday. When she hadn't met Noah.

Oh don't be ridiculous, Willow. You haven't "met" Noah. Not properly. Two FaceTime calls do not substitute for meeting a person. And forget the connection you fancifully think you had with him. The only connection was a digital one, and most certainly not an emotional one. You don't know the guy, so stop being a plonker!

As that last word echoed through her brain, Willow remembered Emma mentioning her recent doomed romance. She'd declined sharing the details with Willow but referred to the unnamed man as a "plonker". Poor Emma. She'd probably give her right arm to have a man like Charlie giving her the full romantic works and a dream proposal. Unlike Emma's mystery man, Charlie was reliable… solid… good looking and – Willow tuned back in – now looking horribly anxious about her lack of response. In fact, her boyfriend looked like he just might burst into tears.

'Please answer me, darling. Please say yes. I so want to marry you, Willow. And to prove just how serious I am, I've gone ahead and booked everything.'

'W-What?' said Willow, flabbergasted.

'It's true,' Charlie nodded. 'I've paid for the wedding to take place here. Goldhill Grange. Saturday the seventh of December. The marriage of Willow West and Charles Goodman. Look.'

Charlie's free hand disappeared to the inside breast pocket of his jacket. It emerged with a folded letter. He passed it to Willow. Wordlessly, she took it. Her eyes widened. Written confirmation for a wedding package… banquet for sixty guests… photographer… videographer… cake… oh my God… these were the "errands" he'd been doing earlier today.

Charlie had been organising a wedding. *Her* wedding!

'And I took the liberty of booking this too' – like a conjurer magicking a rabbit from a hat, Charlie produced another piece of paper – 'our honeymoon.'

Willow silently scanned the document which confirmed a trip to… good *heavens*… the Bahamas. Flipping heck. Charlie must really love her to have gone to all this trouble. She'd be mad to turn him down. Crazy. You didn't refuse your partner's proposal just because a stranger in Australia made your heartrate zoom like a jumbo jet roaring down a runway. And how *dare* Emma ruffle her feathers and imply Charlie wasn't the man for her. Accepting Charlie's proposal would certainly prove to Emma, if nothing else, that Willow was deliriously happy with Charlie.

'Willow?' Charlie implored. 'Please don't refuse me.'

Slowly, shyly, Willow smiled.

'Yes,' she said. 'Yes, I will marry you on the seventh of December.'

And as Charlie closed his eyes in relief, the entire restaurant exploded with a round of applause and even a couple of piercing whistles.

Charlie slipped the ring on her third finger. It was the perfect fit. He'd even taken the trouble to get that right. He moved in closer and kissed her.

'Phew,' he said, over the din of everyone cheering. 'For a moment there, you had me worried.'

Willow tutted and smiled.

'You never had anything to be concerned about.'

And Charlie couldn't help but smile at the irony of his new fiancée's words.

Chapter Fifty-Seven

Willow was awoken on Sunday morning by Charlie's erection jabbing her in the back.

'Is my fiancée awake?' he murmured huskily.

'Well if she wasn't, she is now,' said Willow sleepily.

As Charlie's arms encircled her, she tried not to feel resentful at being disturbed. For the last hour or so she'd been in the sort of light sleep that produced vivid dreams. Her mind had been far away. Nearly ten thousand miles to be precise. In Australia. She'd been walking along a vast deserted beach. Despite never visiting this place, it had seemed familiar.

The white sand had felt like soft flour between her bare toes. Willow had been holding a warm hand. A man's hand. She'd never met the man, but somehow she knew him. They'd strolled along the shore in silence because there had been no need to speak. They were so in tune with each other, words hadn't been required. The only sounds had been that of the waves as they endlessly shushed back and forth. The man had gently squeezed her hand conveying they stop. Together they'd stared at the ocean and the cloudless blue sky, enjoying the warmth of the sun on their faces. And then, wordlessly, they'd turned to face each other.

Willow hadn't been at all surprised to find herself gazing at Noah. His eyes had crinkled attractively as he'd smiled down at her. Both her heart and soul had expanded with joy. The experience had been comparable to a time lapse video of a rosebud swiftly blooming to full flower.

'Willow?' said Noah, finally speaking.

He had looked at her with such love.

'There's something I need to tell you.'

But now she'd never know what Noah had been about to say thanks to Charlie's dick nudging her.

What makes you think Noah was going to tell you something profound? sneered the little voice in her head.

And a very good morning to you, Willow replied. *Why don't you just butt out?*

Why?

Because my dreams are private.

Not to me they're not. Anyway, shouldn't you be dreaming of your fiancé?

I DO dream of my fiancé.

Hm. Not recently. Not slushily.

And your point is?

It's not me making a point. It's your new fiancé, cackled the little voice as the tip of Charlie's penis edged between her thighs.

Willow had an overwhelming urge to slap Charlie's willy away. Opening her eyes and catching sight of the ring on her left hand, she was immediately overcome with guilt. She was engaged! This was what she'd always wanted. And she was going to embrace it with open arms. And legs, if Charlie had his way.

'I find you so incredibly irresistible,' Charlie was now saying.

His breath was coming in great whooshy gasps, hot on her neck and whistling into her eardrum. Now he was nuzzling her earlobe and leaving an unappealing wet trail as he tried to roll her over and kiss her on the mouth. Early morning snogs weren't on Willow's Seduction List. There was a lot to be said for minty breath and mouthwash.

'I must have a wee,' she said, wriggling out of Charlie's arms.

He sighed and flopped back against the mattress.

'Don't be long,' he called after her.

Willow made sure she was in the bathroom for a good ten minutes. First, she flossed her teeth. Then she thoroughly cleaned them. Then she decided her skin looked a little lacklustre, so applied a face mask. It had been one of the presents Emma had given her for her recent birthday. Willow read the instructions. It had to stay on for fifteen minutes. Oh. She might as well go and put the kettle on while it worked its magic.

When she came out of the bathroom, Charlie did a doubletake.

'What the hell is that?'

'A face mask. My skin looked dull.'

Charlie wrinkled his nose.

'It smells peculiar.'

He recognised the scent. He'd once caught Kev wearing one.

'It has avocado in it,' said Willow. 'Let me go and put the kettle on.'

'The kettle can wait, but I can't... with or without the avocado face mask.'

At that moment Willow's mobile – resting on her bedside cabinet – began to vibrate.

'Leave it,' Charlie instructed.

'But it's Emma,' Willow protested.

'All the more reason to leave it,' muttered Charlie.

'What?'

'Nothing.'

'But I want to tell her my big news,' Willow reasoned, diving over Charlie to reach the phone.

As she threw herself across the mattress, her knee accidentally cuffed Charlie in the groin.

'Ooof,' he groaned, clutching his privates.

'Sorr-eeee,' Willow trilled, trying not to feel relieved that Charlie's erection was now deflating faster than air leaking out of a party balloon.

She snatched up the mobile.

'Ems? Hellooo!'

Willow was now dropping bits of face mask all over the duvet, but she didn't care.

'Blimey, you're sounding very chipper,' Emma laughed.

'I am, I am,' said Willow, bouncing around on the mattress with barely contained excitement. Another blob of goo parted company from her face.

'I was feeling a bit bored so thought I'd ring for a natter.'

'Be bored no more!' Willow giggled.

'Why, what's going on?'

Emma felt herself perking up. Willow's mood was infectious.

'Omigod, you'll never guess!'

'Probably not, so just spit it out,' said Emma, laughing again.

'Last night, Charlie and I got engaged!'

There was a stunned pause before Emma replied.

'W-Wow. That's… amazing. Congratulations. To you both,' she added.

Emma was doing her best to sound delighted. This was Willow's big moment. She must be pleased for her. But try as she might, she wasn't.

Chapter Fifty-Eight

Over the week that followed, the news of Willow and Charlie's betrothal was met by others with mixed feelings.

'Hey, matey,' said Ben to Charlie. 'You've finally done it.' He clapped Charlie on the back. 'Brilliant news. I'm so pleased you've seen the light and are going to make an honest woman of Willow. She's a cracker.'

'She is,' Charlie agreed. 'From now on I'm going to be Mister Happily Married Man.'

'Good to hear. And don't forget. You said that if you popped the question, I could be your best man.'

'I haven't forgotten, and it goes without saying that I want you in that role. So you're still up for it?'

'Try and stop me,' Ben grinned.

Willow was walking across Mosley Library's car park when she heard footsteps coming up behind her. Turning, she was surprised to see Anna.

'Hello,' said Willow. 'Whatever are you doing here?'

'Well it's not to borrow a book,' said Anna brusquely. 'I'll come straight to the point. This is something that needs saying face to face.'

'Oh?' said Willow, as a nasty feeling began to unfurl in her stomach.

'I've rescheduled a work meeting in order to say this,' said Anna gruffly. 'That's how important this is.'

'Could you come to the point, please,' said Willow.

Outwardly she was calm. Inwardly her insides were knotting with tension.

'Ben told me that you and Charlie are engaged. I'd like to say congratulations. But I won't. Willow, you need to listen to me. You really do. You mustn't marry Charlie.'

'How dare you!' Willow exclaimed.

The two women stood facing each other, oblivious to their surroundings until a car tooted at them to move. Upon shifting, Anna grabbed Willow's left hand and inspected her engagement ring.

'Lovely. Unfortunately, Charlie isn't. Look, I know I'm upsetting you. And I apologise. All I ask is that you think long and hard about what you're doing.'

'Now you listen to me,' said Willow angrily.

Her cheeks had turned pink from both the cold morning air and fury at Anna's outrageous comments. It took a lot to make Willow mad, but she could feel herself getting justifiably worked up.

'I'm sorry that you and Ben didn't work out. And I'm sorry Ben never asked *you* to marry *him*.'

'Hey, this isn't about–'

'Yes, it is,' Willow interrupted. 'You're jealous, Anna. Jealous because I'm with my man, but you threw yours away, and now you're with no one.'

'Who says I'm not with someone?' Anna challenged.

'Right,' said Willow, momentarily wrong-footed. 'Well, if you have a new man, bully for you. That's brilliant.'

'Yes, it *is* brilliant. It will be even more brilliant when he's properly available.'

Willow shook her head. So that's why Anna was being sour. She'd found another guy, but he wasn't completely free. Well there was no need for Anna to take it out on her.

'But this isn't about me,' Anna continued. 'It's about you. I'm not quite the bitch you believe me to be, Willow. All I will say is, don't throw yourself away on a man like Charlie.'

And with that, she turned on her heel and stalked off to her car.

Willow watched Anna until she'd started the engine up and driven away. She was tempted to phone Charlie and say, "Guess what? I've just been flagged down in the library car park by Anna of all people. She had the audacity to warn me off marrying you. Can you believe it?" And then Charlie would say, "Darling, take no notice. Anna is nuts. That's why Ben extricated himself from the relationship."

Willow dithered. If she told Charlie what had happened, then Charlie would tell Ben. Poor Ben would be so embarrassed about his ex-girlfriend trying to rain on Willow's parade. Instead, Willow decided to ignore Anna and do her best not to let her words upset her.

Taking a deep breath, Willow pushed open the library door. She was sure that Jean, Fiona and Theresa would be thrilled for her. Willow decided to tell her colleagues at the earliest opportunity in order to restore her previously happy mood.

'Congratulations,' said Fiona, as Willow showed off her ring.

'What's this?' said Theresa, sidling over to see what her colleagues were gossiping about. 'Oh my goodness. You're wearing a diamond. Woohoo! You're so lucky,' Theresa gabbled. 'I've seen your Charlie, and he's lush.'

'Why are you girls talking and not working?' said Jean, bustling over. 'Ah,' she said, as Willow flashed her sparkler. 'Now I understand. That's beautiful. Congratulations from me. From what I've heard about your Charlie, he's a good'un. I hope you'll both be very happy.'

Emma couldn't concentrate. Willow was marrying Charlie. The date was set. Charlie had wanted to get married sooner rather than later, so much so he'd seized the opportunity of a cancellation at Goldhill Grange.

There was no doubt that the wedding was going to be a very classy affair. Willow had already asked Emma to be her bridesmaid. Despite accepting, she'd wanted to scream, "No! I absolutely *won't* walk down the aisle with you. No way can I witness you making the biggest mistake of your life."

Even Emma's mother had noticed her glum mood.

'For goodness sake, Emma, what's the matter with you?'

'Willow is getting married.'

'Really?' said Karen.

'Yeah.'

'When?'

'Soon. Ridiculously soon. The seventh of December.'

'I must buy a new outfit,' said Karen, before carrying on filing her nails.

Noah didn't give much away when Emma later Facetimed him.

'I really thought you and Willow had a connection,' said Emma in despair.

'Yeah, me too,' said Noah with a shrug. 'But I guess I got it wrong. Hey, sis. Let's put things in perspective, eh? Willow is a gorgeous girl, but I've never properly met her and... well, now I guess I never will,' he said sadly.

'That's where you're wrong.' Emma's brain was racing. 'You're coming to her wedding.'

'Am I invited?' said Noah, looking astonished.

'No. But I'm allowed to bring a plus-one. And guess what, bro? You're my plus-one.'

'Willow?' said Jean, looking irritated. 'There's a telephone call for you.'

'Oh, I'm so sorry,' said Willow, hurrying over. 'I've told everyone I know not to ring me on the library phone. I don't know who it is, but I'll be sure to tell them–'

'No matter,' said Jean, passing Willow the phone. 'Just make it quick.'

'Hello?' said Willow.

She was met with silence. Willow experienced a sense of déjà vu as, seconds later, a female whispered down the line. The message was only slightly different to the last time around.

'Don't marry Charlie.'

But this time Willow was going to say something.

'I know that's you, Anna. Well thank you for your call, but please don't ring here again.'

Kev pressed a tissue to her wet eyes, desperately trying to stem the tears without wrecking her mascara. So, it was finally happening. Charlie was marrying Willow. Kev had lost him. And despite her knowing that Charlie was a cad, a bounder, and would never remain faithful to Willow, she couldn't deny that the news of his impending marriage had devastated her. If only there was a way to make Willow change her mind.

And then she thought of something.

Chapter Fifty-Nine

The wedding machine roared into action and the weeks that followed passed in a blur.

Charlie's stag night went without any hitches. Yes, he got drunk. No, he didn't make a play for the gorgeous stripper hired by one of his work colleagues. He was glad he'd resisted temptation too, because "she" had turned out to be a "he".

Willow's hen party was very tame. She'd booked a spa weekend with a girly gang. Even Jean had come along and abandoned her stuffy librarian image by getting terribly tiddly on two glasses of wine. She'd then astonished Willow, Theresa and Fiona with a very blue bridal joke.

'I believe sex between two people is a beautiful thing, but between five it's fantastic,' she'd cackled, and then had a tipsy giddy turn.

Emma and Karen had made Jean drink water, then sat her down with her head between her ankles.

As autumn gave way to an approaching winter, the nights drew in and the temperature dropped. Christmas was on the horizon and the beginnings of festive magic filled the air. Mosley Village sparkled at night with numerous fairy lights that residents had threaded through garden trees. Wicker reindeer seemingly grazed on front lawns, Christmas trees appeared in the downstairs windows of houses, and holly wreaths adorned front doors.

Meanwhile, Charlie had asked his mum if he could get ready on the morning of the wedding at her house, but Grace had declined.

'Absolutely not,' she'd said. 'No way are you monopolising my bathroom, thank you very much. Use your own house.'

'But Willow will be getting ready at our house.'

'Too bad. Ask someone else.'

So Charlie had asked Ben if he could get ready at his. After all, Ben had now moved into his new flat. However, the apartment had loads of snagging problems. This included a faulty bath and defunct shower. Charlie's request was consequently pre-empted by Ben who asked Charlie if *he* could get ready at *his*. Charlie had no choice but to say yes, but obviously this impacted upon Willow. She was now despairing. Willow didn't want Charlie seeing her getting ready or wearing her bridal gown until she walked down the aisle.

As a result, Willow ended up asking her parents if she could get ready at theirs. After all, her father would be travelling in the wedding car with her, so it made sense they leave together. But when Willow telephoned her mum with the request, Anita immediately began flapping.

'Oh darling, you're not going to believe what your father has done.'

Willow instantly noted her mother's use of "your father". This ominous wording was always trotted out when her dad had messed up over something.

'What's happened?' Willow asked anxiously.

'Daddy has told all the Scottish relatives they can stay at ours. Not a *thought* about bathroom availability or bedroom space,' Anita ranted. 'And if he thinks I'm giving up our bed, he's very much mistaken. I'm the mother of the bride, and no way am I sleeping on a sofa the night before my daughter's wedding.'

'Ah, yes, quite,' Willow sympathised, her heart sinking.

'Anyway, we'd assumed that your wedding car would be picking Daddy up first before making its way over to you.'

'Oh my goodness. The wedding car!'

Willow clapped a hand to her forehead. It was the one thing that Charlie had overlooked when he'd arranged everything, and it had completely bypassed her attention too.

Willow's dilemma about where to get ready was thankfully resolved by Karen and Emma. They invited Willow to leave as a bride from their house, and she gratefully accepted the offer.

'We can get ready together,' said Emma cosily.

Frantic phone calls were then made to source a wedding car. At the last minute, a vintage Rolls Royce was successfully booked. The Roller would arrive – with Willow's father – at Karen's house. Meanwhile, Emma and Karen would travel to the venue, ahead of Willow, in the Mercedes car that Noah had hired for his duration in England.

Noah had now – much to Karen's reluctance – arrived

from Australia. Karen had been wildly discouraging of Noah's visit giving any number of excuses she could think of: her house was too cramped... he would have to sleep on the sofa... the sofa was lumpy... until she realised her protests were falling on deaf ears. Noah's ticket was booked. The son she hadn't raised was coming. He wanted to get to know her. And that was that.

Willow had yet to meet Noah. She'd deliberately made sure their paths hadn't yet crossed. However, she knew their meeting would be inevitable once she arrived at Karen's house to prepare as a bride. By this point Willow was convinced that any chemistry she'd felt on her part had been nothing other than fanciful nonsense, and nothing more than banter on Noah's part. The small matter of Emma suggesting Willow have a date with Noah had been dismissed by both women as a poor joke.

When Willow's wedding day finally dawned, she was relieved to see the December weather was chilly but bright. The forecast promised a dry day with the palest of blue skies. Willow was overjoyed to see a watery blob of yellow bravely shining away.

Charlie tactfully kept out of the way while Ben helped Willow load up her car with everything she needed. The bridal gown – which had been stored out of sight in the spare room wardrobe – was now in a protective wrapper. Ben laid it carefully on the back seat of Willow's car. A small suitcase was placed in the boot. This contained Willow's make-up, toiletries, wedding shoes, veil and, in keeping with the Christmas season, a white faux-fur bolero to keep her warm when travelling to the venue.

'See you there,' said Ben, giving Willow a hug.

'Look after Charlie for me,' she said. 'Make sure he doesn't get cold feet.'

'No chance of that,' Ben assured. 'He's more concerned about *you* being talked out of it by Emma or her mum. He made a weak joke about it. Between you and me, Charlie suspects they don't think he's good enough for you.'

Willow tutted.

'I know Karen isn't a massive fan of marriage because of her own experience, but that's not to say she's against other people getting hitched. Far from it. And as for Emma…'

Willow trailed off. She didn't want to be reminded, today of all days, about the time when Emma had dared to ask Willow if she was truly happy with Charlie.

'What about Emma?' Ben prompted.

'She's happy for me too,' said Willow firmly. 'Despite being let down herself, she wishes Charlie and me all the best. Her heart is in the right place.'

'And that's what matters,' said Ben.

'You should get to know Emma,' said Willow suddenly. 'Ask her to dance later, at the reception.'

'Are you trying to matchmake?' Ben teased.

'Maybe,' Willow smiled.

'Never mind me. Today is about you.' He gave Willow a little prod. 'Off you go. And don't be late!'

Willow grinned and got in her car. With a toot and a wave, she set off. New beginnings lay ahead. Woohoo!

But even Willow couldn't have predicted quite how this next chapter would start.

Chapter Sixty

When Willow turned up at her bestie's house, it wasn't Emma who opened the door. Nor Karen. Instead, she found herself face to face with Noah.

'Hey,' he said, giving her a lazy grin.

His manner was so relaxed, Willow inexplicably felt like she'd known him for years.

'Come on in. I'm afraid you've got me instead of Mum or Emma. They're both busy accusing each other of nicking lipsticks and hair straighteners, and generally behaving like it's their big day and not yours. Here, let me help you with your things.'

Her little case and the wedding dress – still in its protective cover – were whisked out of her grasp. The bag was put to one side in the hallway and the dress carefully hung on the back of a door. He held out one hand.

'It's so good to finally meet you, Willow.'

She stared at the gorgeous god before her. If she'd thought him handsome on Emma's mobile screen during those FaceTime calls, seeing him in the flesh didn't begin to compare.

Noah was far taller than Willow had expected. Even taller

than Charlie. Everything about this man was different. Whereas Charlie was a good-looking blond with piercing blue eyes, by comparison Noah made her boyfriend look insipid. Dark hair curled over his collar and soft brown eyes twinkled at her. His smile was wide and generous, and his teeth looked so white he could have starred in his own toothpaste commercial. And that accent! Here, in this typically British house against an English backdrop, it was so much more noticeable… and having an odd effect on her.

Feeling gauche, Willow took Noah's hand. His touch had an instantaneous effect on her. If she'd thought there'd been chemistry between them on FaceTime, today it felt like someone had lit a faulty Bunsen burner and caused an almighty explosion.

Hellooo! said the little voice in her head.

What? Willow snapped.

Lost your tongue? Say something!

'Hi,' Willow finally croaked.

Noah was still holding her hand and Willow was starting to feel like she'd been plugged into the National Grid. In another minute there'd be such an overload of zinging electricity, fuses would start blowing all over the country.

'How are you feeling?' asked Noah, finally letting her go.

'Peculiar,' Willow admitted.

'Wedding nerves,' Noah laughed. 'Can I get you a cup of tea? Coffee? Or, considering this is a special day, how about a glass of champagne?'

He led her into the kitchen.

'Mum and Emma put some champers in the fridge earlier. What do you fancy?'

You, was the first answer that popped into Willow's head.

'I, er–'

'Of *course* she wants champagne,' said Karen, coming into the kitchen. 'Hello, darling,' she said, embracing Willow.

Karen had already done her make-up but was still in her dressing gown.

'Crack open the bubbles, Noah,' she ordered, before turning back to Willow. 'Have you had some breakfast?'

'No,' Willow shook her head. 'To be honest, I think I'm too nervous to eat.'

'Well we can't have you passing out, can we?' said Karen. 'Good thing I bought some croissants from good old Markies. What more could a bride want on her wedding morning?' she beamed.

A long snog with your son, Willow was shocked to find herself thinking.

And why stop there? jeered the little voice in her head. *Why not just grapple him away from the fridge and push him down on Karen's granite worktop? Then ask everyone to avert their eyes while the bride-to-be has one final fling.*

'Willow!' squealed Emma, clattering into the kitchen on extremely high heels. 'What do you think of these?'

She stuck a foot out for Willow to see her bridesmaid shoes.

'Aren't they gorgeous?'

'Perfect,' Willow nodded.

Like her mother, Emma was still in her dressing gown. However, her make-up wasn't complete. Emma was now regarding Willow through mismatched eyes. One eyelid was sporting eyeshadow in rosy tones, the other was bare. Consequently, Emma looked like she was suffering conjunctivitis.

'We've finished with the bathroom, so it's all yours. Make-up is taking place in Mum's bedroom thanks to Noah appropriating mine with luggage and paraphernalia. Oooh, yummy, champagne. Cheers!' said Emma, grabbing a glass from Noah and toasting Willow.

'Cheers,' she replied, clinking glasses with the three of them.

Willow took a sip and it went straight to her head.

'Speech!' said Emma.

'What, now?' said Willow.

'Yes!'

'Okay.' She cleared her throat. 'Well, thank you, Karen, for letting me get ready at your house. Thank you, Emma, for being my bridesmaid.'

She looked at Noah. Should she thank him for something?

'And thank you, Noah, for…'

Letting my eyes feast upon a face that must be the most perfect in Creation… for making my heart do little flips as if I'm on a rollercoaster… for my loins twanging like a softly strummed guitar…

Oh. My. God. Did you just say your loins were twanging?

'Um, my champagne,' Willow concluded, taking a hasty

gulp.

By the time Willow had picked at her croissant and drunk two glasses of champagne, she felt a little less shy around Noah and able to look at him without quite so many pornographic images dancing through her brain.

'Hey, come on,' said Emma to Willow. She set down her glass. 'The time's getting on. You ought to start getting ready, and I need to do my other eye.'

An hour later, Willow's hair and make-up were finished. Karen and Emma had left her to quietly prepare without disturbance.

Willow now regarded herself in Karen's bedroom mirror. She hadn't needed a lot of blusher as her cheeks were glowing redder than a traffic light. She wasn't sure if this was down to the champagne still coursing through her veins, or the effect Noah had had on her.

She stared at her reflection. Her eyes were sparkling more than the diamond on her left hand. The last time she'd looked like this was when she'd fallen in love with Charlie. But that had been ages ago.

Have you fallen in love with Noah? piped up the little voice.

Shut UP! Willow silently raged. *I love Charlie, okay?*

Turning away from the mirror, she reached for her wedding dress. Taking it out of the protective wrapper, Willow stepped into it and carefully pulled the fabric up to her shoulders. Wait. She needed someone to do up all the little buttons at the back. Where was Emma? Opening the bedroom door, she peered along the landing.

'Ems?'

'I'm in the loo,' came a voice. 'That champagne has gone right through me. I might be a while.'

'Lovely,' said Willow dryly. 'Well try not to be too long. I need some help with my dress.'

'Ask Mum.'

'Right,' Willow sighed. 'Karen? Are you there?'

'She's on the phone,' said Noah, coming out of Emma's bedroom.

Willow caught her breath.

Noah had changed into a suit that made him look like he'd stepped straight off an advertising billboard.

'I'm not sure who she's talking to' – he continued – 'but the bit of conversation I overheard gave me the impression she'll be a while. What's up?'

'Nothing. I just need your mum to do up my dress.'

'I can do that,' said Noah.

'Oh, but…'

'Turn around.'

'Can I just get my shoes?' said Willow, suddenly flustered. 'I'd like to put them on first and then arrange the hemline and skirts.'

'Sure,' said Noah, following Willow back into Karen's bedroom.

Alone with him, the room seemed to shrink. Willow picked up the shoebox containing her satin heels, but her fingers seemed to have turned into bananas. Suddenly clumsy, she dropped the box. The lid flew off and her shoes skittered across the carpet.

'Here, let me,' said Noah.

He stooped to pick up the heels at the same moment as Willow. The two of them banged heads and, for a moment, Willow wasn't sure if it was stars she was seeing, or whether it was possible to have a zinger explode in her brain.

'S-Sorry,' she stammered.

'Whoa, that was a bit of a belter,' said Noah, rubbing his head.

He passed the shoes to Willow.

'Is your head okay?'

No. Her head was everywhere, and it wasn't okay.

Ramming her feet into the wretched stilettoes, Willow felt flustered and thoroughly out of sorts.

'I'm fine,' she gasped.

She needed to still her mind. To think of something mundane. Boris's Brexit Britain. Trump's orange tan. Meghan and Harry upsetting Buck House. At least they'd taken the spotlight off Prince Andrew. Poor old Queenie. What a lot she had to put up with.

'Then if you're not feeling concussed, try and keep still.'

As Noah deftly got to work on the tiny buttons, his warm hands occasionally grazed her skin. Willow couldn't help giving involuntary shivers.

'Cold?' he asked.

'Yes,' she squeaked.

Calm down. Make conversation.

'It's quite a chilly d-day,' she stuttered. 'How are you finding the English weather?'

The weather! Such riveting conversation, Willow.

'Well, it's not like Australia, that's for sure,' Noah laughed. 'It was very warm when I left.

Willow could hardly concentrate on what he was saying. Instead her attention was on those blissfully warm fingers and the gentle pressure against her spine. A million nerve endings were now feeling blissed-out from his touch.

'But there's something about this place that smacks of home,' Noah continued. 'It feels right.'

All Willow could think about was how right it felt having Noah touch her.

'There,' he said. 'All done.'

Gently, he turned her round to face him.

'You look absolutely stunning.'

'So do you,' she murmured.

The words were out of her mouth before she could stop them.

'I-I mean…' she stammered, before trailing off.

Noah's eyes were full of mischief.

'What do you mean?' he said softly.

The chemistry was once again zinging backwards and forwards.

'I mean… you look very nice, and I'm so glad you like England,' she gabbled.

'Oh I *love* England,' he said slowly, his eyes snagging on hers. 'This place has crept up on me and captivated my heart.

It's such a feeling. One that I can't properly describe. It just sneaked up on me and wiggled into my soul when I wasn't looking. People do that too. Unexpectedly. Just when you don't want them to.'

Willow didn't know what was going on here. Aside from the chemistry, and talking about England and Australia, something else was being said. Something that went way beyond a couple of FaceTime calls and a few hours around a man who was having a very challenging effect upon her.

She gazed up at him, hardly daring to breathe, and it seemed as though the man standing before her was somehow branding his soul upon hers. The implications horrified her. She needed to break this spell.

Forcing her legs to work, she took two steps away from him. It was imperative she move away from Noah. But he immediately reached out and touched her arm. Willow was so jolted she stopped in her tracks.

'Where are you going?' he whispered.

'Well, I just…'

'Come here.'

And with those words, he swept her into his arms. She could have easily resisted; he wasn't holding her tightly. Instead she surrendered entirely to his embrace, arching into him. His fingers trailed down her spine as his mouth came down on hers. The kiss wasn't rough or overpowering, just gentle and very tender. One might even say loving. And she responded with alacrity.

Seconds later, Willow pulled away, hands fluttering to her

mouth.

'Oh my God. What am I doing? I'm getting married, for heaven's sake!'

'Perhaps you're marrying the wrong person,' Noah suggested.

'Don't be ridiculous.' Willow shook her head. 'That kiss was…'

'Wonderful?' Noah suggested.

'Lunacy,' Willow corrected.

'I've never been saner,' said Noah, looking faintly amused.

'You don't understand.' Willow shook her head vehemently. 'The wedding invitations have been sent… guests are probably already at the venue… but apart from anything else, I don't even know you,' she gasped.

'Then get to know me,' said Noah simply.

His eyes were full of warmth and sincerity.

'Willow?' said Emma, barging into the room. 'Your car is here. Come on, Noah. We need to get a move on. I'm meant to arrive at the wedding venue before the bride. Mum's finally off the phone. I have my posy' – she waggled a pretty ball of petals at Willow – 'and here's your bouquet.' Emma placed it in Willow's hands. 'Are you all right?'

'Yes,' said Willow in a small voice, just as her mobile pinged a text.

'You don't look it,' said Emma, frowning. 'Here, pick up your message.'

She passed Willow her phone before turning to her brother.

'Can you give us a moment, Noah? Go and sort Mum out. You've no idea what an airhead she can be. Make sure she's got plenty of tissues. She always cries at weddings.'

'Sure,' said Noah.

Seconds later, he'd gone, quietly shutting the door behind him.

'Last time I looked at you, you were glowing like a wood burner in winter. Now you're as white as February's first snowdrops. What's going on? Have you got cold feet?'

Willow instantly snapped out of her fog.

There was something about Emma's tone as she'd asked that last question. Willow couldn't put her finger on it, but… it was almost as if Emma had – just for one tiny moment – hoped the wedding might be called off. Willow shook away the thought.

'I think I have a touch of wedding nerves.'

Willow pressed her phone's screen. It was a message from Charlie.

See you soon. Can't wait for you to be Mrs Goodman! Xxxxxx

Willow smiled. Back to reality. *This* was the man who mattered.

'My future husband is waiting for me,' she said.

For a moment Emma didn't say anything. Finally, she nodded.

'Then we'd better be on our way.'

Chapter Sixty-One

'Darling, you look stunning.'

Jerry West greeted his daughter with tears in his eyes.

'Thanks, Dad.' Willow kissed her father's cheek. 'You're not going to go soppy on me and cry, are you?' she teased. 'Otherwise you might set me off.'

'Of course not,' said Jerry, doing some rapid blinking.

He squeezed Willow's arm as she sat next to him in the back of the gorgeous old Rolls Royce.

'Your flowers are beautiful too,' he said, nodding at the mixed blooms.

'Heavenly,' Willow agreed. 'Oh, look. Silly me. I still have my mobile. I meant for Karen to look after it. Can I give it to you?'

'Oh dear,' said Jerry, patting his jacket. 'This is a hired suit. The pockets aren't real. Every one of them is stitched at the top. Give the phone to Emma when we arrive. Perhaps she can pass it on to her mum.'

'Good idea,' Willow nodded.

She switched the mobile to silent. The last thing she wanted was a merry tune ringing out just as she was about to walk down the aisle.

Smiling at the thought, she leant back against the soft

upholstery and took a deep breath. Wow. It was really happening. She was getting married! It was her last day of being Willow West. In another hour or so she would be Mrs Charles Goodman.

Her stomach was starting to feel like it was full of fizzing Alka-Seltzers. She put it down to jittery anticipation. However, the truth was that Willow didn't know whether she was nervous about getting hitched or simply suffering the after-effects of THAT kiss.

She closed her eyes. She hadn't dared look at Noah as he'd helped Emma and Karen into the hired Mercedes before driving ahead to Goldhill Grange. She didn't know what to make of what had happened between them. She felt ashamed. And also horribly elated. Her thoughts were interrupted by her mobile silently vibrating.

Opening her eyes, she was surprised to see a message from an unknown number. It said only one word.

Well?

Willow stared at the screen in confusion. Well what?

And then she saw that she'd missed an earlier message from the same unknown number. It was a screenshot. This current text was clearly a prompt to look at a previous one. From the timing, the screenshot had been delivered before Charlie had messaged her. She must have been completely distracted and flustered by Noah not to have heard her phone ping.

The screenshot was too small to read, so Willow clicked on it, enlarging the text. And this time her heart began skipping beats for reasons that were nothing to do with zinging chemistry but everything to do with horror.

It showed an exchange of texts between Charlie and the anonymous sender who, Willow now deduced, was female.

Charlie: This evening. You, me, and chocolate body paint!

Her: Yesss, babe. Tonight's dessert is on me, ha ha!

Charlie: I wish Willow had half your imagination.

*Her: Why did you mention your girlfriend? *scowling emoji**

Charlie: Sorry, sorry, sorry. I miss you, sweetie.

Her: Good. You'd better show me how much xx

Willow looked up and stared blindly ahead. Shock was reverberating through her body. Who the hell had Charlie been texting? Had he been having an affair? No way! She would have known. Wouldn't she?

A part of Willow's brain simply couldn't comprehend the idea of Charlie cheating. This screenshot had to be fake. Since when would Charlie have had time to conduct a secret liaison? The idea was preposterous. He was far too busy working late. Or soothing irate clients in Cambridge and Brighton. Or… Willow gulped as realisation slowly dawned. There hadn't been any irate clients or any real need to work late. He'd lied to her.

Her eyes widened as the phone vibrated with another message. And then another. And another. Suddenly the car was filled with the sound of low buzzing as Willow's mobile received photograph after photograph.

'My goodness, you're popular,' said Jerry, smiling benignly

at Willow.

'Yes,' she gasped. 'I have tons of goodwill messages from people who aren't able to be with us today. Lucky me!'

'How lovely. I'll let you read them in peace while I admire the passing scenery,' said Jerry, gazing out of the window.

As Willow clicked on the images, she was relieved that her father was looking the other way. Here was Charlie, resting his head against some pillows. He'd gone to sleep, apparently with a fishnet thong on his head. Another showed her boyfriend in a shower that Willow didn't recognise. His face was obscured by a plastic cap covered in unicorns, but Willow had seen that large mole on his left butt-cheek a million times to know it was him.

The remaining photographs had seemingly caught Charlie unawares. He was mostly asleep and sprawled out naked with chocolate body paint smeared across his torso. But… what was this?

The sender had cropped herself out of *this* picture but, at the very edge, Willow spotted a lock of dark wavy hair. Her stomach lurched. And… oh my God… in *this* one Charlie was awake but not looking at the camera. Had he even known the sender was photographing him? Probably not. He was far too engrossed in what he was doing. Eyes closed. Face ecstatic as his lips kissed their way up the inside of the sender's thigh… upon which danced a pretty butterfly tattoo.

Chapter Sixty-Two

As the Roller swung through the gates and arrived at its fairy-tale destination, Willow's mobile buzzed with a final message:

I'm not sure I would marry him, but will you?

'Ready, sweetheart?' said Jerry, turning to his daughter.

Willow stared at her father with huge eyes. Ready? She felt so traumatised, she couldn't think straight. Her brain had turned into a pressure-cooker threatening to blow up. She couldn't eradicate the images of Charlie with this woman. Even worse, there were sickening clues to her identity, from the tantalising glimpse of wavy brown hair to THAT butterfly tattoo. Willow felt so crushed by the woman's betrayal even the simple act of breathing was becoming an effort.

The Rolls Royce purred to a standstill. There, on the stone steps of Goldhill Grange, was Emma. Her long wavy brown hair had been threaded into a bridal up-do. The cool December breeze was tugging at the hem of her bridesmaid's dress, but not enough to lift the skirt and reveal the butterfly tattoo on her left thigh. She was clutching her posy… along with her phone.

Willow was so numb she didn't register that the chauffeur had opened the door for her.

'Darling?' Jerry prompted.

Her father was now out of the car and waiting for Willow

to do likewise. She realised that shock had given her a temporary protective cocoon. She couldn't even cry. No doubt the tears would come later. Jerry was looking at Willow curiously.

'Come on, sweetie. It's cold out here. Emma's arms have goose bumps. Let's get on with the show.'

Jerry noted his daughter's pinched expression but deduced she was simply suffering a dose of old-fashioned nerves.

'Ready?' said Emma.

Willow didn't deign to answer the question.

'You're holding your phone,' she said instead.

The words came out in a flat monotone. Willow didn't recognise her own voice.

'Oh, yeah. I should have given it to Mum earlier, but I was taking last minute pics. Not to worry. I'll hide it in my posy. Like this. See?'

She demonstrated, sliding the flower ball over the phone.

'I have some great shots of you arriving. I think you'll be really pleased with them, especially as the official photographer and video guy weren't out here to greet you. They said they had to go inside and get in position.'

Willow didn't reply.

Emerging from the Roller, she found herself copying Emma, tucking her own phone into the bouquet while her free hand took her father's arm.

On autopilot, Willow allowed Jerry to lead her inside the hotel. Moving through the vast reception area with its twelve-foot-high Christmas tree, two uniformed staff guided them to the ceremony room. Every available surface was lined with flickering candles and there were enough Christmas garlands to rival Santa's grotto. The venue looked utterly magical. It was completely at odds with Willow's heart, which had turned into a winter wasteland.

Pausing at the entrance, Willow could see that the guests were now inside and in their seats. Many were aware the bride had arrived. Heads were turning to look at her. Admiring looks were being given.

Dust motes danced in the air, lit up by the fairy lights strung around the room. As she stood there, Willow likened the specks to suspended particles of bright glitter as they whirled around her veil. Now they were blurring with the images of THOSE sexy snaps, and suddenly the glowing sparkles dimmed from an arc of colour to a swirl of fog so that everything became grey.

Willow spotted Charlie's boss, Drummond, in an aisle seat. She was astonished to see Ben's ex-girlfriend sitting next to Drummond. Anna was looking very proprietorial. Good heavens, was Drummond her new man? Anna was holding her mobile. She pointed it in Willow's direction, presumably to take a photograph. Or was she? Was it a secret signal that it was *her* who'd sent those pre-wedding texts?

Willow stared at Anna. At her long wavy brown hair. *She* had a butterfly tattoo on her left thigh. Both Willow and Emma had seen it peeking through her fashionably ripped jeans the day she'd come a-calling at Willow's house.

Was that why Anna had also turned up the library,

pleading with her not to marry Charlie? Could it be that *she* was the other woman? And even though Anna now had a new man, could this be her way for taking revenge on Charlie?

Willow didn't know. She didn't know anything any more. If Anna was Charlie's mystery lover, why had she rung the library anonymously? Why not just say, "Hi, Willow, it's me again." After all, Anna had taken the trouble of turning up in person at the library. It made no sense to hide her identity on the phone.

And then Willow wondered if Ben knew about Charlie's cheating. Was that why he and Anna had split? Because Ben had sussed his girlfriend was cheating? But… if Charlie had had a fling with Ben's girlfriend, surely Ben wouldn't have stayed friends with Charlie, or agreed to be his best man?

Willow was starting to feel dizzy with the possibilities of which woman Charlie had been seeing. She'd once been in Anna's and Ben's bedroom and seen those same patterned pillowcases that had been in *that* photograph. But… then again… she'd seen them at Emma's too. It was a popular brand. Willow shook her head, as if trying to bat away the whirl of thoughts bombarding her.

Her eyes homed in on the lady celebrant waiting to signal Willow and Jerry. She was standing opposite Willow, at the other end of the aisle. To the celebrant's left sat Charlie and Ben.

Willow's face was a mask as she observed both men. Ben was whispering something in Charlie's ear. He must have been relaying that his bride had arrived, because now Charlie's head was swivelling round, seeking Willow out. His eyes locked on hers and he gave a smile that conveyed he was blown away by the vision patiently waiting at the entrance. Willow gave him a hard stare. She watched Charlie's look of delight ebb away and become replaced by something else. Consternation.

The opening bars of Vivaldi's *Four Seasons* rang out. Willow was instantly reminded of another time when she'd heard Charlie humming the same tune. It was the day he'd returned home after running "errands". He'd been so pleased with himself after secretly and successfully booking their wedding. It was also the day he'd brought her here, to Goldhill Grange, and gone down on one knee in front of a packed restaurant.

She'd contributed nothing financially to this wedding. Charlie had insisted on paying for everything. His generosity had been unprecedented. Had he been making up for a guilty conscience?

But, then again, if he'd been having an affair, why had he asked her to marry him? He'd once been marriage-shy. What had changed his mind? And why the hurry? Willow could come up with only one answer. To try and break off his affair. To prove to the other woman that she meant nothing. That their relationship was over. But the woman had been reluctant to comply. And now that woman was angry.

An "Old Wives' Tale" floated through Willow's raging thoughts.

Hell hath no fury like a woman scorned.

Was that why Anna had turned up at both Willow's home

and place of work? Because she was hellbent on pre-empting any marriage proposal? It still didn't explain the anonymous phone calls at the library.

The celebrant was now smiling and nodding at Willow and Jerry. It was time to begin the slow walk down the aisle. Emma stationed herself behind Willow, and gave her a gentle prod.

Tentatively, Willow put one foot in front of the other. She was going through the motions, but her body felt like it had been hi-jacked. A part of her had detached and floated upwards. That part was now looking down on the beautiful bride walking towards her betrothed. There was her father handing her over to Charlie. And now Emma was lifting Willow's veil and trying to take her flowers.

Willow whooshed back into her body and clung on to the bouquet. Emma gave her a puzzled look but didn't object. Nobody had noticed the mobile nestling amongst the roses.

From the moment Willow had received that first text, everything had slid into slow motion. Maybe it only seemed that way because her mind was working flat out, flitting around like an adrenalised bee that had supped from a spilt energy drink.

Her brain had taken charge. Emotion had been shoved away. That could be dealt with later. Instead her mind had shifted into "Logic Mode". It was sifting through facts at lightning speed.

Fact One: Emma and Anna had the same wavy brown hair as the unknown texter.

Fact Two: Emma and Anna both had a butterfly tattoo; but

Fact Three: neither seemed devastated to be at their lover's wedding.

Something was off.

Tugging her eyes away from a worried looking Charlie, Willow scanned the guests at the front of the room.

There was her mother. Anita was giving Willow a watery smile. In one hand a lace hanky was ready to deal with any waterworks.

Her father had now slipped in alongside her mother and was staring at the celebrant, his eyes very bright.

Emma was fiddling with her posy. Was she texting? Willow half expected her mobile to give another buzz, but it remained silent.

Standing next to Emma was Karen. Like Willow's mum and dad, Karen was looking emotional.

Next to Karen was Noah. He looked both handsome and utterly bereft. He met Willow's gaze and the depth of his expression reminded her of long-ago lyrics about a picture painting a thousand words. Suddenly Willow knew what she had to do.

Tearing her eyes away from Noah, Willow gazed at the celebrant. Words were being said. Guests were being welcomed. There was a bit of chat about winter weddings and a day full of joy. And suddenly formal lines were being said. Willow automatically found herself repeating the celebrant's words. There was then a pause. Guests were informed that

Charlie and Willow would now say their own special vows to each other, before being pronounced husband and wife.

Charlie looked at Willow, before taking both her hands in his. For a moment he struggled to speak, but then, hesitantly, started to pay tribute to Willow.

'Sometimes we don't realise love is in our lives until we're in danger of losing it,' he began.

Charlie's voice was so low, Willow doubted whether anyone else could even hear him.

'Sometimes we make mistakes,' he continued.

He was picking his words carefully. So carefully that Willow suspected Charlie had abandoned any previously rehearsed speech. He'd caught her expression as she'd waited in the doorway and thrown away the script. Now he was speaking from the heart. And possibly his words were also for someone else in this room. Someone he wanted to pay attention as he rammed home these words. Charlie's voice was getting stronger as he now asserted his message.

'You are the only woman for me, Willow, and you are the only woman with whom I want to spend the rest of my life.'

Out of her peripheral vision, Willow observed someone losing a battle with tears.

'Willow?' prompted the celebrant.

She looked at Charlie. He was looking more relaxed now. Like a weight had been removed from his shoulders. He was on the home stretch. Willow was by his side. The marriage was well and truly underway. They were only another minute or two from being legally wed. Charlie gave her a nod of encouragement, and Willow cleared her throat.

Her first words were croaky.

'Marriage is about love. And trust.'

As her words began to flow, she found her stride, warming to her task, one eye on Charlie, the other on their guests.

'Today I was given a gift.'

Charlie squeezed her hand.

'And that gift was truth.'

Willow withdrew her phone from her bouquet and pressed the screen.

'Those at the back won't be able to see these images.'

As Willow held the phone aloft, she saw confusion amongst the guests. She also noted the colour draining from Charlie's face. He was starting to make an awful gurgling sound and was quite incapable of speech.

Emma was looking horrified. She was staring at Willow as if she'd sprouted two horns and a devil's tail and was clutching her own mobile as if a crucifix.

Willow ignored them both.

'There will be no wedding today. Instead there will be a celebration of truth.'

Charlie couldn't take another moment. Breaking away, he stalked down the aisle and slammed out of the ceremony room. For a moment Ben looked like he was going to go after Charlie, but then had a change of heart.

His eyes flicked back to Willow. Her finger was hovering over her mobile. What was she doing? Ben didn't know. All he *did* know was that Charlie might have paid Sophie off, but there had been another woman. A woman who wouldn't go away. A woman that Charlie had needed to wine and dine in order to smooth the path of severance. Ben had only known that person as *Kev*.

Willow's finger touched her phone's screen, and Ben instinctively knew that this woman's identity was about to be revealed.

As the merry tune of another mobile filled the ceremony room, all eyes swivelled to see who the mystery person was. Willow stared at her. It was a look of utter contempt. She turned back to the congregation.

'It's a shame to waste a beautiful wedding breakfast and so much champagne, so everyone is invited to join me at the reception. Everyone apart from you' – she pointed to the owner of the still ringing mobile – 'Karen.'

Ben stared at Karen in shock.

Karen Everest.

K. Everest.

K. Ev.

Kev.

Chapter Sixty-Three

Karen had always enjoyed basking in a spotlight of attention. She loved nothing more than being flattered and feted and having people say, "You have a daughter of thirty? No way!"

There was no need to admit that she'd started young. *Too* young. All that mattered was the positive reaction of people feeding her sense of self-image.

It pleased her that others thought she was a woman in her mid-thirties, not forties. It was one of the reasons why she'd always fluttered her eyelashes at younger men… to see if she could still "pull". It salved her ego.

However, lately Karen's self-esteem had taken a battering. Charlie had been the first one to deal a blow. He'd been up for plenty of no-strings fun in the bedroom until he'd got bored and wanted to give her the brush-off. That had hurt.

The second man to upset her ego had been the tattoo artist. Jezz. Karen had thought that sparks had been flying between them in the studio, but it had turned out he'd merely been leading her on. She had a nasty feeling that Jezz had regaled his mates with the story of the middle-aged woman who'd thought she was going to get lucky with him. The discovery that he'd been having a private laugh at her expense had been humiliating.

Karen knew she should embrace growing older gracefully. Hell, she was *forty*-six, not *eighty*-six. But it didn't matter how many times she reminded herself that age was just a number, deep down that number jarred, because inside her heart she felt *twenty*-six.

Karen hadn't meant to hurt Willow. And if she'd left her blasted mobile in Noah's car, instead of trying to stuff it inside her tiny clutch bag with her lippy and box of confetti, then she'd never have been caught out. Unlike Emma, who was almost umbilically joined to her mobile, Karen was always losing phones. Consequently she only ever bothered with pay-as-you-go Sim cards and ancient mobiles bought off eBay. She'd intended, after today, to "lose" yet another phone. Emma had long ago given up programming her mother's number into her own phone for this very reason. If Willow *had* shown Emma the unknown number of the person who'd sent those texts, it would have been unlikely that Emma would've twigged they'd been sent by her own mother.

Threading her way through the chuntering congregation, Karen elbowed her way over to Emma.

'I'm sorry,' she said.

'I think you're apologising to the wrong person,' said Emma coldly.

Karen dared to look at Willow.

'It was only ever meant to be a bit of fun,' she implored. 'It didn't mean anything.'

Which wasn't strictly true. Her feelings for Charlie had got out of hand long ago, even if they hadn't been reciprocated. But there was no need to tell Willow that.

'I didn't want you throwing yourself away on a man who cheats.'

'How incredibly thoughtful of you,' said Willow sarcastically.

The guests were getting noisier. Fingers were now pointing at Karen. She could see that Jerry and Anita were attempting to push their way over. It was apparent that Anita was revving up for a noisy exchange of words. Charlie's mother was slumped in her seat. Grace's eyes locked on Karen's. Her expression was an open book.

My son's wedding has been wrecked because of you? A middle-aged woman! WHAT was my Charlie thinking of?

Now Grace was hauling herself to her feet. Her mouth had morphed into a mean line. It looked like she was going to join forces with Anita and have her say. But both women were going to have to get in the queue.

'You've wrecked my best friend's wedding,' shouted Emma.

'Mum, please tell me this isn't true,' said Noah, catching hold of Karen's forearm.

Karen might have loved the spotlight, but this was one occasion where she wasn't going to hang around and soak up the attention. She wanted out of here.

Shaking off Noah, she held up her clutch bag like a mini riot shield. Guests were starting to circle her like a predatory school of sharks. Shoving her way through them all, she followed Charlie's footsteps and fled.

Willow watched Karen's departure. Would she go after Charlie? Willow wondered if they might even end up together. And then she decided that she didn't care. They both had the same appalling morals. They were welcome to each other.

Chapter Sixty-Four

Willow was still on autopilot. She knew that, when alone, emotions would descend like a wrecking ball. For now, she was managing to keep her chin up and her eyes dry.

The celebrant had offered Willow sincere condolences and said that hers wasn't the first wedding where drama had been witnessed, and likely wouldn't be the last.

Meanwhile, Noah and Ben had taken charge. On their say so, catering staff had hastily dismantled the top table, rearranging it to blend with the others. The seating plan had been speedily removed too, for which Willow was grateful. Everyone had stayed, apart from a couple of Charlie's relatives and his devastated mother. Grace had been taken home and put to bed with a large medicinal brandy.

An outraged Jerry had insisted on making a completely revamped father-of-the-bride speech which had included what he'd do to Charlie if their paths ever crossed again. Everyone had then tucked into the wedding breakfast and, despite the awfulness of the occasion, there had also been some subdued laughter. Even Willow had found herself managing to raise a smile here and there.

Noah and Ben also took charge of warning the evening

guests what had happened. Appalled, they paid their commiserations to Willow. She urged every single one of them to stay and celebrate her "day of truth".

Throughout, Emma had been sticking to Willow like superglue. Unlike the bride, she kept periodically bursting into tears.

'I can't believe Mum would do such a thing,' she kept saying, over and over. 'I'm so sorry.'

But before Emma could say this mantra one more time, Anna had broken away from Drummond and was now approaching both Emma and Willow. Ben spotted Anna making her way over, and quickly followed suit. Willow didn't notice Emma glancing first at Anna and then Ben. She looked horribly uncomfortable.

'I can't keep my distance from you any longer, Willow,' said Anna.

She was agitated and very red in the face.

'I've been biding my time to speak to you and waiting until you're not surrounded by people. You see, I owe you a huge apology. Will you accept it? Even though I knew Charlie was a cheater, I should have kept my gob shut. It wasn't for me to tell you not to marry him.'

'Well thank goodness I didn't,' said Willow giving a mirthless laugh. 'How did you know he'd been unfaithful?'

'Because I told her,' said Ben, interrupting. 'I've known Charlie for many years and, rightly or wrongly, I've been loyal to him. But I've loved you like a sister, Willow, and have come this close' – he held a forefinger and thumb a millimetre apart

– 'to telling you. However, prior to his marriage proposal, Charlie promised me that he really *had* changed. And I believed him. He was over the moon that you were wearing his ring and said he couldn't wait to be a married man. But I guess you won't have him back now, will you?'

Willow shook her head.

'No. Absolutely not. He might insist he's changed but, then again' – her thoughts flipped back to Noah's kiss – 'something in me has changed too. Let's just say that I think today's outcome was actually a good thing.'

'He's not all bad,' said Ben.

Willow shrugged.

'Charlie is no longer of any importance to me.'

'Brave words,' said Ben.

He put an arm around Willow's shoulders and gave her a quick squeeze.

'Can you forgive me for not telling you about his infidelities? It's been horrible having divided loyalties between the two of you, which was why I confided in a couple of people. Anna was one of them.' He nodded at his ex-girlfriend. 'If I'd kept it to myself, I'd have gone bonkers.'

'And once Ben had told me,' said Anna, picking up the reins of conversation, 'I then wanted to tell you. But I was scared to lose your friendship. So instead, I tried to warn you off but without giving the reason why. And, in hindsight, that was the wrong thing to have done because I lost your friendship anyway. After all, you didn't invite me to your wedding. I came as Drummond's plus-one.'

'I'm glad you're here now,' said Willow sincerely.

'And while we're being honest' – Emma piped up, looking sheepish – 'it was *me* who made those anonymous phone calls to the library.'

'What?' said Willow looking dumbfounded. 'But how did *you* know Charlie had been unfaithful?'

'For the same reason as Anna,' said Emma, now looking timorously at Ben's ex-girlfriend. 'I'm the other person Ben confided in about Charlie. You see, Ben and I were seeing each other. Seeing… but not seeing. If you get my drift. He wasn't a free agent. So I owe you an apology too, Anna. But, unlike Charlie, I promise you that Ben was never a cheater. We had feelings for each other. But nothing happened. He was with you and he wanted to make things work.'

Willow was so gobsmacked she couldn't say anything. How many more surprises was today going to hold?

Anna gave Emma a rueful smile.

'Ah, well, there's something else I also need to confess. Ben and I wouldn't have worked out in the long-term anyway. I'm not proud to admit that I'd started seeing Drummond while I was still with Ben.'

Her eyes swivelled to her ex-boyfriend, who was looking flabbergasted.

'I'm so sorry, Ben. I was too much of a coward to properly end our relationship, so I used to create ridiculous arguments in the hope that *you'd* be the one to call time on us. And before you go decking Drummond, he didn't know I was once your girlfriend. In fact, he still has no idea.'

'Good God,' said Ben, his mouth dropping open. 'Well, rest assured I have no desire to punch the guy's lights out. He's my boss, and I'd quite like to keep my job, thanks. But…' – he stared at Anna incredulously – 'you and *Drummond*? He's old enough to be your father.'

'And your point is?' said Anna, her tone suddenly icy.

'Nothing,' said Ben hastily. 'I wish you all the luck in the world.'

'Thanks,' said Anna, looking slightly mollified.

'Forgive me for asking,' he said. 'But I'm curious. How did the two of you even get to meet?'

'The way most people do these days. Online,' she added, upon seeing Ben's baffled expression. 'Yes, that's what an awful partner I was, Ben. One who was actively seeking another relationship and creating arguments with you in order to get the green light to justify what I was doing. And it worked.'

She had the grace to look embarrassed.

'I guess it's all water under the bridge now,' said Ben in bemusement.

'But I really do mean it when I say' – said Anna, looking at Emma again – 'I'd be delighted if you and Ben properly got together.'

Before Emma could say anything, Ben had thrown his arms around Emma's shoulders.

'Darling Ems, I'm so sorry to have made you wait. Will you forgive me? Because I really do want to see you. I just didn't want you to be a rebound, because I have a feeling about us.' He paused, looking both awkward and embarrassed. 'Hell, life's too short, so I'm simply going to spit this out. Will you be my girlfriend?'

Emma looked at Ben in astonishment, joy lighting up her face.

'There's nothing to forgive,' she whispered. 'And yes, I'll be your girlfriend… I'll be your anything… your everything.'

She hugged him hard.

'And I'd like to apologise to the two of you,' said Willow addressing both Emma and Anna.

'Whatever for?' asked Emma, tearing her eyes away from Ben.

'Yes, why?' said Anna.

Willow studied her fingernails for a moment.

'Because, when I received those anonymous texts, I had reservations about one of you being Charlie's lover. Now I know otherwise, and I feel ashamed for doubting either of you. I just wish' – she looked at her best friend – 'that you'd felt able to tell me that you knew about Charlie's infidelity.'

'I wanted to. So many times,' said Emma. 'I just didn't know how. It crucified me having to wrestle with my conscience. Instead I tackled Charlie.'

'Did you?' said Willow in amazement.

'I didn't want to drop Ben in it, so I simply told Charlie that I had female intuition that he was up to no good. He denied this was the case and instead told me he was waiting for the right moment to ask you to marry him. I still didn't trust him to keep his todger in his trousers, so I took the coward's way out and rang you anonymously at the library. It was also why I tried to encourage you to have a date with Noah when he came to England. Can you forgive me?'

Willow sighed.

'Of course.'

Oh, what a day. What a flipping awful day.

And then she caught sight of Noah. He was heading her way.

'Sorry to interrupt, but the DJ is asking if you're still doing a first dance. I've put him in the picture, but he wondered if you'd like to dance with your dad. Would that be all right?'

'No,' said Willow, shaking her head.

'Okie-dokie, I'll let the guy know.'

'No need,' said Willow, catching hold of Noah's arm.

'Then who are you going to dance with?' he said, looking confused.

Willow's mouth twitched.

'I'm going to dance with you.'

Chapter Sixty-Five

Noah stared at Willow, saw that she was serious, and didn't waste a moment. Nodding to the DJ, he led her on to the dance floor.

'Ladies and gentlemen,' said the DJ. 'Put your hands together for Willow.'

As the opening bars to the music began to play, everybody applauded the bride-that-never-was.

Several guests raised an eyebrow at Willow's handsome partner. He'd gathered her into his arms and was now delivering enough smoulders to start an Australian bush fire. Inevitably, there were some discreet murmurs behind hands. How come the jilted bride looked like a woman who was rapidly falling in love before their very eyes?

'Willow,' said Noah, holding her tight. 'I want you to know that I think you're the bravest woman I've ever met.'

'Not brave,' she shook her head, revelling in his warm hands against her spine.

The last time Noah had touched her back had been when doing up all the little buttons on the back of her dress. Now Willow wished he was undoing them.

Here she goes. More erotic thoughts. Aren't you in

mourning for your fiancé?

Oh hello. I wondered when you'd pipe up. And no. I'm not grieving.

People will talk, you know.

You mean they aren't already?

I mean they'll gossip.

So let them. Now go away. I'm having a moment and want to enjoy it.

'However,' Willow said. 'I've decided that maybe today isn't so awful after all.'

She gave him a bold smile.

'In fact, right now, things seem pretty wonderful.'

Noah met her smile with one of tenderness, and Willow felt her body responding. Delicious zingers were once again making their presence known, and she was loving it.

'Do you remember that day when you were with my sister in Franco's coffee shop?' said Noah. 'We spoke on FaceTime.'

'We did.'

'And… at the time you agreed to me taking you out to dinner.'

Willow could feel herself going pink. She could remember that moment only too well. It was when she'd allowed her mind to wander off on a rather erotic daydream starring Noah Everest. And while her mind had been busily engaged elsewhere, she'd apparently agreed to a dinner date without taking on board one word of what Noah had been saying.

'Whatever must you have thought of me agreeing to have dinner with you when I was engaged to another man?'

'Just that you were being friendly,' said Noah, but his eyes gleamed mischievously. 'Admittedly, my intentions were… er…'

'What?'

'Okay. Confession time. From the moment I saw you on my phone screen, I knew that, when I got to England, I wanted to take you out. Properly. You know, on a date. A *romantic* date.'

Willow grinned.

'Did you now?' she said, arching an eyebrow.

'Yeah. Which was a bit naughty of me. But I want you to know that I'm not in the habit of asking out engaged women, or married women, or women with boyfriends, or–'

'I think I get the picture,' Willow interrupted, still smiling.

'I hope you don't think badly of me.'

'I don't. In fact…'

'Yes?'

'Does your invitation to dinner still stand?' she asked playfully.

He looked at her. *Really* looked at her. And once again Willow had the feeling that Noah was peering right into her soul.

'Oh yes,' he nodded. 'The invitation still stands. Nothing would give me greater pleasure than to take you out to dinner. Do you think… that maybe… you might like to get to know me properly after all?'

Willow felt as though every cell in her body was cheering her on as she replied.

'Yes. I think I'd like that very much.'

Epilogue

Eighteen months later

Everyone agreed they'd never seen a bride and groom look so well-matched and so in love.

As the DJ played the opening bars to the first dance, the handsome man led his beautiful bride on to a dance floor strewn with confetti and petals. Gathering her into his arms, he pulled her close.

'Happy, darling?'

'You bet,' she beamed. 'Who would've ever guessed that I'd marry my best friend's brother!'

'Indeed.' He then shrugged helplessly. 'Shame about your new mother-in-law.'

'Hm. Maybe one day she'll be back on my Christmas card list.'

'In which case, you'll have to include her new husband.'

'Oh?'

'I found out she recently married.'

'No kidding. Anyone we know?'

'I'll give you a clue. You were once engaged to your new father-in-law…'

Also by Debbie Viggiano

Stockings and Cellulite

Lipstick and Lies

Flings and Arrows

The Perfect Marriage

Secrets

The Corner Shop of Whispers

The Woman Who Knew Everything

What Holly's Husband Did

The Man You Meet in Heaven

Lucy's Last Straw

Cappuccino and Chick-Chat (memoir)

Mixed Emotions (short stories)

The Ex Factor (a family drama)

Lily's Pink Cloud ~ a child's fairytale

100 ~ the Author's experience of Chronic Myeloid Leukaemia

Acknowledgements

Willow's Wedding Vows is my twelfth novel. I love to write books that make a reader occasionally giggle and provide pure escapism. As a result, there is absolutely no mention of the foul C word that has caused havoc across the globe this year.

There are several people involved in getting a book 'out there' and I want to thank them from the bottom of my heart.

Firstly, the brilliant Rebecca Emin of Gingersnap Books, who knows exactly what to do with machine code and is a formatting genius.

Secondly, the fabulous Cathy Helms of Avalon Graphics for working her magic in transforming a rough sketch into a gorgeous book cover. Cathy always delivers exactly what I want and is a joy to work with.

Thirdly, the amazing Rachel Gilbey of *Rachel's Random Resources*, blog tour organiser extraordinaire. Immense gratitude also goes to each and every one of the fantastic bloggers who took the time to read and review *Willow*. They are:

Kirsty of *Kirsty's Book Buying Addiction*, Caitlyn Lynch, DJ of *Books and Bindings*, Tizi of *Tizi's Book Review*, Berni of *Brmaycock's Book Blog*, Melanie of *Chapter and Cake*, Louise of *Waggy Tales Blog*, Jane Hunt, Lucy of *Blonde Write More*, Kerry of *Herding Cats*, Kelly of *Dash Fan Book Reviews*, Elaine of *Splashes Into Books*, Yvonne of *Me and My Books*, Finitha of *Know Your Books*, Stacy of *Stacy Is Reading*, Kaisha of *The Writing Garnet*, Pam of *Books, Life and Everything*, Sarah of *Beauty Addict*, Els of *B for Bookreview*, Vikkie of *Little Miss Book Lover 87*, Kay of *Coffee and Kindle Book Reviews*, Berit of *Audio Killed the Bookmark*, Tracey of *@traceysyearinbooks*, Donna of *Donnasbookblog*, Sharon of *Stardust Book Reviews*, Stacey of *just_a_girl_who_loves_to_read*, Fany of *Fany Reads English* and last, but not least, Satabdi of *Book Reviews by Satabdi.*

Fourthly, my lovely daughter, Eleanor, for assisting with proof-reading.

Finally, I want to thank you, my reader. Without you, there is no book. I very much hope you enjoy this one.

Debbie xx

Printed in Great Britain
by Amazon

40013828R00246